Beth Schorr Jaffe

Stars of David

R. BECKER PRESS

This book is a work of fiction. The characters, incidents and dialogue were imagined by the author. Any resemblance to actual incidents or persons, living or dead, is unintentional and coincidental.

ISBN: 978-1-62550-463-0

FOR BERNICE AND JULIUS SCHORR

"When you long with all your heart for someone to love you, a madness grows there that shakes all sense from the trees and the water and the earth. And nothing lives for you, except the long deep bitter want. And this is what everyone feels from birth to death."

Denton Welch (1915-1948 Kent, England)

Stars of David

Among the Mourners

2001

THE PHONE CALLS

Queens, New York

Adam rose from bed, his six-foot frame wrapped in his blue flannel blanket, and plodded across the room toward the window. Lifting the shade, he squinted at the fresh snow piled along the gutters, burying parked cars that obstructed the close shave of city plows. The road shone.

Eli's call this morning was as much of a surprise to Adam as Eli's plea itself. "It's a nightmare!" Eli blasted into the receiver. "First he goes off to China and now we've got to bring him home! Adam, you'll do this for me." Eli's father, Adam's uncle, Cantor David Kaplan, had just died of a stroke, according to the Shanghai Medical Examiner. Eli sounded awful. "You *have* to get to Shanghai and retrieve my father's body."

Unnerved by the implicit way Eli worded the request, Adam brooded, *Retrieve David's body?* After he crushed *my* father? Adam couldn't tell if Eli was begging him or demanding, his tone rising from deep and resonant to shallow and stringy. Holding the phone's handset against his ear, Adam closed his eyes, trying to concentrate only on the words in Eli's tantrum.

Eli could not make the trip to China himself, Adam knew this. Eli had been diagnosed soon after birth with cerebral palsy—but that didn't mean Adam had to obey the order of a cousin he hadn't seen in twenty years. Adam pictured his

1

cousin as a toddler: sweet and cheerful, black-haired, blue-eyed, his legs long and elegant in their skewed position. To the eye, it looked as if his handicaps were limited to his right foot, which turned in excessively. A full head of curls made their way over his ears until he was three.

Their families had once shared a Gramercy Park two-family brownstone. Adam Oppenheim and Eli Kaplan were first cousins—Adam was now forty-seven, older than Eli by ten years. But when Eli's father, David, caused such mayhem and searing discomfort for the family, segregating Eli from everyone the way he did, among other disasters, it just seemed easier for Adam to let the Kaplans go their unarticulated ways: not quite family, not quite strangers.

"You'd always said it was all right if I called you, so it's all right?" Eli asked, his tone already faltering. "Because this is urgent."

Adam shut his eyes and saw his toddler cousin slinging his twisted right leg from room to room—giggling, thinking his own disability comical. "Of course it's all right. I'm listening." It made him uncomfortable that Eli was defensive with him. "I'm sorry about your father," he said. Actually, Adam couldn't care less that David was dead. He had endured the cantor's intimidating presence throughout his boyhood, and the man had sabotaged Adam's own father.

But that wasn't Eli's fault. He felt a spasm of love for his helpless cousin. "I would do this for you, but the snow, and the airports. Visas? I would need one and that takes time." Eli said nothing but Adam heard something flung to the floor in Eli's room. He felt as if he'd been hit. "And I have my own business," he offered feebly.

Eli shouted, "My father was a great man!" Then he whispered through tears, "If I could, I would move heaven and earth to bring my dad home to me."

2

It occurred to Adam at that moment that his cousin's childhood lisp had noticeably improved. "Yes, I know you would," he said.

"We are honorable men in this family. Your father, may he rest in peace, you wouldn't have traveled around the world to get him? Honor him?"

Why are you still pretending that my father's death was honorable? He breathed to subdue the rattling in his chest. "I'll try to go."

He leaned his face against the bedroom window until he felt his skin freeze against the glass. "Who's with you?"

"Why? You think I can't stay by myself?"

"I didn't mean anything." Jeez. "No one should be alone when they lose their father." He thought, *You should be singing Hallelujah.* After he had been as cruel to Eli as he had been to everyone else.

"I'm not alone." Eli cleared his throat. "I'll be waiting to hear from you. Today."

Great. And if Adam decided to do his cousin's bidding, he would have to convince his wife Diane he had to do it, which might be harder than actually going to China.

Eli's call was a surprise because his older sister Liora, whom David had sent to live in Israel when she was sixteen and Eli was three, had called Adam an hour earlier, from Tel Aviv. She too wanted him to go to Shanghai and had asked him to telephone a rabbi there, a Seth Giacalone—a name that struck Adam as so curious in its hybrid ethnicity that it typified the peculiarity of David's decision to travel all the way to China in his advanced age. Adam had been shaken by her call, her voice, her sudden re-involvement with the family.

Adam was the chosen one. Just call me Moses, he thought. He was to get his uncle home within the next four days or the Shanghai Lubavitch community, of which the cantor was a guest, would rally to escort him to and bury him in the Jewish cemetery in Beijing. Yes, Liora assured Adam, there was a Jewish cemetery in Beijing. Liora spoke at times in Hebrew and at times in English, but Adam understood enough. "If this rabbi, this Seth Giacalone, can't get permission to bury him in Beijing, and if no one goes to claim the body, then, as Shanghai law requires, my father will be cremated by the seventh day following his death, put in a box with any personal information they have on him, and buried by the city."

It had already taken the Shanghai rabbi a couple of days to locate Liora. Uncertain of Eli's state of mind, the rabbi hadn't thought it wise to first deliver the news to him. Everyone was frantic about the lost time. "This Giacalone schmuck," Liora told Adam, was unwilling to accompany the cantor's body back to the U.S. She had also called him an "absolute imbecile." Jewish religious law dictated he be buried within one day and now, days after the death, they all, Liora, Eli, and David's rabbi in Shanghai, just wanted to get his body into a pine box under ground. Liora had been the one to break the news to Eli.

Adam was sold. He began agonizing; it was now nearly three days into the cremation *dead*line. Liora and Eli's orchestrated appeal was brilliant, and he found himself searching for his passport and the stomach medications he relied on almost daily.

Considering that his uncle David was a castrating prick, Adam wondered if it was possible that the son of a bitch had arranged to die in China. David had called three months ago to tell Adam he was going to China. "Take care of Eli in case of an emergency," he had said flatly. The request seemed so incongruous, so removed from the reality of his present relationship with Eli, that Adam had pushed it from his mind.

Like his dead father Seymour, Adam Oppenheim was a plumber, financially comfortable enough to turn down inconvenient jobs. But when he and Diane met twenty-five years ago, Adam was a twenty-two-year-old college dropout, working for his late father's onetime partner installing new toilets at the courthouse in Brooklyn, where a twenty-one-year-old Diane worked as a court stenographer. Adam had blockaded the ladies room with orange cones and forbade her from entering. He had beautiful white teeth that were exposed almost to his molars when he smiled. He knew that and smiled when it was necessary. Sullen, confused by his father's death, he was effectively soft-spoken. Diane was dumbstruck, she said later, by his Paul Newman jaw. He was equally struck by her chestnut eyes, so perfectly long and wide that it seemed her face existed solely as their pedestal.

After a nonstop three-month sweep of lunches in the cafeteria, dinners at a local diner, and promises of fidelity and passion, they were married. Within one year they had a baby boy, Jamie, and settled in a suitable Tudoresque ranch style one-family off Hillside Avenue in Jamaica Estates, Queens. Their home was no estate, just a quaint brick house with two bedrooms, and narrow hallways.

They affectionately came to call their only son Boy. When he was a toddler he had long blond curls and a smile that showed off a deep dimple on each cheek. Even in a blue shirt, overalls and baseball cap, he looked so precious that strangers thought he was a girl. Once Jamie reached two, Diane insisted they introduce their son as "Boy." References to Tarzan were inevitable.

Now, as Adam stood next to Diane in the bedroom, she exploded. "You are not putting your life at risk to gather up the dead bones of an old man you hardly spoke to anymore!" Then she cried, "You'll be in the air for twenty hours!" At five-five, with enough cleavage, and long skinny legs, wearing white panties topped by her cheetah print camisole (she knew to keep her animal prints to one item per outfit), Adam thought his wife was too smart to act so idiotically, but he also thought she was too cute for him to disallow her self-protective absurdities. He knew she was scared to death. Diane followed Adam from the bedroom into the bathroom. In some lopsided logic understood only by Diane, planes were not capable of routinely staying in the air for more than five hours. It had something to do with engine exhaustion. The fact that they did she disregarded as a fluke. Fortunately for them, Boy, now twenty-four, did not live more than five plane-ride hours away.

"Flying is safe," Adam said. "We've flown three times a year for the past four years. No fatalities. So, taking into account the deer I hit on the Garden State Parkway, it's safer than driving."

"Call Eli and tell him they have helpers for the handicapped that will get him on and off the plane." Her voice softened. "He can get his father himself." She sat on the toilet seat lid, crossed her legs, and waited until Adam looked. He blew a kiss, and then opened the mirrored cabinet over the sink.

"What the hell was the old man doing in China anyway?" She went on. "What kind of old man goes to China alone? Uuch!" She hit Adam's leg with the back of her hand. "He probably went to China to die on purpose. Leave him there." She hit his leg again. This time he swatted her hand away.

Adam suspected Diane was right, that his uncle had wanted to cause more havoc. He pushed a few bottles around in the medicine cabinet before finding the Tums. "Angel of mercy that you are, you could be on to something."

"What did you get out of Liora?"

"Nothing very helpful, rude and evasive as she was. She must think I kept up my Jewish studies. She slipped into Hebrew so often I didn't have the strength to keep stopping her." He avoided talking about his conversation with Liora and repeated what Eli told him. "Eli said his father was with some lost tribe of Jews, getting them prepared for the holidays, teaching them Hebrew or something."

"Lost Jews? That's Ethiopia." Diane smirked, then grabbed the Tums from his hand and sat with the plastic bottle between her knees. "I have a terrible feeling about this. What Jews? And why *you* for god's sake!"

"I don't know what Jews. I didn't say I was definitely going" — even as he said that he knew he was definitely going — "but I feel, I don't know, horrible about Eli, like I owe him something. Big. No, really big!" Why had he been so apathetic toward Eli for so long? *I'm an asshole.*

"Guilt trip. That's what this is! It's China!"

"I know it's China! You think I want to get on a plane at the drop of a hat and go around the fucking world!" Adam's stomachache became more aggressive, angry as much at himself as at Diane. He grabbed the bottle from her knees, opened it, and popped two Tums in his mouth before switching off the light and leaving her on the toilet seat. "Someone's got to go," he muttered around the half-chewed tablets in his mouth.

The loose toilet clanked against the wall as she pounced off the seat and shouted into the back of his head, "I'm getting online right now and buying two tickets. If you go, I'm going with you." She shuffled in her flat black slippers to the computer muttering about the goddamned cost of family obligation and the lack of government support for the physically handicapped. "I'm experiencing genuine trepidations Adam," she yelled down the hall. "I am now so overwhelmed that I am becoming neurologically impaired!"

Adam knew she'd get insulted if he laughed when she lapsed into the pretentious affect that so characterized her mother. He worried that he would have to fix that toilet before he left.

"But why can't Liora go?"

"She said she had four of her six children serving in the army and no one else to help their families with her numerous grandchildren." He backed away from Diane and shouted, "And why the hell would she go?" He hadn't heard from Liora since she had left New York thirty-five years ago. Her voice sounded familiar, except for her Israeli accent. He assumed that David kept in touch with her. She had told Adam, "I will not exhaust my savings by further indulging my father's foolishness, still after his death."

Adam began to sweat inside his flannel shirt. Diane reached for him and squeezed his torso, and he closed his eyes. He smelled her baby powder deodorant. He whispered into her ear, "Let's go online, check out flights," then kissed her shoulder. "No decisions yet."

They walked into Jamie's old bedroom, now a den. Jamie was doing all right, having left New York after one year at City College, heading off to Denver with a boyhood friend, Mark, both of them living for the past four years as carpenters. Adam and Diane each spoke to him at least twice a week. They saw Jamie only at the usual holidays: Thanksgiving, Passover, and his birthday in June, when they would take him on a trip. Last year they went to Cancun. Jamie never came east.

Adam watched over her shoulder as Diane started typing in search words: China, China-Jews, which led to Jews of Kaifeng, Jews of Singapore, Shanghai. Diane shrieked when she saw that Singapore Airlines had a major crash in October and announced she would not be joining him on the flight. By four that afternoon, they had read about the history of the Shanghai Jews—by god there was a Jewish cemetery in Beijing—and the arrival of thousands of European refugees during World War Two; ordered three books on the subject from Barnes and Noble, realized that in addition to his passport Adam needed a visa and could get one issued for an emergency in one day, and locked in one ticket to Shanghai for Monday afternoon. Adam made the reservation, though he told Diane he was still not sure he would go.

Late that Sunday night, as soon as Diane went to bed, Adam snuck into the basement to pull a backpack from the storage closet. Every time he had to go down into the mildew and damp he felt his blood rush through his ears. Adam's father had descended to the basement of the Gramercy Park brownstone, slit opened both his wrists and bled to death, as if unzipping his pants to relieve himself of all waste. Adam never got to see the body, although its situation was later described by the family friend who found him; never got to see the chair his father bled on, or the towel beneath its legs. Seymour Oppenheim's body was carried away on a Monday morning, the day after Thanksgiving break while Adam was rearranging, for the fiftieth time, the speakers in his dorm room at SUNY Binghamton. Every death Adam encountered since meant reliving that Monday morning.

The overhead fluorescents were off; the better to wallow. With only the small closet bulb lighting the corner, he sulked in the litter of dark thoughts: David's corpse—still whole, Eli's need to have it home, and the flurry of black-clad arms throwing handfuls of soil atop a coffin in which his own father lay. Blasphemy, David had shouted about the godless way Seymour Oppenheim had discarded the sanctity of his blood. Adam was horrified by his uncle's damning assaults, ashamed of his father's disgrace, afraid there was insanity in his blood, and he became angrier with both men from year to year to year.

He kicked an old folding chair out of his way, checked the sump pump, then felt the walls for moisture. There was some. Diane would know what to do in case of an emergency while he's gone. Pulling the backpack over to the sofa-bed, he stood holding its handle for a few minutes before he found the courage to sit down and ponder why he felt so determined to go to retrieve his uncle. David had been a misery for years, selfish and dictatorial until he was old and sickly. They had hardly spoken to one another since Adam's grandfather passed away and David solely inherited the brownstone from his father's estate. When David ultimately shipped his sister, Adam's mother Ruby, off to a condo in Miami to console her and to be rid of her, a rift in the family opened and was never resolved. A teenaged Eli, reclusive and already difficult to befriend, became a near stranger to Adam as well.

After an hour in the basement, Adam traipsed upstairs to the bathroom, peed, then turned on the shower and yanked the metal shower rings, jolting him as they shrieked across the bar. If Diane was asleep, he knew that sound would wake her. Standing under the hot water, unable to move as it beat against his back, he ruminated about Eli. He thrived as an infant and with the aid of small crutches and braces was a chattering and rambunctious toddler. Adam remembered Eli, at four or five — his fine motor skills adequate — helping to replace a wheel on a model of a 1967 Thunderbird.

Adam slumped, feeling in his own back the creeping spinal tingle of Eli's insidious decrease in activity. By the time the boy was six, Liora had been gone for three years and he was much less physically functional. There were temper tantrums, bedwetting, unexplained days of silence, a lisp that made his reluctant words sound even more childish. As hard as Adam tried to recall it, he could not remember seeing Eli out of doors since his toddler years. At some point during that time and Adam's father's death, Eli became not only physically challenged but a recluse.

It was for these reasons, Adam guessed, that Eli had been home-schooled. When Eli was eight or nine, a student teacher from NYU — her name, he remembered, was Sharon — came for two hours every day until Eli learned to read fluently. To everyone's amazement and relief, Eli's mind was quick, he had a sense of humor — mostly about himself — and by the age of ten, he had learned to read Hebrew as well as English, do simple mathematics, and win at chess. Adam competed with him for checkmate but always lost.

A towel around his waist, his hair still dripping onto his shoulders, Adam went into the bedroom, turned on the light beside the bed and found Diane sitting up with her hands folded across her chest. He said, "We have to talk about this trip."

The bed was covered in layers of down and quilted comforters. Diane had a weakness for textiles. On cold nights they would lower the heat to sixty-two and sleep in a cocoon. She turned toward her husband and sat up higher, smoothing the linens under her hands. "They had no right to ask you." She threw her back against the pillow and sighed.

He felt water run from his hairline down his back and grabbed his blue blanket. "What? You think weirdo Liora would handle this?" He sat next to her on the bed.

"I don't know that she is a weirdo. I never met her." She lifted the curls from the bottom of his neck. "You're getting all wet."

"My uncle sent her away, didn't he? You think fathers send their children away just like this?" He snapped his fingers in the

11

air. "She is a weirdo." He tried desperately to believe Liora was a monster; he knew in his gut that declaration was untrue.

She was actually a beautiful teenager, as well as Adam could recall. She had her father's blue eyes and mother's long black hair. Adam remembered her wickedly cute giggle, her graceful hands welcoming the Sabbath in prayer, and the feel of her poke when she tagged him in hide-n-seek under her dining room table. She was also the only girl he knew who cursed. As a ten-year-old boy, he had a mild crush on her. And then things got complicated with the birth of Eli, and the death of his mother Miriam, with all the fussing and arrangements that had to be made and changed and adjusted because of poor Eli.

The day after Eli was born, Ruby told Adam that they were not going to the hospital to see his new baby cousin; instead they were going to a funeral. Miriam had been like a second mother to Adam, always there, always cooking and watching and doting upon the only little boy in the house, and now she had died during childbirth. She was forty-two. The umbilical cord had been wrapped tightly around Eli's neck. Every time his mother pushed him out a little, the strangulating rope pulled him back. Miriam was diabetic, and the prolonged labor was too much for her. She suffered a fatal heart attack.

In the days that followed, thinking Ruby said the baby had "sighed and nodded," Adam believed that the baby's breath and movement had caused his aunt's death. Adam was twelve when he learned Eli was "cyanotic." He was being suffocated during birth and lacked enough oxygen. The family didn't know the severity of Eli's disability right away, but for years, they endured an existence of constant waiting and watching—to see how bad the damage would be.

Adam never understood why Liora was sent to live in Israel. Adam heard his uncle cry on and off for days before she left.

David had intermittent weeping jags ever since his wife had died. Adam had grown oblivious to the sounds of his crying. The night before Liora left, her shrill shouting permeated the carpeted floor that separated his family's apartment from theirs. Adam was almost thirteen, and though he was just beginning to isolate himself from his parents, on the cusp of teen-dom, he sat on the edge of his bed with his mother and bit his nails. Adam's mother got up to pace when the screaming became prolonged, while his father stood in the hallway pounding his fist against the wall.

"Why are they yelling so much?" Adam asked, terrified, but all his mother did was stamp her foot and tell him that David insisted Miriam would have wanted her sister in Israel to raise Liora. Ruby and Seymour were devastated once Liora had gone. Adam didn't know what to think.

For months after his cousin's departure, Adam walked around his uncle on tiptoes. His stomach jumped to his throat every morning as he heard David downstairs, first the squeak of his old bed right beneath Adam's room, then his thumping footsteps. Adam knew his mother would hand David a copy of *The New York Times* on his way out, but Seymour would stay in the kitchen behind a closed door. Adam would sigh in relief when he heard the front door slam and knew it was safe for him to leave the house without seeing his uncle.

In high school, Adam would spy on his uncle in the street. David walked hunched, as if always in the bends of his prayers, his knee-length black coat swung backward as he shuffled to and from shul. David became a man who wore his grief like body odor. Adam feared his uncle was floating somewhere between death and insanity.

At the time of Adam and Diane's wedding, David was an impressive six feet tall, his salt and pepper hair curly and wild, the white silk tallis draped regally over his broad bony shoulders. David sang soaring, pitch-perfect, weepy songs. He disarmed the women with the charm of his talent and his European looks: almond-shaped blue eyes with dark lashes, pinched straight nose, and his fair skin always shadowed in thought. All of Diane's girlfriends at the wedding wanted to know if the cantor was single.

David became practically estranged from Adam and Ruby after he pushed her to move to Florida. The wedding had put them in the same room for the first time in a year; Adam had been annoyed at seeing them together, however inattentive they were to each other. He wished they had talked about his father.

"Diane, Liora also talked about something else." Sitting next to her in bed, his chest tight, Adam pushed Diane's bangs from her eyes.

She stiffened. "What, for god's sake?"

"Liora is sure there isn't enough money in David's estate to provide care for Eli forever. He sold the old house to put Eli in this new one. She thinks Eli has nothing. Nothing."

"What are you going to do? What does Liora think we can do?"

"She said if her father had so much love for his son that he chose to spend his whole life surrounded by only one of his children" — Adam stopped and caught his breath — "then he should have seen to it that he'd be taken care of." He turned to Diane. "David must have had something left besides the brownstone. Right?"

David was out of the house a lot after Miriam died, but there were no European trips or art collections, no fancy cars or new spoiled wives. His uncle was a cantor and could not have earned a fortune, but when David's father died he left everything to his son: the deed to the brownstone, shares of his law practice, stocks, the contents of his West Side apartment. Ruby had been long since dismissed as his daughter because of their feeling toward Seymour, and consequently, to placate her from being left out of her father's will, David had bought Ruby the Florida condo, but there should have been millions. Could it all have been spent?

Five years ago, Eli was moved into a group home in Brighton Beach, Brooklyn that David had bought with the proceeds of the sale of the brownstone, with various health aides, and the added benefit of income from other male occupants. Adam had at one time phoned Eli fairly regularly, once a month or so, but after Eli rebuffed several attempts to arrange a visit, Adam got the message and stopped asking.

"I still don't see why you have to risk your life for them," Diane repeated.

Her whining angered him. "First, I am not risking my life! This is for Eli. Eli is debilitated in ways you and I couldn't tolerate. He must feel so, I don't know, claustrophobic, frustrated he can't do this himself." When Eli was a teenager, Adam and Diane and baby Jamie had visited Eli and found him sitting in a wheelchair, cutting photos of cars from a magazine with a cuticle scissor. Adam was shaken. When had Eli become this dependent on a wheelchair? Eli had developed asthma as a boy; maybe as an adult he had trouble breathing. Adam squeezed Diane's hand, horrified. "I have absolutely no idea what condition Eli is in."

Diane was so lonely that she ran to the phone and called Jamie as soon as Adam's cab was out of sight. After telling Jamie Adam's tale of woe, Jamie said, "So, Dad really did this for Eli. Cool." Jamie's voice was mellow and flat.

She had a headache and swallowed two Motrin tabs without water. "You don't sound very surprised," Diane said.

"Actually, I knew."

Diane's headache got worse. "You knew what?"

"I knew about David. *Dying*." He was crunching something in his mouth.

"Stop chewing! Did Dad call you?"

"I've been sort of emailing Ariella."

"Who?"

"Ariella? You know, like your niece? Liora's daughter? My cousin in Israel?"

Jamie's revelation left Diane feeling irritated and out of the loop. Jamie had searched the web several years before, looking for his cousins in Israel. One link led to another and he finally hooked up with her at her high school email address. They'd been email pals since. Jamie told his mother that David had sent letters to Liora over the years and she gave them to Ariella to read. Diane was shocked. Jamie went on to say that Ariella had called him that morning to tell him about her grandfather's death, asking him to find out information about Eli and to go to see him. She was very concerned about his living situation and begged Jamie's confidence when she told him she wanted her mother to go to New York to see the family.

"What? See whom in her family? Her brother? Us?"

"Yeah. Everyone. When she asked me to go see Eli she didn't realize how far it is from Denver to New York." He crunched again—ice. "So, like, why don't *you* visit Eli?"

"Me? I should visit Eli? Alone?"

"Well, his father just died and he told Dad to go to China to get him. I think he'd welcome your interest."

"Eli didn't seem to like us." Diane was reluctant to go into this now. "Did Liora say something to you?"

"I've never like even *spoken* to Liora." He cleared his throat. "But listen, the main thing is that my relationship is with Rella, that's what she likes to be called, not with her mother, so I'm asking you to see Eli for *her*, so then I can tell Rella what's going on with him."

"What does she want to know?"

"Rella just feels that if Eli is, like, too bad-off to ask for help, now that his father is dead, her mother would do something for him."

Jamie made it sound reasonable that such an inquiry into Eli's life would be the customary expectation. What did he know about life-long hostility? But why shouldn't Diane investigate, with David dead, and Liora for all practical purposes removed from the family? It very nearly felt not only reasonable but also expected, for her to offer condolences and to assess the condition of her cousin by marriage. If it hadn't been for the argument between Adam's grandfather with Seymour, Diane assumed that Adam and Eli would have remained close.

"You're right, Jamie. Maybe I will go see Eli. But first, tell me what Ariella knows about David."

"I don't know. Her mother told her he was some famous American cantor, a poet and paragon of the greater *tri-state* Jewish community." He sighed like his mother. "So, you'll go see Eli tomorrow?"

"Tomorrow?" Diane felt an unfamiliar assertiveness. "If the weather is clear."

The seating area at the Shanghai Air departure gate was almost empty and Adam had a moment of panic. He was ready to go— why wasn't everyone else? Was it the wrong time? It was still an hour before departure. Adam walked to the desk, and shrugged at the woman behind it. She kept talking into the phone, but mouthed, "Delayed." Adam could tell by her chatty laughter that this was a social call. He interrupted. "Can you please help me?"

She hung up and explained to Adam that there was bad weather expected in Shanghai.

"How do they know what the weather will be in twenty hours? I have a dead man waiting for me!"

"I'm terribly sorry for the delay, but you see, there appears to be a storm at sea and it could come down on Shanghai tomorrow."

"Guess I have no choice." He looked behind him. "Phones anywhere?" She pointed, and as she got back on the phone she said, "I'm so sorry for your loss." Hers was the first condolence anyone had expressed.

The next difficult task of the trip was telling Diane about the delay. He knew she would take it as an omen.

She responded as expected. "Adam, I'm afraid. Please don't go."

"Stop acting like a child. I'm going." As abruptly as the arrival of a twenty-four hour stomach virus, he had an almost violent need to bring David back. He also knew that until he walked back into the house, Diane would be tearful and sleepless. "I have no choice, Diane. Would I go through this if I had any other choice?"

"And I supported your decision to go, but maybe I'm wrong."

Suddenly, Adam was sure he had forgotten something he needed for the trip. "Have you called Jamie? Does he know about David and that I'm leaving?

Diane rabidly spewed the entire conversation with Jamie until Adam finally heard the words he was waiting for Diane to say. "I ended the call by promising Jamie I would think about seeing Eli."

"Wow. Jamie is full of surprises. Liora's daughter?" Adam was annoyed with the notion of Jamie hooking up with that side of the family. "How long has—" He looked up at the information board. "Jesus, Diane. They've announced boarding. They said we had an hour! I gotta go." He waited for her good-bye as he watched the flood of passengers, draining their coffee cups feverishly, as if savoring their last Starbucks ever. His nerves jittered at the apparent mayhem.

Diane shouted, "Call me as soon as you land."

"Don't worry," he shouted back.

"Adam? I am going to try to visit Eli. All right?"

"I don't know, whatever. Love ya." He hung up and took his position at the end of a long line. He tried to remember what it was he forgot.

A male airline worker pushing a wheelchair whistled to the flight agent to wait. A Chinese woman was in the chair holding a small girl on her lap. She looked about eight years old, and she was crying, the back of her head leaning into the woman's chest. Wrapped in a red and blue knotty woolen cape, the woman herself was tiny, the mushroom of gray hair that sprouted on the crown of her head proving her the older party. Her short legs dangled above the footrest. She and the girl wore identical white sneakers with the Nike swoosh on their sides.

Adam filed behind them as the agent tore their tickets and helped the crying child to stand. The woman rose from the wheelchair, hurriedly put Little Mermaid sunglasses on the girl, took her by the hand, and whispered something into her ear. The child sniffled and got quiet. The two practically had to run following their escort, the woman tugging on the girl's arm. At the entrance to the plane, she threw her three satchels easily over her left shoulder before hoisting the girl onto her right hip.

The three of them—Adam, the woman and the girl—were being escorted through the plane, which to Adam seemed the size of a small city. The door closed immediately and the flight attendant directed him to the bulkhead row of the economy cabin. Handing him a pillow and blanket, she smiled and told him that he had the whole row to himself. The three vacant seats emphasized his loneliness, challenging his instinct to stay on this flight and do the right thing.

Lift off was quick.

He was entrusted to *retrieve* a dead body! That word! He might as well be on a mission to pick up a recovered MIA. Adam had a boyhood friend whose brother Frankie had been missing in action from the Vietnam War. Last year, out of the blue, the family got a call from the Air Force that a land mine had exploded and in the debris they found the missing boy's crashed helicopter, along with the remains of three soldiers. DNA proved some of the remains were Frankie's.

For all Adam knew, Eli was sitting in his chair envying Adam's big adventure, how his cousin was free of restraints, doing his mitzvah, when in his heart, Adam felt just as wheelchair-bound, cornered in his world, the only hope for uncle David's return, as though the world had suddenly frozen and Adam was the last matchstick. For her part, Liora had spoken as though the effort was his familial duty and the Kaplans were asking no favor at all.

As the plane continued to climb, Adam scanned the aisles trying to find a flight attendant. Reaching in his backpack checking for the stuff Diane had crammed in, he clamped his hand around a bulk of paper. He shuffled the deck of forms and certificates looking for that address and phone number of the contact in Shanghai Liora had recited. Foreseeing endless boredom, he wished he could pass the rest of the flight with a marathon showing of *Law and Order*. Adam was in awe of A.D.A. Jack McCoy, his ability to convey sincerity, compassion, and contempt all at once. Adam guessed he felt this affinity with McCoy because law was in his blood.

Closing his eyes against the audible separation of the atmosphere as the plane rushed adamantly forward, he thought he might go back to school, finish college, become an attorney, go to work in a white shirt and come home with it still white. Ruby had never thrown away her husband's white shirts. Seymour Oppenheim, master plumber, had previously been Seymour Oppenheim, *Esq.*

Arriving home, mid-semester, following his father's death, Adam hid from his uncle for three days before mastering the courage to tell him he'd taken a leave of absence. David had been furious. He was the only father in the house now, and he used his voice as if its sound alone bore parental authority. Adam's final disobedience in not returning to school, he believed, was what pushed David to formally ask Ruby to vacate the apartment upstairs, claiming he was preparing to sell the house. Ruby was shuffled off to her condo in Miami and a year later, Adam was walking down the aisle with Diane. The house did not get sold for another twenty years.

Before Adam was born, his father Seymour graduated second in his class from Brooklyn Law School, immediately secured a position at a Park Avenue firm, and then married the boss' daughter, Ruby. Fives years later the judicial inner-circle chatter of Seymour's bribery of a judge had humiliated the firm beyond tolerance. After Seymour's suicide, Adam learned from his mother that her father thought Seymour was unethical, at the

21

very least, an incompetent lawyer, and therefore failed as a husband and father.

~~~Adam aged five and his mother Ruby are riding in a Checker cab, uptown from Gramercy Park to Park Avenue and Seventy-Fifth Street. She is sniffling. It is May. She wears a long-sleeved, ankle-length dress, blue with tiny white flowers, and the fancy shul wig; sweat drips from her temples. Ruby, her father and brother, uncle David, are very religious. Adam sits on the small flip-down seat between the backseat and the driver, holding an empty cardboard box on his lap. His mother is taking him to help clean out Daddy's desk. Daddy quit his big job. "Just like that," Ruby tells him.

It is the only time Adam gets to see his father's office. Its big windows look down from the twentieth floor, and Adam holds onto the brown chair, afraid of falling out through the glass. His father bends to kiss the top of his head as his mother unlocks drawers in the big-as-a-house wooden desk. This is also the last time he sees his old, wooden-like Grandfather Jacob Kaplan, still and stiff at the doorpost as his daughter and grandson file out past him. Seymour is behind them as they leave the office building, but he doesn't follow them into the cab. Adam whines, thinking they have lost him. He doesn't know why his mother brought him on this stupid trip.

Adam heard whining as he sat alone in the bulkhead. He opened his eyes, turned toward the whine, and looked to the row behind him to see the Chinese woman and girl, squeezed in the two middle seats between an obese lady on the girl's side and a middle-aged man, blowing his nose, on the mother's side. Without giving it too much thought, he got up and went over to the woman with the girl and made eye contact. "Do you speak English?"

"Yes. Fine," the woman said and smiled.

"Do you want to change seats and sit in the bulkhead with me? There are empty seats," he said, watching to see if his words had made sense to her. The woman whispered to the girl.

"My daughter say, yes, thank you, we can seat on you."

Adam hoped they knew what he asked them and blushed, fearing she misunderstood his intentions and thought he was trying to pick her up — or something worse. The two collected their jackets and various small bags and knapsacks, side-stepped past the man with the cold, and followed Adam. Now he saw why the two had needed the wheelchair at the airport. The child, her closed eyes, without the Little Mermaid camouflage, held onto the woman with one hand while her other tiny hand outreached, feeling the air. Her small, pale face was round, with pursed red lips, and her neck was long and held taut, with short straight black hair cupping her cheeks, and Adam thought she looked like a doll that was molded to appear asleep, preparing for a kiss in her dreams. Pity crowded Adam's heart, and for a second he was lost in her darkness.

After he sat, the woman took the seat next to him and pulled down the girl into her seat on her other side. More chatter ensued between them, most of which sounded angry.

"Are you her mother?" Adam asked.

"Yes. She my girl. Blind?" She pointed to the girl's eyes.

"Yes, yes." He nodded his head and made a sad face. "Can I help her with something?"

"Yin sleep whole way." She slapped the girl's knee and spoke the angry words again. Then the woman turned to him and shook her head, as if exasperated. "Doctor he say she need sleep more. Yin never sleep all night to day. I go mysef craz." She hit her own forehead with the palm of her hand.

Adam didn't want to ask any more questions and he wanted to ask a hundred. The first food service began, and they were handed their trays.

"Here." Adam offered her the first tray. "I'm Adam Oppenheim. And you are?"

Shaking her head at the tray, she said her English name was Lucy.

"Lucy? No food? You don't want to eat?" Adam asked.

"No. I have food here." She pointed to the small knapsack stuffed against the bottom of her seat.

"And what about Yin?"

"I have for Yin," Lucy said, her voice succumbing to anger.

Adam turned to the flight attendant. Shrugging at each other, they smiled and blinked a sign of criticism. He asked her, "When the service is over, do you think you can come back and go over what will happen when we arrive in Shanghai? I don't even know how to use the phones or the money." She assured him she would.

About halfway through the chicken and rice, Adam glanced over to see the little girl eating what looked like a peanut butter sandwich, and he cleared his throat to speak. "So, Lucy, how did you learn to speak English so well?"

"I work in Shanghai for American. Busiman and wife."

He assumed she meant businessman. "I see. And you came to the United States for, um, for a visit?"

Lucy lowered her head and pulled her sweater tighter over her ribs. "I go for Yin. See doctor for eyes." She took the empty paper bag back from her daughter, crumbled it, and covered Yin with a blanket. Adam backed off when Lucy closed her eyes and curled her body away.

Morbidly lonesome and already becoming uncomfortable an hour and a half into the trip, he took one stiff drink of scotch and played with the earphones until he found music he could tolerate. "Don't Cry For Me Argentina" came on and he closed his eyes.

He woke to the nudge of the flight attendant offering him breakfast. Six hours had passed as he slept and woke and slept, but there were more than that and then some left in this flying prison. He could hear Diane telling him that the plane was flying on luck now. Yin and her mother were awake and sitting quietly hand in hand. Lucy started squirming in her seat and tapped Adam on the arm. He smiled at her but was almost afraid to ask anything, worried he would cause further discomfort to the woman. Then Lucy spoke as if they had become fast friends. "You go to Shanghai for vacation? Is very beautiful."

"No, no. My uncle died." Adam closed his eyes and stuck his tongue out the side of his mouth, pantomiming death to her. She laughed. "I have to go retri—" He started over. "I have to go get his body to take him back home. The government wants to cremate him, you know, burn him to ashes?" He waited for a facial sign that she understood. Her face did not flinch, but he went on, speaking slowly and emphatically. "We're Jewish. I have got to get him home in one piece." He held his hands in front of himself as if holding a solid ball.

Lucy's face lit up. "You Jew? My boss, Mista Cohen, he Jew." She showed the kind of excitement a person might express when discovering something very rare and astonishingly amusing. "You got special rule all everything. Oh, yeah Mista. I learn all rule about food, yeah, and special dishes."

"Yes, well, it must have been hard to learn all that." Adam patted Lucy's hand, then pulled back not knowing if that was allowed. He could see her blushing. "I'm sure the man and his wife appreciate it and I hope you're properly compensated for your considerate service—"

One look at Lucy's bulging eyes and Adam stopped talking. Then she smiled and continued. She told him about her husband's desertion after Yin was born blind ten years ago. Yin was older than she looked. Lucy had found a job with the Jewish businessman when Yin was two years old. Last year the Cohens did some research and paid for the two to make this trip to the United States for a medical consultation. While in New York, they stayed with Mr. Cohen's friends. Unfortunately, the doctor could do nothing except advise them on the proper schooling for Yin, encouraging Lucy to teach her to read Braille.

"And so you are going to do that, right? She has got to learn to read." He smiled, relieved that the doctor had brought that fact to her attention.

"I no can work and worry for she reading." Lucy said bitterly, glancing down at Yin who had seemed to fall asleep.

Lucy's attitude pierced Adam. He could find no words to respond to such resentment at a child. How dare she deny Yin an education?

The captain came on to announce that they had made good time and would have been landing ahead of schedule, except that another rainstorm was pounding Shanghai and they were being diverted to the International Airport in Xiamen. There was a universal groan and a surge of service bells.

"Xiamen," Lucy said to Adam, "is big city." She seemed undisturbed.

A flight attendant spoke over the PA system, first in Chinese and then in English. "We will get you to Shanghai as soon as the storm has passed. You don't want us flying into a storm, do you?" She giggled. "We will be detained in a holding area, as we won't go through customs in Xiamen. Food and restrooms will be provided. The captain is sorry for the inconvenience but regrets there is no choice." No choice. Adam, drained of all his human powers, was more grateful that Diane was not with him than he had been for anything in a long time.

An hour later, the plane landed softly in Xiamen. The room the passengers poured into was large enough to seat them all in rows reminiscent of a courtroom. The walls were white, devoid of decoration. Along a wall sat a machine for cold drinks and candy snacks, and a row of telephones that immediately had a queue circling the room. First class, being first off the plane, got dibs on the initial run, but Adam was able to make his call relatively quickly. The flight attendant remembered Adam's request and briefed him on placing a credit card call, but warned that not all the other airport attendants spoke English and the only English he would hear from employees once she left was from the loudspeaker announcements—maybe. Adam dialed Diane and kept an eye on Lucy. He already felt estranged from humankind and needed her bilingualism to ensure his communicability. The phone rang a dozen times and Diane did not answer. He hung up and called Jamie, who picked up on one ring.

"Dad! You there already? We were worried about your weather. Mom almost had a coronary that you were delayed!"

"Boy!" Adam shouted into the phone. "Where is she? I tried to call the house and no one answered."

Calmer, Jamie drew an audible breath and filled him in. "She went to spend the night with Joe and Nancy. She was, like, so flipped that snow was coming. She tried to change the message on your machine from their house but couldn't figure out what to do. You know she's not too—"

"Oh Jamie, never mind about that. I'll call her later."

"I'll try her too. But hey, I can't believe you went to China!"

Oh, yes, yes. Went to China. No big deal, he told him. "We haven't quite gotten to Shanghai as planned. Not to worry, everything is good as gold on the plane, and I'll get there and back home on schedule." Should he ask Jamie to keep news of this unscheduled stop from his mother? "Look, I have to give this phone up. Call your mother and tell her I'm fine and I'll try to call there later. Okay?" He waited for Jamie's consent. "And tell Joe he can run the business himself till I get home."

"He's your partner. I don't think he needs approval from you."

Adam couldn't tell if Jamie was being sarcastic or trying to be helpful. He heard his stomach growl with hunger. "Listen, I love you. Talk to you tomorrow. Okay?" He wasn't going to ask about Ariella now.

"You're like the adventureman. Hey, I think you're doing a really big thing."

"Thanks, Jamie. Love you."

Hanging up, he drew a breath, slung his bag over his shoulder, and scanned the room for a seat. Boy had sounded sweet on the phone and feelings akin to releasing your child's hand on the first day of kindergarten pervaded Adam's gut. Reward and regret spun into the generalized nausea of his adulthood. Adam let Boy's pride echo in his head: I think you're doing a really big thing.

A food cart came around the waiting room with what looked like dried pork and beef jerky. Adam dug into his bag for Fig Newtons from home.

Disappointed that he hadn't gotten to speak with Diane, Adam sat back and closed his eyes, picturing her giving birth to Jamie, recalling how he studied the boy those first three months, looking for signs of a birth defect. He thought he understood how Eli had been damaged during birth, but he had heard stories while listening through his parents' wall, eavesdropping on their nighttime debates over whether Eli might have developed abnormally in utero. What if Jamie had been born abnormal? How would he, as his father, have lived with that, with Diane, not knowing if she or he were at fault, not knowing how to make his son feel whole? Adam had shown his baby to Eli. Diane had insisted the shy teenager Eli hold the boy, insisted he kiss his forehead and talk to him, placing her baby in his arms and closing Eli's hands securely around Jamie's body. Eli batted his long dark lashes and looked stunned, or amazed, that the baby would stay still in his arms, and warmth rushed through Adam as he watched his cousin's mouth open, mimicking Jamie's yawn. Then he raised his head to look beyond Adam's shoulder and his gorgeous, snapshot-perfect smile fell away. David had come into the room. He walked over to his son, patted his head tenderly, then removed Jamie from his arms and handed him back to Diane.

A static filled, highly accented announcement told Adam that their delay might last several hours. They would now go through customs in Xiamen and find comfortable seating and food within the airport. Adam figured he had one day left to get to his uncle before Rabbi Giacalone hauled him to Beijing for burial. There was no way on God's earth the Lubavitch would let the body be cremated. The rabbi would drag the corpse across China by foot before he would let that happen.

Adam had grown up under close rabbinical scrutiny. David's cohorts continued to interfere in Adam's life even after he and Diane were married. Jamie had been born eight days before the start of Passover, which meant his bris would be on that first day of the holiday. The highly respected and precise moyel Adam and Diane hired from Brooklyn would not drive to New York City on the holiday, and so they felt forced to wait an extra day for him to travel. David caught wind of their plan to postpone the circumcision and was enraged. He told his nephew that he would have a moyel walk across the Brooklyn Bridge to Manhattan so that the ceremony could be performed on the proper day. Diane became hysterical. How could they let a strange moyel who'd walked ten miles cut her baby's penis? Was David out of his mind? The man had already pushed Ruby out of the house, and he still had the gall to interfere in his nephew's life. Adam might have succumbed to his uncle's demands if Diane hadn't objected so passionately.

The bris was done a day late, by their moyel of choice, while David stood over the rabbi and Jamie with a prayer book, bending at the knee and whispering, bowing and praying for who knows what. For the next six months, Diane believed her darling son was cursed because she disobeyed the laws of God. Adam was furious with his uncle for frightening Diane, and for months he wouldn't speak his name in front of her. They left their Manhattan apartment and moved to Queens, as far from David as they could afford.

The sun had lowered outside the airport. Adam searched the benches for Lucy and Yin. He ran to catch up with them as they were leaving the holding room. Latching onto Lucy's trail, he followed along with them through the terminal. He'd pay her if he had to to stay with him until the flight out. At four-foot-ten, she and the little doll girl she pulled were Adam's security force. Lucy yelled up into his face, "You stay for me?"

"Yes. Yes. Yes because I hoped we could stay together." He mimed a circle around their heads, making them one unit. "I'll pay you to stay with me, translate for me, until the plane leaves for Shanghai. Do you understand what I'm asking you?" He shouldn't have asked the woman for anything. He saw himself being arrested for soliciting sex from a mother and child. Diane would have to make the trip across the world to get him out of prison.

"Yeah, I know what you say. You pay me. Okay? Twenty bucks?"

Adam reached in his wallet and handed her a twenty-dollar traveler's check. "Okay?"

"Oh yeah. American Express. I take that." She pulled the check out of his hand, then tugged on Yin again and motioned with her head for Adam to follow.

"Yes, I'm coming. May I pick her up?" Before Lucy could respond he picked Yin up and handed her one of the hard candies Diane had stuffed in his pockets before he left home. Lucy said something in a calm voice to the girl and she settled into Adam's arms without resistance, put the candy in her mouth, and sucked it while her head rested on Adam's shoulder. Adam fell in love with the girl at that moment and his guilt ran roughshod through him, as if he had been the one to desert this child and to allow her blindness to turn Lucy into a servant and the child into a resentment.

He put Yin down, but continued to hold her hand. What could he do for them before they parted ways in Shanghai?

"Move fas, Mista. We get seat by TV."

It was a typical airport, very clean and organized. There was a fee going through customs that he was told supported the airport, kept it open. The signs were all in Chinese with the universal pictures for various instructions. He was very impressed, both with the signs and his ability to follow them. The bathrooms were modern, but Adam saw Lucy hold her nose as she approached the entrance. He handed Yin back to her mother who abruptly yanked on the collar of Yin's shirt, leading her into the women's room.

"Lucy!" Adam couldn't help himself. "Don't tug on her," he said as if she were the older of his two daughters. Then he remembered she was his mouth, and he smiled at her.

"Wha? Yin no move. She pee in pant if no move fas."

"Well, she's tired," he said, his voice softer and apologetic.

"Yeah, she blind. I take her. Go mista, now go you pee." She shooed Adam with her hand and marched away from him, pushing Yin, who lifted her head and marched alongside her mother, as if she could mimic her mother's familial strut via its sound, looking like a straight haired Shirley Temple in a movie about a courageous orphan.

In the larger waiting area, the three settled in seats in front of a television. Yin turned her face toward the sound on the screen. Adam watched the time on the world clocks tick away. If he got to Shanghai a day too late and they had buried his uncle, he would wring his own neck. God, he wished Eli and Liora hadn't asked him to do this.

They had been waiting for three hours when an announcement blared in Chinese and Yin jumped off the chair. It was not followed by an English translation, and had Lucy not been with him he would have missed the flight. Boarding the plane took an hour, and take off was yet another hour, and it would surely be past midnight by the time they arrived in Shanghai. Day six, post-mortem.

Lucy and Yin grabbed the two seats behind Adam on the final leg of their trip and were right there with him when they disembarked in Shanghai. He gave Lucy another twenty in traveler's checks on the flight so they would stay with him until he made contact with Rabbi Seth Giacalone. Adam was exhausted. He could not remember being this tired since Boy went missing after his high school prom and Adam and Diane stayed up for two days until he schlepped into the house, wearing bathing trunks, his tuxedo jacket crumpled, and his bare chest underneath. Adam had not known such depth of feeling. The ache turned the room and everything in it gray. It stung far sharper than even the pain of losing his father. But that feeling had lifted the second Jamie walked in, and Adam became instantly lightheaded, exhaling as if after an exorcism. At the beach, Mom. Where else? Those were the words that brought Diane to her knees, weeping.

Adam's eyes were tearing as he walked from the plane. Lucy and Yin tagged along behind him until he found a vacant phone, and then Lucy helped him to put the call through. While Adam waited for someone to answer on the other end, his heart thumped. He bounced his back off the wall and scanned the long Shanghai Air terminal for an exit sign. The woman who answered the phone had a voice with an Asian inflection but spiced with the Lower East Side. When Adam asked to speak to the rabbi, she told him she was the rabbi's wife, the "rebbitzon," Elana Giacalone. Adam told her who he was and asked to speak with her husband.

"Mr. Oppenheim? I will come out with it. You've missed them. They've gone to Beijing and I'm relieved to tell you that with Rabbi Giacalone's pull they got permission to bury Cantor Kaplan, may he rest in peace." He heard her draw, then exhale, a long musical breath. "It's almost midnight. Rabbi Giacalone, Seth, should be here first thing in the morning." Adam was speechless. "Mr. Oppenheim?"

"What!" He sank against the wall, squatting, and let the phone dangle. The Fig Newtons he'd eaten rose in his throat. He

33

heard Lucy on the phone telling the rabbi's wife to hold on. He rose, put the phone back up to his ear, and laid his right hand over his heart, as if holding it in. "I've been counting." If he sounded soft-spoken and genteel, it was because he thought he was having a heart attack. "Unless I'm really confused, I had until today to get here. Why has he ignored the agreement? I have *got* to take the cantor home."

"You misunderstood. Yes, today is day seven, but you see, they had to have him already buried by today. The Chinese were ready to cremate him!" Adam heard her sigh and recite a quick Yiddish phrase he could not translate. "You're not in Kansas anymore, Mr. Oppenheim," she said, with a half chuckle.

So the rebbitzon had a mean streak. "Jesus Christ."

"I don't think that kind of talk is helpful."

"So, what do I do now? Am I supposed to go to Beijing and dig him up? This is ludicrous. Damn it to fucking hell." He shook his head. "Sorry."

"And I am sorry as well, for your loss and for your unsuccessful trip. But this is what David would want. I can assure you of that."

"Did he actually say as much? Did he tell you, If I die here, bury me in Beijing before someone in my family comes to get me? He said that, Mrs. Giacalone?" Adam felt the blood rush in his head. *Who are you and the rabbi and why am I asking you for permission to get my relative?*

"You must calm yourself." She allowed a beat, as if bestowing on him the chance to collect his wit. "Of course this is what the cantor wanted. I mean, he would want this. You think he should be cremated? We could let it come to that? No! Of course, no. That's all I'm saying."

Someone could have brought his dead ass home. "Where am I calling?"

"I'm here in Shanghai, the lovely HongKou district."

"I have to come right over there! I know it's really late at night, but it's only right, for Christ sa...I need to come and see your husband without any further delay. Please give me directions."

"You needn't be so assertive, Mr. Oppenheim. Yes, you'll come to me. I'll explain as much of this as I can. But any formal account can only be communicated to you through my husband." Adam was too weary to respond. She said, "So then, we can eat and rest and see the Rabbi in the morning." Neither said anything for a few seconds. "Hello? You there?"

"Yes. I'll have to come." Adam's arrogance embarrassed him, and he was grateful for her offer. "I will just have to come to you."

He was thrown by her Asian/New Yorker convergence of accents. Her tone was neutral, but Adam envisioned her bosomy chest puffed out and her hand on her well-rounded hip. As she recited her address slowly, he scrawled it on scrap paper, with reference points and landmarks. She instructed him to secure a Friendship tourist's taxi. "Fine. I'll find you," he told her. "You don't have to feed me. You merely have to give me information about David's death and make sure your husband gets home and gives me what is mine!" He had already lost track of his own rhyme or reason. He wouldn't let her know that. He held his voice firm. "How long is the trip from here to there?"

"About forty-five minutes. Take this time to relax. You sound jet-lagged."

"Yeah," he said with a mock chuckle, but he wanted to scream, Fuck you! The phone disconnected. He didn't know if time ran out or she hung up.

He stuffed his note into his shirt pocket and tried to remember how to place a call to phone Diane. Where were Lucy and Yin? They were not next to him; they were not sitting near him. He slammed the receiver. *Not in Kansas anymore? I'm not in the fucking world anymore.* He closed his eyes to count to ten. When he opened them and saw no one he recognized from the flight, it was then he heard a sweet sound: squeaky wheels from an oncoming wheelchair. Lucy had stuck Yin in a wheelchair again and was pushing her around. Yin giggled and kicked, loudly repeating to her mother a word that must have meant "faster." He didn't know whether to smile at Lucy or slap her.

She stopped at Adam's feet. "So, Yin and me go now. You know where you go?" Lucy asked as she tied a scarf around Yin's head and whispered to her. Yin raised her hand toward Adam.

"No. You have to stay with me." He shook Yin's hand, then lifted her out of the chair and tickled her belly. She giggled and laid her head again on his shoulder. He realized this was not the first time he imagined taking her home to New York with him.

"Where you go, Mista. I no go do sex. You give back Yin now!"

He handed Yin to Lucy. "No, no. Don't scream. I'll get a taxi. Taxi? Yes, and I'll take you to Mr. Cohen and you tell the driver to get to this address." He showed her his note.

"Okay. One hour to here." She pointed at the address. "We go in taxi firs here den to more far in Xuhui. You pay all way." She raised her finger to Adam's face. "Don't touch Yin. She blind."

Adam's jaw tightened. "I *know* she's blind." Lucy turned her back to Adam and started walking, forgoing the wheelchair. Yin held her hand and tilted her head toward Adam, as if to listen for his footsteps. "Wait for me, Lucy," he said after her. She walked fast for such a little woman. Yin plodded with heavy and sure feet, followed every whispered instruction her mother gave her, and seemed happy, smiling—when her mother wasn't pushing her around.

Adam paid his airport tax with his Visa, was cleared to proceed through a diverted exit set up for national flights, and followed Lucy to the currency exchange just before he passed through to the waiting hall, using his Visa once again in the ATM machine. Adam made the girls stop at a bank of phones and Lucy helped to place his call. This time he was able to leave Diane a message on her machine. "I'm fine. They've buried David in Beijing. I'll call you later from this Rabbi Giacalone's house." He figured she had followed the route of the plane online and knew more than he did about where he was. They made their way through the spanking-new airport, passed smoking rooms and restaurants, hotel booking desks and banks, and headed into a misty rain that smelled like an overstocked candle store at the mall. Incense.

The arrivals had just started to land, dribbling in, and it was easy enough to choose from an array of taxis, varying colored Jettas, outside the terminal. The three crammed into the back seat, their bags hanging from their shoulders and balanced on their laps. Lucy instructed the driver, in a tone Adam thought to be arrogant, and the driver took off at aerodynamic speed. Adam shut his eyes and held onto the seat while Yin giggled and Lucy yelped the Asian equivalent of oiy-vey.

Wrapping its way along the Bund River that separated them from Pudong—the side that glittered with the skyline of modern skyscrapers—the expressway reminded Adam of the FDR Drive, curling its way along the East River. Pearl TV Tower stood tall, triangular and brightly lit at the top, a cross between the Eiffel Tower and the Empire State Building. It was late, and dark, but

Adam had no sense of real time. The bouncing and honking were constant as the driver weaved in and out of his lane, heavy with cars and bicycles, and teased oncoming traffic by entering their lanes head on to pass, slowing only barely to make wide turns around bicycles, which were riding alongside, in front and in back. Amazingly, Yin and Lucy had fallen asleep against Adam's shoulder. Even though he was glad for the warmth, he leaned in toward them and tried to straighten Lucy up so they would not be touching.

The driver slowed along a park, then stopped completely and pointed out the window. "HongKou Stadium," he shouted. Adam smiled and looked, nodding briskly as if very impressed, and asked what sport was played there. The driver frowned, threw the gearshift back into drive, and screeched out from the curb. Holding onto the door handle, Adam watched the blurred yellow and red lights of the Chinese lettering on the buildings. He glimpsed what seemed to be a Buddhist temple among the incessant construction. After about forty-five minutes, the taxi thudded to stop beside a McDonald's golden arch. Adam hoped he had reached his destination. The driver told him he had. Adam shook Lucy and asked if they were in the right place. She looked at the address on his paper and then at the building, got out to read the name on the street sign, then sat back in the taxi and told him, "Yeah. Lady say Mickey Dees. Now you pay man to take me for Mista Cohen in Xuhui." Adam was both amused and pissed by the use of this western icon as the landmark to his Far Eastern adventure. He got out of the taxi and stood in front of twin twenty-one story apartment buildings.

About to ask the driver how much he should give to Lucy to cover the fare, Adam turned to see the man opening the back car door and pulling Lucy and Yin out. Lucy was yelping and Yin cried and kicked the man. Adam ran around and pulled the driver off them. "What is going on?"

"He no take me in Friendshy taxi without you. He say this for touris. You have to come wit us or we stay wit you."

Adam lifted Yin, and Lucy took his arm, holding it snuggly against her side, as if they were a family. He tried to reason with the driver. The man spoke no English and Lucy refused to translate; she just kept shouting at the man in their language. Now Yin started her soft weeping again and Adam helplessly watched the driver pull away. Lucy, standing staunch and proud, turned her chin up to Adam. Before he could speak he had to rub his nose and sneeze three times in a row. Lucy told him the women burned garbage along the river and used incense to keep insects away.

The lobby of the building appeared spacious and clean, as in a typical New York City apartment building. He found the rabbi's name, Giacalone, on the intercom and buzzed up. Announcing himself to Elana, he quickly decided not to mention the other guests with him. He'd explain on the twentieth floor.

As they got onto the elevator, Adam watched the now ritualistic whispering between mother and daughter. Lucy lifted her daughter to the buttons on the panel, but as soon as Yin put her fingers to them and the elevator started to rise, Lucy got angry with her and put her down.

"Lucy? Why doesn't Yin speak English?"

"She speak good. She no speak to you. You strange man."

"I'm a stran*ger*. Not a strange man." Adam shook his head and tried to smile.

The doors opened onto the twentieth floor and Adam held out his arm for Lucy and Yin to step off before him. A woman approached them as soon as they turned the corner of the corridor. She was tall and thin with jet-black hair, straight and tapered long past her shoulders. Her knitted dress was red, with black and yellow flowers embroidered down the left side, and hemmed right below her kneecap. A black woolen shawl covered her shoulders, but not in the way an old woman would wear it; the ends draped over her breasts and were tied in a knot below and between them, fastened with a polished ebony and inlay pin. She smiled broadly and Adam assumed she was the au pair or a friend of the Giacalones, because she could not have been more than twenty-five and was Eurasian, and pretty enough, lovely enough, to be a model. She greeted them with her outstretched hand. "Adam Oppenheim, yes?"

Adam recognized the accent instantly and was silenced by his disbelief. Elana Giacalone.

"I appreciate having you here. Next time, God willing, under happier circumstances." She smiled the way a woman smiles at a man in his wildest fantasy, her eyes half closing with the rise of her cheekbones, and blinking slowly as her mouth returned to relaxed solemnity. Adam felt his knees give.

"I'm Adam. Yes." He put his hand to his chest to reiterate that he was the one who was Adam. "And these are my friends, Lucy and Yin. We met on the plane," he said, then mouthed, "I'm sorry."

"Well," Elana took a breath and bent down to the child. "Aren't you adorable. You speak English?"

"Yes," Yin said, startling Adam.

Elana told Adam, without trying to be discreet, that she spoke Chinese but encouraged children in China to learn and speak English. Lucy stood silent until Elana looked squarely into her eyes. "And you? You are her mother?"

"Yes. Yin blind." Lucy bowed her head. She seemed to cower in Elana's presence.

Adam was bewildered by her sudden submissiveness. He felt even less adequate than he had for the past thirty hours. Lucy, evidently pawky as a call-girl wearing grandma's pearls, had been what Jamie would call *dissing* him.

Mrs. Giacalone looked back at Adam, smiling and dimpled, and tilted her head with curiosity. She seemed to welcome the extra company and be quite willing to house and feed them if needed. "I am so happy to have you all," she said. "Please, follow me to my apartment."

They walked single file behind her. Adam was snared in the narrow roundness of her buttocks. *What portal of paradise had the rabbi fallen through to find her?* Brooklyn didn't grow women like this. A Jewish Eurasian? She could have converted, he guessed, though rabbis usually don't take to that kind of thing. He was loath to bring up the subject of his uncle and ruin this encounter, but the image of Eli and Liora rose up in him and he felt the hours of this seventh day melting into oblivion, the soil hardening around David's pine box. He heard his cousin Eli crying for the rest of his life and Liora giving the order to the Israeli army: Storm Adam's house. As Elana opened the door to the apartment he bluntly asked, "Mrs. Giacalone? What should I do about my uncle?"

"Elana. Call me, Elana." She motioned for them to take seats in her living room. Stick lamps with simple yellow cone-shaped shades lit the room from the ends of every piece of furniture. The linear tan sofa was flanked by identical floor lamps, and the simple Scandinavian oak-looking dining table had twin ceiling fixtures over its ends. The room was cold—not just the decoration, but the temperature, which felt only marginally warmer than outside. He saw the electric heating units along the floor. Disappointed, Adam felt as if he were in a very large suite at a Holiday Inn.

41

Elana hurried in with a tray of cold fish framed with cut raw vegetables and tofu. The fishy smell was pungent and spoiled the pot roast in Adam's hopes.

"I'm sorry I have no hot meal for you. We eat a lot of steamed or boiled fish because the cost of kosher meat is prohibitive," she said. "And the oven, well, we have none. They've promised we are next on the list." She sat across the room, nibbling on crackers.

Lucy placed a dollop of fish and tofu on Yin's tongue. Adam felt obliged to mimic their protocol. Elana broke the awkward silence by turning on some soft background music, an Arabian or Israeli instrumental, then sat on the floor, her knees tucked back and under her skirt. Adam remembered Eli sitting like this as a little boy, the better to keep his balance. Elana smiled at Lucy and Yin, then turned toward Adam. "In between your call from the airport and now, Seth called to inform me he'd be landing at about six in the morning."

"With or without my uncle?"

"Without, of course," Elana said intently. "You must understand, before the rabbi returns and you upset him." She stood; her shoulders lifting as she silently caught her breath. "He's gone to tremendous trouble to do the proper thing. The government almost made him leave Beijing with the cantor. Seth said they had no space and the nearest consecrated earth was in Dalian! But he got around it. So, please don't upset the rabbi when he returns."

Adam chuckled sarcastically. "Don't upset the rabbi?" He asked softly, "What about David's son and daughter? It's all right if I upset them?" He recognized her attitude towards her husband. It was typical of the women Adam had known while growing up in a house that catered to his uncle's cantorship and the multitude of rabbis that passed through his house visiting David and Eli. Adam resented the fact that his mother and aunt showed little respect for his hard-working father, and yet extended toward the men of the shul extreme courtesy. Now he fought to remain polite. He was in a foreign country, in a stranger's home, and he didn't want to frighten Yin.

"Elana," he said, feeling uneasy calling a rabbi's wife by her first name, especially, he had to admit, such a beautiful rabbi's wife. "I have not come halfway around the face of this earth to go home with *nothing*. There has got to be a way to please everyone." But Adam knew a fair deal was one where all parties walked away dissatisfied. He would lay it out for her simply and logically. "Cantor Kaplan is dead. His children are alive. They wish—no, they *ordered*—me to bring him home." He felt infused with his cousin's urgent rage. "What right do you people have to abscond with his body and throw him into a grave that no one will ever be able to visit and just before I get here?" His voice rose and he immediately looked at the little girl. She was obviously absorbing the tension; her mouth formed an O, yet she sat still. She was such an unusual child, but aside from her poise, Adam could not quite put his finger on what was so magical about her.

"*You people?* And we did not *abscond* with him, and we certainly didn't *throw* him into any old grave," Elana replied. Her voice was like children's cough syrup, smooth, but delivered like medicine, yet Adam was having trouble suppressing thoughts of resting his head between her breasts.

Elana crushed her cloth napkin in her hand and took a step closer to Adam. "He was our guest for three months. He died right here on that couch." She pointed with her chin to where Adam was sitting. "We knew him better than you or his children, I can tell you that."

"What the…heck does that mean?" He could feel himself flush and lowered his voice to a conversational tone. "I basically *lived* with him through my entire childhood. I've known him for forty-seven years!"

He rose, patted Yin's head, and asked Lucy to take the child into the bedroom he saw just beyond the living room. Lucy gave him a scolding look, but then turned to Elana, who nodded her head as if to say it was okay. Adam watched the girl as she held her mother's hand and skipped into the other room. He didn't think she realized she was impaired, even though he had no doubt Lucy reminded her ten times a day. Running his hands through his hair, searching for words, he retook his seat and asked Elana to sit.

Elana did, then gazed at him hard. "You did not know him as a grown man would know him. Regard him from an adult's perspective. We spent entire days and nights turning his life inside out. I feel I understood him — and — your relationship to him."

"Then you had to know Eli would want his father home." He didn't believe there was any way she understood his relationship with his uncle. "Why couldn't the rabbi have brought him back? The Lubavitch would have paid, I'm sure."

She blushed, then lowered her face. "I would be betraying my husband's trust to go on about his reasons. I really think we should wait for the rabbi to return." She clasped her hands and flattened her hair behind her tiny ear.

She was not going to clarify their relationship with David. Adam was fuming. "I am his nephew. My uncle loved me. Unless you know something I don't know." Part of him was waiting for her to say he was mistaken, because he secretly suspected his uncle loved no one. He glanced up at the clock and saw it was already one-thirty in the morning. He had five hours to pass before Rabbi Giacalone got back.

"Of course he loved you, Adam. You and Eli and Liora. He loved you all. That's what made him so distraught in these months with us." She slapped both hands gently on her thighs. "But please, it's very late. Let me make up your rooms and we can pray for my husband's safe return and sleep until he arrives. Then, whatever he thinks is proper we will discuss." She held her finger up as if already the queen mother of five dutiful sons. "Remember, your uncle sought us out, through the Internet at his temple's computer."

She made it sound as if he chose them specifically. Adam asked himself, How could I have come here not knowing *anything*? He pretended to know what she was referring to.

"He came to us," she said. "We did not ask for him. Heaven bless him, we were so thankful to be able to help him in any way we could. He trusted the rabbi and me and I simply don't feel comfortable talking about him like this. It feels as if I'm holding his peace in limbo between our disagreements. Let David rest. At least for tonight." She popped herself out of the chair, like hot bread in a toaster ready to be eaten, and said she would go set up Lucy and Yin, in the room that served as her husband's study, and told Adam that he would be sleeping on the foldout sofa.

"Elana?"

She stopped in the archway and turned half-around.

"Just out of curiosity, can I ask how someone like you came to marry a rabbi?" She laughed out loud, and maybe didn't hear Adam ask, "Is he Italian?"

"You mean how could Seth, a Jew, who happens to be a rabbi with an unlikely Italian name, marry someone of my race?"

Adam felt even more uncomfortable. Well, you have to admit it's weird, he thought. "I just think, since you know so much about my *family* relationships, I can a least ask you that."

45

"At least!" she said sarcastically and turned to face him fully. "Actually not. You have no right to know anything about me," she said, her cocky petulance bubbling as she sat again, girlish and animated on the chair opposite Adam. Elana delivered her vita as though filling out a college admission's form: She was the granddaughter of an Italian Jewish woman who escaped the Nazis from Italy, making her way to China, and living in Shanghai from 1941 until 1946. She married a Chinese man and they moved to Brooklyn and had a daughter. "My mother was raised Jewish. She married a Jewish man. I have strong Asian features."

"And how did you and Rabbi Giacalone...?"

"We met at a seminar about Jews of multiethnic parents." She stopped talking and clapped her hands once before twinning her fingers together. "And we were both theology students at Columbia University. End of story." She turned pink at the thought and rose from the chair to attend to Lucy and Yin.

She had teased him, deliberately he believed, leaving him with more questions than answers. Especially as to why the rabbi refused to bring David home. That seemed sinfully thoughtless. What had Liora called Giacalone? An absolute imbecile? Adam stood stiffly, too jumpy to sit. The wind was firing bullets of rain into the uncovered windows, the lights of the Bund dripping like long colored tears down the glass. His hands in his pockets, his face only a breath away from the glass, he asked his reflection, What came first for David, China or the Giacalone's? Seth or Elana?

Adam squinted into the lights and heard Liora's angry urgency, *Get my father buried next to my mother. She's been alone long enough.* He heard Eli, *Bring my father back to me. I have to tell him I'm all right.* The idea occurred to Adam now — here tonight with blind little giggling Yin, sheltered only within the care of an abusive and ignorant woman—that Eli held his inability as his expression of self. As though the essence of an orange was its color—Eli became *a* disabled.

Feeling doped by the inescapable responsibility, Adam tried to think, *Can I get to Beijing*? He pictured a cemetery with pagoda monuments surrounded by bonsai. He would stroll through at dusk, remove and unfold from his pocket his Brookstone travel shovel, and start digging, open the simple pine box, fold his frail uncle into thirds, and stuff him in a jumbo lawn bag and carry him off the premises like a bag of fallen leaves. Then what?

A zap of lightening broke the sky in two. He hoped the rabbi's plane wouldn't run into problems landing due to the storm. Adam was determined to stay up waiting for him. He had to know why he and Elana were working in Shanghai and why David wanted to be here with them. Given what he knew about the chatty nature of rabbis, Giacalone would fill in the blanks, and then some.

Elana brought him his linens and pillow and tried unsuccessfully to help Adam call Diane. He could imagine the horrors Diane was conjuring about him. Elana showed him how to place a call and told him he was free to try again any time during the night. As she left him sitting on the sofa, he found himself unintentionally respecting her closed-lip smile and downward gaze, as if she were a self-reliant hooker. Just how much did she know about his family that he didn't? Did the Giacalones so-called information amount to misconceived extrapolation? Surely they knew about the tragic death of Eli's mother Miriam, and about the grotesque death of Adam's father. Did they think Eli was retarded? Eli was not retarded. Adam sulked, feeling a burst of protectiveness fiercer than he'd ever had before for Eli.

At three o'clock in the morning Adam's call went through but the message machine again came on. He hung up on it and thought, This shit blows.

The sound of the front door jerking open startled Adam from light sleep. He sat up. The windows spilled the bleach of the rising sun around him. Just as he began to remember where he was, he turned to the sound of a man speaking. In the shadows he saw a tall, narrow man coming toward him. "Rabbi Giacalone?" Adam asked.

"Yes. Mr. Oppenheim?" His baritone resonated with confidence and pith, like the voice of a game show announcer.

"Yes. I'm Adam." Adam climbed off the sofa and extended his right hand. "How was the flight?" He felt false — evading the obvious.

"Fine, just fine, thank God. I'm here safely." He put his briefcase on the floor. "Can I turn on the lights?" He reached under the lamp and Adam was able to finally, clearly see the face of the man who was attempting to ruin his life. "Adam, please call me Seth."

Seth Giacalone looked to be in his early thirties. His skin was pink and raw around his blond beard and the ends of his mustache. A small nose and deep-set blue eyes made him seem handsome. He wore no hat or yarmulke on his sandy, free-for-all curls, and he was dressed in a dull brown corduroy suit and blue oxford shirt and tie.

Working to keep his voice steady, Adam said, "About the situation? My uncle?"

Seth spoke loudly, without any consideration for his sleeping wife. "Let me tell Elana I'm home, and then we will sit together, all right?"

Seth marched lead-footed to the bedroom. Adam badly wanted to shower and change his clothes, brush his teeth, at least appear to be formidable, at least show that he too was a man, a fully experienced, educated, damn good-looking man who was here to take his damn dead uncle the hell home. But Seth was not going to give him time.

Seth peeked out from around the corridor, his jacket off, shirt and tie loosened. "I don't want you to think we are being rude to leave you out here for any length of time alone, but my wife and I will say our morning prayers and then we'll be out."

"How long? I mean, I understand, but is there time to just do nothing?" Come on!

"Praying is not doing nothing. I can lend you your uncle's prayer book."

More guilt. "Sure." Against Seth's commanding posture, Adam felt he had been drafted into hand-to-hand combat.

VISITATION RIGHTS

D iane's night had turned into a sleepless marathon of worry, waiting to hear from Adam. She thought she'd lose electricity from a storm that had threatened to arrive and so she asked Joey to take her to his house. The snow hadn't come. Joey drove her back when he left for work at dawn.

Mid-morning, Diane heard Adam's obscure phone message about David's burial only when she came out of her shower. Confused, irritable, and disappointed, she called Jamie and was even more sickened now to learn of Adam's unscheduled stop in Xiamen. "I wonder if that extra time would have made a difference with David," she asked herself out loud. "Can you believe the degree of control *weather* has on all our lives?"

"But the weather in New York is okay now, right? You said if the weather was okay you would go to see Eli."

She felt childish enough about her storm-related escape to Joey's last night and had to save face no matter what meteorological event occurred. "I think I'm going. The weather seems fine, so I'm going."

"You know, like if it's safe to go."

Oh sweet Jamie. He worries like a mother hen. As soon as they hung up she started rummaging through her closet, trying to find an outfit that would be both respectful of Eli's grief and cheerfully optimistic about Eli's future. She would help to find him a respectable job, maybe something in the courthouse where she had worked; it was handicapped accessible. He did speak two languages after all. He could be an interpreter for Israeli immigrants! Diane grabbed her courthouse telephone directory and threw it into her handbag.

It had been at least thirty years since Diane had traveled these streets of Brighton Beach, Brooklyn. An old synagogue on Neptune Avenue, evidenced by the remaining stained glass Star of David in the window, was now an Islamic temple. Instead of finding kosher delis and families resembling those in a Neil Simon play, she hurried past Russian stores — and these Russians were not your grandmother's Russians, not refugees from the pogroms — as well as Pakistani, Mexican, and Asian shops. The sun had still not broken through the clouds, and now, about noon, Diane thought the overcast sky was a sign that today would prove to be disappointing.

She finally saw, for the corner sign, Eli's street, about five blocks from the ocean and a few hundred feet from the busy corner of Neptune Avenue. The block was made gloomier by the shadow of the elevated Q train, which rattled her insides when a train screeched above. Who could sleep with the windows shuddering every two minutes? She saw some new buildings rising at the far end of his street. Renewal? That could be a good thing.

She parked, lowered her visor mirror, reapplied her lipstick, and checked to see if her nostrils were clean. Tying her orange chenille scarf tight around her neck, she eyeballed the sidewalk for a path clear of ice. Christmas lights still ran along the bare tree trunks, their branches topped with lines of narrowing white snow. She braved against the wind toward the house, trying to compose a greeting for Eli. She envisioned his face pressed against the window, watching the trains rush past.

The Kaplan and Son Group Home was a modest, cedar-sided bungalow.

KAPLAN AND SON GROUP HOME

The wood sign on the aluminum-framed storm door looked as if it were made in woodworking shop, its letters burned-in with a contraption that Diane remembered Jamie played with in the Boy Scouts. Up close, she sensed the inside of his house would be clean. The walk and steps were shoveled, the siding had been recently painted, and through the windows she could see healthy hanging plants, which she never managed to grow. Diane's stomach rolled. Eli the youth, who was quiet and intense, might prove an angry old man. Thirty-seven years could wear on a life if that life was based on compressed fear. Diane was sensitive to the personas of fear, and she felt when she had last seen Eli's plastic half-smile, half-grimace, that he too was lost behind his plated behaviors of self-preservation.

The woman answering the door was a lovely looking forty-something, wearing black slacks, white shirt, and a camel hair blazer, with reddish waves of hair scattered in uneven lengths approaching her shoulders, and a slim figure with the kind of small high breasts Diane had always envied for their ability to look good in everything. The woman's mouth grew a tender and schoolteacher smile. "Hello. Do you have an appointment?"

Appointment? Diane had not anticipated that necessity. "My name is Diane Oppenheim and I'm here to see my cousin, Eli. Eli Kaplan?"

"How wonderful! Does he know you're coming?" The woman took Diane's hand in an oddly familiar way.

"No, we haven't spoken in a while." She thought of mentioning the connection between her son and Eli's niece Ariella, but thought better of it. "Will I be able to see him?"

"First come in from the cold," she said and stood back to allow Diane to enter the house in front of her. "Have a seat in there and let me go see what Eli is doing and tell him you're here." She pointed to a room on Diane's left. "By the way, my name is Sharon Manila, like the envelope, and I'm the director and senior counselor here. Social worker."

Something in the woman's voice sounded hopeful to Diane. She had said, "What Eli is *doing*," as if there could be any number of things he could be *doing*. The woman withdrew. Diane looked around. The room to the left was a large parlor with its television on, but no one there to watch. Diane swept the room with her eyes. She recognized furnishings that were brought from his home in Gramercy Park. The sofa was covered in a forties slip of oriental motifs: the lotus and the pagodas, Chinese bonsai, women dressed in geisha costumes. She shivered remembering David's corpse in Beijing. Diane suddenly felt discovered in a lie, as she had after rushing to get home to her mother from a girlfriend's "nude séance," when she had realized her blouse was on inside out. Flustered now with the realization that she might actually see Eli, and being unprepared to offer him anything, she looked toward the unoccupied brown Naugahyde recliner that was facing the television, and thought, Stay calm.

In spite of the chatter she heard from another room, Diane crept past the foyer, around the hallway, where she saw the kitchen. It was clean, very sixties — avocado and harvest gold everywhere. A small black woman stood in front of the mismatched white sink, washing dishes, her back to Diane, while three male adults, ranging in age from around twenty to forty, sat around the white laminate table and ate; the older, wheelchair-bound man was doing all the chattering, while the other two men chewed and took drinks from a thick pink concoction through a straw. Diane speculated on their conditions, but felt relieved that they seemed to be harmless and relatively self-sufficient. She heard Sharon calling her name. Diane jumped, scooted back to the parlor, concocting a tale about looking for a bathroom.

Sharon met Diane smiling at the end of the hallway. "Mrs. Oppenheim?" Sharon tilted her head and waited expectantly. Diane stood unable to verbalize her fib. Sharon asked her to join her in the parlor. She turned down the television's volume before sitting next to Diane on the sofa.

Diane smiled. "So, can I see Eli now?"

"I realize you don't recognize me," Sharon pushed her curls off her forehead. "So I have to assume your husband Adam has never mentioned me to you."

"No. Have you two met?" Diane's heart thudded. When an attractive woman mentioned Adam in a familiar way, Diane still felt the cramps of adolescent jealousy.

"Many, many years ago. When I was Eli's teacher at the house in the city."

Diane recalled a vague mention of her and managed to repeat softly, "You were one of Eli's teachers. Okay. And you knew Adam in what regard?" She smiled desperately.

"Well, he lived in the same house, the apartment upstairs, you know, until they left when his mother moved—I believe it was to Florida? We saw each other in passing occasionally." She sat up straight and smiled. "Eli was such a handful, and such a blessing."

She must have started teaching before Adam's father died, Diane thought, wondering if she knew the details of his death and the reasons David had pressured Adam and Ruby to move out. "I remember how he loved to read," Diane said, relieved but grossly confused. She looked toward the stairs that went to the bedrooms. "Excuse me for interrupting, but is Eli dressing or something? Am I waiting for him to come downstairs?"

"I'll get to that in a moment. May I continue establishing my credentials?"

"You're a social worker, correct?" Had Diane asked for her *credentials*? She tried to be polite, but felt defensive. Right then she began suspecting the woman of foul play.

"I was an education major at NYU," Sharon said, still smiling. "Eli was nine years old already and no one had been successful in getting him to advance his skills above second grade level. I'd received his case as an assignment, at first, and then I stayed with him until he read above grade level." In all she had stayed four years, she said, one year past her graduation "I taught for a few years, then went back to NYU for my MSW, partly because of my work with Eli, really."

Now suspicion rose from Diane's insides out. Sharon was acting like a kid in love and she was a good ten years older than Eli. What's with the giggle? "Did Cantor Kaplan buy this place and hire you to run it coincidentally?" Diane asked. "That would be so uncanny!"

"Uncanny, indeed." She laughed. "No, I'd kept in touch, sporadically, with the cantor and Eli over the years, and when it was time for him to think about Eli's future, his father called me to work with him." She nodded, remembering something. "When it was decided to start this home, I was put in charge." She pulled at the knot in the small scarf around her neck. "It's a complicated arrangement." The home Eli shared was established with the cooperation of other families at the cantor's congregation who required living arrangements for their children, Sharon told her. This year one of the families could no longer afford it and took their son back home, leaving the Kaplan business in the red.

"Those other men that live here? Are they like Eli?" She didn't even want to think about what she meant by *like* Eli.

"They have mild handicaps that necessitate assisted living housing."

Good. Fine, Diane thought. Your highfalutin credentials are established. "So, you asked Eli if I could see him?"

"I did. Unfortunately he's not up to company today." Sharon screwed her mouth in a puzzle of a look.

"Today? Does that mean he's seen guests on *other* days?" Diane had learned to cross-examine during her years in court.

Sharon brightened as if she remembered something wonderful. "His physical therapists! They come every week." She looked toward the ceiling briefly. "He did send his love and asked about Jamie."

"That's a relief." Diane felt her heart rate ratchet down from rage to mere anger. "You know, that he remembered his cousin."

"He remembers *everyone* and *every*thing. He's not retarded! He has some neurological impairment that affects motor control, Mrs. Oppenheim." Sharon stared at Diane, then said in an undertone, "And he was housebound for years. And became agoraphobic. He suffers from intermittent depression. As do we all, I suppose."

Diane caught a quick lesson in what stirs Sharon's rile, and felt ashamed she had let her bias slip that way. "I'm very sorry," Diane said. "I just didn't know how he's managed over the years." Sharon nodded, and Diane wondered if Eli spoke to anyone else besides Sharon on a regular basis. She removed her sweaty hands from her pockets and wiped her palms against her coat.

56

"To give you some context until you do see him," Sharon said, "you should know he's had a hard time of it, coming to live here. I retain my apartment in the city, but I spend some nights in a room here — to ease some caretaking burdens. Until his father's departure, Eli was constantly improving. He has a very good, strong mind, and his looks have not diminished during his time of adjustment." She raised her brows and smiled.

Sharon had thrown so many innuendos at Diane that she didn't know which to field. "His looks?"

"You must remember him as a handsome young man. Handsome men have a better chance of fitting in, given Eli's circumstance. He is still very handsome."

Diane was stunned. "Tell me how he looks."

"He had long black curly hair, and until last week used an elastic band to hold it back. He just cut it." Sharon blushed. "There are the soft brushes of gray appearing now."

He sounded as if he looked like Adam. Diane looked into Sharon's eyes; the glow was daunting and defensive. She noticed the other men from the kitchen waiting in the threshold of the parlor, motionless and speechless. She whispered, "I think they want to come in and watch TV. Can we talk somewhere else?"

As the women stood to vacate the room, Sharon said, "This house is good for them, but for Eli? He doesn't need to live this way, and honestly? It's a fortune to run — the help, professional and domestic, the food and upkeep. This house was not the best investment idea Cantor Kaplan could have come up with for Eli." She tilted her head toward Diane. "We could be, or I should say, *Eli could* be in dire straits before long. Financially." Sharon turned to see if anyone else were around. "If we can't start to work this facility in the black," she said even more softly, "we'll have to sell the house."

We'll have to sell the house? When did it become hers? Diane wanted to say, That's why I want to talk to him, you finagler. David should have had millions. Diane swallowed. Feeling as if she were caught in a scary movie, she shook her head to clear it. "Who handles the bills and receivables?"

"David's attorney." Sharon's lips stayed poised but Diane could see her eyebrows furrow.

She herded Diane to the front door and unlatched the deadbolt. Diane's back arched in alarm. "I have more questions. Eli's lost his father and I need to know how he is! You can't make me leave now!"

Sharon gave her the prissy smile of a schoolteacher reminding a third-grader who was the boss. "Actually, I can tell you to leave. I think you should go and come back in a few days. And in the meantime, I'll talk to him and try to convince him to see you soon." She smiled sheepishly. "He needs time to strengthen himself for a visit. You understand."

First the woman welcomed her, then blocked her from seeing Eli, then shared financial secrets as if talking sister to sister, and now she was pushing her out the door! Diane thought about the long drive home and Adam's perilous journey, made to secure a proper burial for Eli's father. "This is ex*a*sperating, and your protective attitude toward Eli is condescending and inappropriate. I've come all the way from Queens! In the snow! With my husband flying to China to meet up with a farshtunken rabbi, who says he took care of David! Do you know my husband had to make an emergency landing?"

"Emergency landing? Yes, yes, I know he is in China. But—"

"But? But nothing. You tell Eli I want to see him." She took a deep breath. "There are important issues we just have to get settled. Issues of critical consequence to Eli's welfare." She remembered her mother using those exact words when Diane was instructed to care for her invalid father.

Sharon took Diane's hands by the fingers. "I understand there are things to take care of. I've been brainstorming in calls with Liora."

"Liora calls? I thought she and Eli don't speak."

"She and I speak. She's trying to get hold of the lawyer who is handling the cantor's estate. That rabbi in China has been evasive." She gripped Diane's fingers harder. "Please believe me when I tell you that Eli's welfare is my only concern, but we don't even know who the executor is. Liora thought it was me!"

Diane was hooked into her forceful stare, but more aghast at the very thought that this person, this outsider, might be considered as executor to David's estate. Diane pulled her hands from Sharon's and put them in her coat pockets. "Why would she think that you —"

"I implore you to trust me. Come with Adam when he gets back with the cantor. How would that work for you?"

Sharon had just set her up: She would not let them see Eli if Adam did not return with a corpse. "Do you at least have a few moments to talk?"

"Certainly." Sharon and her friendly smile stood firm in the doorway.

"You see, I'm afraid there has arisen a predicament that might contribute to the possibility that Cantor Kaplan will be irretrievable. But that should have no bearing on our visitation."

"Excuse me? I don't understand. What?"

Idiot. "If David can't come back, I trust that will not stop you from allowing us to see Eli." Let's see her sling her bullshit.

Sharon laughed lightly, warily, "Don't be ridiculous. Tell me what you know."

"Will you swear to keep this from Eli until Adam gets back?" Diane whispered, not only to keep the secret from Eli, but Adam would choke her if he heard her rambling about his *predicament* this prematurely. "You know, the situation could change in a second." Diane snapped her finger.

"What situation? Please, Diane. What has happened to David?"

"Swear!"

"I swear. Stop being a baby and tell me already!"

A baby? "Don't ridicule me."

"Okay, I apologize. Now can you tell me?"

Diane shook a chill from her shoulders and pulled her coat more tightly around her body. "It seems the people David knew in China have *buried* him."

There was a good ten seconds of silence before Sharon sighed. "So what does this mean? I don't know what this means."

"I don't have any details. But as far as I can figure, they had to bury him because of the time element. Jews believe in a quick burial. You can't have dead bodies just hanging around and rotting. I don't know if Jews can be exhumed, or if that country allows it. The reason I have brought this information to you before I have any facts" — she took a deep breath — "is because we want to see Eli and, to be perfectly honest, I do not appreciate the way you've blocked my right to visitation." She would be disappointing Jamie — he seemed so anxious to please Ariella.

"I am not *blocking* your right, Diane. Truly, I'm sorry if you have that impression. I would love Eli to have company. He is not up to it. *He* said no."

Sharon sounded sincere. She looked sympathetic. Diane sniffled and blew her nose into a paper towel from her pocket. "I'm just trying to help."

"Diane, listen. Eli and I are...close. But I won't say anything to him about David until you call me and know more."

She knew it. Close. If that weren't a euphemism for lover, she'd eat her fake-fur boots. Her back was aching from standing in the drafty entrance hall, but she had to push it. "How close are you?"

"Well, I've known him since he was a boy. I consider myself his most trusted confidante."

"So, you're a kind of mother figure?"

"No, not a mother." Sharon looked aghast. "A professional relationship that evolved...I'm too young to be his mother figure. You think I look old enough to be his mother?"

Diane charitably appeased her. "No. Of course not! A sister perhaps?" Ten years was not that big a deal, though socially Sharon had to have been decades ahead.

"Diane, stop. Look, why don't you come back to Brooklyn and we'll meet for lunch." Sharon sounded patronizing. "You know where Kings Plaza Mall is? Tomorrow is my day off."

"If Adam comes home tomorrow I have to be there." Diane immediately anticipated Jamie's disappointment at her failure to see Eli. And she had to admit that she herself — as an extension of Adam — felt responsible for Eli's care. "All right. I'll come tomorrow. Noon?"

"Sounds like a plan." Sharon reached to shake her hand. "It was a pleasure meeting you. Please drive home safely."

Diane got into her car and circled the block a few times. She tried peering through the side windows of the house, and parked again across the street, watching the house for movement, but decided after a few minutes to just go home. The fact that Sharon was in cahoots with David and Liora did nothing to lessen the possibility that this woman had Eli locked in a room, sequestered from everyone except those she chose for him to see.

When Jamie finally called his mother back, three hours after she returned from Brooklyn, Diane had just frenetically cleaned out the fridge and was preparing to go to bed. She had been at a loss for a mindless activity and left piles of emptied deli food containers from the fridge in the sink. When she told Jamie about Eli and Sharon, he began laughing so hard that Diane had to pull the phone away from her ear.

"Mom!" He yelled into the phone when he caught his breath. "The last time I saw Eli he was in a wheelchair and wouldn't make eye contact with anybody. You think she hung around all these years because she wanted to have sex with him?"

Diane was put out. "This is ridiculous. There's a basic attraction between men and women. Can you understand that?"

There was a startled silence in the phone. Diane wanted to eat her words. Jamie would either assume she meant he was immature, in which case she would have insulted him and he was pissed, or he would assume she thought that he was gay, in which case she was not sure how he'd react.

"So what are you saying?" Jamie asked. "You think I'm gay?"

Caught by the unordinary directness of his response, Diane could not locate an answer inside her. But did she think he was gay? The question was in her heart enough to take the risk to ask it. "Are you...gay?" She heard the words echoing into the mouthpiece, and cringed at having set them loose. She held her breath.

Jamie cleared his throat. "Mom? I'm gonna answer your question. You really want to hear the answer?"

"Yeah." Her heart quickened, and she felt the excitement of being trusted with a son's confidence. Such moments—when a son shows his genuine feelings—prove the solidarity of their bond as mother and child. She prepared herself.

His voice was firm but level. "The answer is that I, sort of, live with Mark, you know?"

She reached to the bedside lamp, and then stopped herself from turning the switch when she realized her hand was shaking. He had caused her to tremble at other times, such as when he tried to explain why the police found pot in his school locker, and he explained how it should be legal anyway, and how it was more illegal of the police to invade his privacy. She remembered his curly hair, long and falling over his wide and singing eyes, his mouth falling into a frown after each attempt to use logic to displace his mother's anger.

"You share a house with him." She asked gently, "What do you mean you *sort* of live with Mark?" She squirmed, grinding her teeth, afraid she had pressured him, embarrassed him. "You don't have to answer me." She felt caught between his modesty and his maturity, afraid that with his answer everything could change between them forever.

"*Sort* of, in that..." He sighed. Diane waited, frozen.

He finally spoke, his voice low and solemn. "I'm sorry. I don't know how to explain it. I'm happy with Mark, is all there is to it." And then quickly added, "You knew that's why I moved away."

"I wasn't sure." She was hardly horrified or shocked by his confession. Somewhere when she had seen him with Mark on their last visit to Colorado, she had known. Still, she tried desperately now, for her son's sake as well as her own, so she'd be able to eventually respond with an evenhanded, enlightened tone, not to picture him having sex with another man. All she wanted in the world now was to hold him.

"I'm just in love with a man instead of a woman," Jamie said.

Her son used the word love. Diane felt her eyes fill. She lifted details into their places before she had time to swallow: He was gay. It was all right. She would have two sons.

Jamie asked, "Are you disappointed? Are you angry?"

"Jamie, Jamie. I'm not angry. You're my only child and I always hoped you'd have babies." She'd heard about a gay New Jersey couple that had adopted. A sharp stab of guilt hit her in the chest. She was again thinking about babies. Selfish. But she wanted Jamie to have, and to give her, that settled, traditional life. Had Jamie, at age twenty-four, even seen enough of the world to settle with a partner? Was he settled in? He said he was in love. "If you're happy...are you happy?"

"Yes," he said softly.

She was unconvinced. "I'm worried, you know. I'm always worried." Where else had Mark's penis been?

"Don't worry. Please don't worry about me." His voice was wary.

Diane imploded, and her thoughts escaped like smoke from her mouth. "AIDS, Jamie. I'm worried about you dying." She could accept his life with an open heart, but this was her son and to imagine him with Mark, even for a flash of a second, made her squirm. She pictured Mark naked and Jamie too. The scenes were insuppressible.

"Mom? I'm getting pretty freaked out. I'd rather poke hot daggers in my eyes than discuss this with you."

She heard him tap something against his tooth, a habit he developed when he had braces on his teeth and liked the way the tapping felt against the tension of the metal.

Don't lose him now, she thought. "I'm fine. Mark is a great guy! He's charming and smart and adorable."

"Whatever. Believe me, please. I'm not going to get AIDS. I'm careful."

"I don't believe in *careful*. There is no such thing." She knew this as well as she knew her own name.

"Oh god, Mom! Can we end this here? I need to hang up. I need to chill."

"You need to chill! Three days ago I lived the most mundane existence in the world, except for my unusually active middle-aged sex life."

"Mom!"

"Got you back. Ha, ha." Would anything ever be funny again?

"I thought you'd cry, or I don't know"—his voice peaked—"just go all, like, out of control crazed!"

Diane could hear him gasp and then she heard him moan as he started to cry.

She cradled the portable phone in her shoulder and finding the bedroom chair behind her with her hand, she sat, unfocused, staring into a blurred, blue space. "Honey, for an only child, you know so little about your mother." He knew her best of all.

He kept crying.

"Jamie, I've known you've been having sex since you were seventeen. It's not shocking to me. I don't care that you use your penis"—her heart pounded—"or with whom." She waited for him to signal he had recouped. "Stop crying. *I'm* supposed to be crying, not you." She exhaled an excited plea. "Come home." Tears came to her eyes, hurting for him and for all he had felt he had to withhold. "Jamie? Why are you crying?"

He sniffed hard. "I don't know. I just wish. Like, I thought being far away I'd protect you from this."

"Protect me or protect you? I do not need your protection. Your gayness does not hurt me. Your crying is what hurts me." She gasped at the first possibility that might explain his tears. "Jamie, if you're not sure about this, if that's why, then come home so we can talk, face to face."

"I'm sure about this." He started to cry again.

If he was sure, that was fine. But he had needed to protect her. Diane started to cry. She tossed a throw pillow across the room, angry with Adam for being in Shanghai, and angry that Jamie moved away because of this. "When Daddy gets back we'll come to Denver and talk. Okay?"

"How is Dad gonna take this?" Jamie blew his nose into something. "Don't tell him. Just don't tell him. Okay?"

"Never mind about him. He loves you. He'll, well, he'll adjust." She sing-songed, "Heee'lll adjuuust. Life is a constant flux of adjustments within the fundamental rules of our erroneous set of beliefs."

"Grandma?" A laugh escaped him.

"She said something to that effect." Diane could hear he was still afraid to blow his nose completely, preferring to leave it stuffed than feel that feeling he detested. Mucus in motion?

She said, "Blow your nose better."

"When do you think he'll be back?"

"I hope the day after tomorrow. All depends on how long he'll try to exhume and export Uncle David. One way or the other, he should be home in two or three days. By Sunday for sure." She took the portable phone to the bathroom and ran the cold water in the sink. Gulping a glassful, she calmed down. "Where's Mark now? Is he home with you?"

"No. He's at work. Overtime."

She loved him even more than she had when she'd loved him more than she thought a mother could: every day since he'd been born. "You're all right now?"

"Yeah, Mom. Go lie down and wait to hear from Dad. Don't say anything to him about me."

"Of course not. But when he's home, you'll talk to him. I don't want you to feel guilty about this. It's your life, not his, and he will accept it. I swear to you he will accept it." She waited for her son to say his reliable and deliberately enunciated "I love you."

"Okay, okay. I love you."

"Love to Mark." She hoped that didn't sound patronizing.

"And Mom? I don't feel guilty."

"Good, sweetheart. That's good."

"And you don't need to attach me to Mark in all your thoughts."

She didn't like the defensive way that sounded. "Okay. Love to *just* you."

Diane wandered from the bathroom and sat at the kitchen table another hour until the winter night had stilled around a half-moon. Quiet, drained, she was thinking about Jamie's baby clothes, which she had saved for her grandchild. In high school, he was so gorgeous; the girls never left him alone, especially Toni, that jazzy little Latino girl. Months after they had broken up, in April, about a week before taxes were due, when Diane and Adam had been doing the books, preparing to give the accountant their bank statements, something didn't add up. There was a check or withdrawal missing and the account was out fifteen hundred dollars. Adam admitted to giving Jamie and Toni the money for an abortion.

Diane had been devastated. For years, she and Adam had tried to have another child. Diane did not believe in abortion if there was a competent guardian out there somewhere for the baby. Adam had secretly colluded with their son and committed a terrible injustice; deceiving her was the least of it. She didn't speak to Adam for a week and almost threw Jamie out of the house. Adam's explanation had been pitiful but honest. He said the girl, 15, Latino and Catholic, was hysterical and near suicidal, and Jamie, 17, was so guilt-ridden he was threatening to run away with her to South America. Adam regarded Toni's suicide threat literally and said he was under so much pressure from both of them that he just handed them the money. Diane had cried, Why didn't you come to me? I would have helped. I would have taken the girl into our home. Now she realized the aborted baby probably would have been her only grandchild.

It was ten p.m. when Diane opened her eyes from her nap, squinting at the LCD on the clock, wondering if it was morning. The snowy glitter blew outside her window. Jamie: gay. She missed him. She missed his smile and his frown, his bony-broad shoulders, the peaceful way he slept with the corner of the blanket folded over his forehead and a pillow against his chest. Jamie's word *careful* burst behind her eyelids and she worried.

She reached for the phone and dialed by feel. "Jamie?"

"Hello, Mother. Hear from Dad?" His voice was cheerfully firm.

"No. I was just wondering about something."

"Oh no. Is this about me and Mark?"

"No. It's about you, hon. I want to know if this relationship is permanent. At the very least what I'm asking is do you intend for this to be permanent. You know, are you committed to making it work?"

"I don't know. Can't this conversation wait until you visit? Or better yet, can we not have this conversation, ever?"

"I'm upsetting you. I'm sorry. I just can't..."

"So much for asking you to leave Mark out of this!" Jamie shouted into the phone. "You just can't shut up! That's what you just can't do. I never should have told you. I never should ever have thought you would leave me alone. Don't come to Colorado with Dad. I don't want you here and I don't want to give you all your little worry-free answers about everything being perfect!"

"Jamie, I'm not asking for you to be perfect." Am I asking for him to be perfect? "I'm asking for you to be responsible for your decisions and take care of yourself! If that's perfection then give your father and me a medal, because we're perfect!"

Jamie went quiet. "Well, then, congratulations," he finally said in a flat voice. "What do you think I've been doing here in Colorado all these years? I take care of myself."

And you hide, Diane thought, but knew enough to leave it unsaid.

"My life is today," Jamie said. "Today I have a happy life. So, if there's nothing else you need, just call me when you hear from Dad." Jamie sighed theatrically. "I'll be here waiting, happily."

Diane hung up the phone and felt lonelier. She was used to spending nights alone. Plumbers have emergencies, especially in weather like this, but Adam was always a beeper away. She had yet to have a live phone call from him. She could not begin to imagine what he was doing, why he hadn't called with more news of his mission. She ruminated about *Issues of critical consequences to his welfare.*

Diane's father had suffered his first debilitating stroke when she was eight and he was only thirty-two. Unable to hold a job, he stayed home, and Diane babysat for him after school while her mother worked. Her mother instructed Diane in what to watch for: slurs, falls, lapses in memory, drools, droops, and unexplained bruises. When Diane was sixteen, wanting to flirt with the boys at the handball court, she stayed late after school. She thought she'd be home by five, leaving her father to manage alone for two extra hours. What she hadn't counted on was getting home at six o'clock to find her mother still not home and her father dead on the front porch, his fist wrapped around his special Independence Day

69

American flag that he had evidently decided needed hanging. It was April. She had let someone die, her father, no less. The binging and purging began. To this day, Diane and Adam celebrated Independence Day on April fourth.

Diane left her bedroom to try her luck on the bathroom scale. She hadn't eaten much since Adam left for Shanghai and was thrilled to see she had lost a pound.

TO DIG OR NOT TO DIG

The chill in the apartment had lessened. The kitchen garbage bag smelled noxious from last night's cold fish, vegetable, and tofu. Adam waited in the Giacalone kitchen, drinking tea, watching the sunrise and the streets below as they were activated with truckloads of goods, from produce to hardware, on the backs of bicycles—listening to the Hebrew prayers seeping from the rabbi's bedroom through the wall-without-an-oven on his left. Lucy and Yin colored the words with sounds of their pen and ink life from the hallway near the bathroom. He shook his head. Adam's mood sank lower. He could not relinquish the notion that he should be fixing something.

The streets below moved in a convoy of glittering multicolored draymen; from Adam's elevation, the city seemed riddled with urgency, as if each of the hundreds of vehicles, from barge to bike, was scrambling for the front of the line. Adam smiled at their willingness to strive and wished Diane was here with him. She loved hard-working people. How was he going to get back home without David—and without Yin? He had awakened before Seth arrived with the fierce urge to take Yin back home with him, leaving with her before anyone else roused.

Yesterday when he saw Lucy slap Yin for crying, he felt blood rush to his face and now he vaguely recalled fifteen-year-old Liora slapping her toddler brother Eli as he sat in his high chair. What for? Had he watched Liora do it in response to Eli's behavior or had he merely seen her hit him as he entered the room? All he clearly remembered was his own response: he stood in the doorway and stared, afraid. Should he have bullied Liora away from Eli? Would Eli's mother have hit her children if she had lived to raise them? Adam could not recall ever being slapped by his mother.

"I see you've fixed yourself tea," Elana said, appearing from nowhere.

Adam exhaled a sleepy sigh and turned toward her sweet voice. "Yes. I couldn't find any sugar though, so I'm afraid it's pretty tasteless."

Elana scuffed her slippered feet into the kitchen and handed him the sugar bowl, which sat in plain view atop the microwave. Embarrassed, he took it from her and shook his head as if to say he was dazed and confused.

"Long night? Did you get to speak with your wife?"

"Only briefly on her message machine. I didn't want to charge up a big bill for you. I'll reimburse you of course. You'll let me know." She was beautiful without make-up and for a very short moment Adam was single and she was a girl he'd met the night before. He imagined pushing her long hair from her neck, but quickly came to his senses and lifted his gaze from her mouth to her eyes. "You look very lovely this morning." How could he not compliment her? She deserved to be told she was lovely.

"I appreciate you saying that. Thank you." Elana flattened her skirt and instinctively raised her hand to tuck her hair behind her small and perfect ear. "Seth will be out in a minute. I heard the girls up and about. I'll go tell them they can come out of the room. I think Lucy is afraid of you."

He laughed. "Not of *me*. She's afraid of *you*!"

"That's silly," she said, blushed, and turned to get them. Adam watched her leave the room and had to smile at the way she turned to catch him watching her.

He had not heard the shower start, but he noticed when it turned off. Seth entered a few minutes later in a fresh shirt and slacks. "Good morning again. Sleep at all after I woke you?"

"Not really. I'm very anxious to talk to you." Adam walked closer to Seth. "You know I can't afford a protracted stay here in Shanghai. I have got to get back to New York—with my uncle. Can we sit now to talk?"

The rabbi led his guest to the sofa and removed a pack of cigarettes from his shirt pocket, offering one to Adam.

"I don't smoke," Adam said. He felt his pulse stab in his throat when Seth struck the match and lit the tobacco; the rabbi was so relaxed and smooth. "There must be someone you know who could get permission for me to take my uncle home," Adam blurted out.

Adam watched him take a drag from his cigarette. In the morning light, Seth looked more Sicilian banker-handsome and less Flatbush Yeshiva teacher. His round eyes, straight nose, and full lips were outlined with steady-handed intention; his cheeks were pale and sunken. "It would be best," the rabbi said gently, "for you and the rest of David's family to accept the fact that he has had a proper burial and is resting in peace."

Some oddly familiar shadow in his personality made Adam's anger crank up a notch. Adam spoke loudly. "Well, I need to *un*rest him and move him to another *more* proper burial place." Immediately his bravado faded and he saw Seth close his eyes in what seemed an effort to maintain his composure. Adam said, "You're not going to assist me, are you? You decided before I even left New York to hold him here and thwart any attempt I made to bring him home."

Seth smiled at Adam, stamped out his cigarette, and placed his hands, palm against palm, in front of his reddened face. "You can raise hell if you wish. You can go to the government and fill out papers to your heart's content. You can do anything you wish and I will not try to deter you. But I've done the only, only thing your uncle would have wanted me to do. He is a buried soul." Seth recited a quick Hebrew prayer and took a clean cigarette from his pocket.

Adam felt bullied. A man's got to do what a man's got to do, he thought. He sat quiet for a few seconds, envisioned his uncle resting with a smirk on his face, and felt the dissipation of pressure that had been mounting since Sunday morning. The sensation in his head was stunning in its lightness. *Pissed* never felt so right. Dry-mouthed and weary, he glanced around the spare and commercial looking room, three butt-filled glass ashtrays, a Brooklyn-bought painting of an old man with prayer book, the gray of his beard not quite the same color as the hair under his yarmulke, and he yearned for his old flannel blanket. Had David come to China and died here learning so little about its culture? "So, why, Rabbi?" Adam demanded. "Why was he here? Did he come here just to die? I mean, you know, we're his family. We would have helped him at home."

Seth took a long drag. "It is not a simple spool to unravel."

No, Adam thought. It's never simple with a rabbi. He didn't want to hear the story from too many hypothetical angles, because he was determined to leave Shanghai within twenty-four hours. Adam wished he were ready to have the rabbi write a note of explanation and release him from any further obligation or responsibility. "Can you just explain, with reasons that have more to do with his personal wishes why David wanted to be buried here?"

Lucy walked in with Yin in Elana's arms. The three of them giggled, thwarting Adam's query. "Lucy and Yin are ready to take the train home," Elana announced. She turned to Seth on the sofa, and asked in Hebrew if he would pay for a taxi for them to return to the Cohens.

Adam stood. "No, no, no. I brought them here so it's my responsibility to see they get home safely." He lifted Yin from Elana's arms, smoothed her hair, and set her down on the sofa, a seat's length away from Seth. The child smiled and said something to her mother. Lucy shut her up with a word. Yin looked abashed. Adam was alarmed. He bent and kissed Yin's cheek, and asked her if she were hungry. When she nodded, Adam asked Elana, "Would you come into the kitchen a moment? Help me get some breakfast for Yin and Lucy?"

She followed him to the sanctity of the ovenless wall, out of sight from the others. "Adam. What is it?" Elana asked, looking at his face. As she reached for his hand his stomach cramped.

Adam asked, "What did Yin just say to Lucy that she shut her up so fast?"

"She said she loved the man from New York." Elana smiled.

A lump formed in his throat and he whispered, "I can't send her back like this. The girl won't get any help from her mother." He took Elana's elbow. "We really have to do something." But when she spoke, even though Elana was young enough to be his daughter, he felt himself wilt at her authority.

"Adam, what did I tell you when you first called me from the airport and asked about your uncle?" She pulled her arm gently to release it from Adam's hold.

He had to think for only a moment. "I know. We're not in Kansas anymore. But we are in a civilized country. There has to be a school or someplace that could help her. She'll grow up to be a servant like her mother. This child is special. She could grow up and do something wonderful with her life."

"Actually, pretty as she is, she'd probably become a massager." Elana nodded in sympathy with Adam. "I had a feeling you'd have trouble letting them go. I saw how you were so protective of her last night. I told Seth." She smiled and touched his cheek briefly, then dropped her hand. "He mentioned a school for the blind in Shanghai, but he agrees with me that we can't impose our wishes for the girl on her mother. We have to let them go on their course. Lucy will never ask for help. It is not in their culture to ask for help, and what's more, you'll only bring hurtful attention to the girl's disability. She'll resent you."

"Everything in this god-dammed...forgive me." He took a deep breath. "Everything in this country cannot be *out of my hands*! And haven't you listened to Lucy speak? She asks for favors constantly, and no one in the world brings more attention to the girl's disability than her mother! I resent *her*!"

Elana looked unperturbed. "You are quite the shepherd, aren't you Mr. Oppenheim? Come to lead everyone home?"

Adam fell back against the wall. "Jesus fucking Christ."

In the living room, the rabbi was singing the English alphabet to Yin, who now sat on his lap. Adam approached them, nervously. "Rabbi? You said there's a school for the blind in Shanghai?"

"Absolutely! Are we going to take Yin to visit?" He winked at Adam and then looked at his wife. Adam smiled with relief. Yin had gotten to Seth. He saw Elana flash her wide eyes with illuminating warmth he had not seen before. Seth looked up and asked, "What do you say, Lucy? Can we make a visit?"

Lucy started out meekly but her color increased, her resolve blotching her face. "I no have money. Mista Cohen say school too far from house." Her voice rose, "Mista Cohen no pay and Yin blind with no money. She no can work for she school!"

"Ah! But I happen to know that the government will pay for her school," Seth said. "I know a boy who learned to play piano there!"

Lucy grabbed Yin from his arms, the woman's eyes welling. "You no take Yin. She my chil. You no take!" The tears rolled down her face. She looked terrified, like a prisoner of war.

Adam took a few steps back before he spoke. "No one is taking Yin. She is your child. Yes, we know." He was so tired of her rhetoric. But why would she believe Mr. Cohen wouldn't want to help Yin if he had already paid for her visit to a New York doctor? Maybe the Cohens just wanted Yin to see. The girl would make a better servant with eyes. Adam thought about their conversation on the plane, and about Lucy's pride that she knew about Jewish traditions and rituals and the reverence she showed toward Mr. Cohen. "We want her to learn to read. We want you to take her to school. You like the *Jewish* Mr. Cohen and Jews like to read." He turned to Seth and nodded enthusiastically. "We can help Mr. Cohen get Yin to read if you let her go to school." He didn't know what he was promising or how he could follow through. "Lucy? You have Mr. Cohen's phone number?"

She nodded her head tentatively.

Adam stepped closer. "I'll get a taxi for you, and pay for it, but let me have his number so we can talk to him. Okay?"

She reached for the pen and paper Adam had been using at the side table and wrote the number. Adam showed the paper to Seth to check if it looked real. Seth nodded, shrugged, then looked squarely at Lucy. "Is this the *true* number? I am a Jew like Mr. Cohen. You wouldn't lie to a Jew, would you?"

Adam looked at him and rolled his eyes. That last question was pushing it.

"That good number. That Mimi Cohen bed phone."

"Very good, Lucy," Seth said. "Now, have some food, and then Mr. Oppenheim will take you downstairs and find you a taxi. We will call Mr. Cohen later. We are not going to take Yin from you. I swear to God." Seth held up his hand.

"Yes, I go home. You leave Yin lone."

"Okey-dokey!" Seth said cheerfully. He stood, spread his fingers over their heads and lyrically recited another prayer. Yin and Lucy bowed their heads as if they understood the reverence of his words. As Seth took the piece of paper and phone number and slid into the bedroom he turned and mouthed, "I'll try the number." The women went into the kitchen and Adam paced around the dining room table, dizzy with self-doubt, thinking about how easily he had let the focus on David slip away.

Two minutes later Seth reappeared and gave a thumbs-up to Adam. Coming close to his ear he whispered, "I got another of the Cohens' housekeepers. They're out for the day, but the number's kosher."

"I'll take them to a taxi. When I get back upstairs you'll be here and ready to discuss David, right?"

"I won't move until you get back."

Adam hated leaving people with nothing more than their promise to remain.

~~~Adam doesn't want to leave home for college.

It is August and his maternal grandfather, whom he hasn't seen since he was five, is dying. Ruby wants to visit her father in the hospital and there are bitter fights with Seymour. Adam's father will not allow his wife to see the man who wrongly accused him of misconduct in his law firm and forced him out. Adam listens from his bedroom. A metal folding chair hits a wall.

Storming into the living room, Adam argues with his father about letting his mother do as she wants, and about letting him take time off from school.

"Your prick grandfather fired me!" Seymour screams, "I am the man who made *you* flesh and blood!" But the more Ruby cries about visiting her father on his deathbed, the more depressed Seymour becomes. He goes to sit in his dark bedroom, wrapped in his woolen overcoat on Labor Day. If Adam thought his father could hear him he would try to talk, but Seymour Oppenheim is unreachable. Adam is afraid of what will happen if he leaves for college: afraid for his mother. His father is irrational, and could he trust David to keep an eye on Ruby *and* Eli? If David is drunk, whom could Adam trust to defend his mother?

Seymour emerges from his room that night after midnight, coaxing Adam from his room by saying softly, "Let me speak my piece with you." His hair is a tangle of oily strands; rings of perspiration stain his shirt under his armpits. Seymour puts his arm around his son, promises Adam everything will be fine and insists he go back to Binghamton. "Your mother and I will be fine." David, sitting on the living room sofa, also insists. Adam doesn't know when his uncle arrived.

The room is brightly lit and Ruby is standing behind the easy chair. Adam squints, his gaze darting from his mother's bulging and reddened eyes to his uncle's flat expression. His skin prickles with goose bumps, feeling the difference between his father and David. His father, with his lean physique and small features, is plain looking, smart and opinionated, yet warm and affectionate. David has a sculpted face, a towering presence, though he is unpredictable and loud; he keeps physically distant from everyone, as if he were a Chassid. "Never mind your rebellion against your father," he tells Adam. "You will go to school and you will do as I say."

A bicycle, loaded with flattened cardboard boxes tied into a high heap over the rear tire, rode through a puddle and splashed Yin. Lucy yanked on her daughter's jacket, pulling her out of the gutter and onto the curb. The girl reached down her leg, cupped her small pink hands over her knees, and wiped the dirty water from her pants. Adam watched, smiling at the efficiency of Yin's intuition and ever more disturbed by Lucy's behavior. She had pulled her daughter out of harm's way without telling her what was wrong. Lucy simply peered down the busy avenue looking for a taxi.

Adam watched the traffic and waited, ignoring oncoming taxis until they had already drifted by. He was holding onto the girl's hand, lost in the fog of his own what-ifs. What if it starting pouring rain again? What if the rain made Lucy realize Yin needed to be somewhere safer? Lucy seemed utterly self-absorbed. What if he told them he would like to take them to America and they said yes? Lucy looked up at Adam and gave him a nasty stare. Finally, she held up her hand and waved a taxi to the curb.

"Wait!" Adam shouted and grabbed her arm.

"Mista Oppenhi, I no can wait. Mista Cohen get mad I no get back."

"You must put Yin in school. Just tell me you will." He wouldn't have believed her if she swore up and down. The taxi driver began to yell.

"Lucy. I'll call you at Mr. Cohen's house and maybe come to see you there. Okay?"

Lucy waved, like a two-year-old, and pushed Yin into the back seat. "G'bye Mista. You find died uncle and go home. You craz." Wide-eyed and snide-faced, she circled her finger into the air near the right side of her head, then slammed the door shut. The taxi drove away. Adam was left resisting the urge to get in a taxi and give chase.

He looked at the sidewalk where Yin had just been splashed. Tears filled his eyes. He loathed the idea of going back up to their apartment, talking about whether to leave David resting in peace or start an international furor, looking at Elana and fantasizing, worrying about Diane and needing her, feeling sick about failing Eli — his cousin's discontent so much a part of him now that he felt doubled in size — and missing Jamie, the one man in the world who might be on his side. Stoned on apprehension, Adam walked back to the complex, buzzed Elana and Seth on the intercom, and told them he was going for a walk.

Finding himself two blocks from the Giacalones' building, Adam stood in front of an English sign directing him to the Yu Yuan Garden. Standing still, gazing into the park, he saw the ancient-looking pagoda building and a long wall topped with the scales of a dragon. He followed the slate walkway, which led him to a pond where tour groups had already gathered and vendors were setting up their carts of souvenir-quality pearls and silk. He wondered if Mr. Cohen was abusive. Why hadn't he wanted Lucy to send her to school? She had to be saved from becoming a statistic.

The height of the scaffolding looming on the building across from the pagoda struck him as surreal. Ships blew horns on the Bund; smaller barges, their flags made of laundry lines strewn across the decks, paddled their way along the canal. The waterway was wide and the noise was overwhelming. If not for the blatant majority of Asians, it would be hard to believe he was so far from home.

81

At nine in the morning the sun felt warm, maybe fifty degrees; he found a table and chair with a view of the pond and rock garden, but it was February and few flowers floated on the sparkling shallow water. The table belonged to an outdoor tearoom; a waiter bowed and knelt, drying tealeaves especially for him. The area was becoming mobbed with tourists and Adam found himself bobbing his head this way and that to glimpse at the park through the crowds.

Diane had asked Adam to look for something unique and old. After consulting the map on the walkway, he walked a short distance to Shanghai's flea market. The streets were crowded and loud and familiar. The old European stone buildings between skyscrapers, and the laundry hanging between the small old houses that were somehow left undisturbed: it was the parallel world of the Lower East Side's Chinatown.

Adam stomped through the paths of the market, thinking about possible motives for his uncle's trip to China, while he picked up a few gifts for Diane: a silk scarf, some exotic collection of teas. If David had spent his long and rigid life keeping Eli's world in order, trying to control the destiny of his extended family's lives, why had he abandoned them to come here? Did he intend to leave Eli and never see him again? Before Adam left, he would have to find out what had gone on with his uncle and this odd couple. It was all too strange to let anything they said just slide by as the truth. If Seth remained stubborn, he would have to get through to Elana, charming her to the point that she would insist Seth dig up the body. How tough could she really be? She was barely older than Jamie! And he had to make sure Yin was taken care of.

He passed a telephone booth. Diane. He had put off calling, afraid she would cry and order him to come home. The public phone worked beautifully. "Me. I'm on the street. Everything okay?" He couldn't have been more drained of energy — or anxious about the impending confrontation with Seth.

"What is going on over there? I'm scared to death!" Diane could not have sounded more unnerved and ravenous for his attention. He heard her start to cry.

"Diane, Diane. I'm sorry. It's such a mess." He suppressed his need to talk about the little girl. "I haven't had time to actually discuss David with the rabbi yet. He prays a lot. But I'm going up to talk to him now. I really don't think I'll be able to bring David home. I just hope I get some proof that it was his decision, his choice, to be here. Maybe that will be enough for Eli and Liora." Adam closed his eyes then opened them and realized, for the first time, that he really was in China. "Shit."

"Well, get what you need, draw up some kind of plan to get David later, and catch tonight's flight out of there. There's a seven o'clock flight your time into Kennedy. You hear me?"

"I can't promise. I'll try." He was contemplating what to use as an excuse if he found he just couldn't leave. "Did I give you the number of the rabbi?" He recited the number off a piece of paper. "His name is Seth, and his wife is Elana. They're young. If you get panicky, call me there. Okay?"

"Adam! I have things to tell you. Do you want to know what things? You didn't ask me what I have to say."

Fresh out of patience, he consciously tapped into his supply of empathy for bereft Diane. "What, what. What things do you have to say?"

"I went to see Eli. I didn't see him, but I'm going back to Brooklyn and I'm going to see him. So? You think I'm doing a good thing?"

"Good. Go. Do. But don't give him any news or anything! Tell him I love him and I'll make it up to him. No, just tell him I love him and he's in my thoughts, always. Okay?" Adam felt the tears in his throat.

"What are you crying about? You and Jamie with the crying. You're getting morbid. I don't like to hear you morbid. You know what? You get Liora on the phone and tell her to get to New York. You need help with Eli and she has got to come."

"We'll see. Lemme go now. They'll be wondering where I am. I love you, Diane. And love to Jamie too." His heart sank. "Jamie was crying?"

"Yeah, well, we're going to visit him soon. I think he needs company from home. All right if I hold some seats to Denver?"

"Yeah, sure. Just scoop me up and throw me. Is he feeling okay?"

"Just some, um, relationship problems."

Adam remembered Boy's high school predicament. "Don't tell me someone's pregnant."

"Nothing like that. No, no, no."

"We'll talk about it when I get home. I gotta go, sweetheart. Hang up."

"Wait, this rabbi, did you see any documents? Is he really ordained or what?"

"Documents? I can't ask him for proof. He'll get even more hostile." Adam shook his head. "Look, I'll get everything out of them I can." Firmly he added, "Hang...up." He hung up before he heard her disconnect, wondering now if Diane's intuition was right. Were Seth and Elana con artists?

By the time he walked off the elevator toward the Giacalones' apartment, he had sunk so deeply into despair about David, Eli and Yin, that he feared he would start to cry the moment they sat down to speak. He walked slowly toward Bonnie and Clyde, and then knocked on their door with two hard thumps, as if he were a detective ready to make an arrest. But as soon as Elana opened the door, she smiled and Adam was ready to treat them like the exotic rabbi and wife team they were, and respectfully engage in a rational exchange of ideology.

The apartment felt chillier. Elana had set the table for brunch: hard-boiled eggs and salad, tea and muffins. She had changed her clothes and wore a bulky knit turquoise sweater and a long brown woolen skirt that hugged her round hips and flat belly. Seth was standing casually with his hands in his pants pockets, leaning against the wall between the living and dining rooms. He spoke first. "I hope you enjoyed your brief tour of the city, but we have a great deal to tell you and little time, I'm afraid. You have to get back to the states and we have our work, so, Adam, shall we begin or shall you?"

Adam circled the living room and then stopped center stage. "I can start with the facts that are not in dispute. Three months ago my uncle lived a quiet religious life in New York. A sick man, yes, but surrounded by his loving family and community. Suddenly" — he opened his hands as if releasing balloons — "his body turns up dead in Shanghai and buried in Beijing. There seems to be missing trips in the itinerary. So" — he looked at Seth — "why don't you begin by telling me what he was doing here with you. And if you don't mind, what you two are doing in Shanghai?" Then, feeling like a cad, Adam added, "And if you'd be kind enough to show me some document attesting to your ordination? I'd be, let's say, more comfortable. After all, you are a stranger to David's surviving relatives."

Seth set his eyes briefly on his wife, who was now standing at his side, then said to her, "My files are in the bedroom desk drawer. Would you mind fishing out my diploma from Columbia and certificate from Yeshiva University?" Adam tried to hide his surprise as Elana left the room to retrieve the papers.

"Let's start with your uncle. First of all, Adam, take a seat please. This is not a one-two-three story." Elana came back with the documents and showed them to Seth, who handed them to Adam. She went to get the plates with hard-boiled eggs and muffins while Seth waited for Adam to take his seat. Seth sat beside him. "That all look okay to you?"

Staring at the ornate papers, a master's degree from Columbia in Hebrew education, and his rabbinical ordination from Yeshiva, Adam worked to brush away his embarrassment. He tried briefly and not entirely successfully to replace his regret with a sense of entitlement.

Seth retrieved the papers from his hands, set them carefully on the coffee table, and seemed deliberately unannoyed. "To begin, David didn't live an internally quiet life. His family was in upheaval. He was tormented." Seth shook his head.

"Tormented!" Adam thought, *My* father was tormented!

"He was looking for—no, desperate for—some truth that he hoped would give him peace."

Adam's uncle had read every book in the library. What was it David didn't know that he had to know now? From this pink-faced rabbi! "Truth? What kind of truth? Something was a mystery to the man who knew everything?"

Seth remained serious. "Are you looking for real explanations or are you looking for a neatly wrapped story to bring home to Eli and Liora? Because I can offer no such packages."

Elana leaned forward from her chair. "My husband and I are only trying to help you, as we tried to help your uncle."

Adam stood and walked to the table, debating whether or not to be patient or indignant. He sat backwards on the dining chair. "Okay. No neat packages. Tell me, Rabbi, as tidily as possible, what was so important that my uncle had to learn. You have to tell me, really, because he was just about the sharpest, most informed man I've ever met."

"And darkest. Your uncle had lost his faith in God."

When Adam heard how Seth said the word "God," as if he were talking about, well, God, he felt his ribcage tighten around his lungs. Discussing a question of this religious magnitude, losing one's faith in God, required convictions Adam had lost long ago.

"He was being eaten alive by the belief that he was an atheist," Seth said. "That was his real cancer!" Seth raised his eyebrows, as if delighted with his diagnosis. "He came here searching to prove himself mistaken. He came searching for his cure."

Seth appeared to be dead serious, but Adam found the notion of his uncle an atheist so ridiculous he had to stifle a laugh. "Are you *trying* to turn this into a situation comedy? His whole life was about being a Jew. My uncle not only wasn't an atheist, he thought *he* was God!"

Seth frowned. "On the contrary. It was David's fear of atheism that brought him to us." Seth looked at his wife and she absorbed his words knowingly. "Your uncle had lived an identity wearing a false face of piety."

"False face of piety?" Adam shot back. "What could a vague statement like that possibly mean to me? I lived with him for the first half of my life! There was not a renegade pebble in his body!" He remembered the fanatical way David stood over and watched Jamie's moyel at his bris. "Why would he have lost faith now?"

"I'm trying the best I can to give you an overall explanation," Seth said softly.

"So tell me, do you think he lost faith in God or in himself?" It didn't make any difference to Adam what Seth answered. Either way, he thought Seth was mistaken.

"Both, as one. Finally," Seth explained, "before David ran out of time, he had to know, to the best of his ability to know such a thing, if the notion of a God was a belief he had actually relinquished. He taught torah all his life, but he had lost his faith many years ago." He sighed, as if in delicate pain. "During our time with your uncle, he made some sad admissions that made it clear he had been living a lie so complete, all-consuming, that there was not a single cell in his being he believed to be authentic."

So all right, the guy was a fake, didn't believe in God, blah, blah, blah. "But why here, to China, to you?"

"He felt dishonorable in the face of death. That was the major reason for this pilgrimage. He hoped to find a small crack in what felt to him overwhelming evidence that he had not been honest."

"Excuse me a second. You are talking in paraphrases. Your explanation is so vague it's making me crazy!"

"Of course, as with most things, there was much more to it," Seth said. "David was ashamed to face his community one more day, and he was pushed to act by his ill health. He found me and Elana, and we welcomed him in our home."

"Your home. Here in Shanghai." Adam contrived a wide-eyed expression. "You said you'd tell me what you two are doing here. So? Briefly, of course."

Seth said, "Briefly, we are teachers." Elana had scooted to the small space on the sofa beside her husband. Seth took her hand. "There are some Jews here. We sought out a place that could use our help, and so we've come to teach whoever cares to learn. You'd be surprised at the outpouring on some days—Lubavitch students needing Hebrew teachers, Jewish expats working here, Chinese with Jewish ancestry. You know some are kosher and they don't know why? Anyway, Elana speaks Chinese and Hebrew and she has roots to uncover, and — well, we came to get away." He smiled. "We all run sometimes from something, somewhere. Don't we?"

Adam felt chilled. "Running? From your family?"

Seth laughed. "I can understand why you might think that. Families get complicated. But my mother died several years ago and when she did, you see, when she died I just felt I needed to leave for a while. But these are things I wouldn't go into with you even if you had time to hear me. They are private."

Adam was still suspicious. Why was Seth's home so open to anyone, and yet Seth the man was so closed? "Will you come home, back to the US?" He would like to meet Seth on his own turf.

"It's not in our immediate plans, but who knows? I'd like to keep in touch with you. Maybe next year...Jerusalem."

Maybe. Adam didn't doubt the incidental facts the Giacalones supplied, but they were world-class bullshitters. "Yes, Jerusalem. Too bad Uncle David never made it there to see his daughter. Any clue he gave to why that was? And why he should be kept from her now?"

Seth stood and walked toward the bedroom. Elana flung him a warning look and he calmed her with a slight wave of his hand and a muted *Shhh*. She had tried to argue the point by biting her lower lip. Adam watched the communication of lovers, partners, and didn't interrupt their silent messaging.

After Seth left the room she stared at the floor and Adam stared at her — uncomfortable in the silence and pissed off at the rude intermission. "Is this all really necessary?" he asked tersely.

"My uncle is buried in a remote corner of the world and you two sit here entertaining me existentially about my, *my* uncle!"

Elana had no time to respond, save for a deepening of color to her cheeks, before Seth returned holding two letter-sized vinyl folders, each black and an inch thick, containing a messy accumulation of papers held together with a dirty elastic band. It looked like a package of junk mail. Seth held them chest-high toward Adam. "These are your uncle's notes. We read them with him, and together we tried to piece his thoughts into a bed he could rest in for eternity. Did you know he was actively dying?"

Dread fell over Adam, as if David was still alive and his death had suddenly become imminent. "I knew about the stomach cancer, I didn't know *exactly* how sick he was."

"Yes, well, he said it was inoperable and he chose not to treat it again chemically. So, you see, we had to find his faith in these scribblings." Seth placed the folders on the dining table.

Regretting his outburst toward Elana but unwilling to apologize, Adam turned toward the folders and removed the thick elastic band that held them together, flipping the cover open. Inside was a compilation of different sized and colored paper: folded yellow sheets from a legal pad, index cards, backs of dry-cleaning tickets, fine ragged stationery. "They're in Hebrew!" Adam was alarmed and disappointed.

"David said he could at least limit the possibility of snooping housekeepers reading his private thoughts if he wrote in Hebrew. It was bad enough they got to see his underwear in the laundry." Seth chuckled. "He said some really funny things."

"That's my uncle. A comedian if ever there was one." How was he going to make heads or tails out of this Hebrew haystack?

Seth offered a tiny smile. "He'd been writing similar type notes to Liora for years, but he said over this past year he just kept them."

"To Liora?" Adam said.

"He said he wrote to her often, whenever he had something he had to tell her."

David had that much contact with Liora? But how would Adam know what David and Liora did? Adam wrapped his big hands around both folders, feeling he should take them. "Aren't the notes really Liora's, if he was writing his…thoughts to her for so long?"

"My wife has hinted to me, that perhaps showing them to *any*one is premature. I believe David left them to me to do as I see fit." Seth went to gently remove the folders from Adam's hands. "Obviously, David withheld them from Liora for a reason."

Reluctantly, Adam handed the folders back. "They were meant for Liora. David could have destroyed them, but he didn't."

"His decline and death was more rapid than we'd expected. We were still talking about his life when he died. He hadn't yet assigned the inheritance of the notes."

"If they're not meant for Liora, than for whom, you?" Adam heard *inheritance* and the word hit a nerve. Why would Seth and David have discussed such things?

"The writings were a way for him to explore his feelings," Seth said, "to explain himself to himself. They aren't even addressed to anyone in particular."

Elana looked at her husband. "Because he mentioned sending previous notes to Liora, we only assumed they were written to her, but it's unclear whether he wanted her to actually read them."

"We were trying to sort it out," Seth added. "Trying to help him find his faith in God."

Adam groped for sense in this absurdity. This stranger was going to hold not only the remains of David's body, but also the remains of his mind. "So? Did you find his faith for him?"

"One man can't find the faith of another. I did read faith in what he wrote. In the end, he asked to be buried as a Jew. I took that request literally. I took it to mean he remained connected to God."

Doubletalk. "But you don't know for sure that David meant 'buried as a Jew' in the strictest sense of Jewish law? Don't you think Liora and Eli's wishes, his children, should trump your intuition about the man?"

"But he hasn't seen Liora in over thirty years," Elana pointed out.

"But he said nothing specifically about not wanting someone to bring him home." This was the deal-breaker for Adam. He doubted he would be convinced even if Seth said, Yes, Cantor David Kaplan wanted to be buried here.

"Nothing as specific as that," Elana said.

Adam felt a baby step ahead. He turned away from her and fisted his hands to keep himself from pointing at Seth. "Yet you are *certain* enough about things to keep his body, his end-of-life thoughts, under your control." Adam grimaced to show his disbelief. "How dare you?"

Seth pulled his head back and said, "I would be arrogant if I thought I had the power of certainty about anything."

Elana spoke up loudly, "Arrogant, my foot! I am sure. I was with him at the end and I tell you I am sure he was looking toward the light of Hashem." Elana looked at Seth and began to weep. Just as he reached to touch her cheek, the phone rang.

Seth picked it up, spoke cordially, and handed it to Adam. Adam hoped it was the Cohens calling about Lucy and Yin, but it was Diane, reminding him that his plumbing business had come to a halt and telling him that she had reserved seats on a flight to see Jamie in three weeks. "Adam, call the airport *now*, and get a seat on tonight's flight."

"Yes, okay," he told Diane, and hustled her off the phone. Adam shuddered while visualizing Liora and Eli furious that he didn't even go to Beijing to inspect the gravesite. He could think of only one more thing to convince Seth to return the corpse.

"Seth"—Adam put his palms together, prayer-like—"Eli is homebound, alone, completely lost without his father. Please, have compassion for him, for Eli—cooperate and have David shipped home. There must be a way you can arrange it."

"I can't do that."

If Adam weren't so focused on his flight home, he would have screamed. Instead he gritted his teeth and nodded. "Fine." His malice toward Seth grew by the nanosecond.

But Adam was going to bring Eli something. For the next hour, as the phone calls went back and forth between Adam and the airport and Adam and Diane, and the Giacalones did their best to look busy, Adam was scheming.

Before leaving town, Adam asked to call Mr. Cohen and make sure Lucy and Yin arrived safely. Elana dialed and handed the phone to Seth. There came his introduction, and his inquiry, an "uh-oh" a few "uh-huhs," and then he hung up. "I hate to have to tell you this on your way out, I know you'll be that much more upset, but they never arrived."

Adam felt lightheaded and plopped onto the sofa. "Oh my God. Yin is lost."

93

"Oh, I'm sure they'll turn up. Forget about her." Seth waved his hand.

"Forget about her!" He was unnerved by Seth's presumptuous suggestion. "You forget about Yin if you want to! Do you know *any*thing about love?"

Seth took a seat next to Adam. "It is not that difficult to see how you could mix up your feelings for Eli with your feelings for Yin."

"She needs my help."

"You will not be able to save Eli by saving Yin," Seth said.

Save Eli? "I'm telling you right now. David will be returned to New York, and I will not forget about him or Yin."

"You're a man with a cause. I wish you good luck."

"To begin with, give me the notes to read and give to Eli."

"You won't understand them," Seth retorted. "Your uncle wrote in old Hebrew and I think some words he actually invented." Seth smirked, shaking his head. "You'll misread and think you remember things—you'll think of better ways to have done this or that. Life-altering, mishandled situations might seem tragic." Seth, even with his Brooklyn accent, sounded infuriatingly all knowing. "You are the kind of man who would allow himself to become drugged with regret and failure." He nodded sympathetically. "This failure is in all our lives." The rabbi placed his hand on Adam's shoulder. "Go home. Your uncle was burdened with profound frailty. Let him rest now."

Frailty? "What situations? Life-altering? Am I responsible, is my uncle responsible for someone's death?" Adam wasn't home when his father slit his wrists, but David was. "You have to know that you're scaring me. You're being cruel." He slumped deeper into the sofa, thinking, That old prick killed my father!

Elana kneeled near Adam and gently said, "Adam, no one caused anyone's death. My husband"—she looked up to him—

"in his zeal to protect you, has frightened you with his directness. Your uncle realized he did many things wrong and blamed himself for his son, but mostly for the reason he sent Liora away." She stood and walked closer to her husband. "It shocked him when he realized what he did wrong. But what he did and believed in the end, was right. Does that help you at all?"

Adam stared at her. "So! He did *force* Liora to go away. Oh jeez, she wasn't pregnant, was she?" Pregnancy seemed to be his misdemeanor of choice today.

"No, it wasn't anything like that," Elana said, lowering her eyes.

"So what then? Give it to me in a sentence and be done with it. I'll leave." He held his hand up as a sign of his pledge. Maybe this would be something he could bring to Eli.

Seth leaned forward. "A single sentence would drive you mad."

"You have already driven me mad. Say it."

"I understand your frustration. You have to keep in mind this mea culpa about Liora is only part of your uncle's journey." Seth took a deep breath.

"What was it?" Adam tensed.

They were momentarily stilled by his demand. Elana finally broke. "In a sentence, David claimed to have witnessed Liora trying to kill Eli."

"What!" Adam could feel the initial rip of his heart. "What could he possibly have meant by that? Was he delirious or demented? I mean, my God, why would he say that?"

"You got the sentence you wanted." Seth put his arm around Elana. "The rest is incidental. Who would it help to know about all the tumult that tore your uncle apart?"

"Who would it help? I think you mean, who it would hurt." This smart-mouthed, hole-in-the-wall creep of a rabbi, who the fuck does he think he is, messing with me? I should wring his neck. He held his lips together, shook his head, and stared deeply into Elana's eyes. There was no movement on her face, but he saw her eyes move to David's notes on the table. Adam said, "For one, it would help me and I think it would change everything to know about 'all the tumult.'"

"Knowledge is not always for the better," Elana said.

Seth was flat as that morning's tea. "It's time you go or you'll miss your flight."

Elana and Seth went to the kitchen to prepare Adam a travel bag of sweets and leftover breakfast muffins. Adam eyed the two folders marked 1 and 2. He didn't know if these were all the notes David had written, if they were only some of the notes Seth had, or if these were the only folders the cantor brought to China. Adam slid one folder into his backpack. He would have taken both if he thought he could get out unnoticed.

DEGREES OF SEPARATION

E li Kaplan alternated between humming the tunes of prayers and crying. The aluminum awning over his bedroom window pinged with icicles breaking off the gutters. The sooty morning snow would soon mist into a putty-colored day. His father's face did not quite manifest itself in a shadow beneath the window where yesterday's snow caked on the hedges, as Eli stared, frustrated that first Liora's face, and now his dad's, seemed vaporized from his memory. He whispered, "Where is my father?"

Sharon sat with him this morning as he prayed. She didn't know a single word of Hebrew, but listened to him and bowed her head. The words of the prayers became insignificant beneath the melodies Eli had heard as a boy from his bed, where, listening to his father in the next room, he sometimes pushed his face so close to the wall his nose smashed flat. Smelling the oil-based paint, Eli would try to concentrate as hard as he could, to miraculously penetrate the plaster barrier between them.

When he finished his prayers he tried to relax by talking to Sharon about his upcoming SAT exam and the summer school course—either Introduction to English Composition or Introduction to Abnormal Psychology—that he hoped to register for at Kings County Community College. It had been such a leap of faith even to consider attending the school, and now it was that much harder to imagine going to college without the life of his father breathing with him. He feigned optimism for Sharon's sake.

When he had first heard Liora's voice delivering the announcement of their father's death, Eli had been awakened from a deep sleep on the cushions of a brown velvet sofa in the laundry room. Sharon had come barreling into the room with the portable phone and shook Eli awake. The small space was warm from the clothes dryer. All the loads had been washed and dried, but Eli had neither the strength nor the desire to go to his bed. Saturday night and into Sunday morning, stomach cramps had disturbed his sleep, and he was more comfortable here. Eli had awakened to Sharon's hysteria.

"It's Liora from Israel," she had shouted. "Get up!"

In the second or so it took him to realize Sharon was talking about his sister, his heart had started pounding and his head spinning. Eli knew it was bad news. He sat up, disoriented, staring into Sharon's wide eyes, not knowing whether to comfort her or speak to Liora.

"It's not good, Eli." Sharon sat beside him and squeezed his hand.

Eli fell back against the sofa. He took the phone and listened to his sister for the first time in over three decades. Liora's voice was piercingly familiar. She had developed a gruffer, militant tone, but as small as Eli was when she left, he never forgot her sound. Eli had felt Sharon's pulse through her hand and barely heard Liora's "Hello" before he said to her, "Daddy has died."

"I'm sorry, after all this time I have to call with this. Yes. Your father has died in China."

A strong hand had gripped Eli's chest, dug in, and ripped his heart in two; his brain unable to instantly assimilate how his father could be dead *and* in China, and not understanding why it was his estranged sister who has called to give *him* the news.

Liora had recited the details to Eli, one miserable fact at a time, and declared she would try her best to get their cousin Adam to go to Shanghai, and "retrieve his remains."

Eli, wearing the clothes he had laid down in the night before, a gray button-down cotton shirt and black corduroy pants, listened intently, trying very hard to be still and listen to Liora's ideas about asking Adam to rectify her "*incredible inconvenience.*"

"I have to call Adam myself," Eli told her. "I will ask him because he always loved me." Eli thought, And he hates you! We all hate you. My father hated you.

"Give me a few hours to get in touch with him and if we don't hear back from him, then you call him."

He hung up abruptly, angry that he could not jump hard and purposefully to his feet and punch the wall. Liora in Israel and a so-called rabbi in China, somehow able to contact each other before getting a simple phone call through to him in the United States! "Why do you think my father's friends called Liora first and not me?" he yelled at Sharon. He covered his mouth with his hand, knowing he was about to start bawling, not wanting to disturb the others in the house. "I am his son! I — am — his — son!"

"Liora said the people in China weren't sure you'd be able to accept the news from strangers."

"But he just called me a few days ago. What did they think was wrong with me?" He had cried more softly, deeply grieved and flooded with disappointment. It was an hour before he would dial Adam's number and burst again into vocal grief across the phone lines.

By Liora's third call that week, she used more familiar language with Eli, confiding, "I was back in the US, once, years ago. So, maybe soon, we'll visit."

Visit? He was furious with her suggestion, but Eli could summon no energy to hate her. Right now he was more concerned that his father had kept a secret from him. "Did you see our father?"

Liora laughed. "Of course not. He had his life, and I have mine. And never the twain did meet. And so now we never shall."

~~~Three-year-old Eli is up early in the morning and watches Liora carry her clothes in long bags, as she is passing his room through the hallway. But he had seen her take clothes from the house before, and then bring them back on hangers in clear bags and they would smell funny. He waits days for that oily stink to drift past his room. Neither Liora nor her clothes return. He cries and can't fall asleep at night. His father sits beside him, his breath pungent, smelling the way Eli's hands smell after he holds pennies in his fist. "Your sister," his father says in a dark voice, "is gone *forever*." The word sticks in his brain, as does his father's biblical declaration of Liora's misconduct. "She took unfair advantage of God's gifts and tried to use her power against weakness."

Eli begins getting pains that start deep behind his heart and spread through his chest until he feels hollow and hot. He comes to define that feeling as hate.

Diane sat in her car, winding through late-morning traffic, frustrated in her eagerness to meet Sharon. Adam's airplane is flapping its exhausted ailerons toward the New York sky. She was meeting Sharon at Kings Plaza shopping center on Avenue U and Flatbush; they were not meeting to shop, so why exactly Diane had been asked to meet her at this place escaped her. She hoped Sharon would bring Diane back to Eli's house for a short visit. Thinking wishfully, she had bought an apple cake to bring to Eli and had filled an envelope with pictures of Jamie and Adam to show him.

When she rounded the exit from the Belt onto the Flatbush Avenue extension, the cake and the envelope slid off the back seat. From the corner of her eye she could see that the cake had landed bottom first and was probably still in solid form. Photos had spilled from the envelope. Jamie's fourth birthday party. Was he gay at four? On the verge of tears, she wondered if he had been in pain for so long and she didn't know.

The windows started to fog. She stopped behind a parked city bus in front of the mall. As she wiped the windshield with her coat sleeve, the bus pulled away and she spotted Sharon in the line of shoppers just off the bus. Her navy blue, military-looking coat, double-breasted and fitted at the waist, covered her long figure from neck to toe. A pale putty pashmina, the color of any number of office machines was wrapped around her neck and head; red tendrils blown from the edges of the scarf lashed over her face, partially covering her eyes. Diane rolled down her window and shouted, "Sharon! Come on in. We'll go park." Sharon got in, removing her glove immediately to shake Diane's hand, then shivered.

Awkwardly reaching over the console between them, Diane extended her still-gloved hand. "The bus take long?" she asked. Diane was aware that she was constantly asking people about the convenience and comfort of their transports. Sharon's hot hand seeped through Diane's glove. "Are the buses over-heated?"

"They're fine, but with all the stops, it took half an hour. Not too bad, really."

Diane drove around the labyrinth of parking levels at the mall until they found a spot near the Macy's entrance, thinking it would be easy to remember. She stood at her locked door for a moment and watched Sharon as she made her way to the rear of the car and waited. Sharon looked pretty wearing little make-up, and—with her fitted coat—sophisticated, cool. Diane decided the heat that transferred from hand to hand was more likely the onset of Sharon's menopause than the warmth of her soul.

They each bought a large coffee and took seats at the open-mall café. Sharon took out her eyeglasses and put them on the edge of her nose, as if she were about to read a contract. "So. What's the latest word from Adam?"

"God willing, he'll be home tomorrow morning." Diane felt the truth choking her and couldn't help blurting out, "And David is still in a grave in Beijing, most likely because Liora didn't go and force the issue, and Adam was unable to convince the rabbi that his uncle needed to come home."

Sharon made no comment, looking as if she were waiting to hear the important stuff.

Diane said, "So we, Adam and I, will need to see Eli tomorrow and tell him. I won't tell him when I see him this afternoon, but I'll try to lay some groundwork."

She watched as Sharon drew a silent breath and unbuttoned the length of her coat. "Not today, Diane. Today is his birthday and his housemates had secretly planned a small party for him, but besides that, Eli is out of the house and won't be back until maybe five or six o'clock. It was an appointment he had to keep. With his doctor in the city."

Diane felt herself flush. "You didn't know this yesterday when we spoke? You could have at least reminded me of his birthday, and now you've made me come here for nothing?" She cocked her head.

"As a matter of fact, I did not know about the appointment yesterday because it just came up an hour ago. If you check your answering machine, which by the way doesn't seem to be working correctly, you'll at least be able to tell, I hope, that I tried to leave a message to tell you, but you had already gone."

Diane relented. "Is he okay? Is it something new?"

"He's fine. He's going to start more aggressive physical therapy. An opening in the doctor's schedule came up for his pre-therapy clearance exam. Eli was very anxious about it. I would have preferred to go with him, but I wouldn't have let you come here and wait for me." She sipped her coffee and leaned back into the chair.

Diane was confused. "Now what? Now what do we do?" She tapped her nails against the side of the cup. If she were not going to see Eli, then Sharon was going to give her some party favor to take home. "Can we talk more honestly about what's going on?"

"I have been nothing but honest with you, Diane," Sharon said promptly. "I don't know what kind of story you're looking for, but you have the truth." She turned to regard some commotion behind her. A small boy was kicking his mother in a rage. "He should be disciplined more," Sharon remarked. She shook her head and then looked squarely at Diane.

Diane blinked the remark away and watched the mother lift the boy from behind with one arm while he flung out his feet and she covered his mouth with her other hand. When the screaming stopped, Diane focused on Sharon. "I really wanted to see Eli yesterday. I found it all very strange. And today. First that we had to meet here, and now, seeing your face when you told me about his appointment, well frankly, you seem to glow with the mere mention of his name." Diane blushed. "I wonder if you're more involved with him than you've let on." Her words sounded accusatory and demeaning. "I mean, I know he's dependent on you and relies on you, I'm just wondering if you perhaps…" She closed her eyes, then looked away and couldn't continue.

"If I'm perhaps in love with him? Is that what you're trying desperately to ask?"

"Yes." She waited.

"You know what, Diane? I have had enough for one day. The bus was crowded and yes, it was overheated. I thought that getting out of the house to window shop would be nice, but the mall is ugly and noisy. And you? You are rude." She stood and tied her scarf. "Eli is about to embark on a life without his father and I should be with him. Call me as soon as Adam lands, please." She turned and strode away.

Diane sat with her mouth open, heart pounding, watching Sharon walk toward the center staircase, until her head descended and disappeared from view. Sharon had not asked one question about David, did not seem to be disturbed or surprised that he wasn't on a plane with Adam. Diane found her disinterest both fascinating and conspicuously narcissistic. After dumping her coffee cup into the trash, she dashed out into the crowd and sprinted to the parking garage, hoping she could find her way to Brighton Beach and get there before Sharon. At the corner gas station she asked for directions—a second opinion of sorts—and proceeded back to the Belt Parkway and drove west to Coney Island Avenue.

After exiting the parkway, she didn't know which way she was facing, whether the ocean was to the left or right, and made what she would later that evening tell Jamie was a seriously mistaken calculation: she drove at least ten minutes heading in the wrong direction. Once she did turn around, she drove along Shore Parkway into Brighton Beach.

Diane drove past the Kaplan Group Home. She wasn't sure if Sharon already returned. A parking spot was being vacated about twenty feet from the house; opportunity was at hand, yet in all this time she had yet to decide what she hoped to achieve by coming here. She pulled into the spot and watched the house. Was Eli out of the house or had Sharon lied? Remembering the apple cake, she thought to bring it to the door, tell Ludie it was for Eli's birthday, and casually ask if he were home to receive it. The wind kicked the tops of snow-banks, forcing a spiraling whiz of flakes around her body as she got out of the car.

Behind the storm-windowed screen door, the front entrance to the house was shut. Ludie answered after the first ring and smiled a capped-tooth smile. Diane wondered who paid for her dental work, and then speculated it was probably paid for with funds embezzled from David. "Hi. I was here yesterday? Eli's cousin?" Diane always expected no one remembered her; Ludie's non-verbal response indicated this time Diane was right. She said, "I have this apple cake for Eli. For his birthday? Is he here?"

"No, hon. Won't be back till nighttime. I'm sure he'd love you for leaving it, though. Apple's his favorite." Ludie smiled more warmly.

Diane handed Ludie the cake, rummaged frenetically in her bag for her wallet, and slipped a ten into the woman's hand. "Don't mention to anyone I was here. Just keep the cake for yourself." She ran to the car and drove back to Queens, fretting the entire way that she had done a really stupid thing.

Adam's flight from Shanghai departed three hours behind schedule. When he asked and was told that half the business class section was empty, Adam was able to evoke sympathy from the check-in clerk by telling her about his failed mission, and she offered him and his casket of notes an upgrade. Adam had initially felt high from his impromptu confiscation. But now, with the strap from his backpack digging into his shoulder, lugging his booty out of the country, his sneaky self-indulgence struck him hard and he questioned his decision.

With his first course of shrimp dumplings devoured, Adam pushed his body as deeply into his seat as he could and elevated his feet. No one was sitting beside him so he lifted the center arm, covered himself with a blanket and opened David's folder to a yellow sheet, looking creepy with a stain that could have been spilled black coffee or dried blood. Maybe it was a Pandora's box and Seth was right to try to withhold it. Adam just knew he was going to get punished for his theft, but here he was and here it was, and if the plane was going down it was going down.

He spread the yellow sheet across his lap and began. Although Adam had been taught Hebrew as a second language and had been able to hold a conversation with Liora if she spoke slowly, he was accustomed to reading it only in the form of prayer or torah. David had been stunningly fluent in Hebrew. His writing would no doubt be sophisticated, and — Adam feared — rendered in the complicated prose of a gifted thinker.

He decided he would begin by attempting to decipher the words literally, rewriting them in English, making liberal use of his imagination and inference. He would, if necessary, later review a word's meaning with Jamie. Diane didn't speak Hebrew but Jamie had been an excellent Hebrew student and kept studying it as a second language for years after his bar mitzvah, maintaining straight A's through high school. But starting to read the first entry, Adam felt paralyzed by hesitation. The passage was dated exactly one year ago, February 18, 2000. Today was also Eli's thirty-seventh birthday. This was surely coincidence, but the improbability of it happening was just about as eerie a way to start this project as Adam could tolerate.

Adam spent about ten hours of travel time with a notepad in front of him, translating his uncle's words into English, and trying to maintain a sense of detachment from their meaning, as if he were doing Hebrew school homework. He concocted a system: if he remembered an event David mentioned he made an asterisk; if he was unsure of a word he put a question mark beside it. Adam kept reminding himself that the writings were his uncle's thoughts and had presumably been written for someone to read, yet before the readings by Seth, had actually been seen by no one. Adam shook off a twinge of guilt. The first note's language was stiff, the words written with a hard hand, with some lines cutting the black ink deep into the paper. He heard his uncle speak in anger.

white index card/ February 18, 2000: On this day I should celebrate the birth of my first son, but I feel only grief on this thirty-sixth anniversary of my wife's death. I visited Miriam's grave alone. I no longer have a being, human or spiritual, to share my thoughts. I have not been to see Eli for his birthday. I hope he does not guess that I am too frightened for him to see me. Who can he rely on to love him if he sees me so sick?

back of doctor's "Dear Patient" homecare memo/ March 22, 2000: The doctor wants more aggressive testing to plan treatment. I fear what is to be found. I have fallen into the world of an invalid and there is nothing to do but watch and wait for my complete debilitation (?). The doctors have not given me an ounce of help, and I am suffering crippling pain.

white index card, front and back/ June 6, 2000: Tonight I go to teach my three students their Haftorahs. I find myself needing to concentrate hard to keep His spirit as part of my song. I am weary from a growing impatience (?) with such an all-knowing Lord, yet I fear His disdain for my skepticism (?). I hold onto the fear of the wrath of a God I no longer believe in, and I shake with shame trying to cover the lies of living as the man I portray. / Shame overwhelms me. I look forward to the tears I know will come when I curse a God who has not stretched farther to touch me. I will become afraid when I find myself at last in bed denouncing (?) Him. I talk to walls. Tomorrow I will wake and call my son and silently begin again the day's graceless requiem. I've learned I am dying.

The flight arrived at Kennedy just after 5 a.m., an hour ahead of the revised schedule. Adam had been unable to sleep. He collected the notes strewn across the seat and floor in front of him, and stumbled into the aisle dizzy with exhaustion. He had accomplished very little, but was already convinced that his uncle was in the throes of a breakdown. Liora was not mentioned. Had he written to her over the years, remaining so removed from her feelings that he couldn't even use her name?

Adam still couldn't imagine why, after a diagnosis of cancer, David had brought himself around the world, like an elephant finding his burial spot. And what of this nonsense of losing faith in God? He sounded agnostic, not atheistic. Who hasn't had moments like that? Those moments come and go, but in the end? Adam was not sure, in the end, what he himself believed anymore. But religion was David's life, and Adam, in this first peek at the notes, had yet to read anything that would indicate why his uncle had been led to Shanghai.

Business class emptied. Adam checked his seat. He had a sinking feeling that he had left something behind in China. Oh yeah, *him*.

Diane waited inside her black '97 Volvo by the curb at Shanghai Air arrivals. It was nearing six a.m. and the airport was crowded, the police continually asking her to move. Determined to stay put, she tucked the Volvo neatly out of the policemen's sight. Her car was meshed between two cabs and beside a shuttle bus when she spotted Adam swinging his carry-on, shielding his eyes from the blowing wind. The relief in her stomach was overwhelming and she cried as soon as she knew he saw the car.

Adam ducked inside quickly, a gust of wind helping him to slam the door shut. Diane leaned over and cupped his cheeks, kissing him hard on the mouth. "Hello, hello, hello. Oh god, I'm so happy you're home." She could smell that he had just put on after-shave and was tickled that he thought to do that for her. "The flight was good?"

"I'm here, so I guess it was good." He lowered the folder of notes to the floor at his feet. "I'm tired as shit. You okay driving in this weather?"

"I've been to Brooklyn and back twice in this weather, so yes, I'm okay with it." Diane was bursting to tell him about Eli and Sharon but was saving it until Adam told her what happened with David. Easing him into talking, she asked, "What's that folder thing you threw on the floor?"

"Believe it or not, it's David's," Adam said, turning to Diane, letting his face go deadpan. "He kept notes."

"You mean, like, diaries?"

"More like letters to Santa. Letters to no one."

Diane put this information together with what Jamie had confided about his communication with Ariella. "Could they be letters to Liora?"

"Why would you think that?"

She told him about Jamie's relationship with his cousin Ariella and her grandfather's letters.

Adam shook his head. "The boy gets stranger by the day. He doesn't tell us anything anymore."

Diane didn't know whether to laugh or cry.

Adam said, "I need Jamie's help." He yawned like a lion. "The notes are all in old Hebrew, so I've only gotten through a few pages." He threw his head back against the seat. "Let's get home and sit down with coffee."

As soon as they walked into the warm and lamp-lit house, they kicked off their wet shoes, dropped their bags, and briskly threw themselves into a bear hug. "Oh, I missed you," Diane said into his shoulder, breathing deeply to inhale his smell. He squeezed her tight and let go. They walked arm in arm toward the kitchen; dawn shone through the window of the back door, all hard shiny surfaces gleaming.

Diane put the coffee on. Adam placed four slices of rye bread into the toaster-oven and stood staring at the orange coils while Diane looked at him and made funny faces, waiting to see if he'd notice. He didn't.

"So," Adam said, still staring at the coils. "David is in Beijing."

"Yes, I know." She tapped Adam's shoulder so he would look at her. Adam wasn't ready to talk and she couldn't wait any longer. "I went to Brooklyn again to see Eli's social worker, Sharon. You know, his old reading teacher? She remembers you, Adam." Diane watched to see how he'd react.

"Sure, sure. I remember her. What is she, like ninety? She takes care of Eli?"

"She's your age and runs the house David put him in. Anyway, I saw her twice while you were gone."

110

Adam looked at Diane. His face scrunched, as if bearing a toothache. "How's Eli?"

She waved her hand in front of her face. "Didn't see him. Whole other story."

"So you went to Brooklyn twice and didn't see him?"

"No, Adam! I didn't get to see him. We'll see him when we go today. Okay?" She was relieved at his reaction to Sharon and lost the desire to go on with her story. "Now tell me about your trip with the abundance of detail that I'm entitled to"—she took a breath—"given the enormity of our altruism."

Adam took the scorched bread from the toaster and told her about Yin and Lucy— Lucy was the meanest and Yin the most adorable person he had ever met—and about the beautiful, exotic Elana and the arrogant, bright, tediously evasive Seth. "He wouldn't give me a goddamned straight answer about anything." Adam told her, briefly, about Seth's claim of David's tango with atheism and about his health. "Why didn't he tell us he was so sick?"

"Why, because your uncle was such a forthcoming person in general?"

"You're right. I should know a lot more about him after I read his notes. Wait till you hear this one." He proceeded to tell Diane the one sentence answer he had demanded of the rabbi. "Did you ever hear anyone in the family allude to Liora trying to *kill* Eli?"

Diane was shaken. "That's insane. She left when he was only three years old."

"*Insane* works for me. I don't know why I should, but I believe Seth." He looked at his buttered toast and bit into it hard.

"So, this Seth is very *evasive*, but he gave you David's memoir?"

"I wouldn't call it a memoir."

Something was not scanning and Diane tensed. "You're the one who's being evasive." She squared her stare into his eyes.

"I *took* them. Okay? I'll explain when I have the strength." He closed his eyes. "Don't ask me to explain now. Could you please do that for me?"

She knew he must be furious with himself for leaving David there; she could see his weariness and relented.

They finished their breakfast and Diane walked behind Adam to their bedroom. He looked in and stopped short. "You left the house and didn't make the bed?"

"I thought you'd want to get right into it." She felt a pleasant thump in her chest that rose to her cheeks. "It didn't even bother me." She stepped in front of him.

"Lie down with me." He put his hands on her shoulders and guided her into the room. "I need a few hours sleep before we drive to Brooklyn." Adam shook his blanket out flat across the bed. "Where exactly is Eli's house?"

Diane slid under the quilt and pressed her cheek firmly into the pillow, yawning. She wanted to fall asleep quickly. "Brighton Beach. His street is not too nice. You're gonna get depressed when you see it."

"*Get* depressed?" He turned over with his back to Diane. "You never told me. How's Jamie? You said he was upset about something."

"He's good." With her stomach jumping, she rubbed his shoulders and scratched his head and neck. Diane chewed the inside of her cheek and debated whether or not to just drop the bomb or wait. "It's just that..." She began. She looked down and saw Adam was already asleep.

At eight o'clock Diane picked up the ringing phone. Sharon was checking up on Adam's arrival. Whispering, she said to Diane,

"Listen. Liora just called me for the second time about shiva. She said now that his father is buried we must tell Eli to start to sit. The Chinese rabbi, Giacalone, called her yesterday. I told her Eli was showering, but she's going to call back later and demand to speak to him! I'm going to tell Eli as soon as he comes downstairs."

"The Chinese rabbi? I don't think Giacalone is a Chinese name," Diane said sarcastically, then told Sharon firmly, "Wait until Adam gets up and tells you how to handle Eli."

"I'm an adult, Diane. I'm also a mental health professional and a friend of Eli's. Why do I have to wait for Adam to tell me how to handle him?"

"Because Adam is his closest relative, Sharon, and Adam is the one who flew to China, and Adam is the one who will make this decision!"

"Well, fine. When can I count on hearing from you?" Sharon's voice was clipped, distressingly professional.

"By one o'clock. I'll wake Adam at noon and we'll discuss it. Then we'll call you back. All right?" She wished Adam would wake up and take care of this.

Sharon said, "I just hope his sister doesn't call again before then."

"Well, we'll have to take our chances. Adam needs some sleep. And by the way, it was such a surprise to me, so I'm curious, why aren't you more disturbed about the news of David's aborted return flight?"

"If you knew David as I do...oh, never mind!" She hung up on Diane.

"Bitch."

Adam was dreaming he was traveling through Brooklyn on a kid's bike, riding along the elevated train tracks until he saw Eli

113

in a wheelchair at the bottom of the exit stairs. Adam jumped off the bike and ran down the street, away from his cousin, and into a butcher shop where they handed him an urn and told him it contained his uncle David. Adam began to argue with the butcher about why he had cremated the body, but Eli came into the store and told him it was all right: He would keep his father's urn in the basket beneath his seat of the wheelchair. Adam screamed at him that it would be like using the urn as a toilet.

He woke up breathing hard and sweating. He put his hand up to his head and Diane grabbed it. She was standing above him. "That was a horrible dream," Adam said. "Let's get dressed and go see Eli."

"Well, I am dressed, but there's a ton of snow outside. A blizzard flew in ahead of its estimated time of arrival." Diane made a sour face. "Sharon's waiting to hear from you. She told me that the Seth Giacalone person called Liora and told her to start sitting shiva. Liora called Sharon and she wants to tell Eli about David."

"Oh Jesus, she didn't, did she?"

"No. I told her to wait to hear from you. You think he'd go nuts if he finds out that he didn't know he had to sit shiva?"

Adam sat up and looked through the window. The snow was piled high on his small lawn. He stood and wrapped the flannel blanket around himself, not sure of where to go or what to do. He felt stupefied with sadness. One week ago he had looked through this window and Eli had begged him to retrieve his father. Adam shivered. "I actually went to China, and I fucked up. What do I do about Eli now?"

"I'll give you the phone number. Call him." She started to leave the room but turned back to look at Adam. "You're going to talk to Sharon first?"

"If she answers the damn phone I'll talk to her first. Otherwise, no."

"Don't be nasty with me, Adam."

"I'm sorry. Do you think she'll answer the phone?"

"She'll answer," Diane declared. "She'll make you tell her what you plan to do before you speak to him. She runs his life." Diane walked back to her husband and grabbed Adam's shoulder, pulling him toward her. "You have to listen to my story about her before you call."

"Tell me the story, but please, please, don't get caught up in too many tiny details. Eli has to sit shiva, and he'll need time to prepare and get started."

Rapid fire, Diane recounted her adventure, interspersing interpretive commentary, up to and including the part about speaking to Ludie about the cake. It took her all of five minutes. "So, Adam, I was too freaked by that time and too afraid that Sharon would show up any minute and crucify me. I'm sorry I didn't wait and get to see him."

"That's all right. But you can't be serious." Adam was entangled in one particularly exuberant element of Diane's account. "You don't actually think she's in love with Eli."

"Actually, I do think so. She has devoted her life to the man. What's more, she has the look of love about her."

Adam raised his eyebrow. "You're nuts."

"Maybe, but she's involved somehow." She leaned into him like a conspirator. "She said he's starting more aggressive treatments."

"I'm going to make the call and get it over with."

"Wait. What are you going to tell her?"

"To put Eli on the phone!"

"And then?"

He didn't know. They both sat on the edge of the bed as Adam thought. Adam suffered from the sometimes unconstructive belief that bad things happened for good reasons and ultimately would all turn out for the best. It often relieved him of disrupting the course of events and lessened his guilt over a bad outcome. He went to China because of that guilt, but left without his uncle, totally unprepared for a complication of any kind, let alone the steel determination of Seth and Elana. He had decided even before he landed at Kennedy Airport that he would go back to Beijing if he had to, this time armed with details and legal documents. Now, was this blizzard going to stop him from going to Brooklyn? Recognizing he was making a too-easy concession to nature, Adam felt the prickly and hot drops of guilt sticking on his body.

"I could walk to the train station and ride out to Brooklyn," he said.

"You could do that. It will take you four hours to get there. But I'll go with you if that's what you think we should do." She stood up straighter.

"I'd like that. Let me call and tell him we're coming."

Sharon answered the phone, and at the sound of her voice, Adam's head split into a right-sided migraine.

"Adam, welcome home," she said. "I have already spoken again to Liora, who was outraged that her brother had not started shiva."

Adam wanted to calm her and shut her up, but he looked out the window at the driving snow and had to admit before he spoke that the trip was not going to happen.

Sharon said mildly, "Liora was in hysterics over the debacle in China, angry as hell with you. I must tell you, she said that you'd *pay*, whatever that means, and insisted Eli be told the whole truth immediately. I put him on the phone with her."

"So she told him everything?" Adam felt drugged with fatigue.

"Yes, and after she told Eli, she called me back yet again, and instructed me on the laws and customs of shiva for Eli to follow."

Adam heard no mention of Eli's inability to sit on a small wooden bench for seven days, as Liora undoubtedly told Sharon shiva required. He didn't want Sharon's opinion about Eli's condition. Instead he asked her to put him on the phone, but as Diane had warned, Sharon would not relinquish sole communication. She claimed he was sitting shiva and was forbidden use of the telephone, per Liora.

FAILURE AND OTHER FAMILY PATTERNS

Eli had stood in the hallway outside his bedroom, by the communal telephone table, talking to Liora, still praying for a miracle even greater than the one he saw when he caught sight of his reflection in the hall-mirror. After days without good news he felt bad news was all the more possible, but he was shocked just the same when the worst news actually came. On top of the fact that his father's body would not be coming home, Eli was rattled by the moral his sister drew from Adam's failure. What had her phrasing been? "A lesson for you. You can stop counting on people to help you. They've all failed, failed, failed." Stunned, focusing on a cobweb between the table and the wall, he was having trouble distinguishing between the time before the phone call and after. Light seemed to fade and brighten. Was he dreaming?

In breaths that sounded all too calculated and calm, Liora had said, "Eli, do what need be done and start your shiva today." She held on for a few seconds. When Eli had hesitated, trying to find words to respond, she said, "Have an easy shiva," and she hung up. His eight-day-long prayer marathon to bring his father home ended.

Facing the wall he shouted Sharon's name. She was standing behind him. Startled, yet not turning to face her, he asked, "Did you listen to the call? Did she really say he wasn't coming home?"

"Yes, Elias. I'm so sorry." She took his free arm and put her forehead against his shoulder. "Is there anything, anything at all I can do for you?"

118

"Yes. Get me a hard bench. It's time to start shiva."

"Eli, you can't possibly be serious. There must be an alternative."

"Get me a fucking hard bench!" he shouted, like a man whose character had been defamed. And instantly, as if her frown had scorched his eyes, shame engulfed him. His cane slipped from his hand. Eli caught his balance, arched his back, walked toward his bedroom in a gait that was quick for him, and then took a seat on his wooden desk chair. He listened to Sharon's footsteps coming toward him and hoped his throat was capable of murmuring how ashamed he was for cursing. "Please understand and just call the shul for me, can you? Have them arrange for services here tonight and ask them to deliver a bench."

Her voice was not angry. "Which shul. In the city?"

"No. The one around the corner. And Sharon? Tell them we need another six men for a minyan." Eli heard her hurry down the stairs.

It was September. Nine-year-old Eli sat in his chair watching from the window, waiting for the arrival of the young student his father had interviewed the day before. The cantor was busy preparing for the Jewish holidays and Adam was packing to leave for college. Eli's Gramercy Park room had windows on both corner walls. There was his chest of drawers, a large mushroom colored velvet chair at the east window, a wall of bookcases, and a single bed.

Sharon came up the side street, visible from the east window. She was pale with auburn hair, shoulder-length but baby-fine, and the noon sun lit her face as the wisps of red flew back from her. She wore a long dungaree skirt with a man's shirt, the front tails tied around her waist, allowing a small section of her belly

119

to peek out under the knot as she walked. Eli grew intent on the pink oval of skin. When she disappeared around the front of the house he listened hard for the moment she entered the house.

Eli overheard Ruby tell her, "Cantor Kaplan says he wants you to remember that you're here to tutor him." He was to study and eat in his bedroom. Ruby opened his bedroom door and introduced them to each other.

"Hello Elias. I'm going to help you read and we'll have fun. Okay with you?" She approached him and extended her hand to shake.

"I can read." Eli looked into his lap and kept his hands against his stomach, humiliated that this pretty teacher thought he was illiterate, praying to become totally mute so he would not have to read aloud and make a fool of himself. He knew that whenever he spoke, the sounds of his speech made his father's eyes shut.

"Oh, he can read, Sharon," Ruby jumped in. "He's a good reader. We just want to help him do a tiny bit better. Isn't that right, Sharon?"

"Yes. I know you can read, Elias. I'm going to work with you and maybe you'll be able to sit in a real classroom someday." She lowered herself to Eli's eye level, smiled at him and then at Ruby.

Ruby smiled back. "Eli is happy learning here. Don't get his hopes up."

Eli watched, made more anxious by Sharon's questioning eyes. He loved that she called him "Elias." It was an adult name.

Ruby approached Eli and put her finger under his chin, tilting it up for Sharon to see. "He's still a small boy."

Eli wanted Sharon to be quiet; he feared she would get fired for asking to take him outside; he feared more that she'd get permission to do it. When he concentrated hard on what it would be like to be in a real classroom, he became short of breath, and had a coughing fit and forced elongated wheezes. He was a good boy, and Eli knew his seclusion was not a punishment; his father was clear about that. Eli understood he was just not yet good enough for the rest of the world. Adam was quite special, Eli was sure, because he was permitted to study with the cantor's Hebrew class, and though Eli longed to be like his cousin, deep in his heart he knew he himself was not special enough to enter The Talmud Torah.

For four years after that first day, Sharon came each week loaded-down with the public school curriculum. Twice a month she would bring along another coed, and they would have gym class among the three of them, playing knock-hockey sitting on the floor in the living room, or tossing a volleyball from one side of his bed to the other.

Barely six months after Sharon departed, he became a bar mitzvah on a makeshift bema in his dining room. A photograph of his mother Miriam was positioned on a chair in front of him. The picture spooked him. He was relieved that he didn't have to recite his haftarah in shul. Sharon's friendly post-teaching visits had slowly dwindled to never, and so Eli promised God that if Sharon showed up he would lift himself from his wheelchair and run to her. Adam and Diane were there, and Eli's Hebrew teachers came, but there had been no need to walk at all.

After only five minutes sitting in his hard desk chair, Eli's back began to ache. Where should he sit shiva? What would his father expect from him? Eli looked at the floor and lowered himself carefully down to it. With his legs folded comfortably behind him, he rested his back against the bed frame. Eli waited to hear back from Sharon about the rabbi, anticipating that without his father, the world would ignore him.

Weeping quietly, he sat not knowing how much time was passing, thinking time would never pass. After a period of tears, his anxiety ebbed, as his sister's call pushed its way to the front of his mind. Why did she say his father failed him? She was a wicked and ugly woman. He was relieved he could not remember her face, though her voice would ring in his head forever.

He went downstairs and made a shiva bench out of the top step of a three-step kitchen stool. His back leaned on the frontside of the upholstered sofa arm. Sharon approached, bringing him tea. Unnerved by the blank look on her face, he asked, "Did you get through to the rabbi? Is he coming?"

"Yes. I just hung up. The rabbi *and* the cantor will be here before sunset. They've assured me a minyan will be here in time for the service. They said they would need information from you. About your father and such."

He suddenly felt drunk with relief, as if a coffin had been lifted off his chest; he briefly believed he would make it through this. Almost happily he said, "They'll want his Hebrew name. Maybe his parents' names. I know all that."

"And your mother's name? You think they'll need that?"

Another coffin thudded into him. He slumped from the hit. He doubted he could bear it all.

"And they asked if your sister would be here with you."

"God, no. My father would turn over." He shivered; the thought of his father dead in China, turning over, sent drips of icicles down his back.

"She has a right to come. Your father has no further say in matters of his children. He no longer has a say about what you or Liora do."

"Just stop it." He nudged her away from him. "Can't you see I want to be quiet? Show respect for his wishes now that he's dead." He wondered why she so often spoke against him.

"I showed your father respect while he was alive. But I have more respect for you, and you're a man with wishes too."

"Liora has to stay the hell away." Eli's voice grew louder—he didn't care who in the house heard him. "You don't want to see the ugly side of her. My father couldn't even speak to you about her ugliness, but it was always clear to me. She cannot come here."

He looked at Sharon. She had the face of an easy life and it calmed him, with its absence of middle-aged laugh lines at the corners of her eyes, and no bags beneath. She had perfectly clear skin that was only slightly made-up with rose-colored lipstick, barely-pink blush, maybe a single swipe of mascara. Eli loved her face. Even moments of contentiousness with her reminded him he had a body. He put his hand on the back of her neck—feeling her fine hairs stippling against his finger tips—and urged her with his eyes to bring her face closer to his. "Forget ugly Liora," he whispered.

The snow was falling hard and heavy. Eli wondered how the rabbi would travel down the street, how a minyan would get to the house. He kept a keen eye on the drift of snow across the front sidewalk, as if staring at it would melt the mounds and open a path.

At three-thirty in the afternoon the cantor and rabbi arrived, along with the shul's two shammosim bearing two benches, the rabbi mistaken in believing that Sharon needed one as well. Rabbi Weinreich and Cantor Jacobs looked a few years younger than Eli, nice looking men, with slicked-back, shorter hair than expected, and their bodies tall and trim in their clean black suits and semi-clean white shirts. The four men from the shul surprised Eli with their youthfulness and he realized, again, that he had never experienced the rituals of his religion with anyone but old men.

Seeing the rabbi remove something small and silver from his pocket, Eli offered his neck tie, a visible cloth the rabbi would cut. He listened as the rabbi said the prayer, understanding the words and recalling the ritual. They said, "Amen" and Eli waited as Rabbi Weinreich sawed his way through the silk with his pocketknife. The bottom of Eli's tie fell away and he felt as if a stranger had barged into the house and slit his middle open.

Eli followed behind the men as they walked around the house, sizing up the place. The cantor stopped the rabbi before he set foot in the kitchen, to warn him not to touch the food. Eli knew the kitchen had *Kosher-Questionable* written all over it. Theirs was supposed to be a kosher household, but time after time the rules were broken: Ludie would buy cookies that contained lard, or the residents would serve themselves and mix the dairy with meat utensils. Even so, the young rabbi and cantor laughed and kidded with the men in the kitchen. The rabbi explained politely why the television should stay off and asked Ludie to place sheets over the mirrors in the house. She turned to Eli to check this instruction with him. Eli knew no one in the house but her would have dared argue the point with a rabbi. He felt strangely relieved, and one stone in his chest instantly dissolved as he told Ludie, "Cover all the mirrors."

By four-thirty the house was filled with twenty men, ten women, two teenaged boys with scraggily beards and black hats, two trays of kosher delicatessen donated by the temple's Ladies Auxiliary, and a variety of miniature pastries. Eli regarded what was transpiring among the mix: a noisy, respectful shiva call. The only other shiva he'd experienced was noticeably weepier; it was his uncle Seymour's.

Eli listened intently while his callers said prayers, the cantor gave instructions, and Eli accepted condolences graciously.

Whether in sympathy and generosity or in nosiness, members of the congregation were paying their calls on him. Eli was overwhelmed with gratitude.

Ludie cleaned the puddles from boots and umbrellas after the last caller had gone. Sy and Ted, two of the men who shared the house, helped pack and store the food for tomorrow. Eli heard them chattering like yentas in the kitchen, boasting about the leanness of the pastrami and the amount of raisins in the cookies, while Sharon helped him upstairs. His heart gathered strength with each step.

Sharon asked, "You think it was all right? Did the rabbi do it the way you wanted?"

"He was fine. He's a warm man. And the cantor was very nice too. Beautiful voice, although his pronunciations were awkward. My father was better." Eli caught himself hoping his father heard that. "I'm thinking about starting to go to services in the spring. I'll find a shul that's better for me. Conservative." He hoped his father didn't hear that. He let his cane fall to the floor. He lowered himself onto the bed, ready to remain fully clothed, including the sawed necktie. Eli didn't want Sharon to leave the room. His eyes filled with tears, but he was not crying about his father's trip to China and death and burial there.

Right before David went to China, Eli had overheard Sharon talking to his father on the phone, accusing David of making this trip with the sole intention of separating himself from Eli. Eli had lifted the extension outside his room and listened silently as Sharon's voice grew tearful. "Now, of all times in your life, you leave, after you've spent your life undermining Eli's progress. You're the one who petrified him."

Sharon had gone on to tell David that she never had the heart to accuse him legally, to ever officially report any abuse, because

Eli loved him so much. Eli waited for his father's response. But all that came was the sound of his father's weeping, then the black sound of a dead connection. The first thing Eli had assumed Sharon meant was that David beat him, or kept him dirty or starving. He alone knew none of that was true, but he was terrified at that time to ask Sharon what she meant.

A few days after their phone conversation, David gave Sharon power of attorney over Eli's health-care expenditures and added her to their health insurance policy. Eli had an uneasy reservation about the necessity of anyone having power of attorney, but he was equally uneasy about relying on himself in legal matters. Now that his father was dead, Eli needed to know, wanted to know, what Sharon had meant that day confronting his father on the telephone.

The other men, Sy and Ted, were still carrying on in the kitchen, and Eli knew Sharon had to get back to her evening responsibilities, looking at the day's mail, paying bills. "Will you stay and talk for a while?" he asked her.

She pulled the desk chair next to the bed, put her head down near his arm, and let him play with her hair. He silently condemned himself for having an erection in the middle of shiva for his father. "Sharon?" He smoothed some wisps of hair from the sides of her face. "What is it you think my father did that was so terrible? Why did you accuse him of mistreating me?"

His hand stopped stroking her hair and rested on the crown of her head.

She looked at him. She sounded tired. "Did he tell you I said that?"

"I heard you saying those things to him." His voice was weakening, but he recouped. "You do understand how hard a job it was for him after my mother died, with me, and my horrid sister? I know he wasn't home much, but he had to work a lot.

126

Men of the shul have to work very long hours to serve the congregation. You see how they had to show up here today on a moment's notice. In your life, you must have known a priest like him."

"But it was your father's behavior towards you! The staying away, and finally his going so far from you, he...but mostly his *isolating* you."

"It was all out of love for me. I was the one afraid to go out. You know that!"

"He loved you, of course." She shook her head. "But he gravely misunderstood his role as a father. Obviously, you're capable of a full and rich life."

He took a breath so deep it shook him. "My father misunderstood *very, very* little in this world. You don't know, and now you will *never* know him like I do."

She stroked his arm.

He relaxed under the stroke of her hand, as her words rumbled in his head. When they all settled into intelligible thoughts, he knew there was something about her accusations that rang true.

Sharon closed her eyes. She rubbed Eli's chest and he opened his eyes, his heart racing, wanting her to stop because it was shiva and wanting her to continue because he wanted her so badly.

She looked into his eyes. "Listen to me. Your father, when he went to China — remember I left the house that night? You were here and you said you were okay about his trip and wouldn't mind if I go out?"

He nodded, his eyes and attention sharpening, as she continued slowly. "He called me that morning, asking me to meet him at the airport. I went because I thought it was important to hear what he had to say." Sharon lowered her head, angling her face away. "While he waited for the flight he rambled about his emptiness. He used the word *Godless*. And he was reciting a long, involved speech about" — she stopped — "just all kinds of foolishness."

"Foolishness? Now you think my father was foolish?"

Sharon tried to explain calmly that she thought David was paranoid, even to the point of psychotic; she explained how she tried to pull him out from his blabbering and pry admissions about Eli from him. "I tried to get him to stay. He obviously left anyway, but before he went through security he grabbed my wrist and said he was *entrusting* some bunches of papers to me. And there were others he'd written, that he took with him, but he wanted to leave some behind in case anything happened and they got lost." Perspiration appeared on her neck. "And he said to give them to you after he died." When he handed them over to her, he boasted that the papers were filled with the most interesting observations. He had said, "Just give them to Eli. It explains everything."

Sharon told Eli, "I was more frightened than anything else."

"Hold on!" Eli shouted. "Are you saying he gave this to you to give to me and you didn't?"

"I promised him I'd wait until he died. But then I held onto it without showing you because I was afraid for you. That was a mistake. I tried to protect you. I should know better. I don't know what they are because they're in Hebrew. I swear I was going to give them to you after you finished shiva." She spoke fast so Eli wouldn't be able to interrupt.

Eli's face was soaking wet. "Where are they?"

"I'll get them." As she rose, she said, as if a warning, "He told me the stories were mysteries, or maybe he said mystical. He was hard to understand." And she seemed suddenly to remember something and asked, "Do you know a Mike? I think he told me, 'Mike knows.'"

Eli knew no Mike.

Sharon returned to Eli's room with the notes. Eli sat a few minutes without opening the package, staring at it. A two-inch-thick stack of folded sheets from a yellow legal pad, torn lined paper from a spiral notebook, and various different sized, different colored scraps were held together with a fat, gray elastic band.

Sharon asked, "Will you be able to distinguish between what is reality and what were the delusions of a sick man?" She spoke softly, the therapist mien overtaking her tearfulness. "I've watched your father decline over the years. It's my professional opinion that your father started becoming paranoid after your mother died."

"Are you saying he was out of his mind? I trust you would know, so is that what you're trying to tell me? Cantor David Kaplan was a lunatic!"

"*Lunatic* is not a word I'm particularly comfortable with, but I believe your father suffered from major depression and paranoia. And I'm convinced his cancer had a deteriorating affect on his brain and mind. I'm sure some things he told me as truth he imagined." She squeezed Eli's hand. "Before you start reading I should tell you what else he told me at the airport."

"This is going to be terrible, isn't it? It's going to kill me."

"Eli, don't be absurd." She sat at the far end of the bed and smoothed her hand across the tops of his feet. "Your father said he thought you were in danger. He thought certain people, unidentified people"—Sharon rolled her eyes—"had been a threat to your life. I think it's why he sent Liora away, and why he locked you inside. It's why he didn't believe in God."

"My father didn't believe in God?" Eli slid his feet away from her touch, as if her hand was contaminated. He was disgusted.

"That's what he told me when he left," she said. "I don't know if it was true. He could have been angry when he said it, or maybe just speaking it out loud to test himself, see if he could stand the thought of it. I don't necessarily believe anything he said at the airport."

Eli threw the package of notes across the bed. "So what am I to assume from any of these writings? It could be all lies or all truth?"

"Any of that, or small truths mixed with delusions."

"Delusions of what?"

"Reasons for leaving you. Whether your father was conscious of his motives or not, he hurt you in the process of protecting you."

"You're not making sense."

"This is going to be hard, Eli. It's hard for me to understand and I've been trying to do that for years. Do you have the strength for this tonight?" She leaned over his legs and lifted the pack of papers. "Should we read this after shiva is over?"

Eli shrugged hard and held his breath for a moment. "You said Adam is coming tomorrow." He was not going to appear to Adam as "the baby." "There are things he and I will have to discuss. Let's just get this done."

Sharon removed her shoes, put Eli's terrycloth robe on over her dress for warmth, locked his door, and got into bed next to him.

By sunrise, Eli had read through the notes three times, practically memorizing them. He didn't understand why his father's life fragmented so decisively into categories of love, hate, and revenge. Whether or not David believed in God had quickly become the least troubling revelation emerging from his father's notes. He crammed himself up against the wall to give a sleeping Sharon enough room. Wiping away tears, Eli reminded himself to breathe. He still believed that if his father had questioned his beliefs, it was his cancer talking and not his soul. And the writing was strange. It didn't sound like the stoic and assured man he knew his father to be. But Eli was sure that Sharon was right about one thing: his father was delusional. David's confession of the existence of an illegitimate son was a figment of his father's imagination.

Where were the other notes Sharon said he had with him? Had these Giacalone strangers stolen them? Maybe Adam knew. There was so much Adam might explain. He put the stack of papers under his pillow and slid as quietly as possible to the far end of the bed, hoping Sharon would continue to sleep.

Lowering himself to the hard floor, he opened the bottom drawer of the desk and removed the bottle-green velvet pouch that held his father's great white silk tallis and satin skullcap — the set he used only during services in shul — with his Hebrew name embroidered beneath the pouch's zipper. David had given it to Eli when he stopped working. The yarmulke had belonged to David's father and was soiled inside with the hair oils of both men. Eli kissed the rim, said a brief brocheh, then took the cap in both hands, laid it over his face, breathed deeply, and filled his senses with the vinegar and musk rituals of his father and his father's father.

This morning, in the first light of this second day of shiva, he longed to feel his father's hand beneath his face, melt against the lean touch of shoulder against shoulder, feel his father kissing him good-bye. Eli felt intimacy stroke his hands as he placed them over his eyes. He prayed this featherlike touch was his father, finding his way through the eternal portals between life and death, telling his son he loved him.

He pulled himself up and shook the tallis until it opened fully. His father was a taller man, and Eli had to roll the collar so the shawl wouldn't drag on the floor. He kissed it and draped it over his shoulders. He took his siddur from his desk, attached his brace, and made his way to the living room to find his bench and meet the day with Kaddish. At the stair landing, he could hear Ludie stirring in the kitchen. He looked through the hallway window and saw the sooty breakers of yesterday's storm ebbing to stain the day's new light. Entering the lamp-lit living room, hoping for nothing, he found ten men from the shul, a minyan to davenen and say Kaddish, and he was shocked to tears.

A MASTERS IN SOCIAL PIECES OF WORK

Sharon came down the stairs and stared at what Eli had written on the residents' daily wall schedule for today: *Second day of shiva / No TV. No Music.* She sat close enough to Eli's bench so that her leg was touching his; his body was warm. She felt him pull away trying to straighten his back. How far they had come.

When Sharon received the call from David that he and Eli needed her, she could not return soon enough, almost two decades after she started her career as a student teacher. The housekeeper, Izzy, sporting a thinning roll of Bounty in her apron pocket and a can of Glass Wax in her hand, let her into the house. She led her through the apartment to Eli's room. The Persian rugs were recently vacuumed, the lines of peaked pile alternating direction up and down the room. The slipcover on the sofa was taut over the seat and the corners tucked snugly beneath the roll of the arms. Either they had just been smoothed in place or no one had sat in the parlor for a while. Passing the dining room table, Sharon saw the silver Shabbas candles in place at the center. She reached Eli's closed door and instinctively twitched her nose at the smell, reminiscent of her days on the pediatrics ward at St. Vincent's Hospital. She smelled urine.

His condition shocked her and she heard herself gasp. Eli was sitting in bed in his underwear, his legs in the W position, unshaven for days, his hair long and visibly dirty. He stared suspiciously as she walked through the door, but he said nothing. She asked herself a question that would haunt her: Why had David waited so long to call her for help? Eli, nearly thirty years old, had stopped all effort to groom himself.

Sharon turned to Izzy. "Where are his clean clothes? He needs to be washed and dressed." She whispered, "Does he soil himself?"

Izzy whispered back, "He just doesn't bother to get up sometimes. He knows what he's doing. He would get cleaned up within a few hours."

Sharon approached her student, smiling. "Hello again, Elias. Remember me?"

He nodded. "Yeah."

"You seem to be in a mess here. I've asked Izzy to get you clean things. I'd like you to dress."

He adjusted his position so that his legs were straight out on the bed, and turned his face to the wall. Izzy brought his clothes to him and the women turned away while Eli stirred enough to put on clean shorts and pants. Sharon peeked to see how he was doing, and gasped again when she saw Eli's legs. His calves and thighs were thin as an anorexic's. Izzy stripped the bed with Eli still in it. Sharon saw there was a rubber liner under the sheet and asked neither of them in particular, "My god. What on earth has gone on here?" Eli closed his eyes and seemed to escape. Sharon's chest filled with sadness.

In the dusty racecar magazines, she saw the evidence of his past hobby, how he had once busied himself cataloging them, keeping pictures and articles of engineering innovations and documenting on a child's writing tablet cars' times at zero to sixty miles per hour. The signs were everywhere; he could have been a regular kid. When Sharon lifted a magazine and inquired about his hobby, Eli blushed.

By late afternoon, after Sharon told Eli about her life and struggled to force a dialogue with him, he asked to be left alone, ostensibly so he could sleep, and good manners forced Sharon to eat a salami sandwich Izzy made for her. Chatting with Izzy, Sharon learned that Eli was afraid to leave the house. Except for some outings with his father, he had basically lived inside for at least the ten years Izzy had worked there. She had seen the cantor take Eli out for long car rides, late at night; sometimes they got home in the early morning. "Where? Why?" Sharon asked. Izzy shrugged and Sharon grew more daunted at the prospect of coming back to work here.

David had not yet come home at eight p.m. Sharon was furious that he failed to appear before she had to leave for home. She wrote out a detailed letter for the cantor outlining her objectives for Eli's rehabilitation. The single fact that David had sought her at all cemented her intention to help Eli. In the fifteen minutes it took to write the note, Sharon decided that if she really was to help Eli, it would have to be on a live-in basis. His care would demand her full-time attention. She was already willing to resign from her job at the hospital to take on his case. She gave an ultimatum to the cantor: that he release Eli's medical records for her review or else she would contact NYC Adult Protective Services and say she suspected abuse.

At home in a housing complex on Second Avenue and Twenty-eighth, Sharon awoke the following morning desperate to get back to Eli. She recalled the look in Eli's eyes when she first entered his room yesterday and saw it as a spark of persistence. She flew out of the house to catch the train to him.

In Gramercy Park, Cantor David Kaplan opened the front door, standing tall in his old but clean black suit, his beard grayed, his chin sharp with arrogance, the bright morning sun forcing him to squint. When Sharon heard his voice she felt her knees buckle. He was direct and discomfortingly robust. "Morning, Sharon. Seven-thirty. Right on time. Come in." He turned from her and walked, slightly hunched, into the kitchen. "Sit here, won't you." He pulled the kitchen chair out from under the table.

"I'll stand, thank you."

The cantor turned on the light over the sink, and in the dim glow Sharon could see a crystal decanter half-full with Burgundy on the counter near the dish drainer, with two stained but empty glasses. She forced herself to stop judging David. She could not however force herself to stop growing angrier. "You've seen my note?"

"I have. It's quite a memorandum you've drafted. You think you can do what I haven't been able to? Have you become that educated about cerebral palsy?"

"I've seen much worse than Eli do a heck of a lot better than he has. If you expect me to work with him"—and if he said he changed his mind, she would run to Protective Services—"then you have to trust me to work with him how I see fit. Because, yes, I am that educated." Her heart pounded, and even though she felt that morally and ethically she had an upper hand, he remained a powerful presence; she could see him throwing her out, and probably throw his weight around Protective Services too.

"Trust you? I have no reservations about your trustworthiness. Your note to me, however, was an indictment of my humanity. I take offense, but I refuse to defend myself where Eli is concerned. He has consistently had a fine roof over his head, hot meals and"—the cantor raised his voice and his face reddened—"servants and teachers all his life." With what appeared to be a stiff neck, David held his head steady as he turned, opened a cabinet door above his refrigerator, and removed a green folder.

"Here you have them. Medical records from the very day he was born. Some of them you will remember from your last mission in this household."

Stunned, Sharon took the folder, which seemed awfully thin for a thirty-year-old. "Thank you." She really wanted to ask, *What the hell happened here?* but asked, "How has he been?"

"It's not as though his life is unaccomplished." David's face remained firm. "He has tried hard and has the rewards of love and protection."

"Yes."

"You have your *new* mission then," David said. His face was set for poker. "Eli is not up yet, but you should begin his day by getting him to start reading again." David flicked his hand toward Eli's room, his cuff too short above his wrist. "He only reads those car magazines. You probably saw them. I hope there is some master plan in that portfolio of yours."

"No. No master plan. It will be a while until you see results. *If* we see results. My goal right now is to get him to go out of the house. That's as far as I hope to get for awhile."

David nodded stiffly. "He is totally inept outdoors. He's frightened. I never felt that was particularly safe for him." He cracked his knuckles and they stared at each other for a moment. He said, "You'll let me know before you do anything like that."

Sharon could feel his lasso being thrown, trying to restrict her work before she'd even begun. She removed her sweater and rolled up the sleeves of her cotton shirt. "You have a good day, Cantor. Should I expect to see you at any point?"

"I couldn't say. If I'm detained and don't get back before you leave, write me a note. You're good at that." He smiled. "And include, if you would, a proposal for your salary. I suppose there is a usual and customary going rate, so to speak."

"I am a professional, so my fee will be commensurate…"

"Yes, of course." He waved her concern away with another flick of his hand.

Nodding, knowing she had to say something else before he left the house, she followed him to the front door, building her nerve. "Cantor? Is there an extra bedroom?" She explained the need to work around the clock. And she offered to take a leave of absence from her position at St. Vincent's. Sharon was relieved to have said it out loud and commit herself to working with Eli. For the past two years Sharon had been dating a fellow social worker, Howard, and though their relationship was intimate, both were gun-shy about marriage. His job was his life, and so Sharon was sure he would not have a problem with her spending weeknights sleeping out, caring for a client.

The cantor had to run—he had to make minyan, he said—but he hastily agreed that he would try to work it out so that she could stay over a few days a week. His study was a mess, filled with books and papers and God knew what. If he could see his way to clearing it out, he would set up a cot for her. He said, "If that would suffice, I'll do my best." She said that was fine, and within a week *his best* was good enough for her needs.

Meticulously going through Eli's medical records over the course of several nights at home, Sharon saw that his last full physical exam was at fifteen, when he was noted as having the flu. She could not even be sure he had been fully vaccinated. It said his medical care had been transferred to a new doctor when his pediatrician retired, but no new records were recorded.

Trying to track the rest of his recent history by calling the office of that last newly assigned pediatrician, Sharon was told that yes, they had received his history from his former physician—the computer showed they were still in storage, somewhere in the basement—but there was no new record of him, and no one remembered him personally. "He's nearly thirty years old now," Sharon told the receptionist. "Will this doctor take a look at him?"

"Sure, we see patients through their twenties. Let's get him in, at least for an evaluation."

A week later, Eli would be taken by ambulette to the doctor. It was April and Sharon kept watch across the skies, praying it wouldn't rain. She had been able to slowly alter Eli's clock with minor adjustments in his sleep patterns—he was used to sleeping from midnight until noon—and for several days before their outing she had been preparing him to venture outdoors. Sharon asked about the long car rides with his father. His reply was a mere whisper: He said, "We've gone to see mountains and slept near lakes." Not wanting to alarm him, she asked gently, "Slept where near lakes?" He said innocently, "In the car." His smile seemed unnatural. He spoke reluctantly about where he'd been— a car ride upstate, a stop at a farm stand on a country road. When Sharon asked him where he might like to go, he shrugged and looked away as he sat in his chair by the bedroom window.

She had not accurately estimated his fear. She assumed that their trip to the doctor would be almost routine, a matter of another car ride with a secretly welcome change of scene, but on the picture-perfect spring morning she tried to get him to sit in his own backyard, she realized he was terrified. When Eli lifted one foot over the threshold he claimed he was dizzy and began sneezing. Sharon attempted to assure him that he just had an allergy to pollen, the kind of irritation everyone suffers from. But he sat down at the kitchen table and said he couldn't breathe. His body trembled and he yelled to Izzy for help. Sharon realized she was witnessing a panic attack, and deferred the backyard excursion to the following day. It didn't happen.

On the day the ambulette arrived to take him to the doctor, he had already worked himself into a whirlpool of anxiety and had to be pushed in a wheelchair, gasping and crying, to the van. "I'm really shaky," he said to her.

"I know you are." Sharon placed her hand on his elbow. "I've got you." She sat with him in the back seat of the van. She watched as he held his breath for one city block after another. She rubbed his hands and felt the jagged edges of his bitten fingernails. Taking his hand into her lap, Sharon removed a nail file from her handbag, and as they rumbled along the bright streets, she filed his nails into even lines across his fingertips. Eli began to breathe more often. When she finished, she put her palm under his wrist and held his hand. Eli looked at her, his awkward smile making a brief but now familiar appearance.

From the pediatrician's waiting area with its sniffling and squabbling toddlers, she and Eli were ushered to an examination room, where they were left alone for several minutes, sitting hand in hand. Sharon said gently, "There is nothing to be afraid of," and knew immediately what a hollow statement that was to an agoraphobic, suffering from irrational, pervasive terrors. Was his syndrome the reason the cantor allowed him to stay indoors, at a loss for any other way to treat his son? But what came first, the phobia or the lockdown? Was David the perpetrator or the protector of Eli's disease?

Eli had a documented history of some degree of neurological impairment, his stiffened leg and dropped foot being the prominent and obvious symptoms, but after Eli's examination, the pediatrician went so far as to question the actual diagnosis of cerebral palsy. Given Eli's fragile condition, he let the diagnosis stand until Eli was strong enough to go through more sophisticated testing with a surgeon specializing in neuromuscular involvement.

His medical exam made it certain to Sharon that Eli's most severe disability was psychosomatic.

Sharon spent several weeks setting up a schedule that would allow Eli time for school studies, social interaction, psychological counseling, and physical therapy. She repeatedly told him what she had told him in the ambulette: "You have all treatable conditions and we're going to open the doors to the outside for you." He seemed afraid to believe her.

Eli worked with a variety of professionals everyday of the week except Saturday. Whatever insurance didn't cover, David agreed to pay for out-of-pocket. Sharon took it upon herself to serve as his teacher, friend, and psychotherapist. She knew that crossing those boundaries would chisel deep holes into the foundation of her professional rules of conduct, and she went back to her texts and read again about counter-transference, how she could grow subconsciously too attached to her client, but she didn't accept the phenomenon in this case. She'd known him as a boy and was able to leave him then, after all. And she had no supervisor, no one to challenge her treatment plan, which relieved her. Howard surely would argue against such an inappropriate relationship—if she had asked him.

Sharon kept her mouth shut as David dragged his feet arranging for Eli's appointment with the neurologist and filling out the necessary insurance forms. But within a month the doctor had examined Eli, and recommended the simple procedure of releasing his Achilles tendon, that would greatly correct the position of his foot. David acted overwhelmed at the idea of this minor surgery. "The forms, the transportation, the pre-surgical testing!" he shouted. "How on earth can I coordinate so many things? The insurance company alone will hold things up for months!"

141

Sharon fought to keep her cool but couldn't. "The doctors said it should have been done many, many years ago!" she exclaimed. David looked at her hard, but Sharon could not access what was happening behind his wild blue eyes. "Improvement would have been more dramatic, would have saved Eli so many struggles."

David's eyes grew moist. "You have no idea what struggles he has been spared."

Once Eli's surgery was completed and he began to walk with new balance and confidence, the anger that Sharon was hiding from both David and Eli dissipated. He started taking newer medications that were prescribed for his other pains and symptoms caused by inactivity, atrophy, and emotional instability. Sharon and Eli were told by the neurologist he believed Eli never had cerebral palsy, but a mild case of arthrogryposis, a congenital condition, that in Eli's case affected only one limb with stiff muscles and joints—Eli's ability to walk markedly compromised by the turned foot. The new doctor did concede that although Eli was not spastic, his condition could be mistaken for cerebral palsy. Sharon felt relief and chagrin at the new explanation of Eli's condition. Eli responded with a curious incuriosity.

He was not stupid, but Eli was very naïve—and Sharon knew he would accept his father's story about old-fashioned doctors with old ideas and valid differences of opinion. She was mystified by David's stubbornness, but she worried more about what Eli thought; she wanted him to know that she would be vigilant about his care, yet feared he would lose his ability to trust his father, or her, if he really allowed himself to understand his news.

A few mornings after Eli returned from the hospital, Sharon stalled David's departure for shul and asked him, in private, if there was anything else he could think of that would be responsible for the mismanagement of Eli's development. David's face grew fierce. His words whipped across her face. "I am assaulted," he said, "Your insinuation that care of my son was ever discontinued is unconscionable. Management of his life was my sole reason for getting up in the morning!" He caught his breath and stared at her. "Perhaps the differences in our backgrounds led you to your misconceptions about how I cared for and protected my son." She knew he was referring to her Christian upbringing, but did not react. "I have done everything humanly possible to keep him active and engaged. He's had teachers in every conceivable subject, including religious instruction." He pointed his finger at Sharon. "And by the way, he was mortified when *you* missed his bar mitzvah." David went on to assert that his son had "an unusually traumatized childhood," which developed into "adolescent agoraphobia" — a term he had trouble saying in a full breath. "I asked psychologists, several in fact, and they all said to leave him alone, he'll outgrow it."

Sharon didn't believe he'd spoken to any such professionals. Again she had to swallow her anger. It was clear, if unspoken, that David held the ultimate power: he could separate Sharon from Eli with a single word.

Gently and in small doses, Sharon introduced Eli into a new way of daily living; he still had trouble walking and wore a brace, and swallowed Klonopin three times a day to ward off panic attacks and Paxil to lessen his depression and fear of meeting new people. Eli resumed assembling car models with the help of a teenaged boy on the street whom Sharon had seen repeatedly working on his dilapidated Honda.

Within a month, Eli was able to sit on the front stoop. One rainy afternoon, as he exercised on the interior steps that led to the upstairs apartment, taking them up and down with the therapist, he stopped halfway to the top and looked down at Sharon. He imitated Jerry Lewis. "Hey lady, throw me up the stairs my keys."

Sharon was taken by surprise, and amused. "When did you start doing impressions?"

"That was my first time for an audience," he said, his face faltering. He pulled himself closer to the railing and carefully started his descent.

"You've passed the audition!" Sharon called. She knew he had taken a chance with that performance and wanted to kiss him.

When he reached the landing he touched the back of Sharon's hand and said softly, "Thank you."

It was late August, after he had recuperated fully from surgery, when he and Sharon started walking to the corner. She would awaken from her cot in the cantor's study and through her morning shower she imagined showing the world to Eli. Sharon was still involved with Howard, and he had finally asked her to marry him—someday. She declined his proposal, but continued to spend some nights away from Eli with the man she supposed she still called her boyfriend.

By the return of springtime, when he was venturing significant distances, Eli insisted on bringing a wheelchair, but his arms got stronger, and he worked with a trainer to build up muscle. He still had a slight lateral lisp but people understood him well enough when he spoke. Shopkeepers handed him what he asked for, and neighbors offered him gossip on the street. He spoke two languages fluently and he had things of interest to say. That winter he completed his high school education and earned a GED.

The first time Sharon asked David for the keys to his sixties-something Cadillac, he laughed. "I dare you to deny him this ordinary pleasure," she told him.

David left her standing in the kitchen. Five minutes later he returned, dangling his keys between his thumb and index finger in front of her face, smiling like a madman, he said, "And I dare you not to let him get hurt."

She drove Eli over the Verrazano Bridge to the Staten Island Zoo, and the next time to the Catskill Mountains, parking at the dead end of a country lane where he'd led her, telling her he'd been there many times with his father. They didn't get out of the car, just looked around. Eli explained how different the stream looked in sunlight.

They often took rides to Brooklyn's Brighton Beach. Eli loved that neighborhood, with its homes, stucco and terraced, close to the water, and he ate with a voracious appetite at the restaurants in Sheepshead Bay, restricting himself to fish and dairy. When they drove under the jolting, clapping sounds of steel wheels of the elevated Q train, Eli tilted his head back and playfully screamed, "Aahhh!"

For Eli, it seemed a natural evolution to fall in love with Sharon, but he knew he was merely her client and hardly a suitable partner for this perfect woman.

David was home more often, saying he was too tired to get out of the house early enough for services at shul, and when he stayed home he kept to himself. On the mornings that Eli didn't hear his father leave the house, he would round the corner of the hall to his father's bedroom to see if the door had been left open. If it had, he knew it was safe to wander in and check on his father's condition. If the door was closed, Eli listened for breathing, creaks in the bed, coughing, withdrawing only when he was satisfied that David was alive.

Eli and Sharon routinely got silly and offered David outrageous situations for the Kaplan household: The rain is dripping into the toilet and it keeps flushing and running over onto the oriental rugs, to which David would become stone-faced, until he became aware of himself and then might say, Yes, as if that were the required response to whatever had just been put before him. "I'm teaching you to be cruel to your father," Sharon once cautioned Eli. He told her she was refreshing. "Refreshing like what?" She had asked. "Refreshing like a girl's navel to a ten-year-old boy." He enjoyed the quizzical look in her eyes, not knowing what he had seen from his window the day she first arrived twenty years ago.

Eli and his father's time together was strained by David's physical discomfort and Eli's distress about it. He told David about the Brooklyn beach neighborhood. Within weeks, the Gramercy Park brownstone was put on the market to be sold, and David quickly settled on the mid-century renovated, now two-story bungalow in Brighton Beach. David's plan was to have Sharon direct a small staff, and set up the house for a few other men who needed assisted living arrangements; create housing for Eli with a built-in business.

Just days before Eli moved into his new home, sharing oranges with Sharon on a bench in Gramercy Park, she took his hand and looked at him squarely. Eli felt his pulse go rapid-fire and expected bad news. Instead, she said she thought he was beautiful looking and that she had fantasized about being with him. In spite of all the barriers, she was willing and eager to become romantically, sexually, involved with him. She glided a finger across his cheek. "These feelings caused my break up with Howard," she said. Eli was trembling by the time she asked, "Do you have feelings for me?"

Eli was suffused with awe and anticipation. "I have nothing *but* feelings for you," he told her. All he could think of was getting her to the waiting house in Brooklyn and ravishing her in the empty bungalow, hearing her moans echoing through the vacant rooms. But he tensed and felt his penis shrinking, painfully aware that his sexual expertise was just like the rest of his life: inadequate.

Eli and Sharon left the park and returned to the brownstone. He was in an emotional fog as they sneaked inside his bedroom and undressed quickly. Sharon's pregnancy-free adulthood had left her body lean and taut. He kissed her neck, smelling her clean and sweet skin from her shoulder to her chest. There was a musky film of perspiration between her breasts. He shuddered when he realized it was Sharon he wanted to do all those sordid things to, and he went limp. Embarrassed by his inability to remain erect, he pushed Sharon away. "Stop!" he told her.

"We can wait. If you're not ready." She lifted her fallen shirt up off the floor and over her breasts.

"You don't understand." Eli sat on the bed and covered his face with his hands.

"I do understand. You...haven't done this before." She sat beside him. "Trust me. Tell me what you want me to do."

Do? He was sure she couldn't do what he wanted: erase his history, absolve his sin, and engorge him! He sat impotent, but his heart was busting to tell her.

He steeled himself to extend his hand and touch her. He fingered her cheek and pushed on it gently so her face would be directly facing his. Her eyes reflected the window behind him and he watched himself dive through it. If he ran from her he knew there would be no other opportunities for him. He wanted nothing more than to connect to life through her. He forced his lips to move in the same way he had forced himself to read his haftarah in public. She would listen, hear him, and he felt the nausea that accompanied the often-ruminated story engulf him.

147

He would try to explain it to Sharon. Maybe she could untangle it for him. Eli told her he had been sixteen when it happened. "It was three years after you left. Three years I had spent in the house, without your warmth, without anyone's warmth." Then Eli said to Sharon, "I did have sex."

He told Sharon how days on end had passed with only the young Hungarian housekeeper Lulu and her burly superintendent lover, Ferdinand, as company. The two of them spent most of their time fooling around together in another room. Lulu and Ferdinand knew the cantor did not come home straight from temple on Shabbas; he would stumble home in the middle of the night half-drunk.

~~~The moon is up and Eli, aged sixteen, is sitting at his bedroom window, looking for something outside to count and occupy his mind. Four squirrels are leaping wildly, and he follows their frenzy. The reading lamp on his night table is shining over Lulu's shoulder as she sits cross-legged on his bed, tearing coupons from the local supermarket flyer. Eli hears glasses clink in the kitchen as Ferdinand dips into the cantor's schnapps, and then hears the man's clomping feet as he enters the room. Eli watches wordlessly as Ferdinand sits close to Lulu, their bodies touching.

Lulu and Ferdinand are giggling. Eli giggles with them and Lulu says, Look, Eli thinks we're funny! She stands and puts her hand on Eli's cheek and he feels her girl-spirit tickle through his body. His heart pounds.

Ferdinand puts his hand on her back and says, Go for it, my Lulu kitten. Touch his little puppy.

Lulu looks at Ferdinand.

Eli looks at her, his heart rams his chest and he thinks, Go for it Lulu.

148

She seems to feel his consent and touches his pants on his fly. He doesn't move.

Ferdinand laughs in a drunken gurgle. Go! Jerk his little puppy off.

She is looking into Eli's eyes for his permission while her fingers unzip his pants and her hand begins to rub his penis. He nods for her to go. He wants to reach for her breast but is afraid and can only do what Adam once instructed him to do with a girl. He peers as far as he can down her blouse. He looks over Lulu and sees her lover is on the bed trying to make himself hard with his hand. Eli closes his eyes, becomes Lulu's lover, lets his body jerk with his climax, and it is fantastic.

Lulu cleans him up, helps him into bed, and kisses his lips goodnight.

Eli has trouble falling asleep that night. He is too frightened, still in shock by the touch of a woman, humiliated at having an audience, and afraid his father will find out.

"That was abusive," Sharon said. "I'm sorry I wasn't here with you."

Eli was confused by Sharon's failure to react with more horror. Releasing the story from his vault of humiliation only served to increase his shame. "Lulu and Ferdinand disappeared about a week later," he told Sharon. Eli felt unworthy of even the couple's abuse. "I was never sorry it happened." He remained afraid of something, having still not forgotten enjoying Lulu so much. "But I can't do that with you until I feel better."

"What do you mean by *better*? About yourself?"

"I don't know what I mean. I just can't."

"Was that the last time?"

"You mean, the last time I had sex?"

She nodded.

"It depends what you mean by sex." When he was twenty, David came into his room one morning, smiled at his son, and placed a brown bag on Eli's bed. "I would be reprimanded sorely if anyone found out about this," David told him. He looked handsome, a man of the world. "Don't open the bag until I leave the room." Inside the bag were copies of *Racecar Driver*, and *Playboy*. Then they would talk for an hour about current events—Eli half-removed from the conversation with thoughts of the pages waiting to be seen—until David looked toward the bag, stood, and Eli watched his father's straight feet carry him out of the room.

Eli knew by the wrinkles in the pages that his father looked at the magazines before he brought them to his son, which he would do every month, and found comfort in the fact that they were both unattached to a woman. Reading the articles about the escapades of other men, Eli understood less and less about his solitary life. Rationalizations about his fears clotted his head with meaningless words. He couldn't comprehend why thoughts of being let loose on the street brought his body to a stifling panic—from the feeling of a cord around his neck to pins stabbing the heels of his feet.

"Eventually," Eli told Sharon, "I guess I lost my will to wonder." He helped Sharon button her blouse, silently hoping the vixen she had become on the park bench would return and that he would somehow summon the prowess of a sexual animal. As they dressed, he concentrated intently on pictures from Playboy, and he revived Lulu's touch, but he remained soft. Sharon straightened her clothes, adjusted Eli's shirt collar, and told him to wait as long as he needed, until blamelessness erased his shame.

The couple already had begun their lives in Brooklyn when the cantor learned of the brewing romance. Celebrating the installment of a new water heater and sharing a bottle of wine, Eli boldly and proudly announced his relationship.

David looked at his son, his eyes clear. "I have cancer." He reached across the kitchen table, held Eli's hand, and said, "So, you will end this affair now."

Eli felt his brain plummet to his gut. "You're sure it's cancer?" Frightened beyond anything he ever knew, he was also hopefully suspicious that his father was lying, in an attempt to get Eli to do as he said. "What? Are you sure? What should I do for you? Anything."

David rose from his chair and peeked around the kitchen doorway, as if for an all-clear. "It is cancer and I'm doing what needs to be done. Now you have to do as I say."

Eli believed his father; David had never lied to him. He reached for his father's other hand. David pulled back and rubbed his palms on his pants. "I know how you could get caught up in all that. I know all about it. But not with her."

"We are not having an affair. But we do love each other."

"I said you will break ties with that old shikse. How can the family name, our legacy, go on if you don't have a Jewish child?" Tears coasted down his father's cheeks.

Eli pushed himself to speak up. "She's given me a life. Don't ask me to give that up for your legacy." He looked hard at his father and noticed his jaundice, his shrunken face, and felt guilty he had not realized sooner that he had become so gravely ill; he had been just as preoccupied as his father, just as self-centered.

David slumped in his seat. Eli watched as he dug his chin into his neck and seemed to will wrath up from his heart. "Then I'm finished worrying about you, Eli." He wiped his eyes with a crushed handkerchief. When David smiled, Eli saw cynicism. "Welcome to the world. It's all yours."

RAISING DAUGHTERS

The first time Adam had to stop and catch his breath—literally, go outside for fresh air—was after reading a note implying there was a woman in David's life. His best translation of his uncle's sentence was: "I wonder if Eli has the need to be touched the way my lovely June touched me."

Adam had only been ten years old when his Aunt Miriam died, but he had vivid recollections of a distraught David who spent time out of the house a lot, and when he was home, attended to his work and his children, fussing over baby Eli's cleanliness and his teenaged daughter Liora's education. He sulked around his apartment teary-eyed and often, between his studies and going out again, came upstairs to visit his sister Ruby for tea and company. Adam felt David was ignoring him, except to criticize.

Translating David's notes was much more arduous and tedious than Adam thought it would be when he stuffed them into his backpack. He had sat with Diane through last evening, eating graham crackers and jam as she listened to every word he interpreted and wrote down.

"I have to get out of the house." Adam kissed Diane's cheek, grabbed his jacket, and stormed out the front door. Hit in the face by a northern wind, he gritted his teeth and begged David's soul to rest in peace. Not that the bastard deserved to.

Light snowflakes fell on his hatless head. He shoveled the walk and started digging his car out, preparing for tomorrow morning's expedition to Brooklyn. Diane called to him a few times, forced a wrapped sticky-bun into his hand, shook an Excedrin bottle at him, and finally brought him a thermos of hot chocolate. He ignored her nagging, and pulled the wax paper more tightly around the bun and placed it on top of an evergreen branch, but gratefully accepted the thermos.

As buses crept down the plowed avenue, the sky filled with gray and eggplant striations, a sharp sliver of teal underscoring a low break in the clouds, the streetlamps, splattered across the sidewalk in an upside down V shower of yellow light. Exhausted, Adam finally stopped shoveling. Where was Yin? What if Shanghai had flooded and that inane mother of hers hadn't gotten the girl to safety? How can I call Seth to ask about the girls? I've stolen from him!

Adam pulled a folding porch chair from under the steps, unfolded it, and propped himself in the middle of his eight-by-ten lawn. The chair legs sank into the powder and brought his seat level with the snow mound. Adam prayed. He realized he was praying to a God his uncle had dismissed. He sat on his chair in the snow waiting for a response of some sort—maybe a frozen bird falling to the ground in front of him. Diane appeared and covered Adam with his blue flannel blanket. He stood up, wearing the blanket like an Indian in an old cowboy movie, then took the frozen pastry from the branch and buried it in the snow at the curb. When it thawed the birds would have a treat.

Prepared to stay awake all night to finish reading the notes before he saw Eli, Adam called Jamie to confer on some of the language. Jamie confirmed that David definitely said something about being with a female, and wrote of her in the familiar way someone speaks about a close friend. Jamie cleared his throat. "I know I kept my relationship with Ariella from you," he said, "but I swear she never mentioned anything about this woman."

"Yeah, well, doesn't mean they didn't know something." After Adam hung-up from Jamie, he wondered if David was so secretive about another woman in his life because he felt shame. Maybe he knew that Liora wasn't the only Kaplan who reacted badly to Miriam's death.

Resentment wormed its way through Adam's body until he felt it squirming in his chest. The image of David with unknown women was more unbelievable than disappointing and more visually distasteful than unbelievable. Adam told Diane how he could still picture the house as it had been when he was a teenager, his mother Eli's primary caregiver, scheduling his teachers, preparing his meals, providing Eli with the attention she should have given Adam and his father, attention that David should have bestowed on his son. Seymour Oppenheim must have felt abandoned.

Two sheets on identical ivory vellum stationery—seemingly unrelated to each other, written with different color ink— were folded together. On one sheet, dated a week before the second sheet, David wrote of his misgivings about the board of directors at the shul, doubting their spiritual commitment to the congregation. He complained of money that was spent on foolishness, like a new nursery school, and of women trying to make their way to read torah from the bema. He ridiculed the board for being more concerned with economics than with the Laws of God. The other page was written as if it was a note to himself, but he seemed to switch, at once referring to "Liora", and then using "you", as if directly addressing her in the letter.

> ivory velum stationery/ January 13, 2000 Liora repeatedly assaults my humanity. Her letters explain the obvious, that she was lonely. Eli was hard work for her. I know it was hard for you. If anything had happened to Eli I think I would have made a home for myself in the corner of a back room, where light would never enter. Or have I done this? Liora, I miss you. But I will continue to explain, as time permits, so that I will not be remembered as a neglectful father.

Adam suddenly thought of Sharon. She was very pretty. "Do you think David slept with Sharon?" Adam asked Diane. There were many teachers coming and going. Adam remembered those visits because some of the young teachers were "hot-to-trot", as he recalled. He watched them arrive and leave from the Oppenheim's living room window, and with great relief occasionally getting some attention from them.

Diane yawned. "I can't really see David and Sharon fucking." She snuggled deeper against Adam's chest. "You want to call Seth? It's daytime in Shanghai."

The more he'd read from his uncle's stolen notes, the more convinced Adam was that he had the right to see them. Seth and Elana would nonetheless think of him as a thief, and if accusations and name-calling began, he would have to control himself.

Adam held the phone awhile before he dialed the long, detailed number. Waiting for the call to connect, he stiffened and tried to get into a Seth-like self-righteous mood. Then he heard Elana's quirky voice answer the phone and his heart jumped. "Hey, Adam here. Is it a good time to talk?" He felt nauseated.

"Sure, sure. Seth is away, though." He heard her draw a breath. "You know, just after you left it started raining like dragons here."

Adam snorted a laugh, relieved that she didn't sound angry. "Oh, I get it. Cats and dogs equal dragons. Does Seth ever stay home?"

"His business takes him all over. When one man has such responsibility, the job has a life of its own. He's a rabbi. There are no holidays."

Adam still couldn't tell if she was aware that David's notes were missing. "Was Seth upset by my visit?"

She snickered, "Upset by your visit? No. He was upset with your departure."

He tried very hard to keep focused. "What did he say?"

"He knows more than you think about the irrepressible nature of man. Nothing surprises him or throws him into hateful rages toward another human being, Adam."

"Can't you ever say exactly what you mean?" Adam asked. Seth, self-important prick, too high and mighty to get thrown by me! Oh, if only I had the balls to tell Seth to fuck off.

"I've said exactly what I meant." There were a few seconds of silence. "Did you call to see how we felt about you, or is there something else?"

Yeah, there was something else. "I can't stop worrying about Yin. I don't suppose you've heard from the Cohens again?" He could feel the word *please* bouncing from one side of his cranium to the other.

"I have. But there's nothing good to report." Her voice edged toward sympathy. "Lucy has not been in touch with him. Mr. Cohen said it's not completely out of character for her to disappear. Seems she's done it a few times before."

Adam nodded silently, sick to his stomach. "Well, thanks, Elana. You have my number. Please call me, collect of course, and you'll let me know if you hear anything?"

"Absolutely. Don't spend too much energy worrying about the little girl. She seemed all right, really, for a handicapped child. She seemed happy enough. But, Adam? Have you seen Eli yet?"

He felt as if his head hit the wall. "Tomorrow. You can tell Seth that Eli's sitting shiva. There was a lot of snow today, but we'll go to him tomorrow."

"Excellent!"

Excellent? It was as though she were congratulating a student for the right answer to a difficult question. "Listen. Take care."

He sat at the kitchen table, his back aching from writing for hours, hunched over. Elana's faith in her husband—knowing about the "irrepressible nature of man"—left him feeling less troubled about his theft. He kept thinking about what Elana had said about Yin. She was happy enough. Lucy had in fact traveled with her across the world to find help for her. Maybe her motherly nagging was a more natural, more humanistic, grounded way of treating a child like Yin; maybe it would have been a better way to treat Eli.

Adam shuffled softly into the den, tired, but also trying to be quiet so not to wake Diane. He reached for the remote, stretched his legs across the sofa, and started his search for some mindless war movie with little dialogue, lots of guns, and indiscriminate killing. After he'd gone through every channel and found nothing but tits and ass shows that seemed oddly distasteful to him, he dragged himself back into the living room, shook out his hands, forced his eyelids open, and resumed transcribing.

#1 of 2 paper-clipped Index cards/ October 30, 2000
Perhaps my Liora is correct. Perhaps I had not done enough with the boy. Perhaps he could have made a better life for himself; I can never imagine him independent and employed for salary. He could not travel to and from a position of daily responsibility. I suspect Sharon is exaggerating Eli's level of functioning.

index card #2/ November 18, 2000 It has been several weeks since I last wrote. I have begun to utilize a computer at shul and have found it most rewarding. A law student I tutored years ago for Hebrew has been a delightful asset in my discovery of the Internet. He guided me and now I use the computer on my own. Tonight I searched with great success for names and addresses. I will be traveling to Shanghai.

folded white sheet of copy-paper clipped between cards (no date)/ Dear Liora: I had a brief setback and have been in the hospital for three weeks. I was sick with the flu but I am feeling stronger and was relieved to be diagnosed as stable. I permitted a blood transfusion, IV antibiotics and injections of B vitamins, but nothing toxic to me or to my cancer. The lesion in my stomach has not changed or spread to other organs. They have given me morphine to carry with me on my trip.

It is time to make final arrangements for my trip to Shanghai. The doctors suggest I leave within the month so that I might go while I am feeling healthier and also avoid traveling in bad weather. They don't talk to me optimistically. They are trying to manipulate me into enduring chemotherapeutic infusion, but I refuse. The travel agent has begun the preparations. Tomorrow I will write to you about June.

June? Was it the month or the woman he'd referred to earlier? And why hadn't he mailed this letter to Liora? The great success with names and addresses he wrote to Liora about; is this when

David located the Giacalones? Adam was frustrated with his uncle's vague, poetic, random tales of personal woes. It was important Adam understood this accurately, and it was clear his translation had become more inference than discovery.

Marking the page with a wooden toothpick from his shirt-pocket, Adam decided he had read the last of his notes without help from someone fluent in old Hebrew. But there was one thing perfectly clear to him: he had no idea who David was, yet even in death, David was succeeding in keeping himself front and center.

Adam stripped completely and got into bed—under Diane's blanket because he'd left his flannel thing outside on the lawn chair—and lay as snugly as possible against Diane's back. What had she said was bothering Jamie? Adam had totally forgotten to talk to her about him, and neglected to ask his son why his mother thought they should go to Denver soon. Adam shook off a chill.

Diane sighed and Adam took it as a sign that she was awake, or at least approachable. He pushed his lower body into the meat of her buttocks and slid his hand around her waist to her belly. She squirmed. "Hi."

"Hi, hon." He felt himself start to get hard and gave himself a few extra seconds. "Jamie didn't mention anything wrong and you never talked about it." He licked down her spine between her shoulder blades and moved his hand from her belly to her buttocks and then between her legs. He could feel her groin muscle contract under his grasp, his heart pounding harder as he squeezed the fleshier corner of her uppermost thigh.

Diane arched her back and her head dropped slightly so that when she rolled to face him her mouth was level with his chest. She drew a tight circle around his nipple with her tongue and whispered back, "About Jamie." She nibbled gently and then pulled on his chest hair with her teeth. "Later."

The familiar feel and smell of her smooth and solid body, and the sense that her arousal arose from the mere touch of his hands, thrilled him. Adam felt the electricity from her tongue on his nipple shoot to his lower body; overexcited, he stopped himself from throwing her on her back, pushing too hard, hurting her unintentionally by biting her. He lay in wait. He gave in to Diane's hunger to suckle him—and she licked him from his inner arms to his thighs, up and around every surface. He could have stayed like that until he came, but he lifted her on top of him. Adam held back until Diane gasped from discomfort, complaining between moans that he poked her ovaries, and he came; her tightened grip on his thighs signaled the pain had turned to pleasure and Adam rocked her until she climaxed and faded.

After a few hours sleep, Adam was up and churning to understand everything he had read. His plan was to get in the car after morning rush hour and head out with Diane to Brooklyn. Adam wondered if Sharon knew all the details of David's *excellent adventures* with women. He strongly suspected this June was the woman David referred to in earlier notes. But David's affair took place many years ago, and anyway, who the hell cared if old David fucked around? He was a cantor, not the pope; he was a singer, a one-man act, with the inevitable guaranteed packed house of adoring females. Seth and Elana had read the notes, and Adam felt embarrassed for his uncle. Did David really have to tell these strangers his problems, with all the sordid details? Did he really have to go and spread his shit to this particular couple? What did they have to do with him? If anything.

160

Diane walked into the bedroom, wrapped from breasts to tush in a worn burgundy towel, exposing her soft, muscular shoulders. Adam, instantly charmed, smiled, and smiling back at him she said, "Nice welcome home last night." She stretched her neck and planted a kiss on his earlobe.

"Yeah, you were horny. I better go hit the shower too." He didn't want to spend too much time standing still in one place with her. He knew if he started talking about David, her questions would be unending, and they'd never get out of the house.

Adam was careful to get a neat, close shave. He instinctively chose to wear his navy-blue suit with a cream shirt and a silk cream and red striped tie. Diane gave him the once over. "You look like you're either going to march in a July fourth parade or going to assembly in Catholic school. Can't you wear a color that's not in the flag?" She wore her black suede pants, a perfectly pressed button-down white cotton shirt, and her mother's pearls.

"You're not in anything special," Adam said. Diane's face froze. "No. You look great." He thought she needed more. "Prettier than Sharon, I'm sure."

"I'm not competing with Sharon. Competing for what?"

"I'm kidding. Just fooling around." He kissed her cheek. "I'll take off the tie and wear, what? What do I wear?"

"You take off the tie, change into black pants, and wear your camel sweater over the shirt you have on."

He did what she said.

At ten a.m. Adam and Diane were in the car. The day was clear, the roads were clean and the snow showed signs of melting. Icicles that had formed under the overpasses were dripping onto the windshield. "Looks like it's turning into a beautiful day," Adam said through his nervousness.

"It will get much colder in Brighton Beach. Wait until you see Sharon."

He smiled and sighed, debating himself about whether or not to ask Diane what was going on with Jamie. Either he could think about what might be wrong with his son and make himself nervous and guilt-ridden about not asking, or he could just deal with it now. He was reluctant to add another ounce of stress to his day. He swallowed a belch. "We've got at least another half-hour in the car, so tell me — what's with Boy?"

"Let's see. Where to begin." Diane hummed for a few moments, which Adam allowed. Better to let her get the words right than have to listen to her amendments and codicils all day. She eventually would get her story together the way she wanted to tell it. But Diane kept humming.

Adam pounded the steering wheel. "What the fuck is going on, damn it? I'm gonna have a stroke!"

She flinched and then blurted out, "Okay. Jamie is fine. Be assured first of all that he is fine and happy and healthy." She cleared her throat. "So, do you have a good grip on the wheel?"

"Diane!"

"Jamie is gay! He's in love with Mark and he's gay. And that's why he moved away, because he's gay and, and, well, that's it. He's a gay person." Sitting still, hands folded on her lap, staring out the front window she asked, "Does it feel like your blood pressure is elevated?"

Adam held his teeth so tightly clamped together that his jaw muscle went into a spasm, and the cramp traveled from one side of his face to the other. He would swear later in the day that it wasn't anger that amplified him, but he spoke louder than usual. "Is he sure? Because he could be confused. He's only a kid and he could be confused. He's only been with a few girls. Did he specifically say he's sure?" He thought to ask if he'd already had

162

sex with the other boy. It seemed at first that the answer would make some kind of difference. Adam was working hard to maintain control of the car and stay within the lines of the middle lane, but he nonetheless looked at Diane.

"I asked him that, if he was sure. He started to cry." Now Diane began to cry.

Adam reached for her hand and felt his mouth quiver. "So that's why he was crying?" Even when Jamie was an infant and was expected to spend half his day crying, Adam could not stand to see his son in tears. "Why on earth was he crying?"

"I don't know. He felt bad about it, obviously!" Diane pulled her seatbelt away from her chest. "No, not bad about *it*, just uncomfortable telling me. He's such a good kid. I have to believe he knows who he is and what he wants. He wouldn't do anything just to be difficult. He told us. That's the biggest hurdle and now that's over with. Next hurdle will be seeing them and remembering to treat them the same."

"Did he want you to tell me? Because he told *you*, not *me*."

"I know. He wanted you to know, of course. I think, ultimately, he'll want everyone to know. He was hoping to tell you at a better time." And, as if she could read his mind, which Adam was convinced she could, Diane said, "And don't feel cut off from him. I know about you two ogling those dirty magazines, doing boy stuff. You thought you were sharing." She cried softly into a tissue, and then she laughed. "I never felt closer to him. Now I get my chance to raise a daughter."

"That's not funny." At least he didn't think it was funny. He stared at the plowed roadway. "It's one thing for him not to like girls, it's quite another thing to know he has relations with men." The words seemed to enter his brain without permission.

"It's called sex, Adam, and he is very, very sensitive to that. I know from talking to him. He knows what we're thinking and it's hurting him that we might find him disgusting or unlovable."

Adam shot up straight against the car seat. The overpass to Pennsylvania Avenue momentarily gave shade from the sun's glare. "I don't think he's *disgusting*. Does he think I think he's disgusting?" He started to get a little more tearful. "Let's get a cup of coffee at the Seaview Diner. It's right here." They took the Rockaway Parkway exit into Canarsie and pulled into the restaurant lot.

Seating themselves in a booth, they ordered two coffees and one bagel, briefly holding hands across the table until Adam let go. He played with the salt shaker, rolling it between his hands, and pictured Jamie blowing out birthday candles as a three-year-old, then riding his bike uphill in the Catskills when he was ten. What did he look like this morning? "Diane? You know I kind of always had an inkling about this. I can't tell you exactly why, but when that girl got pregnant, the way he acted. He was just so hysterical. So unnerved. Demoralized! As if he was lost in space. More, more than just a kid who got a girl pregnant and was scared shitless." Adam shuddered; Jamie had threatened suicide. "Different. More," Adam murmured. He added three teaspoons of sugar to his coffee and Diane grabbed his spoon to stop him from adding more.

"I'm still upset about that abortion," she said. "I think about it often. I was just thinking yesterday how we all lost our chance." She seemed to get excited and talked very fast. "So? I think we should go see him and assure him we love him. He told me while you were away. It just sort of came out after a few sentences of talking. All of a sudden, he was telling me things. I told him we loved him. I said everything right. I even told him how much we like Mark."

Adam rolled his eyes. "Oh, that must have relieved him." She acted as if everything would be all right.

Diane said, "Jamie might care if we like his..."

"His? His what?"

"Lover." She assumed a pose of assurance and looked into his eyes.

"So, you're sure they, you know, you know." Adam could feel the coffee regurgitating. "He does not disgust me. Disgust is an awful thought and it's the furthest thing from my mind. But I'm not gay and I just can't imagine my son"—he cleared his throat—"I just can't imagine." He raised his hand and motioned for the check.

"Don't try to imagine it. Don't even think about it. That is not the point, who he has sex with. It is so far from the whole point. The point is he's different than we imagined he would become, and we will need to adjust our vision about his life and future. A simple and doable adjustment. Like waking up one morning to find you're suddenly left-handed." While she spoke she wrapped the untouched bagel in a napkin and shoved it into her handbag. "So the left hand works instead of the right. You just have to remember which hand to use to reach for the coffee cup." She offered a delicate shrug.

Left hand verses right hand seemed reasonable enough. "You made a good point. An excellent point!" He suddenly felt lighter. "It's just going to be a little harder now."

Diane sniffled and wiped her nose. "Hard. Yup. What's gonna be the hardest thing?"

"For Jamie to come home again," Adam answered immediately. "We could love him and accept him from now until doomsday, but it will be hard for us to fit into his life. For me, especially. You know, we shared stuff that we just can't anymore." He thought about the late night girlie shows on TV

165

they used to watch when Diane went to bed early. Was Jamie faking interest? Adam's heart turned into hot syrup and spread through his chest, realizing Boy must have simply wanted to spend time with him.

After Adam started the car, but before he started to drive to Eli, Diane turned to Adam and smiled as if she were a little girl with a plan to connive her father into buying her an expensive doll. "I told Jamie they could adopt."

"Are you out of your mind?"

Mutely, they drove to Brighton Beach, until Adam came to Eli's street. "They hardly cleared the roads here! How the hell am I going to park the damn car?"

"Calm down, Adam. You're making a shiva call, remember? You're supposed to offer solace. Drive around and find a supermarket. We'll have to park in a paved lot and walk a little. Thank God I made you wear your boots."

"Oh yes. Thank God for that!"

And thank God for Waldbaum's. There was a store two blocks away and the lot was clear. Adam plowed the front end of the car into a snow-bank at the head of the space.

Diane punched his arm. "Stop being stupid. I have to use this car."

"Our son left us didn't he?" Adam said. "He felt he had to go away. So what did our life together add up to if he chose to leave us? What's that all about? Is he trying to erase his life with us?"

"You're irrational."

Their bagel sat on the car seat, like a secret between them, wrapped and untouched. He felt her breath as she faced him and leaned in saying, "You do realize that you are a forty-seven-year-old man who is thinking like a child."

His stomach churned. Without being asked, Diane dug into her bag and her hand came up with the Tums. "Here, jerk

166

puss. Now get ready to meet Eli and Sharon. What if your son were as crippled as Eli? What if you had to deal with what David suffered—a crazy daughter and a helpless son? Be grateful."

"I am grateful! I love Jamie and think he is perfect." They sat in the car staring through the windshield at the sidewall of Waldbaum's until Adam stopped chewing the Tums.

"And your perfect son loves you too. Now shape up and fly right!"

"You're beautiful when you're militant." He meant that to be an insult, but as he said it he realized he loved that about her.

They walked up the street hand in hand. School seemed to be closed; at eleven in the morning, children were playing everywhere. Diane and Adam stopped mid-block and watched a group of four Middle Eastern nine or ten-year-olds build a fort. Three smaller Hispanic girls watched as they stockpiled snowballs and giggled. Adam squeezed his wife's hand. "I wish we'd had another."

They only walked a few more feet when Diane stopped. "Catch your breath, Adam. We're here."

Adam looked up the stoop, stared at the front door, made a rudimentary check on the general construction and condition of the building and said, "It can be fixed up."

As expected, the door was unlocked. Adam allowed Diane to step in before him. A woman who seemed to be the housekeeper Diane had described approached wordlessly and took their coats before asking them to please wipe their feet, "hard." Adam scanned the room, his chest pounding with guilt and grim expectation. A few people dotted the living room, talking and eating. Diane kicked Adam's foot and jutted her chin in the direction of a woman he realized was Sharon. He thought she looked pretty damn good.

"Jeez. She looks exactly the same," he whispered. Diane threw him a look. "Should we ask her to take us to Eli?"

"We'll find him."

One person was seated on a low wooden bench. Adam's heart jerked. With cropped, neatly brushed salt and pepper hair, blinking his lively blue eyes, a man was chatting effortlessly with a woman who looked to be twice his age. When the man smiled at the woman, the grin was unmistakable. Could Eli be such a beautiful man? Adam nudged his elbow into Diane's arm and they made their way toward Eli. He looked up from his conversation, stopped talking, and smiled at Adam.

Adam's morning thus far had left him disbelieving that he had participated in the same past as his immediate family, so why should things change now? He did not know how Eli could possibly be this vital. He took Eli's hand as he stood. "Eli. I want to tell you I'm so sorry." Adam grabbed him closer and hugged him. He could feel the strength in his baby cousin's shoulders. He shook him gently to emphasize his own sincerity and then put his hands on Eli's graceful face. Adam steeled himself to say what he thought was a simple truth: *I meant to bring him home. I tried, but, no, I didn't try hard enough. I'll go back.*

A startling flash of memory tripped up his tongue, disabling his ability to speak. He saw a vision in Eli's eyes: A little boy trapped under the weight of Liora kneeling on top of her two-year-old brother, then jerking up in surprise and screeching when she saw Adam, and releasing her hold. His skin tingled. "I'll go back, Eli. I'll go back for your father and bring him to you if it's the last thing I ever do."

Eli spoke close to Adam's ear, barely whispering. "Adam. It isn't your job. It's his job. If it's meant to be, he will find his way back to me."

The words, *You sent me to China*, were on the tip of Adam's tongue, but he thwarted them. Eli's odd response to Adam's promise, the suspect generosity, contributed to Adam's sense that he'd lived a different reality than his relatives had.

Eli lowered his eyes and seemed to speak to the floor. "In a while we'll go upstairs." He stretched his chin and looked over Adam's shoulder. "Hello, Diane. Sorry I missed you the other day. Thank you for coming back."

Adam watched her approach Eli and kiss his cheek tenderly. Her soft-spoken words were flavored with wonder when she said, "My God, you look terrific."

ONE FOR THE PRICE OF TWO

Through their first public hour together, Eli could feel—through Adam's stiff carefully selected words—the really personal questions snared just behind his cousin's lips. Questions like: How did you escape from your dark hole of teen hell to become this involved and upstanding, responsible adult?

If Adam actually asked him, he would remind his cousin of the myriad years that had passed. He would detail the exhaustive work Sharon had performed and the money generously spent by his father. He would explain how hard this had all been, equally as hard from yesterday to this morning; and how intense his work remained. Eli had to admit to himself that he could not sit in the living room an entire day on a hard bench.

He had been waiting since last night to be alone with Adam, and now he whispered to him to follow him upstairs. He winked at Sharon, and excused himself from the few neighbors who remained visiting. Sharon left as well, going with another resident of the house, Warren, to a meeting at Social Services. Diane was settled-in with coffee and cake beside the woman, a neighbor, who had been sitting with Eli when they'd first arrived. Eli was happy to see she could be left alone because he had no desire to have her in on his conversation with his cousin.

Eli could feel his limbs quivering as he climbed the steps, trying to convince himself the muscle spasm was due to overuse

170

and not nervous tension. The mere image in his mind of sitting with Adam, man to man, discussing life as if they were equal participants exhilarated him but also made him anxious. The notes absolutely had to be discussed before Adam went home.

In his room, he took a deep breath, preparing his nerves for the inquiries he had for Adam, and for what Adam would have to say about his father. As Adam's eyes scanned the room, so did Eli's. The aluminum-framed red print of an F-50 Ferrari hanging on the wall over his bed was slightly crooked, as though the bumper had been weighted down with dust; his smooth maple bed frame was freckled with a few drippings of the paint Sharon had used to brighten the doors and moldings. Eli regretted not having painted the whole room; the stucco plaster walls looked shaded in the plaster crevices, like the cleaned face of a child whose fingernails were filthy. Yet all else in the room was clean and neat, and it was a light-filled space, the bedroom window and the window in the hallway casting winter light straight onto his bed.

"Nice room, Eli," Adam said. "Sunny. Spacious. You're happy here?"

"It's been an adjustment, moving from the big house to this one, sharing this with the others. The stairs have been a challenge. They force a little exercise, which is good for me. I guess I can't complain." *I'm happier than I ever imagined I could be.* "Diane looks good. Still in love?" He smiled, but he could hear the edge of resentment and old envy in his voice.

"As ever. Things have been good for us. We have ups and downs. Things on the whole are good."

Adam looked older, but no worse for the wear. And Diane, though too perky and chatty for Eli's taste, had looked slightly aged around her eyes, but still very much the same. "Yeah. You said Jamie is fine. Living in Colorado. Twenty-four already?

171

Wow. Handsome, I bet." Eli tried to glance at his reflection in the window. The mirror had been covered; he wanted to see if he looked handsome too.

"Handsome, oh yes. Very. Just found out he's gay." Adam looked at the floor, than quickly lifted his eyes to meet Eli's. "Did I say he was gay? Funny how that came out so fast. I heard myself just this morning."

"I'm sorry." He was.

"No, no. He's healthy. That's all. Healthy. Good boy. Adjustments, you know?"

Eli nodded and had an emotional experience he had never known before: he felt sympathy for Adam. "Will you try to correct the situation? Bring him home for some sort of therapy?"

"No! For god's sake, Eli! The boy is gay, not psychotic. It's not a disease. Did your father teach you it was a disease?"

Eli felt himself blush. "My father taught me very little about anything so aberrant. It's just something I believe." He had no argument for Adam, and he felt himself quivering, losing parity. "We should talk about other things. My father. You met those people, the Giacalone people."

"Oh, yeah."

"And you talked with them about my father? About what he wanted?"

"Well, sort of."

It had been uncounted years since they'd talked with any seriousness, but being with Adam felt as it had when they were kids: he experienced the same familiar, subordinate comfort. Subordinate now because Adam had at least gotten to meet the people who had commandeered his father and kept his body. Subordinate because not only did Adam know his father longer than Eli had, but he had discussed his last days with his father's captors. Eli wanted information, in part for reassurance, and in part to even them out. "Sharon gave me these...notes of his." He lifted the messy bundle from under his pillow and showed it to Adam, then tossed it onto his desktop.

Adam lifted his eyebrows. "That's interesting. I sort of picked up another batch of his notes at Rabbi Giacalone's apartment. Some mind-blowing stuff in there. Were they alarming to you? I mean, they were interesting."

"He took them there? You read them?" Eli felt he was about to collapse under Adam's guarded representation that his father had had so much turmoil. Did Adam believe Eli had been unaware that his father was troubled; that news of his emotional upheaval had now ambushed him? "Don't judge me, Adam. I'm not retarded." He sat on the bed, shook his head vigorously, got the kinks in his neck loosened and put his head face down on his pillow.

"Retarded! Eli, you're about as retarded as Jamie is psycho," Adam said with a soft chuckle.

That didn't make Eli feel much better, but he knew what his cousin meant.

"Let's sit, okay?" Adam said. "Let's talk specifics, because your pile of notes look as hodgepodge'd as mine. And written in Hebrew too, so to tell you what I think he wrote would be unfair, to you and to him. What have you got in those?"

Adam gently closed the door to the room and Eli was afraid of what that might mean. There was only one thing he needed to know from Adam, one claim of his father's, that if true would readmit him to isolation and loneliness.

Eli closed his eyes, imagined himself alone on a mountaintop, and said, "My father had some idea that he had another son." He prepared himself to freeze on that peak if necessary.

"Really?" Adam sounded surprised. "How did he put it? Did he just write he had another son somewhere?"

Eli opened his eyes. Adam looked either truly uninformed or masterfully holding a secret behind his blushing face. "I'll read that part to you, translated," Eli said, and felt his body return to the warm room. He looked toward the pile of paper back on the desk. "Can you reach that for me? It's difficult, you know, to keep getting up and down."

Adam pulled the chair over to the bed, handed him the papers, leaned snugly into the back of the chair, folded his hands in his lap and nodded for Eli to go ahead. Eli shuffled through the pile until he found the yellow sheet with the turned corner, then licked his lips several times. "It's addressed to his father, but his father was dead already." He caught Adam's eyes, level and expectant on his.

two stapled sheets/white velum stationery   My Dear Father—When I now tell of my third child, I speak of my second son. Another father, a less than brilliant man, raised him apart from me.   I had prayed for my son's existence for many years, and though I gave up prayers I always believed in my heart that the woman I loved had conceived this child from my seed. I watched the boy grow for eighteen years, until the day I came to the neighborhood where he had played all his life and I had secretly watched him grow until he was gone. With the help of computer technology I had the blessing to find him at his university. I was in agony and needed your advice. Should I approach my second son? What if he ran away? What if he didn't believe me?

My joy! He not only accepted my love and confidence, he had known the truth for years. His dear mother had divulged the story while her beautiful and nurturing breasts were killing her with the cancer that is killing me.

I was at once lifted into a spiritual realm that had long been closed to me. Hoping for rebirth, I prayed. But the interval between our visits became longer due to his career and then to my illness and my faith once again dissolved into a cloud of hopelessness. Eli too has gone from me into his new home.

Eli took a deep breath and tried unsuccessfully to repress the quivering in his jaw. "No name of another son. Nothing." He waited for Adam to offer facts or denials, but his cousin sat dumb. "I think he imagined it all," Eli said firmly. "He told Sharon the letters were written with me in mind, but he addressed this one to his dead father." If Adam told him he knew of the other boy, Eli would not be able to sit shiva for his father. He held his breath waiting for Adam's response. "So? Anything you can add?"

Adam shook his head. "I know nothing of this. I'm stunned."

Adam thought he would puke. "You know, Eli, Jamie helped me reading these. I had so much trouble myself. I don't know what to make of it right now." He stood and poked through some coins and loose screws and nails on the bookshelf. If what Adam suspected now were true, and if Eli had to deal with Seth, then Eli's grief would be endless. He touched Eli's knee casually. "What would it mean to you if it were true? It might be nice to have a brother. I wish I had had one...although, I always thought of you as my baby brother. While we were kids, anyway." He was rambling and he knew he had better stop.

Eli palmed the wall, then pulled himself into a more solid sitting position. "What would it mean to have a brother? It would mean that my father was a whore. It would mean he was a liar and he cheated me out of his life. What would it mean! It would mean he had me right here but he lost his faith in God until he found another, better son." Eli started to cry, but before his cousin could hold him or find words, he hit his head with his fist. Then he took a breath and spoke softly. "It would mean I was worthless to him. I would never forgive myself for letting him down. I will die of shame if there is another son who brought the light of God into his heart again. The light that I shut when I killed my mother." He threw the clump of notes across the room and fell into sobs that forced Adam to climb into bed with him and hold him, frightened.

The shouts and the choking noise of his crying brought Diane and Ludie upstairs, bursting through the door. Adam ignored the women and said, "You're wrong, Eli. You are so wrong in everything you're saying. None of this is your fault. Nothing you did made your father's life worse." He looked at Diane and Ludie. What could he tell him now? That his father was wrong to lock him away, out of shame, or fear, or anger? He thought of the image that had ambushed him earlier, of Liora hitting Eli. Should he tell Eli his sister actually could have killed him, vindicating David for hanging both his kids out to dry?

Ludie went to the bathroom and came back into the room with a medicine vial. "His pills for panic attacks," she said, flashing the bottle in the air for everyone to see and then sat next to Eli and inserted a pill under his tongue as he cried. "I'll get you some juice. Sharon will be home real soon, doll. Yes, that's it." She rubbed his hands and he quieted.

"Is he all right?" Diane asked Ludie.

"He will be in a minute." She looked at Adam. "The boy was doing so well. What on earth did you say to him?"

Ludie was not that much older than Eli, about forty, and Adam was riled at her insinuation. "The *boy* is a *man* and we were talking about his father. We were just talking. He got upset. It's understandable. Why don't I stay with him now and you go downstairs and assure his visitors that he's okay."

"Well, try to keep him calm," Ludie said. "He has panic attacks. Ever see a panic attack?"

"Yes. A few," Diane retorted.

Adam looked at Diane and slumped his shoulders. His wife's history of anxiety felt like comic relief compared to this.

"I'll stay with you," Diane said to Adam.

Ludie left the room, shaking her head. Adam and Diane took seats on the edge of the bed, held hands, let go, took peeks at Eli, and waited until he simply dozed off.

"What happened?" Diane whispered.

"I can't talk about it," he whispered back. "We have to wait for Sharon to get back."

"What is he so upset about, Adam?" She hissed.

"His father! What do you think! Now shush! Let's go downstairs."

It was three in the afternoon, too early for Rabbi Weinreich and his minyan to show up for services. The guests had gone home to do afternoon business. The house was quiet and Adam took to the sofa, removed his shoes, and put his feet up.

"I'm going to make a pot of coffee. Call me if Sharon comes back." Diane tickled under Adam's toes. "You okay?"

"Yeah. I've got to talk to Sharon. This is all getting out of control. Go. Go make the coffee. Strong. That'll be good." He closed his eyes, drifting. He visualized his family's dining room table at Passover. If Seth was the son — it had to be Seth — Diane would insist he be invited. Now that Eli could get around he would come to Queens, and his feelings will take priority over everyone else's. Except Jamie's, who would now come home with Mark. Lots of new men in the house. Adam breathed deep against the noise in his head.

He heard pot-banging in the kitchen and Diane giggle, and then the hushed conversation of women in cahoots. Adam rolled toward the back of the sofa, working to block out the fact that he was in a stranger's home. He recognized the old slipcover, with the lingering fusty scent of David still in the seams, and wondered why it was dragged along to this house, and then tried, amid bubbling nausea, to remember Seth's phone number, throwing digits in visionary sequences, hoping one would appear that was brilliantly correct. What would Adam say? So, Seth, my man, who the fuck is your father?

The men who lived with Eli came into the room, turned on the television and started watching *General Hospital*. Then Sharon appeared and asked them to respect the shiva and turn it off. Adam had been eager to speak to her, but for some reason feigned sleep. He heard her march into the kitchen and talk to Ludie. Adam was dozing again when a voice rocked him.

"Adam, we need to speak. Adam? Are you awake?"

Sharon could be rude, Adam thought. "I'm awake. Sorry for napping. How was your meeting?"

"Fine," she said flatly. "I hear Eli had a rough day. Care to share what led to his panic?" Adam felt as though he were being scolded at school.

"The notes. Wait. How much do you know?"

"I know enough. He read them all through the night to me, and the cantor spilled his heart out to me at the airport before he left. Why did Eli get so upset with you? What did you *tell* him?"

"I didn't tell him anything. *He* said he had a brother."

"Or that his father *wrote* about having another son."

Adam could tell by her sarcasm that she didn't necessarily believe there was another child. "Yeah. Well, Eli wanted to know what I thought. I told him I didn't know what to think. But the truth is, I think it's probably true." It had come to him so easily as Eli read to him. Why wasn't it apparent in China, in the man's blue eyes, in his deep voice, in his command of a room? Why

178

else would the old man have flown around the world? The idea would scorch Adam's mouth if he didn't spit it out soon.

Sharon's face turned bright red. She grabbed a folding chair and pulled it closer to Adam. "You do know that David was suffering from all kinds of paranoid delusions. That's what I tried to convince Eli of last night. You don't think this lovechild is just another delusion?"

He didn't know who Sharon really was nor why she was so convinced David was out of touch with reality. He wondered if she was after something David had left for Eli, although Liora had pretty much persuaded him that David couldn't have had much of an estate, and that the money from the Gramercy Park brownstone must have been poured into this place. "I would like to know which delusions you are referring to, but I am honestly more concerned about your relationship to Eli," Adam began. "Did David leave you with guardianship or something?" He felt himself blush, knowing full well that if she had half the intuition Diane had, she knew what he was really asking.

Sharon kept her features and voice even. "I have some legal authority over his health care expenditures and the finances to run the house, but our personal relationship is not exactly your concern now, is it? Eli is now the only man left standing in the Kaplan household and he is independent. He does not need a guardian."

"There could be another Kaplan, don't forget," Adam shot back, and when he saw the moisture in her eyes he felt bad; at least some of her stoicism was an act.

"If you are sure about this other person's identity, you have to tell me," she said. "This will devastate Eli."

"I know it will." Adam hesitated, unnerved. Sharon thought the existence of Eli's brother was a delusion. But delivering the news also made him feel potent and proud, and he gave in to the

179

desire for dominion over his family. "I think it could be Seth. The rabbi in China? Certain things are adding up, and well" — his need for authority spontaneously shrank beside his fear of bearing responsibility for his words — "this should wait until we can talk more privately."

Sharon's eyes sharpened. She looked behind her for signs of life. Her voice dipped to a whisper. "If you believe this Seth is really David's son, who is Seth's mother?"

"There was a woman. I'm fairly confident about that." Instantly, Adam regretted confiding this.

"You're *fairly* confident there was a woman." Sharon looked toward the ceiling and seemed to be trying to control her temper. "Adam, the delusions I've referred to, the one in particular you seem to be ignorant of, is David's notion that Liora tried to kill Eli. He exiled the poor girl from her family all these years, not to mention he exiled Eli from the entire world. He was locked away like some feral child." Her face drained to white and her neck turned to cherry ice.

David witnessed Liora trying to kill Eli. Elana's parting sentence sprang into Adam's head. And with it surged his own vision of Liora holding down Eli. A stone seemed to lodge in his airway. Adam raised his eyes to see Diane appear over Sharon's shoulder. "We have to go now," he told her flatly.

"What's this about a feral child?" Diane asked.

Adam said, "We were just commenting on different cases Sharon has seen in her practice. Sharon, we really have to head home."

Adam and Diane left Eli's house before the evening minyan arrived, without saying goodbye to him. Feeling numb, he led Diane through the afternoon wind to their car and sat huddled in the front seat while the car warmed up. "We'll call Jamie as soon as we get home," Diane said. She wrung her hands, and then briefly held her knuckles against her lips. "By the time we get home you have to be comfortable with how you feel and tell him it's all right."

Adam felt the numbness in his face and fingertips. They tingled painfully. Now the entire matter of Jamie's life as a whole would be referred to as "it's." Words fell out of him. "I don't have to be comfortable, but I'll tell him *it's* all right. Of course I'll tell him it's all right. If I said it's not all right would that make things better? It's all right because that's what is." He put the car in reverse but didn't yet back the car out of the space, gripping the steering wheel with his need to hold Jamie. "So, he said he's happy? He's healthy?"

"Yes, yes, yes to everything. He said he knows how to take care of himself. I asked him the exact same things."

"All I keep picturing is him on the news marching for AIDS funding." He closed his eyes and worked to slow his breathing. Jamie and Mark. They had known each other since they were thirteen or so. The boys had been through everything together: junior high, high school, summer camps, first jobs at McDonald's. Adam had seen them showering under the garden hose in the backyard one late summer afternoon after a day at Far Rockaway Beach. They were about seventeen and naked. Mark was a much more solidly built boy than Jamie, with broader shoulders, heavier legs. Adam laughed at them at the time, finding them horsing around and completely oblivious to the notion that it might seem inappropriate to a nosy neighbor to see two boys outside in the nude. He resisted the image of how they might have been minutes before he returned home, touching each other. Had they felt the way he had as a teenager on a date, anxious and scared to touch? He wondered if their freshly washed bodies felt as good to each other as a girl's would to him.

181

Fear gushed up in him. "He's being careful?"

"I believe so."

Twenty-five years of marital trust, but Adam still felt a day short of confident in Diane's belief system.

BOY IS WHERE THE HOME IS

"It's a miracle. Just remarkable," Diane exclaimed. At four forty-five p.m. the sky had morphed into a grayed plum, lined with peach over the horizon. She stared into the sunset feeling the smile spread on her face.

Adam glanced from the road at her and asked, "Why are you happy? It was a miserable day."

"I guess I'm just relieved that we went to see Eli. You haven't even mentioned how remarkably well he is. You never recognize the good stuff. Aside from the panic attack, didn't he seem *remarkably* well?" Diane smiled broadly now.

"Remarkable indeed. Makes me wonder how handicapped he ever really was. Can people really regenerate like that? He appeared so, I don't know, whole."

"Whole. Yes. He moves relatively well, and his speech, well he's got the little bit of a lisp, but he's perfectly understandable. You have got to admit that Sharon is doing something good with him."

"If you mean sexually, I hope you're right. That would be great. Right?"

"Yeah, it would be great. But you think her interest in him could be about his inheritance?"

"If Liora is right, there isn't much to inherit. I wouldn't worry about that."

"No, you wouldn't." She tried for a few moments to pick apart Sharon's character, but she pictured Eli's mature face, and hoped his mother Miriam and father David were able to see him, and within seconds she found herself smiling again. "So, we'll call Jamie when we get home and you'll have a nice talk. Yes?"

"I guess. Don't rush me. I haven't had a minute to think about what to say."

"You say, Jamie, my darling son, I love you. How's business?"

"Brilliant."

She hit his arm lightly. "Don't insult me. Life doesn't get any more sensible than telling your child you love him. What else on earth would he want to hear from you?"

"Maybe it's not about what he wants to hear but about what I want to say?"

"And maybe it's not about you!" Why-oh-why couldn't it all be about Jamie and no one but Jamie, just once?

If only she hadn't worked while Jamie grew up. She wished they hadn't needed the money and she could have been home to watch him more. Once she forgot to wake him for school in the fourth grade and left for work, leaving him in bed all by himself. At the time he was not so disturbed by the event; he hadn't even called her at work to reprimand her. Jamie never let her forget it.

Traffic came to a halt on the Van Wyck near Kennedy Airport. It was six p.m. when their Volvo made it over the ramp, passed the airport, and they were again on their way home. Diane's eyes were closed, and she was thinking about Jamie at eight years old, how he would take garden hoses from the garage and run around the small backyard pretending to be a firefighter dousing fires, how he had jerked his body backward in a mock jolt from the power of a ton of water pouring through the hose. When the fire was out he'd wrap the hose around his sunburned shoulder, tiny and round, and wipe the sweat from his forehead with his free hand; such a hard job he had.

Night had fallen, street lamps lit their block, and children with flashlights climbed over the remnants of snow mounds. Adam parked the car in front of the house and Diane started — every light in the house was ablaze. She said, "You left all the lights on this morning."

"No I didn't."

"Well, the lights are on. Someone left them on." She stiffened. "We've been robbed! Did you set the alarm?"

Adam grimaced. "*That* I couldn't swear to. Stay in the car. I'll check the door." He got out and marched up the walkway.

Diane pulled her cell phone out of her handbag and held her middle finger on the number 9 and her index finger poised over the 1. She watched Adam unlock the door and then he flashed a thumbs-up to her — the door had still been locked. He opened it slowly and she heard him shout, Hello? He walked into the house and disappeared.

She sat waiting, her heart pounding as she watched, squinting at the living room window to discern any sign of a shotgun or blood spurting. Then Adam came back to the door and beckoned her inside.

She lowered her window. "What's going on? Anything missing?"

"Got a little surprise for you. Hurry up." He waved ferociously.

Maybe there was a puppy from her next-door neighbor, Sandie, whose dog had a litter a month before. Sandie was the only neighbor with a key to the house.

"Don't run — you'll slip on ice," Adam yelled at her.

The little surprise stood just beside the front door, his hair spiked on top and cropped short on the sides, a smile as wide as Colorado on his face. "Hiya, Mom. Yippee!" Jamie wrapped his arms around his mother, squeezed gently then let go and stood back.

185

Diane saw the pale olive cheeks of a hurried afternoon and broke into tears. He looked gorgeous in his black bootlegged jeans, and black T under a chambray shirt that matched his blue eyes, his hair darker. She stared into his face. "Look, Adam. Doesn't he look like Eli? Your whole family with those eyes!" It was as if she'd never seen his eyes before. She pulled on his hand. "What on earth are you doing here? Come into the kitchen. When did you get here? Why didn't you tell me you were coming? I would have had more food for you. Are you all right?"

He was laughing, eyeing his father who was shuffling through the mail. "I'm fine. Fine, fine, fine. I just wanted to come home. You know, with the funeral and all."

Adam looked surprised. "First of all there's no funeral, and you barely knew David. I mean, I'm thrilled to have you home, but—oh yeah, you and Liora's little girl, Ariella. What's that about? Did she ask you to come?"

Jamie laughed. "Little girl? She's my age and she's pregnant. And yes, she did ask me to come. But that's incidental." Jamie stood a good three inches taller than his father. He took the Pottery Barn catalog from Adam's hands and flipped through the pages, rocking on his heels as though listening to music. "I came because I wanted to."

"Oh, let him eat and relax," Diane said.

Boy threw the catalog down on the end table and smiled at her. "I'm not really hungry. I've been here a few hours and I've been noshing." He looked more solemnly at his father. "So, how is he? Is Eli going to be okay?"

Diane saw Adam look deep into his face. "Okay? Sure, sure. He'll be okay." He gazed at his son. "I love you, Jamie. If you're scared, or think I don't love you, well, I do."

Jamie turned to his mother. His face turned purple. "You told him? I thought I was going to tell him!"

She felt his fierce dismay and was ashamed of herself. "I told Daddy this morning. It just came out on the way to Eli's."

Jamie's mouth pinched and his chest began to heave. Diane tried to take his arm. He shook her hand off. "For Christ's sake, Mom. I'm okay."

"Sorry. I'm really sorry. I have such a big mouth." She felt like an old fool.

Jamie marched into the den and sank onto the sofa, muttering sounds of disgust sprinkled with words like "fucking yenta." Adam followed close behind and took a seat in the recliner. Abashed, but with no choice but to stay, Diane took a seat on the arm of his chair, patted Adam's head and asked, "You want to talk first?" Adam winced. She regretted her patronizing tone the moment the words left her mouth. When was she going to stop?

"I don't think much talking is necessary." Adam smiled at his son, though his droopy eyes told Diane his affection hid a pasty melancholy. "It's not like I have to tell you anything, or you me. Mom said you're with Mark. So? Do I wish you were *not* gay? Yes, I wish you were not gay. Is that going to change things? I don't believe so."

Diane was frustrated with the distilled version of his fears. "Adam, ask him what you really want to know."

Adam sat momentarily silent and then said, "Are we still the same father and son? That's my concern."

Jamie nodded and said softly, "I know. Mine too."

"I don't know the answer." Adam stood and began to circle the room. "I'm not sure I've known who you are or who you've been. Do we talk about the things we talked about? Politics. Music. Do we share the things we shared before? Your photography, for instance! Have I seen any of your work lately?" He looked at Diane for acknowledgement. "He didn't even tell us about talking to Liora's daughter."

187

Jamie waved his hand at his father, as if Adam's complaint was irrelevant. "People grow up. Everyone talks about different things. So I didn't tell you about Ariella. Big fucking whoop! I'm the same person, Dad. Only what *you* are experiencing is changing. I did hide things from you, but it doesn't change the facts." Jamie lowered his head and glanced at his mother. "I wish so much I could have told you sooner, maybe it would be easier for you. We'd be *there* already, instead of this bullshit *just love me as if I were your human child."*

Diane gasped. "Boy! Your father and I just miss you."

"You know we love you." Adam sat on the sofa again, and reached for Jamie's knee. He turned his face up to Diane. "Your uncle, your father's brother Gary, he was gay. Right?"

"Oh god, Adam. You sound like an idiot." When her estranged uncle Gary had come up in her thoughts she at least knew not to mention him.

"I just have to ask you, Jamie. Are you sure? Because if you're troubled, if you got caught up in an adolescent rebellion and now aren't comfortable and that's why you came home. You can tell us. You seem nervous, so maybe…"

Jamie stood. "Leaving home with Mark was the least rebellious, most calming and natural thing I've ever done for myself." He pointed his finger at Adam and said, "And, you know, like, don't make presumptions about my life based on old teenage shit. I know who I am." Jamie's face was blotchy and Diane knew he was about to cry.

"Okay, okay!" She jumped to her feet and waved her hands to stop the action. "Adam, you have to stop challenging him."

"He's not challenging me, Mom. It's all right. I should have done this by phone."

"No, no, no. I'm sorry," Adam said. "I'm happy you came home to tell me. You look great. You look healthy. That's all I care about. You could have brought Mark. You should have brought him. I haven't seen him in ages and he should know he's welcome here."

"Is Mark in town with you, somewhere else, maybe?" Diane asked.

"Well," Jamie said and became tearful, "Mark left me."

Well, Mark left me.

The words pierced Diane like a black dart. This was the worst thing he could have told her. This is precisely what she feared most. Now what would happen? He'll start with the different men, nights out looking, dating, swinging and drinking, looking for love in all the wrong places. She covered her eyes with a tissue and burst into tears. "Why, why is this happening to you?"

"Mom, shut up!" Jamie came over to her and grabbed her shoulders. "We've been together since we were kids. It's time to stretch, meet new people, you know?" His voice was shaky and Diane didn't believe his explanation. "We might get back together. He hasn't deserted me."

"Never mind *desert* you! You were supposed to be monogamous. You and Mark. You were supposed to have a family and be safe!"

"What do I look like, an infant?" Jamie shouted. "Don't tell me how to be or who to be with! Me and Mark? He doesn't even know who he is!" He grabbed a bunch of hair and pulled it straight up, as if it were something that should be ripped out. "He made me make my hair darker because he said I looked too gay as a blond!"

Diane gasped again. She was sincerely befuddled. She whispered, "He said that to you?"

"Yeah, like, if I said to you, You're breathing too loud. You sound too alive!'"

189

She asked, "Are you comfortable looking gay?"

"If you're comfortable with how you suck air."

"Gasping is involuntary. I can't help it."

Jamie looked at her and said, "Ditto," then looked away. "Mark's not sure. Okay? He says he's not sure that he's gay."

"He could still be not sure?" She didn't understand.

"And you, you're positive. You're absolutely sure," Adam asked.

Jamie reeled back, blushed, and turned his face away. "This is too much for me. What am I supposed to do to convince you? Show you photographs?" He grabbed his jacket from the doorknob, said, "Fuck this," and fled the room. The front door slammed.

Adam sat in bed, pulled his washed and dried flannel blanket up to his neck, and stared at the flat dark ceiling. It looked like a hole in the world that led to nowhere. He'd been sitting in bed for an hour and, dozing, thought: Jamie, just come back already. *Photographs? Am I as insensitive as he thinks I am? Where did the dumb kid go? He doesn't even have friends here anymore. Does he have money on him? Of course he has money. He works. He's an adult. He got himself from Colorado to Queens by himself. He probably went right back to the airport.* Fuck!

He gave up trying to sleep and started to get out of bed. Before he could unravel from the cover, the bedroom door flashed open, Diane snapped on the lights, and Adam could see her swollen eyes, red nose, and the crumbled tissues in her hand. "He's still not home?" Adam asked.

"No. It's ten o'clock, Adam. He's been gone for three hours! Where could he have gone?"

"I was thinking maybe he just went back to the airport. Try to catch a red-eye back."

"Take me to the airport to find him."

"Get outta here. I'm not traipsing around the airport. I don't know where the hell he went. He ran away like always. He'll be fine. We'll just wait to hear from him." Adam wanted more than anything to go to the airport, but it would be a chaotic, hopeless search, and Diane would go mad when they didn't find him.

She was still holding onto the doorknob. "Did he seem hopeless to you?"

"Not at all. Diane, come here."

She sat next to him and squeezed his arm. "Mark left him. Told him he looked too gay! Jamie just told me yesterday that he was in love with him. He has to be devastated. How could Mark not know if he's gay all of a sudden? He's lying to Jamie. He's found someone else! Poor Jamie. I'm afraid he'll kill himself." She started to cry again.

"Don't make up stories. He didn't seem devastated. He was sad, yes, not despondent." But Adam's stomach started turning and the heart attack pain of heartburn rose to his throat. "Let's dial his cell number."

They tried his cell but got only the painful sound of his recorded voice. They called his Denver house. Maybe Mark was there and had heard from him. Recording…message. Adam looked out the window, checking the street from left to right, squinting to peer inside the storefront window of the Korean grocery at the far corner. Stirring in him was the sick feeling he had when Lucy grabbed Yin from him and took off in the taxi to parts unknown. Why hadn't he chased that cab? "Diane. Get your coat. We'll try the airport. How many airlines you think will be flying out to Denver tonight?"

"I'll check online. Give me two minutes."

When Adam walked into the hallway, he felt himself breathe for the first time in hours: Jamie's backpack was still there. He'd left everything he had come with. Adam shouted down the hall to let Diane know. Jamie had every intention of coming back to the house tonight. "Let's go to bed," he told her. "He'll wake us up when he comes in."

"Well, there are no more flights out tonight anyway."

"Good. That's good. He probably went to get a few drinks or see a movie. You go to bed. I'm gonna try to get through to Shanghai and give Seth a call. I have to ask him about Yin. Maybe he's heard from the Cohens or something. Go ahead to bed." Yin was a convenient excuse to call Seth. Adam didn't want to tell Diane of his deductions about Seth's true identity before he was more certain. He had been tossing around the idea of daring Seth to tell him who his father is. Adam was grateful Diane was too preoccupied to bring up Eli's panic attack.

"Don't tie up the phone too long," Diane said, "Jamie might call."

"We have call waiting."

"It might not work, damn it. Just don't tie up the phone. Please!"

After having survived the pronouncements of both Eli and Jamie, Adam knew he could withstand anything Seth might say about the theft of the notes, or of his own paternity. He dialed four times before he finally punched the numbers correctly and heard Seth's phone ringing. His stomach flipped. It rang at least a dozen times. Adam was confused about the time difference, but thought it should be morning there. As the ringing repeated in his ears he practiced his question: Did David tell you he is your father? If Seth said, "Yes," Adam was further prepared to ask, Is he? A message machine came on; he couldn't think fast enough and left no message. He figured he'd wake up in the middle of the night when Jamie got home and try the call again.

At five in the morning, Adam opened his eyes to see Diane standing over him, the phone to her ear, as if waiting for someone to pick up. "I'm calling the police. He's not home and I think something is very wrong."

"Diane, the police aren't going to do anything. He's been gone for a few hours. He's not exactly a missing person."

"He's missing!" she shouted.

"Did you try his cell again?"

"Fifteen times. He's not picking up."

"Did he even take the phone? I'll check his backpack. I bet it's still in there."

Adam dug through Jamie's clothes and found the phone at the bottom of the backpack. The ringer was turned off, and it had seventeen missed messages.

He brought it to Diane and they sat staring at it in the kitchen. "I have to go into the office today." He didn't know if Diane was afraid to wait alone. "Can I leave?"

"Sure. It won't make a difference. You don't seem to care anyway."

He knew her assault was just a measure of her frustration, but her bitchiness pissed him off all the same. "I'm sure he's all right. If something happened the police would have called. His wallet is gone so it must be on him. He's got credit cards. He's at a motel." He shook out his arms, stretched his neck until the knot cracked, and roused himself to full wakefulness. "I guess I can do some paperwork from home today, but I should show my face to Joey. Maybe later."

Diane wrapped herself in a lambskin coat and dragged the week's garbage to the curb. Adam and his wife never entered discussions of whose job it was to take out the garbage. From day one, as naturally as if she were changing potpourri in her underwear drawer, Diane took the filled, stinky bags from the trash containers and carried them to the cans outside. Their house always smelled clean. Elana and Seth's building—for all its concrete and marble, incense and silk—had hung heavy with the scent of accumulating garbage.

Adam passed the early morning hours by listening for Jamie at the door and fiddling with some papers, pretending to review jobs and billing, until he was sure it was dinnertime in Shanghai, and Seth might be home. He called Seth again at seven a.m.

Elana answered, and Adam felt himself smile at hearing her sweet Brooklyn accent, tilted adorably off-center by her Asian ancestry, her consonants softened.

"Adam! I hope you haven't called again for the rabbi, because he isn't here."

Adam pictured her in her long dress, clean and perfect, as she faithfully waited for word from *the rabbi*. "First, hello to you, Elana. So, you say Seth is out again, huh? Well, when do you think he can get back to me? It's pretty imperative that we speak." Did she know the truth of Seth's birth?

"God must be answering your prayers. Seth should be arriving at Kennedy in the morning. *Your* morning. Is it morning there?"

Shock "Yes. About seven o'clock. Why is he coming?" Adam breathed deep, locking the stunning news in his head. He knew better than to inquire from Elana why Seth was coming. "Is he going to call me?"

"He's staying with his aunt in Brooklyn, but I know he will call you as soon as he parks himself. He'll call me first and I'll tell him to call you next. Is everything all right with Eli?"

"Eli is remarkably well, as a matter of fact. I'm calling about David." Shit. Here we go. "Eli is asking about his father. It seems David left him his own set of notes, like yours, to deal with." He wished he hadn't have spoken the word "notes." He waited to hear again about her forgiving husband.

"Oh my. Don't tell me he's read something about Seth." That was it. Adam's throat closed with her confirmation. "You know then."

Returning to stone, she said, "I shouldn't say. You will speak to Seth and he'll know what to do."

Adam was clenching his jaw, both infuriated with her and scared by her inadvertent admission. "You don't have to say another word. I know Seth is Eli's brother and it won't take Eli very long to figure it out. I hope Seth acts fast. Difficult as it's been for Eli, he's accepting his father's death, but he's still a little fragile emotionally." Adam hoped he wasn't giving Elana the idea that Eli was feeble. "He's not happy about the prospect of having an illegitimate brother." Adam felt obligated to harden his warning. "I don't know what Seth is coming here for, but he better not fly into town to screw around with Eli's life." He bit his tongue accidentally and cringed. "It would be kind of him, at the very least, to tell Eli exactly what was done with their father's body." He swallowed the blood in his mouth.

"I haven't confirmed your assumptions, Adam. But Seth has given a lot of thought to this eventuality. The cantor told us he gave Sharon some letters for Eli. But I'm afraid that's all I'll say. Seth was adamant that I not discuss this if you called again before he got there. You and Eli will have to wait a little longer."

He felt snared in her stubborn loyalties. "I guess I'll wait. You'll be sure to tell him I'm expecting his call." He hoped his voice conveyed his attitude toward Seth: Let him know I'm not afraid of his impending accusations about my lifting the notes and God knows what else he has to tell me about himself and Eli.

"He has his own reasons for getting hold of you. You know?"

Adam knew. He had to flush his embarrassment and spit out his uneasy question. "Elana? Have you heard *any*thing about Yin?"

She chirped as if remembering the most marvelous surprise. "Seth spoke to Mr. Cohen just yesterday morning. Seth was on his way out, but I overheard something about Lucy and Yin being in some sort of car accident with a taxicab and Mr. Cohen settling a legal debacle."

"A car accident!"

"I don't know what else. Seth will tell you."

"But they're all right?"

"I think so."

She knew everything there was to know about Yin and Lucy, but she would remain cruelly obedient to her husband's MO—using information as leverage. "Listen. Talk to you soon." He still wanted to tell her it was good to hear her voice, but the sentiment seemed so vain, guiltless, wrong.

After hanging up, he immediately concocted the idea that the taxi Lucy and Yin took from the Giacalones had gotten into an accident and had kept them from arriving at the Cohens as expected. Yin must have been frightened to death. Adam prayed she had not sustained any further life-debilitating afflictions, and fleetingly and guiltily hoped Lucy had, and that Yin was now in the custody of someone who would take more suitable care of her. He never imagined that their disappearance was the result of an accident; he had just assumed that Lucy ran away again. And where the fuck was Jamie? Jamie could have been in an accident as well. He reminded himself that he had his wallet and so the police would have called.

The keyboard on the computer was clicking rapidly under Diane's fingertips, and Adam thought the staccato would drive him crazy. Seth could be landing right now, getting ready to call him any second. Adam needed time to think about protecting Eli from Seth. He considered making another shiva call but vetoed that idea because it might lead to discussing Seth with Eli. Adam's fight for Eli's rights as David's only legitimate son was cornered between urgent and premature; fighting for Eli's rights to his father's love more so than to his money.

Adam jumped into a black fleece sweatshirt, topped it all off with his brown, down bomber, grabbed his cell phone, and was ready to walk until his face froze. He muttered to Diane that Seth was coming to New York, and as Diane gasped, he waved his hands in a *don't ask* gesture and left the house. "I'm going for a walk. If he calls, take a message."

Diane sat at the computer, Googling around for local news of accident reports, trying her best to keep occupied while Adam walked. At last she got up with grim resolve and did what she believed was impossible not to do. She retrieved Jamie's cell phone and reviewed his automatic dial. Mark was listed, and before she could read if the number was home or office, she pressed Send.

Mark answered, groggy, probably still asleep. Diane recognized his hello and could not help but feel maternal and sentimental about her relationship with him. "Mark? It's Diane Oppenheim. I know it's early, but Jamie is missing, and I just felt we had to talk."

Mark's casual—"Sure. Hold on."—infuriated Diane. She heard a man's voice in the background asking what was going on. Mark had lied to her son.

"Hi. I'm back. What do you mean he's missing? He called me when he got into the airport. Did Mr. Op go berserk or something when Jamie told him, well, about everything?"

The nerve! "No, Mark, his father did not go berserk. His father loves him, as do I, as did you, I thought. I'm so upset about you leaving and I don't even know what really happened. Mark? Are you *not* gay? I heard another man's voice, but Jamie said you said..." It was obvious to her Mark was in bed with another person. "Are you with someone?" She could not believe she was asking these questions with a sturdy voice and a sincere heart. It all seemed so natural.

"Well, unless we're both hearing voices, Mrs. Op, I apparently have company." Mark had a forthright, if sometimes obnoxious personality; he was the kind of man who would hesitate under only the most severe circumstances — such as police questioning — from saying whatever was on his mind. Adam had always liked that about him. Mark told Diane, "Look, life with Jamie was becoming unbearable for me." He went on to explain himself with stinging directness. Seems, Mark wanted to party more, experiment, be with other men. He was not "comfortable" with Jamie and Jamie could not accept the possibility of an "open relationship." According to Mark, Jamie was jealous and paranoid, needy and repressed. The words pierced Diane, but she swallowed her retort when Mark said, "I love him. You know I've always loved him. But if I had to live my life a hundred percent *risk-free*, I would have crashed and taken him down with me."

"Aren't you the least bit afraid of AIDS?"

"Sure. But since you're pushing me into a corner here, I have to tell you, I'll take my chances. An open relationship can be done with only *minimally* increased risk." Diane heard him chuckle. "Listen, *Diane*. I have a mother too. And as I told her, we homos have read the literature. Condoms? But thanks for calling."

Diane was shocked. Who would rather take any increased risk of dying than be loved by someone lovable? Whatever was going on with Mark, Jamie was better off without him. God only knows what he would have brought home to her son. "I don't understand what you're looking for. I think you're confused," Diane said.

His voice was braver, louder than at first. "But I'm happier trying to find something real than laying low and safe in that cabin with Jamie. He's a beautiful person, but we are so, so different. He wants strict monogamy, like when we met. He wants something that isn't real and he doesn't get it that he's never going to find his fantasy relationship." He drew in a deep sigh. "I'm here for him, Mrs. Op. I'm here and he's my dearest friend. But I've temporarily moved in with a person who gives me the freedom I need. I have to go with it. Just tell him to phone me when he turns up."

"But, Mark. You're ignoring the reality of risk. You can't be infantile about this." She felt genuine concern for him. "Condoms break!" Diane waited for his response but only heard him disconnect. Diane had witnessed freak accidents and sudden deaths, horrible atrocities that had thus far—save her daring drive to see Sharon in stormy weather—rendered her paralyzed by the prospect of devastating consequence. Yet within moments, begrudgingly, she found herself mildly appreciating what Mark was saying: he just wanted to live a more immediately satisfying life.

And what of her son, who was also absolutely right to want to be careful? Could he trust anyone now to be intimate with him? He had trusted Mark; a man who—in a whirl of a sexual growth-spurt—was gone. Her worry suddenly seemed incestuous, and she felt squeamish. Ever since adolescence she would stop nagging thoughts by sticking two fingers down her throat and forcefully gagging. The disconnected cell phone lingered in her hand, as she leaned over the toilet and tried to get herself to vomit, asking silently, What was Jamie supposed to do feeling so threatened every time he wanted what every human being wants: touch?

The bedroom phone rang just after ten o'clock. Diane plucked it up instantly. Adam was calling from a few blocks away. "Where are you? Where *are* you?" she shouted. She put her hand to her heart. She listened but barely heard a complete sentence.

Adam said, "He was in the fourth motel I called. I told him we'd pick him up, promised him we wouldn't ask any more questions, and I swore we didn't go through his things except to look for his phone." Adam knew the boy fairly well, Diane thought, save a few incidental personal preferences. "We have to go get him. He's okay, at the airport Marriott. Get ready, I'll be home in a few minutes." Jamie had tried to get a flight back to Denver, as Adam had guessed he would, even without having his backpack. There were no flights and he checked into the Marriott. Checkout time was eleven and he was ready to come home again and talk about certain things, Adam said, but would not answer questions he deemed none of their damn business.

She scooted quickly to the bathroom sink, put a comb through her hair, poured a quarter-sized puddle of Oil of Olay into her hand and rubbed it over her face and neck, walked toward the front of the house, and once again put on and snuggled herself inside her sheepskin, waiting for Adam with the car keys in her hand.

Adam came through the door, shivering. "I agreed to all his demands. Now you just leave him alone when he comes back. I'll tell you right now, I won't ask anymore about his personal life, but I'm going to try to get him to move back to New York."

"Thank you for finding him, Adam." She kissed his cheek hard. "Now, let's go."

Diane's blood pressure surged as they drove closer and closer to the Marriott. "He's going to have to find someone else, you know. This isn't *Will and Grace* and he's not going to fuck around with one-night stands and then just have the *funnest* time in the world with heterosexual friends who satisfy his need for intimacy. He's going to need someone to love." Diane started to cry.

"Stop your madness! He's only twenty-four for Christ's sake. And we aren't going to talk about his personal life."

"I agreed I wouldn't ask him about it. But just think—what will he do to stay safe if he keeps changing lovers?" She decided not to tell him about her call to Mark, and his condoms. If Adam wondered why she was so suddenly insightful about her son's needs for intimacy, he would just have to assume she was wonderfully empathic.

Adam was staring at the traffic light. "Do you want me to solve the AIDS crisis before we get to the Marriott or can I hold off till after lunch?"

She stopped crying actively but spoke through tears. "He's either going to end up sick or alone. We have to do something to protect him."

"Not every single gay person in the world gets AIDS. If he's responsible and careful, uses condoms religiously, he'll be fine. But really Di, you and I have no control."

"Responsibility is only *one* part of it. What if he just wants what *we* have? Can a person go through life making love through latex? Could you have?" She knew the answer to that and sickened herself once more at her inability to stop obsessing over sex as it related to her son. The heartache was not that her son was different than she expected, not that he might get ridiculed or bullied, taken advantage of or abused. Those were all parents' nightmares, no more tedious or demanding than parental worries about any children. She knew that at least for Jamie, the big fear was of infection, or of infecting a loved one, and the true heartache was that her son's ability to love would be forever circumscribed.

Jamie was waiting by the curb at the Marriott, squinting into the glare of the windshield, his hands in his jacket pockets, shoulders slumped. He looked tired and didn't smile for them. His short hair, un-gelled, rippled in the wind and Diane could see now how much darker it had been colored. Insensitive Mark made him do that and then betrayed him.

When Jamie scrunched into the back seat, Diane turned to him and blew a kiss. He looked at her hollowly. As they silently drove away, Diane turned to look at her son, hoping he would volunteer a thought. "Are you hungry?"

Jamie remained silent. His legs were stretched from his side of the seat to the other half of the car; Diane took note of his height. He had two days' growth on his face. She turned to maudlin thoughts of toddler-sized clothes and perfectly clean boy's cuffed socks, until suddenly struck by the obvious fact that her son was manly. She said, "You scared us. I wish you wouldn't scare us."

Diane insisted on stopping at the corner deli and plopped the sack of groceries on Jamie's lap. He walked up to the front door holding the bag. Diane could feel Jamie's warm, sad body standing next to her when she turned the key in the lock, with

Adam, tall and stiff, positioned behind his son like a crane operator, his arm reaching over their heads to hold open the storm door. The scene Diane had often fantasized about, the three of them all together again, was painfully tense.

Diane's bladder always felt full lately, but she fought the urge in order to stay with her boys. She said to Adam, "After I check the phone messages I'd like you to call Eli and see how he's feeling. See if he needs us."

Jamie put the tuna salad, bologna, ham and Swiss in the fridge, and then excused himself and went to the den. Diane clicked into the phone. She heard a message from Mark — *Please have Jamie call me* — and her head throbbed. Next was a message from Adam's partner Joey — *The high school pipes froze and burst. Need help! Call me ASAP.* The last message was Seth's voice, deep, officious. Diane saved it without listening to all of it and paged Adam. He moseyed into the kitchen and pushed "speakerphone." Seth's words swallowed the room and Adam froze. *"I'm in New York at my Aunt Rhoda's house in Flatbush. I hope we can somehow meet tonight and talk. The reason I came is twofold. I came to collect what you borrowed from David's estate, and I have David's Last Will and Testament. I'm the executor. I hope to pay my respects to Eli before shiva is over at Shabbas. Please call me as soon as you get in."* He left the number, said *"Shalom,"* and that was it.

"Nice voice," Diane said.

"Dial that number back while I get something to drink. We're gonna have to go to Brooklyn." Almost choking on his last swallow of orange juice, he asked, "Why would Seth think Eli's only sitting shiva three days?"

Diane, bent over with the phone wedged against her ear, packing-down garbage into the kitchen pail, said, "He's right. Sharon said Eli didn't want to resume shiva after Shabbos was over. You've got to make another shiva call. Why is Seth the executor of the will? You borrowed something, wink-wink?" She stood straighter and looked at him, puzzled. "Those papers weren't yours to take, were they?"

"Well, there's a shitload of current events we haven't had time to discuss. I'll tell you in the car. But I don't know what the hell is up with the will. Are you dialing?"

"A *shitload* of current events?" Diane handed Adam the phone. "It's ringing." She whispered, "Am I going with you to Brooklyn?"

"You and Jamie. Go tell him." Adam took the phone. He gave Diane a thumbs-up when someone answered. "Hi. This is Adam Oppenheim. Is Seth there?"

The discussion with Seth was terse and abbreviated. Diane heard no questions about David's Last Will or Yin. Adam was all business, writing Seth's aunt's address and instructions to arrive after sundown but before five o'clock. Diane gave Adam her full attention and got nervous when she heard him ask Seth, "Are you angry with me?" Adam listened to Seth briefly, and then hung up. "The man is a machine," he said to Diane. "We have to be there at exactly four fifty-five or I think his heart will seize."

"Why is he angry with you?" Diane tied the ends of the garbage bag together.

"He's not. He claims to have a non-antagonistic code of behavior." Adam rolled his eyes. "I think he was being facetious."

"Because?"

"Because you're right. David's notes weren't exactly handed to me, but Seth said he expects them back." Adam took the bag from her and stuck it in the corner by the back door. "I am very uneasy about that man. Popping into town like a sick-fuck magician."

"I can't wait to meet him." Diane was truly anxious about the prospect and immediately started worrying about what to wear.

Before choosing an appropriate outfit for meeting Seth, Diane had the awful duty of telling her son that his ex-lover had called and wanted him to call back, and confessing her morning call to Mark. She found Jamie in the den, and watched as he buttoned yesterday's blue shirt against the sofa, smoothed it and folded it as though it were clean, to pack it. Her body became thicker.

"There's a message on the phone from Mark. He wants you to call him." He turned toward her with the first heartfelt smile she had seen on his face, and she prepared herself to wipe it off. She swallowed hard, then spoke softly. "Early this morning, when we were going crazy worried about you, I called Mark to try to find you. You left your phone behind with his number on speed dial and I just wanted to find you."

Jamie's face drained. "You spoke to him? Is that why he called?"

She felt his hopelessness and steeled herself to treat him like an adult. "He was worried that you went missing. He wanted to hear from you again. That's all."

He whispered, "Great," and sank into the sofa. "What did he tell you?"

Miraculously, she thought, he hasn't gone ballistic on me. He must be too tired, or just too relieved to hear even the mention of Mark's name. "Just said basically what you had said." She tried to sound casual. "That he's confused. He wants a different life than what you two had. For now." She struggled with revealing what else he had said, and *who* else she had heard, deciding it would serve no purpose. "Mainly, he's worried and wants to hear from you. So, you might want to call him now because your father is making us go to Brooklyn with him to see Seth this afternoon." She wished as hard as she could for Jamie's easy compliance. "Please just go along with it and come with us?"

Jamie fingered his sweaty bangs, smoothing them away from his forehead, and then walked away from his mother.

THIEVES

It was getting dark by the time Adam, Diane, and Jamie were driving down Nostrand Avenue from the Belt Parkway. Adam cracked his window open and inhaled the smell of incoming rain, murky and cold, blowing off Jamaica Bay; the aroma was a mixture of old waterlogged newspaper and the Good Humor freezer—a stale, frosty cloud hitting his face. The street's brick and aluminum-sided houses and two-story storefronts still, at the end of February, vibrated with colored holiday lights and white-bulb wire reindeer. A mist was falling and when the streetlights went on all at once the avenue turned shiny.

The right lanes in both directions were lined with unattended double-parked cars and delivery trucks, and now at the start of rush hour their Volvo had to crawl the twenty or so blocks from Shore Road to Avenue J where Aunt Rhoda lived and Seth was waiting. The forty-five minute trip from Queens to Flatbush had been just the right amount of time for Adam to brief Diane, concisely but satisfactorily, on the possibility, the probability, that Seth was Eli's baby brother.

As Adam expected, in accordance with her acceptance of all things strange, Diane was excited about the prospect that it might all be true, though she was duly convinced that Eli would "without question regress and fall prey to the continuation of, though posthumous, intentional tort of his father." Then Diane asked sarcastically, "And no one has any idea who his mother is or where he grew up?" As if such passivity was incomprehensible.

Adam wished she had never worked for attorneys. "He grew up in Brooklyn, around here. I haven't asked about the mother." He turned to Diane and pointed his finger. "And don't ask Seth." Immediately after warning her not to ask, Adam found himself hoping she would. "This Aunt Rhoda has to be from his mother's side, so maybe we'll find something out."

"Maybe Rhoda is his mother."

Adam had been thinking the same thing. "That would make things easy."

Jamie had fallen asleep in the back seat before they were even out of Queens, as though he were two. Now he awoke, yawned, and asked his mother if she had any chewing gum. She did and gave him the wrapped grape Bazooka. After blowing a bubble he asked, "So, I'm here with you because you need my stabilizing influence on the family, or just to show me off to the new cousin?"

Apparently, he had been more awake than not. Adam glanced in the mirror and saw him smile. "Both," Adam said. "I want you to meet Seth and I'd like your input when we decide what to tell Eli."

"O-kaaay. The explanation works for me if it works for you."

"I mean it, Jamie. I hope you'll speak up and include yourself in the business of family," Adam said, though he was not at all sure about involving Jamie in family business.

"Cool. Interfering in Seth's life, the life of a total stranger, sounds like a comfortable way for me to endear myself to an illegitimate member of my family."

Diane sighed. Adam saw her turn to Boy and roll her eyes toward her husband. Adam knew she loved being comrades in the field with her son.

"Jamie, tell Seth about Liora's daughter," Adam said. "Ask around about what info the rabbi has. You have feelings and you can contribute your feelings." Adam heard a muffled chuckle from the back seat and hoped he hadn't unintentionally insulted his son. He never would have worried about such things a few days ago, before he was *informed.*

Diane lowered her visor and looked in the vanity mirror. "Jamie? Are you going to stay in Queens for a while? I could bring your real bed up from the basement."

"No thanks, Mom. I'm gonna head back in a day or so. I have a job, you know."

"You could get a job in New York," she said.

"I already have one in Colorado, and a home and a life."

"You rent a house and build houses for someone *else*," Adam pointed out.

"I'm buying my house. I've already put down money."

"You can afford to buy a house?" Diane sounded shocked.

"I can afford to buy *that* house."

She turned around to face him. "I was hoping you would move back, now that you and Mark have broken it off. Why don't you just think about it?"

Jamie tapped his booted heel hard on the floor. "I have. That's why I put the down payment on the house."

"Leave him alone," Adam said.

"It's okay, Dad. She'll get it eventually." He immediately shook his mother's shoulders. "Mom? Do you get it yet?"

Adam and Jamie giggled.

The lobby of Rhoda's three-story postwar brick apartment building was covered floor and walls in one-inch black and white hexagon tiles, better suited for a very small bathroom. There was nothing ornate, save the heavy black and gold wrought iron railing, which led them up the three steps to the elevator. The Oppenheims went to the third floor, where they emerged into a hallway with an over-ambitious heating system and the smells of roasted meat, browned cookies, and someone's boiling cabbage. Diane whispered to Adam, "I hope Rhoda is serving dinner."

Adam pushed the bell on the apartment door and looked at the floor, praying that Seth wouldn't retaliate for Adam's conduct by saying something like, Ah! Here's the creep's wife and son. How *do* you two *live* with him?

Seth answered the door wearing a Levi's work-shirt, half-tucked into his brown corduroys, the pleats folding flat against his slim torso. "Welcome to my Aunt Rhoda's home," Seth said, offering his hand to Diane. A tiny woman stood behind Seth, and with a sigh and a respectful tilt of his chin, Seth turned toward her. "My mother's sister, Rhoda."

Adam and Diane threw a look at each other, as if to say, There goes that theory. Adam studied the old woman, trying to see a familial feature that might have attracted David to her sister. Her face was as plain and sweet as a butter cookie. As Diane and Jamie watched Aunt Rhoda leave the room to check on the food, Seth said in a low tone to Adam, "We'll discuss the notes later."

Adam resolved again to stand his ground, though an excuse for taking the notes escaped him now. In the dinning room, Adam had decided he would sit in one of the chairs on the long side of the table, making sure Seth knew he was to sit at the head, but when people all took their seats, the Oppenheims ended up on one long side of the table and Seth and Rhoda where on the other, as if negotiating on behalf of two armies. Adam felt belittled, as if Seth had made a grander gesture. The moment the initial silence fell, Diane said to Seth, "You have gorgeous blue eyes." He blushed. Adam saw Jamie averting his gaze from Seth's face and wondered if he was struck by the man's good looks, or by Seth's obvious resemblance to their family.

After the hurried dinner of corned beef and cabbage, amid benign chatter about travel, life in China, and the weather, Adam, Seth, and Jamie remained at the dinning room table with the plateful of browned mandlebread, while Seth's Aunt Rhoda excused herself, tied a red silky kerchief around her head and a matching heavier scarf around her neck, buttoned up her probably fifty-year-old alpaca coat, and left the apartment for a visit with a friend across the street. Diane walked her to the door, then went to the window. "I'll just watch until she crosses Nostrand Avenue," she said to the men.

Seth got up, took three cigars from a box inside his suitcase near the door and asked the two men to join him. "They're Cuban." Seth asked Diane if she minded the smoke.

"Just try to blow the smoke over there." She pointed to the far end of the table.

Seth handed Adam a cigar, which he stuck in his shirt pocket, but Jamie refused the offer and got up to retrieve the bowl of M&Ms from a server next to the table. He proceeded to combine pieces of the mandlebread with the candy and meticulously place even-sized pieces in his mouth.

Adam had been suppressing his uneasiness all through dinner, but once Seth's cigar was trimmed and lit he said, "Elana told me Yin and Lucy were in some kind of accident? What's going on with them?"

Seth nodded knowingly and sighed like an old man. "Yin wasn't hurt too badly. Bunked her head. Some cuts and bruises. Seems her mother was quick to grab her before the taxi actually crashed." His acknowledgment of her efforts was blasé. "Lucy broke several bones, in both feet, and suffered a head injury. They're keeping her in an induced coma until the brain swelling goes down."

"Oiy vey," Adam said and looked at Diane, who shook her head and echoed his sentiment. "And where is Yin now?"

"Yin is in a children's shelter not far from my apartment." Seth stretched his arm across the table as if reaching to touch Adam's hand. "I've made visits. She's as well as can be expected."

"Was it the taxi they took from your apartment the day I left?" Adam asked.

"I think so. It was that day, anyway. Mrs. Cohen is keeping in touch with the shelter, although Yin is not the first thing on her mind. Mr. Cohen's business, a dot com, went belly-up while Lucy was in New York." He raised his eyebrows, which Adam regarded as recognition of the Cohens' financial mess.

"But Lucy will get Yin back? I mean, when she's well. The girl isn't gonna get lost in the system, is she?"

"I hope not *lost*. Though she could be better off without her mother. The woman is touched with more than a bit of malice, I believe."

Adam swiped a crumb of cake off his lip. He was starting to feel dizzy and panicky. "You're kidding, right?" He gulped a mouthful of seltzer. "Did I go to China not only to come back without my uncle, but with guilt about leaving Yin as well?" The secondhand cigar smoke rushed to his head.

"I'm exaggerating. Forgive my flippancy. Lucy loves her daughter." Seth slapped his hand against his heart. "But you need to let the girl go, Adam. Her childhood is virtually gone already."

"She's only ten!"

"Dad? Like, what gives?"

Adam waved his hand at Jamie to be quiet.

"She'll have to find her way like the rest of us," Seth said. "There's no reason to feel guilty about Yin."

This man does not have a conscience, Adam thought. I may not show reverence to God as much as Seth, but I sure as hell show more concern about people here on earth. "You don't seem to have much pity for the girl. As I'm sure you recall, *Yin blind!*"

"Of course I pity her. But you talk as though you had a choice, and that you chose to leave her. You couldn't have taken Yin." Seth chuckled, and Adam wanted to bash his head in for his condescending authority. "She is not yours for the taking," Seth added.

Adam stared, straining to contain his rapid burn. "I only wanted to help her."

"Help to save her."

"Some children need to be saved."

Still flat, calm, still wearing that pompous smirk, Seth went on. "All children need to be saved. I don't doubt you've felt abandoned at times. I have." Seth sat his cigar in an ashtray and patted it lightly with his fingers. "Do you believe in God, Adam?"

Adam pointed his finger at himself. "What if I was sent to China to be the way God wanted to save her? You know the old joke about the dead man asking God why he let him die on the roof in the flood, and God says, 'Shmuck, I sent a rescue team with a boat, I sent a helicopter with a rope and basket, but you insisted on waiting for *me* to save you! Who do you think was sending those to you?'" He sipped more seltzer. "Maybe I'm her lifeboat."

Seth laughed. "I'll let you evade my question. As far as your joke is concerned, yes, we have a moral obligation to accept help, a humanitarian responsibility to give help, when we can. Especially to family."

"Are you really saying I've been less than responsible with my own family?" Adam ran his sweaty hand along the side of his pants and reached for Diane's fingers under the table. He would think more clearly about what to do about Yin once he was away from Seth's voice of force.

"I am really saying what I have said, nothing more, nothing less."

Seth sounded anemic, his words hungry, and Adam wondered just how many times Seth had been left behind himself?

"So," Adam said, "You've come to New York to execute the cantor's last will? Should we discuss that, or first talk about you with relation to Eli? It's only a matter of time until Eli figures out if David's claim to have another son is true or not. Eli is slightly *emotional*. Just my mentioning the possibility of a brother pushed him to panic." Adam felt like a cad; he had just knocked Eli down a notch and his cheeks burned from regret. "You've never met Eli. He's a wonderful man. Remarkable!" He looked at Diane.

She nodded. "Unbelievably accomplished!"

Seth responded quickly. "Elana told me about your telephone call, of course, and you have good deductive reasoning." He clasped his hands under his chin, and for all his austerity, he blushed. "Yes. David is in fact my father."

In the spasm of silence that followed, Adam felt a question buzz, unspoken from all three Oppenheims: Who is your mother? And what was your father thinking, cavorting with a woman he could not, until he was at the brink of death, admit had borne his child? What if Seth's mother was a hooker? Adam swallowed his curiosity. "I have to know what you're planning to tell Eli."

Seth turned his eyes toward the floor and then drew his head up and looked at Adam belligerently. "How I intend to go about handling that subject with Eli is my own business, but you can be assured I have learned to be gentle in my rabbinical practice and know how to handle this." He folded his arms across his chest and offered Adam a wide-eyed incisive look. "I can confidently give Eli the gift of knowing that his father loved him, if he is willing to accept it from me."

"Elana told me," Adam said, "that you knew David left notes here for Eli." Cautious looks flew between Diane and Jamie. "He's already read about some other son."

"I wish I'd had time with Eli before he read about me." Seth patted his shirt pockets as if looking for a pen or a key. "David told me there were notes meant for each of his children and they were self-explanatory."

"They aren't," Diane said. Her face grew red.

So much for how well you know David, Adam thought. "David's letters for Eli are more confusing than the load of crap notes I have."

Seth's pitch rose, "From the notes you stole."

"I had a right to see them."

"You had no such right."

"I'm not a thief." He heard his voice resonate through the apartment, but he felt ten years old.

"I did not call you a thief."

"You just accused me of stealing!"

Diane grabbed his knee while Jamie watched smiling, ate his M&Ms, and leaned his chair on its back legs.

Seth lowered his chin, and then his voice. "You did steal. You are guilty of an incident of thievery. As far as I'm concerned, that single act does not a thief make." He chewed momentarily on his cigar. "I can see you haven't brought them with you, but I expect them returned to me as soon as possible. The notes are for us, his children."

Humbled but still resentful, Adam felt his face flush.

"But I would have been relieved reading them to you in their entirety," Seth went on. "By the way, why didn't you take them all?"

"They didn't fit under my jacket." Adam wasn't sure if Seth were bullshitting. "I don't believe you wanted me to read them all."

"I believe him," Jamie said quickly. "Let him get to the will."

"Thank you, Jamie, for offering your trust in my integrity, and honesty about your concerns." Seth reached below his seat and lifted an attaché case to the table. "Before I get to this, I must insist that you send or bring the notes to me so I can make sure Liora receives what belongs to her."

"I can send them to Liora," Adam said.

"Well, I am the executor. I'm asking you to give them to me and I will see to it they go where they should."

"Fine." Adam would first make copies for himself.

Seth lifted a document out of the case. "If anyone wants me to read the will verbatim, I'd be happy to, but the terms are quite simple."

At their shrugs, Seth summarized. Real estate assets were left to Eli. The house in Brighton Beach would be paid off from an insurance policy. David's father had long ago left him his shares in his law practice—David had lived off interest from those assets all these years—which now were also left to Eli. David's wife's diamond jewelry went to her daughter Liora, and he left a few items of memorabilia from his Gramercy Park apartment to Diane and Adam—a painting done by Ruby when she was young, an old Persian rug, and a silver-plated tea service. "And finally, to be dispersed evenly between Eli and myself, there is an additional life insurance policy—a two million dollar life insurance policy. Eli's going to be a rich man."

Adam nodded to himself trying to unscramble the list of assumptions he'd been forced to make up to himself since his father's suicide. One problem he never considered for his father was lack of money. He closed his eyes and tried to calm himself. When he opened them and looked at Diane, he said sadly. "David inherited everything from his father. Nothing was left to my mother." And now, his mother Ruby's rightful inheritance from her father, Adam's inheritance, would be given to Eli and Seth. "Liora thinks Eli's broke!" Adam shouted. He wished David were alive so he could strangle him.

Diane asked Seth, "Does anyone else know about the money?"

"Possibly Eli. Possibly Sharon," Seth said. "The only person I expect a problem from is Liora. David's lawyer is well apprised of all contingencies and is prepared to deal with her if necessary."

Adam could see Diane's face light with fear. She said, "Eli has to be protected from Sharon. She has power over him."

"She told me she knows nothing of any money," Adam added. "But she has some legal power, and emotional sway over him, I believe." He felt strange, falling into cahoots with Seth to safeguard Eli.

Seth nodded. "She has a legal say only over his health-related expenditures. David was careful about that. David thought of everything. He was sharp as they come."

"About Liora, though," Diane said, "first of all, she thinks Eli is being left practically penniless. She doesn't even know about you! And doesn't she have a right to a third of the estate?"

Adam was tabulating his grandfather's net worth. Seth nodded to Diane and said, "Even before David's stroke he was adamant that she not take anything more from Eli."

"Anything *more*?" Diane asked. "What else has she taken from him?"

Adam knew exactly what Liora had taken from Eli, and what Adam had taken from them both. As he read notes last night he sensed the hardball he had tossed into the atmosphere years ago rounding his street corner, and now he questioned if stealing weren't something that had always been in his nature.

Seth held Adam's gaze, then turned to Diane. "You'll excuse us one moment, Diane and Jamie? I'd like to ask Adam something privately."

Diane nodded and Jamie shrugged. Seth led Adam into a small front room with a sad old Hollywood style daybed covered beneath a dark corduroy spread and backrest. Adam figured this was where Seth would be sleeping. The small television in the corner sat on a wood-laminate stand. Adam pushed its antenna down as Seth reached into the back pocket of his pants and found the folded yellow paper he had probably been searching for earlier in his shirt pocket. Adam's chest sank as he saw David's familiar Hebrew printing. "Shit. What now?"

"One of the pages you left behind. Why don't you take a minute and read it?"

Adam was embarrassed, but for the sake of accuracy, asked Seth to read it aloud.

Seth said, "David said the notes were really meant as a 'reverberation' as he put it, of his voice to his children. His songs, if you will. This is one I'd kept separate. It's one of the few David and I discussed at the end." His slight smirk was unthreatening.

Adam stood as far into the dimly lit room as possible, by the window overlooking the wet avenue. Seth turned his back to the dining room, facing Adam, then read the single yellow page in a low voice:

It was a Saturday morning when you wheeled your baby brother back from shul. He was three years old and had been able for the past few months to sit quietly in his stroller and watch the service. You worked hard caring for Eli as a baby. I came home an hour later than you. I had no choice. The house was quiet when I returned. I thought you were napping, as was the usual case on Saturday.

As routine, I went to look in on Eli. I found you in his room, Eli lying in your lap, kicking, with a pillow over his face. When I pulled him away from you, you made no attempt to lie about what you had tried to do, but merely admitted that you had had enough of him, that he had caused your mother to die and had no right to breathe freely. Enraged, I taped your mouth shut so you would feel the hysteria of suffocation. I had to send you away. Liora, tell them I had to send you away.

The hardball Adam had sent swirling into the universe struck him in the chest. He sat on the daybed and dragged his fingers hard through its ropes of corduroy, causing friction that stung his fingertips; he would not have been unhappy if a spark set him on fire. "I know you had to. I know, David," he found himself saying. It was as though a mask had been pulled viciously from him, and he was no longer able to deny his family the discomfort of his real face. Adam and David knew the truth about Liora, and now so did Seth and Elana. He looked at Seth's quiet eyes. Adam asked, "Who did David want Liora to tell?"

"He didn't say."

"You said you discussed it."

"We discussed what Liora had done, not his remedy. But you pose an intriguing question." He held his hand in the direction of the dining room, encouraging Adam to go back.

Shrinking inside, Adam looked at Diane and Jamie. He asked his family to leave their seats and follow him. He took his wine glass from the table and with his head down, led them into the living room, listening to them move and shuffle behind him, and when he turned to sit on the ottoman, they were there, standing above him with curiosity and apprehension on their faces. "I

219

have something to say." Adam simply looked up at them and told what he remembered about an April Saturday, a year before David sent Liora to Israel. Rubbing a scar on his right hand, he spoke into the empty space between his feet.

~~~Eli is two years old, Liora fifteen.

David had demanded Liora stay home with Eli this Saturday morning. She loves shul—gathering and praying, hearing and watching her father sing—and she is furious about missing it. Adam hears Liora stamping her feet on the sidewalk just below his bedroom window; he pities her and begs his mother to allow him to stay home with his cousins, which she allows. He is to read to his cousin Eli or stay quietly in his room. Twelve-year-old Adam adores his pretty teenaged cousin Liora and any chance to spend time alone with her is exciting for him. If they are lucky, Eli will take a long nap, and the two of them can run amuck around the house.

Liora snubs Adam as soon as their parents leave for services. It seems she is not as fond of spending time with her *delinquent* younger cousin. She stays in her downstairs apartment with Eli, and dictates to Adam to stay in his apartment upstairs. *"Play your stupid games in the backyard,"* she tells him, *"out of sight of neighbors who could witness your truancy."*

Most of that April morning passes with Adam watching cartoons, until he decides to turn the TV off, letting it cool by the time his parents get home so they won't know he was *sinning*. He leaves his apartment, slides down the common hallway railing to the lower entry foyer, takes the inside access door to the basement, and walks through the basement door up the five steps to the backyard. A friendly warm breeze blows.

As soon as Adam reaches the center of the small backyard he hears Liora screaming, shrieking, using words he hears only from the men on Dad's poker night. Ball-buster. Asshole. Fuck.

Is a robber attacking her? Adam rushes to the window of Eli's room, makes an awning of his hands over his eyes, and looks for Liora. Eli's tiny body lies on his stomach in his crib, the side railing all the way down, his face against the mattress, Liora straddling him, her knees on his legs, while she screams profanities at him and punches his arms with her fists. Adam thinks his heart is pounding enough to crack a rib. The window is opened just an inch but he can't budge it, so he bangs on it hard enough to break the glass, leaving him with a gash in his index finger. (He later tells his parents he cut it cleaning up glass after the window broke from an errant baseball.)

As soon as the glass breaks, Liora startles and leaps from the crib. Eli gulps for breath and then howls unintelligibly. Adam can't get into the room, but he stares at the scene, dumbstruck and mute, bleeding and in terrific pain. Liora is huffing and sweating, her black curls wet around her face. She screams at Adam, "Get away!"

Adam grabbed the ottoman so he could feel the seat beneath him, looked up at Jamie, and shut his eyes against his son's grimace. "Later that night, Liora told me that it was the first time she hit Eli and she'd never do it again. I never told anyone. If I had said something, anything, to my mother or father that Liora was losing it, that she beat up her brother, someone might have helped them before David had to send her away."

Adam waited for a groan, some swearing, but it seemed as though they were all holding their breath. "Have you been listening?" he asked. "She could have stayed home and I could have helped, and she'd have learned to love Eli, be his big sister."

Diane finally moved to Adam to touch his shoulder. "It's horrible, but you were a little boy yourself."

221

Seth drew an audible deep breath; showing for the first time the ability of his face to look horrified. "You said absolutely nothing. To no one."

"I know I should have, but I was so afraid of her myself."

Jamie ignored Seth. "Was it really that unbearable for Liora?" he asked his father. "Was Eli that annoying, such a burden, that she needed to attack him? My God! She could have been sent to a juvenile detention center. She's lucky he sent her to Israel."

"That's not the point, Jamie," Seth said. He sandwiched Jamie's hand between his two, and transposed from a horrified sibling into a rabbi. Seth arched his back sharply, as if regaining strength. He let go of Jamie's hand.

Seth spoke to the younger man kindly, suggesting neither condescension nor equality. "Okay. Let's try to make sense of it. Acknowledge Liora her misfortune, that she had lost her mother, that her father became despondent and distant, that she believed her brother was a total invalid, and that she was also very young. For her, Eli was to blame. But what your father is questioning is, what should *he* have done with the information he knew, and given what *was* done" — he turned toward Adam — "essentially nothing" — he looked back at Jamie — "how does your father, how do we all, deal with the outcome?"

Adam felt tears collecting inside him. Diane squeezed next to him on the ottoman. He looked at Seth and prayed the man was smart enough to absolve his sense of guilt. "Do you think I ruined Liora and Eli's lives?"

Seth briefly looked up and raised the palms of his hands, as if to alert the ceiling of the dilemma. "Ruined? No. Could you have helped more? If you'd told an adult about Liora, might that have changed things? Certainly. Every action *changes* things. For the better? I don't know. But you were not *willing* to tell." He raised his eyebrows and assumed the fatherly tough-love expression of a much older, less beautiful man. "Your intellectual ability is far different from your, our, willingness to respond." He went on, "Ethically? I believe you had an obligation to tell an adult about Liora, despite your fear of her rejection or personal retribution. For whatever reason, that quality was lacking in you. You were old enough to know Eli's life was at stake."

Feeling reprimanded, belittled, Adam felt a lump grow in his throat. "I tried to keep my eyes on her. I tried to keep her away from him," he said. His face was wet with tears. He wondered: Had David seen other bruising? Adam then felt guilty about passing blame.

Seth's voice was softer. "How could you watch her every moment? Obviously, you did not appreciate her emotional inability to deal with all her disappointment and abandonment."

Diane voiced in, "He was so young!"

Seth just looked at her gravely. Remembering his God joke, Adam wondered if Seth were his lifeboat. God, Adam prayed, Please just let me drown.

"Anyway," Seth said, "it appears David was truthful and evidently not paranoid when he accused Liora of, well, of being hurtful. I wouldn't go so far as to agree with him that she attempted *murder*, God forbid. Maybe the best solution at the time was to send Liora away." He closed his eyes and seemed to say a prayer, and Adam noted this behavior was either Seth's religious ritual or a nervous tic. "Be relieved," Seth added, "that her life has been whole and productive in Israel." His attempt at solace was transparent and hollow.

"She lost her mother, her father, Eli," Adam said, "and me."

Jamie stood close to Seth, tilting his head to his shoulder, looking serious and as attentive as a grad student. "Do you think everyone's behavior, good, evil, or whatever," Jamie asked Seth, "is dictated solely by what they are *willing* to do?"

"Willingness, when measured against our ideals of good behavior verses our ideas of evil," — he tapped his lips softly with his fingers — "is a tremendous issue."

Adam couldn't tell if Seth was with him or against him. Diane said, "But do not forget psychological compromise. Especially in this case! All the children in that house were in a precarious situation."

"Mom?" Jamie waved his index finger as if telling a child, No, no. "This is about the constructs of good and evil," he told her.

His mind already spinning by the turn of the conversation, Adam knew he did not have the strength tonight for an interminable discussion about good and evil. As the question hung in the air, Adam felt so uncomfortable he had to push ahead. "Did you plan on seeing Eli tomorrow?" he asked Seth. "You know he's decided to end shiva tomorrow at Shabbas. He's already in a compromised emotional state. The longer he waits…"

"Yes. I planned on dropping off his copy of the will tomorrow, and having a talk with him, if he is agreeable."

Adam knew he'd have to get to Eli first. Another day of missed work. Joey will kill me. But nothing was going to stop him from protecting Eli this time.

"Or, I can wait until Saturday night, after Shabbas. Would that be better?" Seth asked.

"I think it would be more relaxed." Adam would have more time. "I really wish you would tell me what you plan on telling him. He's been through enough."

"God, yes," Diane said, "so much! What would you say?" Adam saw Jamie give his mother a small kick into the heel of her shoe.

"Yes," Seth said, looking at Diane. "Well, among the personal account of my history, and things I want to share with him that should remain between brothers, I want to tell him how much his father loved him."

"Oh, Jesus," Diane whispered into Adam's ear.

"I wish he'd made his love clear to Eli before he died," Adam retorted. "Because seeing you? Comparing himself to you? And then facing the long future with his father buried in China with *you*?" I have to get David back to the States.

Seth walked up and back through the room in a straight line. "Perhaps my other news will temper his reaction." Seth offered everyone a refill of wine, and took a sip from his glass. "On closer scrutiny, I was convinced that David's will clearly stipulates he be buried next to Miriam, a wish he himself had not made very clear to me before I read the legal document." Seth rubbed his fingers over his lips. "Even if David's feelings for Miriam had changed over the years, I have no reason to believe he changed his mind about his burial, except for his plea when he was semi-conscious to remain near me. I have deep reservations about forcing more suffering on Eli. Besides which, I don't know where Elana and I will eventually settle." He clapped his hands. They all raised their eyes to him. "So, I have decided to bring him back to the United States. We'll be able to bury David in New York early Monday morning, as he will arrive Sunday afternoon from Beijing with Elana. The plot beside Miriam will be ready. A minyan has been arranged for eight-thirty a.m."

Adam's teeth nearly chattered in anger. "My, my, Seth. That's fan*ta*stic," Adam told him. Seth made it sound as though he alone had the power to redirect family history, as though Adam's trip to China were not an overture grand enough, that not until his own *closer scrutiny* of the will would he have reversed himself. Jamie was holding his lips tightly closed, looking as if he were ready to burst into laughter from the rabbi's ludicrous rationalization. Diane looked as if she was in shock and Seth watched her as she carefully rose to her feet.

Adam strode out of the room and gathered all three coats. Seth stood at the threshold of the living room, looking baffled at their eagerness to leave.

"So, I can expect you all at the cemetery?" Seth asked.

Cemetery. Minyan. Does he think we'd attend his party? "Call me before you go to Eli!" Adam demanded. He tried to grab Seth's eyes in his, but Seth was looking with great interest at Diane's black leather boots, probably wishing he could get a pair for Elana.

Seth said, "Let me take the ride down the elevator with you and see you to the car."

"That's not necessary," Diane said. "It's raining and cold."

Seth insisted.

Stepping foot into the old elevator, Adam took Diane's hand and stared at the brass floor indicator at the top of the doors, while Seth leaned against the side wall and stared at the group. His discomfort was palpable. Adam chose to maintain the tension by keeping mute.

The elevator finally reached the ground floor, but the door hesitated a few seconds before opening. "So, Diane, Jamie," Seth said, "It was nice meeting you. And Jamie? Perhaps next time you'll tell me about your theories of good and evil."

"Jamie, tell Seth what you think," Adam said sardonically, nudging Jamie with his elbow. "What d'ya say, huh? Tell him about goodness and evilness!" Evilness? Jamie shook his head as the doors opened.

"Go ahead, tell him," Diane said as they vacated the elevator. Adam could feel her heart pounding through her hands. She

226

repeated, "Tell Seth what you think." The doors jerked and shut behind them.

They walked single-file toward the exit, with Jamie leading. He stalled the procession at the double glass doors by stopping and facing Seth. Jamie spoke softly and seemed to be over-enunciating, his head tilted down. "I think we humans have an idea of perfect behavior, and so we all naturally *have* to digress from that prototype."

"Maybe now is not the time, Jamie," Diane said.

Jamie looked down at his mother's eyes. "You just told me to tell him. So, I'm telling him."

"Please, Jamie. Go ahead," Seth said, smiling.

Adam felt like opening the doors, pushing Diane and Jamie out, and locking Seth inside. But Adam had asked Jamie to come. He had to let him speak.

Jamie went on. "I think it's all about not being God-like. Not perfect. Like, how can anyone be born without something going off course? Little by little, someone gets far enough away from that perfect image we have of what *good* is, and they are suddenly evil." Jamie sniffed and looked from face to face. "Who made up what perfect is anyway? And why would anyone with perfect sense *choose* evil? The premise of evil is illogical." He took a deep breath. "And we judge and punish these people." He nodded.

The street was bare of pedestrians, but cars whizzed on the avenue, plowing through deep puddles that splashed from the middle lane clear to the sidewalk. Diane, Jamie and Adam stood by the passenger door of the car, their collars pulled close around their necks. Although the rain had stopped, it was windy. Seth pulled a Totes from his raincoat pocket, clicked it open, and tried to shield them with the small umbrella. Adam knew he was stalling for time, maybe trying to manipulate a smoother departure, but he was not going to help Seth by cooperating.

"What if you were brutalized by one of your imperfect humans?" Seth asked Jamie.

Diane said shivering, "Oh Rabbi, God forbid."

"Don't put ideas into my mother's head, please." Jamie looked at his mother.

Seth persisted. "Are there consequences? Imperfection is one thing, but I believe a perpetrator of harm has to account to someone. And when we are personally victimized, it becomes a different story."

Adam was nearing the boil-over point. Please, Jamie, don't answer back so we can get the hell out of there.

Jamie raised his head against the wind. "It's totally unbearable when you think what cruel things some people will do. Sometimes our best is *just not* good enough. Sometimes our best is the worst others can imagine." He folded his arms across his chest, looked squarely at his father, and his shoulders rose, his body seeming to fill with air. "Dad, this is so not about you and the Liora crap. I'm not very eloquent. But consequence, Rabbi? Like an eye for an eye? You're left with a world of blinded people." He put his hands in his pockets and then pulled them out.

Seth said solemnly, "God willing, we won't be victimized and have to face that conundrum."

Adam could not contain the mental image of A.D.A. Jack McCoy spinning in the courtroom, screaming, It's about the protection of a free society! Adam was never as sure of his feelings as his son seemed to be. He envied Jamie. "You *are* very eloquent."

Seth put his hand on Jamie's shoulder. "Yes. And thank you."

Adam thought about the summer he was ten, how he saw a teenaged boy hang a cat. Even at that age, Adam knew people were capable of horrible, deadly acts for what seemed to be no good reason. He knew, even at eleven or twelve, that Liora was stricken with some sort of lethal sadness. He'd seen it, but he had dangerously gambled that Eli would be fine.

Adam kissed Jamie's cheek, unlocked the car doors, and then held the door open for Diane. As he turned back to Seth he asked, "Just for clarity, Rhoda is your mother June's *older* sister?"

Seth took a moment to respond, then smiled softly. "My mother's name was Jericho."

IN THE NIGHT OF THE HEAT

Diane's numbness began to dissipate as they drove back toward Queens in the dark. Dampness licked her spine. "I feel like I'm getting sick," she said to Adam. "Everything aches." Diane knew she was not getting sick; she was getting angry to her bones. Seth was manipulative, self-serving. "*Is* it a nice thing Seth's doing by bringing David back?" Neither Adam nor Jamie spoke. When she was certain they were not going to answer her, she asked, "What kind of name is Jericho? Jamie, did you ever hear that as a name?"

"Jericho, Long Island."

She laughed. "Of a person!"

It was nine o'clock when they pulled up to their unlit house. Rain had flooded the gutters, and parking was going to mean getting close enough to the curb so not to step into water two inches deep. Jamie yawned as Adam maneuvered the Volvo. "Please just park the car. I have things to take care of." Diane knew that meant he had to call Mark. He had seemed calm and confident enough in Seth's house, but the closer they got to home, to his call, the whinier he had become, complaining about the weather and his dread of the next two days in New York.

Diane was first to enter the house and get the lights on for Adam and Jamie. She rushed to the bathroom and swallowed two Excedrin by the blue of the nightlight. Amid the cool blue fixtures, matte gray tiles, and the darkness blaring helter-skelter in her head, she asked how Adam could not have told anyone what Liora had done. She never imagined he could be so irresponsible, even as a twelve-year-old.

Diane watched her hands as she cupped her breasts; they felt fuller and pushed against her bra, throbbing with a hard and erratic pain akin to the ache that anger was drilling into her bones; she knew this pain was a sign of her oncoming period. Her cycles were off-kilter, and this cycle was late. Perimenopause was a scourge that was overpowering her relationships with everyone and everything on earth.

She peeked through the door, down the hall and saw Adam in the kitchen handing a large filled goblet of wine to Jamie. They clicked glasses with frowns on their faces. Adam kissed him on the forehead and headed for the bedroom. Jamie retreated to the den. "Good night, Jamie," Diane called out from the bathroom threshold. "I'm so happy you're here." She wanted him to turn and come to kiss her cheek.

He gulped a swig, closing the door behind him as he spoke. "Good night, Mom. It's gonna be a long one."

Moments later, Jamie's low tenor voice bled through the wall between the bathroom and the den. He was talking on the phone. He had the television turned up too loud, trying to cover his words, but the use of volume only brought more attention to the turmoil she could hear in the patterns of his talking. He was generally considerate about noise once his parents went to sleep.

Standing in the hallway, looking into her bedroom, she saw movement in the semi-darkness. Adam had let the blinds land lopsided when he lowered them. The right corner held at about three inches from the sill and formed a triangle of light across the foot of the mattress. Adam sat up higher with a groan and poured himself more wine. It splashed, he said "Shit," and slumped forward, extending his glass-holding hand down his thigh.

Diane felt alone. "We need to talk," she said softly. "Don't make yourself drunk."

He looked at the glass on his knee. "Do you think I have to tell everything to Eli? Do you think it matters to him?"

She was becoming infuriated, but went to the bed and sat in the triangle of light near his feet.

"Do I think *what* matters? That his father was right to send Liora away or that you were — well that you were, what would you say you were?" Stupid? Cowardly? Abusive? Irresponsible? Selfish? Feebleminded? Diane was not prepared to use any of those words against Adam. Angry as she was at him, disappointed and insulted that she had never known the story, she would not use any word that would hang as an assault between them — a lesson learned after many years of marriage.

Adam's voice came out raspy. "Do you think it matters to him, now, that I was largely to blame for the mess?" He waved his free hand, as if calling a time-out. "Yes, I think he should know that David was right about Liora, but should he know I was a chicken and a liar?"

"It might make you feel better." But what could possibly be the end of it? How would it help Eli? She wanted to scream, Look what you've done! "The part about knowing why Liora was exiled may be helpful to him, in a horrible kind of way, but you can't tell him that without the rest of it." Her voice rose slightly. "He might turn away from you and lose you again."

"He should know who he'd really be losing. I'm not the good guy he thinks I am."

"Adam, don't be maudlin. You're as good as they come. True, you acted in an *awfully*, *power*fully regrettable way once when you were a boy. Okay?" She was using strong words and felt bad for Adam, but she knew he would recover. "You *should* have known better. Evidently, something more powerful than wisdom prevented you from —" She placed her fingertips on her temples and pressed, thinking about what Jamie had said at Seth's. "Your best was awful." Diane checked Adam's face to gauge his reaction. He looked unfazed or stupid.

He put his glass on the nightstand, scooted to the end of the bed and put his arms around Diane. "You think Eli will make something of himself?" Adam asked. "You think Sharon is an all-right person and there's a chance he'll have a regular life?"

"I don't know." She didn't know and worried plenty. "We'll go there tomorrow and see how it goes."

"I think I want to sell out the business to Joey," Adam said. "I don't ever want to go back to work."

"You're depressed. Stop drinking that stinky wine and go to sleep. I'll call him and tell him you'll be back on Monday." She nudged him onto his pillow and rubbed his feet for a minute as he closed his eyes.

Tiptoeing out of the room, as if sneaking away from a fussy baby who was finally but just barely dozing, Diane stood for a moment in the hallway. Monday would be the funeral. Decisions about attending would wait until morning. She enumerated her current misfortunes. One, Adam had committed a wrong for which she felt they would be paying interminably. Two, Jamie would be leaving soon, and probably would never come home again. And three, she hadn't gotten her period. Try as she might, she could not remember the train of thought that brought her to that final one. She said to no one, "Menopause. Short-term memory loss. Thanks."

After several minutes of inertia, she realized Jamie's television had been turned off. She went to the den, tapped twice on the door, then heard Jamie say, "Come in, Mom."

The television was animated with a handsome but mute CNN newsman against the backdrop of the White House. A low voltage light on the bookshelf made the room seem serene and scholarly. Jamie was sitting on the couch with his feet on the side chair staring at the TV screen. "How'd you know it was me?" she asked. She didn't know yet whether to be warmed by his intuition or insulted.

"I knew Dad was headed for bed. He doesn't have strength to deal with me tonight."

"*Deal* with you? We don't *deal*. He's very upset about Eli and really doesn't have the strength for anyone else. Can I sit and stay a little while?"

"Sure. Make yourself at home." He wiped under his eyes and drew a deep breath while kicking the leg of the chair, pushing it out for his mother. "What's Dad gonna do?"

"What's to do?" Jamie must have just this minute gotten off the phone because his mannerisms were less guarded. She saw her gay son. She saw it in the way he sat, his legs crossed now at the knee, his shoulders covered with the tight posture of a woman recently dumped and doesn't want to cry. Diane forced a slim smile while she shook her head, utterly uncomfortable with her resentment toward her husband. "You were right at Seth's tonight about doing one's best. If people knew better they would do better. Your father's behavior had nothing to do with being a bad person."

Jamie grimaced. "I know that! For Christ's sake. Do you not understand what I said?"

"I understand." She was not sure exactly what he thought.

"The predicament is not about you explaining his motives as good or bad. It is now about him accepting his motives for ignoring Liora and living with his guilty conscience."

234

She sat and thought. How important was it for Adam to face the enormity of the risk he had taken with his cousin's life? "You're right." She looked into his eyes, still moist. "You spoke to Mark? You all right?"

"Why don't you just burn me with cigarettes." He squinted at her, daring.

She laughed. "When did you start speaking so dramatically? It's not as though you didn't run away last night and take the risk of giving your father and me heart attacks."

"*I* speak dramatically? Gee, where did I pick that up?"

"From me. You picked it up from me. Now, let's begin again. How did it go with Mark? Are you feeling better or worse?" She could see by his eyes the answer to that one.

Jamie squirmed. He pulled his legs to one side on the cushion and used his hand to squeeze them against his buttocks. "I feel lousy. I loved him and he's already living with someone else. A man. He didn't say as much, which is why I suspect it. He said I didn't need to know." He rolled his eyes and shifted his jaw back and forth. "I have a lot of shit to figure out, but at least *I* know what I want."

What do you want? she wondered. He was pouting, and his left hand was flat on his chest, counting beats or protecting his heart. It was clear he wanted to cry, needed to, and she didn't know what in him was ashamed to let go. She leaned back in her chair and got as far from his face as she could, consciously separating the mother and son. "Look, I know you're twenty-four and by this age anyone would have had several experiences with various individuals they had met along the way, so I am not being judgmental. I just would like to know how many…"

He squealed, put his hands over his ears, and then shouted a whisper, "Mom! Are you really interested in how many men I've had sex with? Do you really want me to tell you, so the number

235

will ring in your head keeping you awake nights until I walk down the aisle in a pretty white dress?" He gasped for air and uncovered his ears.

"That many?" Even though he was kidding, the thought of him in a dress made her uneasy. Frozen in place, she watched as Jamie first burst-out laughing and then broke down in tears.

He sang out, "The grand total is, ta-da…one! I've been with one man. Three girls in high school and one man since. Happy?" He started to sniffle.

Diane heard herself say, "Oh." She got up and sat beside him. She was relieved for herself and heartbroken for him. He looked so small and thin when he cried. Diane could think of nothing to do for him but rub his arm and the back of his hand.

He put his face on her shoulder, then after a few seconds raised it, shook his head and laughed again. "I was happy. I thought my life was set. And then Mark started running around and I was too horrified, too afraid, to be with him." He wiped his nose with the napkin from his wine glass. "I'm so afraid of getting sick. He knows that, but it was oh so important to *him* to have experiences."

Diane listened, realizing how Jamie had lied to her on the phone that everything was fine with Mark. "He's not always meticulous or sober during his experimentations. To do what Mark does would be like knowingly inhale powder that had a fifty percent chance of being asbestos. It's all I think about when I meet someone and Mark is oblivious to danger. I'm not." He got an excited look in his eyes and pounded his finger into his chest. "I deliver meals to men with AIDS. I see what happens. Could I trust Mark to protect me?"

"No. Oh, god no, you couldn't trust him." She loved him and respected him and still the wish she fought wishing flash-flooded her head: she wished Jamie weren't gay.

He started shaking his head nervously. "I just want him to love only me. And then he goes and pisses away everything we gave to each other." He tossed his cell phone to the floor. "But you really don't know anything about this."

"Yes. I do."

Jamie closed his eyes and tilted his face away from her.

Diane was feeling sufficiently uncomfortable now. For the first time she had no answer for him.

"I think I need to be left alone," Jamie said. He slid down on the sofa and hugged a pillow firmly against his chest.

"You come to me or your father if you need anything. Promise me you won't go running away again. I have your father to worry about tonight. Okay?" She rose from the sofa and pulled an afghan from the armrest over his shoulders.

Adam was snoring. Diane tried to lie next to him, be near him, but was unable to shake him deeply enough to get him to change positions, and though she was desperate to sleep, she would not be able to rest as long as he carried on like that. He was not a heavy drinker and the few glasses of wine were sure to keep him comatose for hours. Grabbing her pillow and blanket, Diane moved to the living room. She lit vanilla and apple scented candles on the coffee table, then sat on the floor Indian style and tried to relax. The aromas were delicious and she breathed deep, hoping to fill her body with the pseudo-calories in the air. Within seconds she was overcome with nausea and ran to the bathroom retching. Trying to keep from disturbing Jamie in the next room she gagged as silently as possible. She hoped it wasn't food poisoning courtesy of Aunt Rhoda's corned beef, because that would mean everyone else would be vomiting soon as well.

The nausea persisted for a solid hour without producing any serious stomach pains or vomiting. She drank some Kola syrup from the bottle in the medicine cabinet—she and Adam owned every gastrointestinal relief known to man—and felt well enough to return to the couch and lie down.

The candles had continued to burn and the house was filled with the overwhelming sweet smell. When she opened the living room window she unwittingly set off the burglar alarm. The siren screamed through the house as she ran to punch in the shut-off code, but not quickly enough to keep Jamie and Adam from charging in.

"It's okay! It's Okay! I tripped the alarm by accident! Everything is okay." Diane stood in the kitchen near the backdoor keypad and stared at her disheveled husband and son. "Go back to bed. Both of you."

Adam pulled on the back of a kitchen chair, and slumped into it. "I can't go back to bed now. I'm all riled up."

Jamie yawned. "I'm hungry."

"Hungry?" Diane asked Jamie, "Not nauseous?"

"You mean nauseated."

"I was nauseous before. That's why I opened the window. Adam, are you feeling sick?"

"No. I smell vanilla. Do we have white bread? I'll make French toast."

Diane was relieved that no one else felt ill. She decided she either had a stomach virus coming on, in which case father and son would catch it by morning, or she alone had gotten food poisoning. "I'm going to bed. I have a terrible feeling I'm going to be vomiting in a little while." She left the kitchen holding her stomach with one hand and her lips with the other.

Adam and Jamie ate two slices of French toast each, which Adam had fried with olive oil instead of butter, obliging his

238

son's request for reduced fat. They finished an entire half-gallon of orange juice, and belched without shame or disgust. "Good snack, ay?"

"Ay? What are you, Canadian?" Jamie said.

"Too much hockey. You still keep up?"

"Go Avalanche," Jamie said with questionable enthusiasm.

"Traitor."

Friendly arguments ensued but both agreed the Devils would most likely make the playoffs, the Islanders could probably make them, and the Rangers definitely would not. Each man yawned and smiled. Adam's stomach was reacting negatively to the maple syrup, or was he just suddenly nervous being alone with Jamie? He wanted to talk to him about *stuff*. About his work, his money situation, the house he was buying, and his lifestyle. He didn't know where or how to begin.

"The rain stopped. How about we walk outside?" Adam dipped his head up and down—his impression of a rapper: "Roam the dark, misty streets of the hood, man." Adam laughed, snapped his fingers and grabbed his crotch á la Michael Jackson—a move he immediately regretted.

Jamie smiled and seemed impressed with the suggestion. "Sounds good, but could you not like act so, um, dumb? There *are* other people awake at this hour."

They got their jackets, checked the keypad to be sure the alarm was off before opening the front door, and slipped into the lamp lit sidewalk of a wet and clammy night. Adam rubbed his hand against the back of Jamie's leather jacket and inhaled deeply beneath the cataract sky. The cold air pressing on Adam's face felt good.

A porch light was on here and there along the block. Adam felt like clinging to Boy as life intruded. A lone elderly man, bundled into hat and scarf, marched passed them with his leashed dog. The dog sniffed politely, but no one spoke as they sidestepped each other, so close that their shoulders brushed.

Adam and his son walked for an hour in nearly perfect silence, weaving up and down the neighborhood streets, stopping a few times in front of houses where Jamie's various childhood friends had lived. They would look, nod their heads remembering, and continue wordlessly. The dampness finally made its way through Adam's jacket, and with it, worry. When they had walked full circle and were at the traffic light closest to home, Adam asked, "You sure you can afford the house? I could help you out, although your mother would kill me for making it easier for you to stay away."

"I'm good. I have enough money."

Adam was both disappointed and relieved. They crossed the street against the light, running, even though there was no car in sight. Oppenheim instinct. Breathless, Adam said, "So, you'll be living alone then."

Jamie nodded. Adam suddenly felt as if he were talking with a neighbor's son, a casual acquaintance, who had gotten locked out of his house in the middle of the night and came over to kill time until a locksmith arrived. Adam pushed himself to act like the father of this man. "You were very eloquent and forgiving. I admire your clarity about why people are less than good. You have anything more to say?" He stopped walking. "Anything I did to make you lose faith in me or distrust me?"

"Are you talking about after what you told us tonight, or through my life?" Jamie smiled and put his arm around his father's shoulders. "I never have and never will distrust you."

"What I said tonight at Seth's, about Liora, I'm really sorry about not doing anything."

"I don't think you should worry about Liora and Eli so much. How many years ago are we talking about here, thirty-five? Shit. Every living cell on the earth has changed by now. Nothing is the same. Forgive yourself and get over it."

"It's that easy, huh? It's that easy to look at the misfortune and dysfunction surrounding my family, thanks somewhat to me, and just get over it? They're still suffering."

"Ariella never sounded like she or her mother were suffering."

"When did that all start, you talking to her?"

Jamie explained in short, factual sentences that she had emailed him when they were teenagers. She knew some kids in New York who she'd met one summer in Israel, and this that and the other, bla-bla-bla, and eventually she got his email address. "She knew all about David and Eli. Well, she thinks she knows about them."

"Such as, what does she think she knows?"

"Well, she thinks Eli is, like, a total invalid. And she thinks her grandfather is, *was*, a religious zealot who sent Liora to Israel to give her a purer Jewish experience. But she didn't know about my grandfather, your dad. Liora just mentioned to her he was dead a long time."

"Liora sure worked that lie in diplomatically." Liora, Adam suspected, knew more than he did about his father's demons.

"I didn't know much to tell her. You're pretty evasive on the subject too." Jamie laughed self-consciously. "But she did know I was gay before I even told her. And she never saw me, or talked to me until about a year ago." Jamie looked to the ground.

He had said he was gay so easily. As they reached their front door, Adam said, "I did such a good job raising you that your sexuality was evident through computer lines."

Jamie raised his eyebrows, pulled his face a few more inches away from his father's and looked at him squarely in the eyes. "Do you think something you did or didn't do made me gay?"

"I didn't say that, but did I?"

"I'm not about to start to explain this to you. The answer to your inane question is no." Jamie whipped out his house key and unlocked the door.

Adam rushed in behind him, whispering hard. "Don't be mad at me because I feel bad. I've made my share of mistakes and I just want to understand why you are the way you are."

"I am fine! Finer than you are with what grandpa did to you. Maybe you need to untangle some shit and stop obsessing over me." He went straight to his room.

Jamie's proposal pierced Adam, pinning him in place just inside the front door. When Adam had asked his mother why his father spilled that hideous scene in his own home, she would only say that he was a disappointed man. Even as a young man Adam had thought, Who isn't disappointed?

Adam was thirty-seven when his mother died. Emmy, Ruby's cousin, accompanied her body back from Florida to New York. At that time, Emmy told Adam her understanding of the events that led to Seymour's suicide: Early in Seymour's career, Ruby's father had accused him of bribing a judge, and once his father-in-law fired him, no law firm would take him on. Ruby never believed the charges were true, but her father was a very powerful man. Emmy told Adam, "I don't know what ulterior motive her father could have had for wanting to destroy your dad, but whatever, it ended your father's career, and I guess that was too much for him to bear."

All through his grief, denial and anger, Adam had alternately blamed his mother, his grandfather, and himself. It had taken him the three years after he quit college to bring himself to get rid of his father's personal effects. Adam kept the boxes of law books from his mother's basement. He knew his father's heart had been left inside them. Although he had always blamed his father's depression and death on other people, Adam could never answer one question: How could he leave *me*?

Adam moved from the foyer to the kitchen and sat back down at the table, trying to absorb Jamie's beliefs in the penaltylessness of past juvenile delinquency. He ruminated on the widely reported story of the thirteen-year-old Florida boy who shot his teacher, and how terrible both he and Diane felt that the child had been sent away to prison. What did Adam want, now that he had exposed his cold-blooded lapse of reason? Empathy? Jamie had offered it and it didn't feel right. So, what were the appropriate consequences of behaving like a scumbag?

About a week after Liora had been sent away, just days before Adam's bar mitzvah, Adam had received a letter—his first airmail letter ever, in a fancy striped envelope—from Israel. He was afraid to open it, afraid of a threat, even more fearful of a curse Liora might have put upon him, so he jammed the envelope into the bottom of his toolbox. He had always known it was there, unread, but unforgotten, and the letter came to the forefront of his mind as Jamie spoke tonight about Ariella's emails from Israel.

Shutting the kitchen light, moving through the dark house, Adam found himself at the basement door. His hand reached for the doorknob and turned until he heard the lock release. He allowed the door to swing toward him. He held onto the railing, guiding himself down in the dark, and when he reached the floor, stood in the blackness. There was a string hanging from the bulb that would hit him in the face if he moved one foot forward. Adam decided to creep his way in darkness over to the workbench and find the flashlight. He wanted only little light, making it as difficult as possible to find what he was headed for.

With the flashlight blaring, the entire bench area was illuminated. He moved the light from left to right along the table, reviewing the mess: duct tape, the electrical wire, a few wire-cutters and his open toolbox, a box he had since he was a boy, the first one his father had bought him in a real hardware store. It was red with a black stripe around the base, which he painted himself to distinguish the box as his own. Removing the top compartment, then lifting the middle shelf, he pushed his obsolete tools out of the way to see the letter at the bottom.

The corners of the envelope had peeled back some, the adhesive dried and flaky, but the point of the flap stayed stuck and the envelope was still sealed. The ink with his name and address had faded, as did the Hebrew-scripted return address on the back. The stamps lay flat and clean under the postage cancellation markings. Adam shook the envelope, judging the width of the letter, wondering how much could have been written on such small paper. Contemptuous of the childish dread he was feeling, Adam set the flashlight on the workbench pointing at his hands, tore the envelope open, unfolded the lilac sheet of stationery, and stared blindly at the seven evenly spaced straight tracks of cursive, purple-inked words.

It was five o'clock in the morning when he heard Diane calling him from the top of the stairs. "Adam? You down there? Phone call for you. Adam?"

Stuffing the letter in the elastic waistband of his shorts, he bounced to a sitting position on the old recliner and moved toward the stairs. He told Diane he was coming. "Who the hell is on the phone at this hour? Joey?"

"Nooo," Diane whispered to him as he reached the top. With her hand over the receiver of the portable telephone she said, "It's Liora. She's at Kennedy. She wants to go to Eli. Adam, look at me." Adam looked at her. She grit her teeth and whispered heavily, "She wants to go now! She sounds rabid!"

There had to have been a curse. No sooner had he opened and read her letter and she appeared—as if by witchery. He took the phone and swallowed hard. "Hello, Liora." He wondered if he were dreaming and looked around until he fully recognized where he was standing. "Tell me where you are and we'll be right over to get you."

"Yes, hello, hello. I'm at El Al. You don't need to come and get me." Her voice was heavy and impatient. "You need to tell me Eli's address. I seem to have lost it en route. I'll take a taxi. Go ahead, I have paper."

Adam doubted that she ever had Eli's address to begin with. He looked at Diane and shook his head. The morning rush hour had started and streaks of headlights pulsed across the walls from the living room window. "Don't you think it would be better to wait for me to take you?"

"Adam! I long ago gave up relying on you for assistance. Just give me the address, please!"

He owed her the truth—that the body of her father would soon be arriving from China—but he was reluctant to tell her anything just yet; he hadn't even considered whether or not he was going to David's funeral. "What will you say to Eli when you see him?" He went to the sink for water.

"It's none of your business what I say." She became quiet.

Adam could hear her sniffling, and then blowing her nose. "Are you all right, Liora?"

"No. It's too cold here. I just want to see my brother and get back home to my family." They both remained silent for a moment and then she said, "You know what? I know Eli's phone number. I'll call him and get the damn address myself!" The phone disconnected.

Having finally read the letter she had sent him over three decades before, Adam could not hold Liora's bitterness and anger against her. She had written to him, at that time her closest cousin, as an exiled adolescent girl in dire straits, and he was too much of a scared, confused, guilty boy to risk dealing with her message. The day she had arrived in Israel, stealing some privacy in a distant relative's strange home, on a small sheet of lilac stationery, Liora had written:

> Please tell my father to let me come home.
> I promise I'll be good.
> My father won't speak to me.
> Please beg him for me, Adam.
> You are my only hope.
> I'm so very, very sorry.
>   Yours truly, Liora

He thought of the enormity of will it had taken David to push Liora away and change her world forever. Adam's mind zoomed in on the Shanghai street where Lucy and Yin had gotten into their taxi while he stood in the puddle and racked his brain for an excuse that would compel Lucy into staying at Seth's with him. Adam's spirit plunged as he at once grasped how David's selfish bullying had interminably damaged lives. He understood that when his uncle coerced emotion and manipulated living conditions, adulterating circumstance solely to allow himself to fit more comfortably behind his own façade of purity, he had left his family members in one of many unfortunate situations: alone, segregated, dead, or woefully guilt-ridden over the lonely, segregated, and dead.

246

THE SON OF A BITCH

Eli awoke before dawn on Saturday. Pain had kept waking him during the night, first a series of stabbing jolts under his ribs and eventually fiery rods traveling through to his back. By five-fifteen, the burning sensation was terrifying him, and he pushed the intercom by his bedside to call Ludie for help. Simultaneously, the phone in the hallway rang. Had Sharon slept in her room downstairs or had she gone to her apartment? He hobbled over to answer the phone and immediately after his customary "Kaplan Residence" greeting, he heard Liora announce herself and ask for his address. Confused, as if dreaming, he recited his address, thinking she must be mailing him a package, until she said, "I'll see you soon."

At five-thirty Ludie had not yet come to his room. The pain in his abdomen and back intensified, as did Eli's fear, and he started to lose his ability to inhale fully. After several labored deep breaths, his heart felt as if it had exploded and spilled into his mouth. Liora would come to find him dead. He had grown up despising his sister, always speaking hatefully of her, yet now he was pining to live long enough to see her again.

Trying to commandeer his courage he stared out the window as a cast of white blew past, slanted toward the ocean. He forced his eyes to blur, than focus, and made an activity of changing perspectives on the scene before him. Light began to rise through the room like a cloud of mauve dust, and the mere advent of dawn slowed his pulse. Lying on the bed, the pain abated only briefly before a shot of fire from his back to his groin made him fold at the waist, and he used the adrenalin from the dart to turn onto his stomach, hang his arm over the edge of the mattress, grab his brace, and fling it as hard as he could toward the open bedroom door.

The brace missed the door completely, bounced off the wall of the landing, tumbled down the stairs, hit every few steps, and settled at the bottom with a deliberate thud. Ludie began screaming and Eli was relieved to hear the tiny woman's usual and inexplicably leaden footsteps coming up the stairs.

"It's about time!" Eli scolded when she entered his room. He was sitting up and holding his ribs with both hands. "I'm in terrible pain. You need to call the doctor right away. It's unbearable." With another sword-like jab in his back he winced and blurted out, "Get Sharon. Is she here?"

"I don't know." Ludie ran to the phone screaming "Sharon!" Eli pulled off his boxers in a pain-induced fit. The pain was unrelenting and he screamed, "Call nine-one-one!" Sweat rolled down the sides of his head. When neither Sharon nor Ludie arrived, he swung his legs out of bed and hobbled to the staircase, every movement costly. In the course of two shallow breaths, the hall spun and he lost consciousness.

Eli awoke on a stretcher, aware of being carried, his head under a blanket. He heard Ludie crying his name and he lifted the blanket to show her he was alive. The snow flurries felt good on his brow and he left the blanket under his chin. They were hefting him into the ambulance, and he turned his head to smile at the housekeeper, to reassure her, when he saw the woman.

What other woman could have been standing on the sidewalk at the crack of dawn carrying a suitcase and wearing his father's face? He felt the warmth of her eyes touch the corners of his—stinging without pain—and he saw by her tears that she knew he was her brother. And then he was inside the van with the medic busy above him.

Sharon banged on the back door and it opened for her. She was carrying a small duffle bag. The female EMT was busy trying to get an IV started. Sharon took his free hand and he squeezed it. "Eli?" she asked. "What do you think it is?"

The female EMT answered for him. "Acute abdominal pain could be from an ulcer, obstruction, something else. Doesn't seem to be anything broken from his fall. We'll keep him stable and they'll figure it out at the hospital. Any history you know of?"

Sharon said, "Any *history*? I know everything about him."

"Does he have an ulcer?"

"No. I don't know." She looked at Eli. "Do you think you have an ulcer?"

Eli felt a lump at the back of his tongue and, petrified the persistent pain would intensify, instinctively tried to keep his body from moving. "I think something burst... during the night. Like a bullet."

He let the ride jounce him with the rhythm of the broken asphalt. They would take him to Coney Island Hospital. He knew that hospital. His head swirled. I'll be comfortable there. My doctor is there. What's his name? Sharon will know. His vulnerability became unbearable. He wanted to talk about seeing Liora. Too weak to move his mouth, he thought hard: They have to tell Liora. She'll get scared and won't want to go back to school. My father will have to calm her and bring her to visit me. Ludie could bring her on her bike. Daddy will leave Talmud Torah early and stay with me. The bar mitzvah boy will have to sing his lesson without him and Liora will have to call her family in Israel to tell them she'll be staying here.

~~~It is a warm April morning in my backyard.

Aunt Ruby pushes my swing high, higher, and I giggle louder than the taxi's horn. The strap holds my belly against the seat and my legs fly with and then against the sparkling air. Back and up and down and up. I'm so happy. The swing almost hits the sun on its way up, but Ruby always makes sure I come back down before my face touches the fire. It's Ruby's day to push my swing. She said Liora is going in the taxi. Liora will have her turn to push tomorrow.

"Liora had to go far away," Ruby says as we go into the house for lunch. "She won't be back tomorrow." Then Ruby pushes my sweaty hair back off my face, kisses my hot cheek, harder than I like, and promises me a cool bath. "Don't think about Liora anymore. She's bye-bye. Can you say 'bye-bye'?"

I'm three. Why does she think I'm a baby? Doesn't she know I can already spell *bye-bye*? Liora knows.

Roused by the gurney dropping from the back of the ambulance, confused and thirsty, Eli struggled to move his head to peer down at the gray sidewalk. There was no differentiating the snow from the concrete. Dawn was over. "What are they doing with me?" He licked his lips wondering if anyone knew he had to have something to drink very soon.

"You're at the hospital. You'll be fine," Sharon said. "I'll take care of getting you admitted. You just relax." She ran alongside as the technicians rolled the gurney swiftly and roughly into the ER. Sharon asked them please to be careful.

Eli closed his eyes and let the commotion encircle him, as he moved under bright lights, the swerving of a corner wrenching his back, then stopped in a darker space. Then a curtain sliding open, a woman's hand on his arm.

"Eli Kaplan? Open your eyes for me please, sir. The doctor is coming and I have a few quick questions."

Eli opened his eyes, saw the young Hispanic nurse who reminded him of Lulu, and looked at the small space he was in, the walls so near his bed, the curtain closing him inside a box whose meager light reflected off the shiny apparatus hanging over him. He panicked. Who's with me? Who's going to watch me? "Where's Sharon?" He gasped for air. "I need water."

The nurse grabbed his arm and squeezed gently. "All right, Mr. Kaplan. Calm down. Your wife is in the admitting office."

"Not my wife." He took a shallow breath and pounded his fist in frustration and terror. "Klonopin. She has it. Please get her." He began to thrash his head.

A tall, white-coated youthful Asian woman came in from behind the curtain. "What's going on here?"

The nurse said calmly, "Hi, Doc. Mr. Kaplan seems to be having a panic attack. He asked for some Klonopin."

"Piggy-back Ativan and let me have a look." She took Eli's hand. "Okay, Mr. Kaplan? I'm Doctor Su."

He swallowed and nodded while his other hand was pulling the sheets from the side of the bed.

"Try to relax. You'll be fine in a minute. Are you able to tell me why you're here?" She looked at his face hard and directly, then lifted his shirt to expose his torso.

His heart and mind raced. He told himself to just talk; the panic attack would end. "Really bad, sudden pain. Here and here." He pointed to his abdomen and back. "Like I'd been shot. So bad I blacked out. That's all I can tell you." His breathing was already deeper and less strained.

"Just wanted to make sure you were clear-headed. Now just try to relax your stomach." The doctor took a second superficial peek and smiled. "No entry or exit wound. History of this pain before?"

He said something to her about his bum leg and foot. She acknowledged his report without much interest. The doctor had a gentle touch and an unremarkable manner that suggested to Eli he was in no mortal danger. She patted him on the belly, a friendly "okay, buddy" pat, rolled the flow valve on the IV drip, and told him he'd be more comfortable in a minute.

Dr. Su made some notes and spoke as she wrote. "We'll take some pictures, see what's going on. I'll need you to sign a surgical release, just in case." She winked at him.

He heard her tell the nurse to call the OR and make sure they had a room within the hour. Eli didn't care. He wanted whatever had torpedoed through him to be removed. The fluorescent light over the bed seemed to enlarge and grow uncomfortably bright and just as quickly clouded into clay. Eli noted he was floating in some Ativan/ Demerol medical miracle, thinking about swings and tapioca and Sharon's breasts. By the time his medications took effect, two male transporters appeared with a clipboard and smiles. The tall one said, "Goin' to radiology, my man. Gonna fly really smooth from departure to arrival." He pulled Eli's gurney from his cubicle, took a fresh blanket from below, and covered Eli neatly and tenderly from neck to toe. "Warm enough, sir?"

Immediately following an abdominal CT scan, Eli was rushed to surgery. When he awoke several hours later, Sharon was standing over him, holding a Bible with a large silver crucifix painted onto the leather cover. He saw the cross and thought he'd died and been misdirected to the wrong side of heaven.

When he parted his lips to speak, Sharon put her fingers on his mouth. "Don't try to talk. You had a tube in your throat. You had a small perforated ulcer. You're fine. Just nod if you're all right."

He didn't move. Eli didn't know if he was all right. He wanted to ask her questions. He wanted to reach for her and cry and tell her he was so sorry for the trouble. His throat hurt and he looked to her for help. She shook her head and his tears rolled into his mouth.

"You're in good hands here," she said. "I won't leave the hospital." She talked and they hugged and Eli spent the rest of the day in and out of sleep.

By seven that night the incision site was throbbing and he was not in the least bit anxious to have visitors, but he could speak now, however softly. Adam and Diane stayed near the door of Eli's hospital room until he gave Sharon the go-ahead to let them in.

Smiling shyly, Eli waved his cousins into the room. He lifted his face for Diane to kiss his cheek and squeezed Adam's hand when it was offered to him. After their expressions of sympathy and encouragement, Eli told them to sit. Before their backsides hit the chairs, he told them about his sister. "You know Liora is here. I saw her, and Sharon saw her. She was at my house."

"Yes. She called us from the airport," Adam said. "We didn't know she was coming." Adam looked at Diane sideways, and Eli suspected collusion between the couple and Liora.

"Where is she?" Eli asked, fearful of a number of possible replies.

"She took a room at a motel nearby, in Sheepshead Bay." Diane said, apparently sensing his fear. "She's been calling about you all day. She'd like to come here to see you." She winced, suggesting it was not something Eli would easily agree to.

"Can she still get here tonight?" He realized, as he hadn't before, in the moment of a paper-cut, that his father was actually dead. He was desperate to see her, as though Liora was the only other person on earth who truly knew David Kaplan.

253

"Are you sure you feel up to it?" Sharon asked. "It might be too much just yet."

"Eli," Adam said softly. "Wait until tomorrow. She'll stay for a few days, at least."

"She's come all this way. Honestly, I want to see her tonight." He didn't know why he had been taught to hate her, but now he wanted to be made the fool, and to learn that his father lied about Liora's character; he would see the love she held for him and feel for her without the anger that bored this perforation in his stomach. Thinking he was about to die had brought him close enough to his father's death to feel the last bite of cancer. "Please call her, ask her to come."

"Fine, Eli," Sharon said. "If that's what you want." She looked at Adam and Diane. "Can you go call Liora? I'd like to talk to Eli alone."

Adam and Diane left the room. Adam gave a friendly wink to Sharon and Eli saw Diane throw a dart at him with her eyes. Sharon sat on the bed close to Eli's chest and pressed her lips against his neck. "I love you," she said. Then she backed away a few inches, smiled, and stoked his forehead. "There's another matter that we need to talk about before they come back to the room. Especially before Liora comes."

"Tell me." His mind scrambled amidst a throbbing pain.

"This is hard, Eli."

Eli watched her straighten her back and acquire that social-worker look of import. He got scared. "Just spit it out." He thought it had to do with his surgery; he thought he had cancer.

"There's a lot you don't know about your father. Some of the disturbing things you read in his journal are true. It's hard to tell you. It'll be hard for you to hear. But I'm giving it to you straight." She paused and waited for Eli's reaction.

"You're not telling me I have cancer?" Eli looked at her sweet, but drawn, worried face. He felt a tentative ease.

"No, Eli. This is about your father. Are you paying attention to me?"

He nodded. "I am. As long as I don't have cancer."

"Eli. Your father" — she tightened her grip on his hand — "he does have another child."

"Yes, Liora."

"He has another son, Eli. An illegitimate child. And according to Adam, that man is here, in Brooklyn, and wants to see you. He was with your father when he died in China." She wiped the perspiration from her neck and gazed steadily at Eli. "His wife is en route from China as we speak, with your father's body, and they are going to rebury him on Monday, next to your mother."

His heart pounded harder and louder. Had he heard, Another son? With his father when he died? Coming here to rebury him? It was too much to absorb, impossible to separate the important facts from the incidental. Eli looked deep into Sharon's eyes. The abrupt explosion of acknowledgment hit him. Fragments of this other son rapidly assembled themselves in his head. He was furious and confused, hurt, and ready to cry. It was suddenly paramount to know when his father had this child. "Is he older than me?"

"No. He's about four years younger. He came after your mother died." Sharon's voice became softer. "We are hopeful his mother was a woman your father cared about. Adam didn't know about any of this, until this man, his other son, told him that your father and his mother —" She glared at him, flinching.

A woman he *hopefully cared* about? As opposed to what? His throat ached from the tube they'd removed. He could only whisper, "How do we know he's, who is he?" Eli's face was

255

burning. "Is that why Liora came?" His shoulders shook, and then his torso and legs trembled. "I don't have the strength for this."

Sharon smiled. "Of course you have the strength, and I don't think Liora knows a thing about him. You're not alone. I'm here, and Adam and Diane are still outside. We're all here to help you through this."

"Adam and Diane know him?"

"Adam met him in China, but they've just found out who he is."

"Adam met him in China?"

"Your brother is Seth Giacalone. The man who raised him was Italian."

"So this other man could be his father."

"He raised him, yes."

"Stop!"

"But from what Adam gathered, his mother was Jewish and he's Jewish and—"

"I said stop!" Eli blinked frantically against images rushing into his head: urine-soiled bed sheets, aborted outings, silences, interactions avoided. The hospital room was suddenly congested with Eli's first thirty years, with stacks of unread books on dusty shelves in his boyhood bedroom, with the cacophony of unheard prayers his father sang at unattended temple services. Every ignored day now shone like a gravestone against the neon sign that flashed: **RABBI**.

"Get out and leave me alone!" Eli threw a pillow to the floor and waved his unrestrained hand weakly above his head, then he collapsed into sobbing.

Sharon stood and waited. "Are you going to be all right by yourself?" she asked firmly. "I'll go, I'll keep everyone out so you can think, but I'll be right outside the door." She backed out of the room.

He thought to pull at his incision and bleed to death, never encounter this illegitimate person who stole his father from him. Liora would meet Seth and love Seth more. They would spit on Sharon, with her cross and her New Testament. All he had accomplished with her—getting outdoors again, resuming his education, seeing new doctors, becoming a loved man, a loving man—would be mocked, seen as ludicrous, when even his father chose to spend his last precious days with this other son. And now this Seth has brought his father back. Was Eli supposed to be grateful?

The room was silent except for the screaming in his brain. He pulled the blanket over his head and wept, falling lower and lower, until he heard, "Eli!" The voice boomed so powerfully it startled him. He lowered the blanket slowly. The eyes of this female intruder were Daddy's, but her curly sable hair and austere expression were unmistakably those of his mother Miriam, whose photographs had been displayed all over the house in Gramercy Park; from the rarely used dining room table covered with framed portraits to his dresser and the walls of the hallways.

"Eli," she said again with a more girlish tone, "that can't be good for you with that blanket on your face." Liora walked closer. "Look at me."

Eli was dumbstruck. Her elegant features dark and familiar, she was tall, thin but busty, and wore a voluminous multi-colored crocheted scarf that swept several times around her long and slender neck, underscoring the lovely point of her chin. Her beret was purple and the tendrils of sable and gray curls held around her face were tight.

Liora unwrapped her scarf and approached her brother's bedside with heavy feet. "How are you feeling? That Sharon woman out there said you didn't want visitors. I came from Israel to see you, and I'm going to have my visit."

257

Eli said her name, but nothing came out of his mouth. Sharon pushed her way past Liora and took Eli's hand. His heart jumped but he couldn't feel her touch. "She forced her way in," Sharon said. "Adam and Diane are right outside the door."

His big sister had finally come home. He started smiling. "Sharon, this is my sister, Liora. Liora, this is Sharon." He wiped the tears under his eyes, and motioned for the women to sit, the stinging stitch in his belly reminding him that he had been in surgery twelve hours ago; he composed himself, allowing the pain to force calm. "Liora." He looked up from his hand over his wound and faced her. "Why are you here?"

"Am I supposed to talk in front of your housekeeper? Who is she to you?" she asked, as though they were old neighbors whispering condescendingly on the front stoop.

"You can say anything in front of her." Eli glanced at Sharon, scanning her face for a gesture of partnership. When she smiled, he felt ready to hear Liora.

"Yes, yes. Fine, fine," Liora said. "I don't have all the time in the world so I'll just come out with it." She pulled down on her long skirt and used her ring finger to scratch under her beret. "I came to sit shiva with you. Some shiva this turned out to be." She jutted her jaw at his IV drip. "Well, it's not your fault. Shiva will have to be over. And I'm hoping, now that our father is gone, very gone, around the world gone, that we can make amends and fix whatever got broken between us?" She sounded, from the upturn of her tone, to be asking a question and folded her hands on her lap.

Eli looked at Sharon and wished hard she would understand, without his having to speak the words, that he needed her to leave them alone. She didn't move. He whispered to her, "I'd like to talk to her alone. Would you mind?"

Sharon stared at Eli for a moment or two, put a hand to his shoulder, and left without speaking. Liora pulled a chair closer to his bedside, sat and then showed Eli her palm, as if offering a piece of candy. "Your father. Thank *him*."

"Broken between us? Was there ever anything worth breaking?"

"You don't remember me," Liora said. Eli noticed a hint of disappointment in her voice.

The taxi's horn sounded in his head. "I remember you leaving." Liora looked struck, her shoulders pulling back.

"You know what he thought about me, your *father*?"

"He thought you were bad." Using the word "bad" in reference to this grown woman felt juvenile. "Were you?"

She spoke quickly, following through from one sentence to the next without a breath. "I was very bad. I was extremely mean to you. You were an absolute thorn in my eye." She leveled her eyes on his. "But I would have outgrown it." Her voice remained solid as she declared, "I could have loved you all these years, and he wouldn't allow me near you. I'm sorry, Eli. I'm sorry I punched you and hit you and wished you were dead."

Eli was moved by his sorrow for Liora. She was rude and loud and apparently self-righteous, and he was warmed knowing she had come all this way to be with him for shiva. "You wished I was dead?" He assumed she was exaggerating and he found her confession charming.

"I did. You were born and Mommy died. Not only was the love of my life taken from me, but also I was given the unimaginable duties of caring for a damaged infant." She put her hand to her heart. "I wanted you dead and Mommy alive." Her eyes were shiny with tears that must have known better than to fall down her cheeks. "I didn't have to leave you and Daddy forever."

Forever. Eli remembered his father saying that word about Liora's departure. "Why did you wait so many years to come back?"

Liora scowled. "I couldn't look at that man. I wouldn't give him the satisfaction of seeing me. He never even wanted to see my children. I have six healthy children, and now my Edo is without a leg. Blown off in the army. He's fine with one leg." With that she began to cry freely. "It's been ten years since that mutilation, and it has always made me think of how terrible I was to you. Eli, my baby brother." She laid her head on his blanket and cried softly against his body. "Adam told me how beautiful you are. I've missed you."

She was a middle-aged woman, and she looked to Eli like a young girl begging her grown brother for absolution. Unsure of what she had done, he nonetheless remembered the years of yearning for her, and of loneliness without her, without a friend, and he could find no words. He was sad, yet happy just to have her by his side now, and would say nothing that might scare her away. Liora might leave as quickly as she had appeared.

Sooner or later they would have to talk. There was first and foremost the matter of Seth, and the arrival of his father. And there were the tales David left behind in those awful notes. "What do you know about our father's life, my life, after you left New York?"

"Nothing," she said and blew her nose. "I heard over the years" — she waved her hand with the fisted-tissue — "through various grapevines, visitors from New York, that you were not doing well. Vague references to your complete disability. Your father wrote to me every year at Rosh Hashanah, and never mentioned you. To be honest, until I spoke to Sharon last week I was under the impression you were barely able to think."

Shaken by the image she had held of him, he reminded himself that he was a grown man, with a girlfriend, with an education. He said, "I don't know how to feel toward you, but right now I'm happy you're here." He took one of Liora's curls and pushed it away from her face. "You're beautiful too, like our mother."

He wanted to explain to her that it wasn't his fault their mother had died giving birth, that she was diabetic and obese and was warned of her risk factors. Sharon had taken great pains to convince Eli of these facts over the course of several years. He nearly began reciting these facts to Liora, thinking, I almost died today. I can say whatever I want. "Liora?"

"Yes, Eli?"

He closed his eyes and started over, concentrating fully on keeping his eyes closed until all his words got out. "Liora. Try not to interrupt me until I get this all out." She agreed. "Our father is being flown home from China. There's to be another funeral Monday on Long Island." He heard her gasp What! but kept talking as loud as he could manage. "Seth Giacalone, the rabbi in China who was with him—his wife is flying him back." He opened his eyes and waited to see if she knew who Seth really was. He needed a shot for the pain in his abdomen, but he would wait.

"That miserable self-centered rabbi and his snippy wife. They are actually letting him go? Who does that man think he is! *I* won't go. *You* can't possibly go. Well, let them dig him up and rebury the bastard and have their own service." She brushed her hands together to shoo away the dust of it.

Eli was shocked. "He's our father! I love him. I am going to the cemetery no matter what you think. I don't care who's brought him back!" Until just now, he didn't know he was so determined. He put his hand lightly over his wound and held his breath against the stabbing pain.

"I'm a nurse, Eli. I can tell you right now, you are not going."

He had a drain from the wound and an IV in his arm. It was already Saturday night. "Fuck! Why did this have to happen now? There's no way. There's no way I can walk out of here by Monday." He gasped. "Adam's got brains. He'll know what I should do."

"Funny, I remember him as a whiny little spit of a kid." She pretended to spit into each of her hands. "I have never trusted him. He knows about this?"

"I suppose so. Did you see him?"

"He's right outside the room. Boy, did he age." She shouted toward the door, "Adam!" She then quickly whispered to Eli, "He's irresponsible as his father. Remember Seymour?"

Adam entered the room, along with Diane and Sharon. Sharon looked beat. She walked to the foot of the bed, tucked in the corners of the blanket and said, "I don't think everyone can stay here in the room. They've made concessions for you, Liora, because of your long trip, but visiting hours are over."

Liora looked at Sharon. "So leave!"

Adam stepped in and suggested that Sharon and Diane wait in the lounge until the nurse forced him and Liora to go, at which time Sharon and Diane could run in and say goodnight. Everyone cooperated. When Sharon leaned over to kiss Eli, he warned her with his eyes to stop; it was too soon and inappropriate in front of the family. He whispered to her, "Try to talk to Diane. She means well."

Eli stared at his sister for a few seconds, wishing to God he didn't have to ruin their reunion. "Liora. I appreciate how far you've traveled to be here." He was sure she had no idea of Seth's claims and he wanted to be the one to tell her. With Adam and Liora sitting erect as sentries on either side of the bed, his pain quieted; he placed his hand on Liora's on his blanket, and

262

spoke as plainly as he could. "Please listen carefully and prepare yourself for another shock." Eli tried fitfully to string together a series of words to tell Liora about Seth. He concentrated hard to keep the hand holding Liora's from shaking. "There was an illegitimate boy." The words became the world. "Our father had a child with another woman, and he's Seth."

Liora stood, pushed the chair back with her leg, turned to Adam, then back to Eli. Words flew past her lips so rapidly it was as if she had a life-threatening leak. "Your father was a son of a bitch! I should have guessed it then. I saw him looking dead when he woke up hung over. I was the one who got the frantic calls from the shul asking where the hell he was. Hypocrite, womanizer, praying with the torah in hand!" She pointed to Eli. "And God forbid I might ever have told on him to you! That's the real reason he sent me away. *His* shame!"

Eli was frightened by her sheer volume. "You knew he was seeing a woman?"

"I'm not the only one who knew. Ask the Shabbas goy!" She looked at Adam, squaring her shoulders.

Eli didn't even know who or what the Shabbas goy was.

Adam took a deep, slow breath. "It's not as though David was nothing more than a bad father to you. He was also protecting Eli. Liora, you can't give Eli the impression that you were not, at least to some degree, partly to blame for being sent away."

Eli wanted to stop Adam from antagonizing her, but he couldn't speak.

Liora's face grew long as she seemed to get taller. "And there was no other way to protect Eli from his terrorizing sister than to ship me off to Israel?" She was spitting at Adam with the force of her words. "Where were you when I needed help? You were always lurking around, spying on me, and pushing your way into my privacy. But when I couldn't take it any more, did you lift your little lazy finger to help! Did you respond to my letter? No, no, and again no!"

Adam said, "Liora, not now." He walked to the foot of the bed.

Eli looked at Adam, trying to figure out how old his cousin was when Liora was sent away. What could he have done? Adam was eleven or twelve—he shouldn't have been expected to care for him. Eli was embarrassed enough that his sister had been asked to; it was humiliating. "You can't involve him in our family turmoil," Eli said to Liora. He had wanted to use the word "destruction" but if he failed at the "s" he would sound like a child.

Liora looked disbelievingly at Adam. "You were a stupid kid," she said. "You always failed our family. You failed us again in Shanghai. And you don't tell me when to speak."

Adam backed away from her. "Hey, calm down."

"Liora, please leave him alone. What do you want from him?" Eli asked. "This was between our father and us."

Liora opened her mouth and looked at Adam astonished. "Adam, you bastard. You saw me. Go ahead, tell Eli how you just stood there and watched me hit him!" She waved her wand of a finger at Adam.

Adam's face flushed with guilt. Eli felt the hollowness of his childhood spread like mercury through his chest.

"It's not what you think, Eli," Adam said.

Eli's body froze. He saw the nurse and security guard enter the room. The guard pointed individually to Adam and Liora, saying, "You and you. Out!" and walked closely behind the two, escorting them out of the room.

To their departing backs, Eli growled out as forcefully as his surgical pain allowed. "Liora, get back on a plane to Israel and take your chances against the Palestinians." And to Adam, "Just get out of my life."

The guard stood sentry until the elevator doors closed and sent all four of them descending. Outside the hospital's main entrance door, Adam watched as Sharon and Diane hugged goodnight, mystified by their show of affection but too furious with Liora to speak. Coatless, Sharon waved to Adam and rushed back into the hospital. Liora fished inside her purse, pulled out a fistful of bills, and muttered to no one that she would hail a taxi and go to her motel.

Adam grabbed her arm.

"Let go of me," she said.

"What the hell were you talking about in his room? What Shabbas goy? At the old shul?"

A cabbie pulled up for Liora and gave her two small toots of his horn. She yanked her arm back from Adam. "His name was Mike Devlin. You find him for me. If he's still alive he'll tell you why the great cantor was a sham." She tightened the scarf around her neck. "And now that I've seen my brother, I guarantee you, my father had more defects than Eli." She turned to Diane. "Take care of yourself." She dropped her body into the taxi.

THE DEVIL AND MRS. GIACALONE

Adam and Diane came home to find a completely dark house. Switching on the hallway light, Adam saw Jamie asleep on the living room couch, folded into the fetal position, his jacket on and buttoned, and his packed bag on the floor beside him. Adam sat next to him and shook his shoulder gently. "Hey, Boy. Where are you going?"

"Hey." Jamie sighed, and shot up, squinting. "Shit! What time is it?"

"About nine…at night."

"Oh. I'm catching a red-eye to Denver. Midnight."

"Why?" Adam was disappointed. He thought they'd have a few more days to talk.

"Timing. It's time to go home."

Diane was standing out of Boy's view over his head. "I think it's a good idea," she said, walked past Jamie and sat next to Adam. "You need your work and friends." She leaned forward and reached over Adam to rub Jamie's knee. "Just tell me you're not depressed."

Jamie smiled. "No. I'm not depressed. Anyway, I have a shrink and she's there for me." He yawned.

"You're in therapy?" Adam tensed with worry.

"She? A woman therapist?" Diane asked.

"Yup. I really do want to get back for my session on Monday night." He blushed. "She's nuts for me and she understands my problems with Mark."

266

Adam saw Diane entwine her fingers, trying to crack her knuckles. "What!" He said to her. "What is wrong now? Are you jealous of" — he looked at Jamie — "what's her name, Jamie?"

"Margaret," he said and smiled again at Diane. "No, I do not think she's my mother, so chill."

"Oh, please. I'm fine. You came home to me. Your mother." She leaned toward him over Adam's lap and kissed his cheek. "What's she like?"

"A fifty-year-old lesbian. Very stylish. Very cool."

"As long as you have someone you trust," she said.

"As long as you have someone you trust and you don't call her *Mom*," Adam said into Jamie's ear.

Diane let herself chuckle. "Don't be so afraid, Jamie. If you really do know who you are and what you want, you have to take some chances." She tapped her knuckles three times on the wooden lamp table. "You'll be reasonably careful, of course. You're street-smart. You have good judgment. I've opened my eyes to some things and I don't think it's good just being safe." She gazed into Jamie's eyes, watery in his post-nap state. "But you'll be very careful."

"Oh, that wasn't a mixed message," Adam said.

"I just mean that when someone is so afraid, or someone's primary caregiver is so afraid, it has the perpetual opportunity of undermining a life."

"Don't worry," Jamie said.

Adam, though annoyed as usual with her *perpetual* affect, was impressed with Diane's enlightenment. He wondered what she and Sharon had discussed in the hospital as he was participating in the crossfire of his cousins' reunion.

"So?" Jamie asked. "You saw Eli? How is he?"

"Surgery went well. Liora showed up. It's a mess." Adam's chest tightened, struggling in the mix of humility and frustration from his forced hospital exit. He told Jamie about the scene that had taken place in the hospital room after Liora basically accused him of being an accomplice to her assaults on Eli. Adam said he felt both trapped by her ambush, showing up like a shot out of hell, and responsible for her lifelong separation. "I was embarrassed for Liora and Eli." He wanted her reunited with her brother. "Never mind that I feel like a shit." And he felt all the more dejected because Jamie was leaving tonight.

"Rella didn't tell me her mother was coming. Weird. Anyway, sucks for all of you."

Diane rolled her eyes at Adam, squeezed his arm and said, "Yes. It sucks for everyone."

At ten they drove to the airport. The sky over New York was calm; clouds settled in place for the night, with space enough between the pillows to see a few stars. Air travel would be smooth.

Everyone in the car sighed.

Diane waited in the Volvo outside the terminal, tearful, while Adam walked their son through check-in, then kissed Jamie good-bye at the security line. He stayed to watch his son's shoulders sway under his black lambskin jacket, his long thin legs in an athletic stride as he strode down the ramp and out of sight. Adam wanted to shout into the crowd, He's my son! Isn't he the most beautiful man you've ever seen?

The Shabbos goy: Adam had a picture of him. Mike Devlin: bone-slim and six feet tall, middle-aged, with a clean-shaven, weatherworn face and wide lips that never smiled, his gray workman's uniform decorated with soot and grease, skulking around the hallways like a ghoul. Adam and his friends called him The Devil. There was a room in the basement where Adam believed the man slept from Friday night to Saturday night, turning the lights on and off, managing air-conditioning, heat, locks, and toilets—all the work-related necessities not permitted for Jews on the Sabbath.

Adam paced around his house until Liora called at midnight, out of *courtesy* she said, to tell Adam she was leaving the next morning for home; it was for the best. "The horror of the past thirty-something years, my suffering, and Eli's life, trapped with my selfish father, was not my fault!" She declared with conclusive vehemence. She said Eli's childhood was worthy of his pity and insisted, "You look up this Devlin person. I want you to know exactly whom to blame for our estrangement."

"But Devlin could be dead," Adam said. "He would be in his eighties. Why don't you just tell me what you want me to know about your father?"

"Who would believe me if I start disparaging my father? You?" She paused. "It was so long ago. *I* couldn't even swear to my recollections. I pray to God Devlin's alive and can bear witness to...to the soot my father lived in."

Someplace in her silences and verbal postures Adam heard the be-a-big-girl efforts of a brave lost child. Reconciliation between Liora and Eli was unlikely, but through her anger, Adam realized she was right about one thing: he was an accomplice. Now, more than forgiveness, he wanted Eli to have the confidence to match Liora's passion in blaming Adam.

"You need to stay in New York and work this out. Please. Don't leave yet." He promised her he would try to find Mike Devlin, but he couldn't call the old synagogue until Monday. "At least put your trip off until Tuesday."

Liora agreed a little too easily, and Adam suspected she had been bluffing about her speedy departure. "But Tuesday's it, Adam. And it's because of this Seth Giacaloni claim."

BETH SCHORR JAFFE

"*Giacalone.*" He again needlessly clarified the man's name, humoring her.

"Whatever! You think I'm letting that one go? My father was a drunk and a whore, but he wasn't *stu*pid!" She was crying. "My brother, Eli, is so naïve. We *will* order Seth to take a test!"

"A test sounds fair. But your father was not a whore, Liora. One illegitimate child does not a whore make." He liked his new philosophical catch phrase.

"Illegitimate child or not, I cramped the man's style."

Liora sounded like a jealous girlfriend. Even though she had tried to harm her brother, he thought she had every right to feel cheated. If the charge of David's womanizing were at all true, Adam had seen no clue of it when he lived at home with his uncle. Had he been as spoiled and oblivious a kid as Liora claimed?

Adam spent most of Saturday night and into Sunday morning holding Diane's hair off her face and putting cool washcloths on her neck as she retched over the toilet. He was sure she caught a virus when they traveled in the rain to see Seth.

"Stomach viruses don't last this long," Diane said from the bathroom floor.

"A virus could linger, Doctor Oppenheim. Try to fall asleep." He laid a folded towel on the tile floor for her head and threw his terry bathrobe over her legs. She started to doze around five a.m. and he crept into bed.

Adam woke at eight to the sound of a metal object falling onto a tile floor. When he jumped up and ran into the kitchen to investigate, he found Diane on a stepladder, every can from the cabinets on the countertops. She was trying to read the side of a box of Passover Matzos. She turned to him saying, "I think this is from nineteen-ninety-six."

270

"If it's sealed it should be good. Not for Passover, but to eat."

"It's pure carbs. I'm tossing it." The box crashed to the floor next to a garbage bag that was already overflowing with half-used boxes of pasta and rice. "I've let the kitchen go to hell. I'm gonna clean all day."

"So you feel better?"

"I woke up at six and ate an egg. I feel fine."

"Good." He was amazed that she recuperated so quickly. "So I'll call the shul tomorrow and see if they still have Devlin's home number."

"Call them today. Call them right now!"

"On Sunday?"

"The office will be open, Adam. Torah for Tots or something must be going on. The Men's Club? Call." She put some cans into the sink and ran warm water over them.

Adam left the kitchen and dressed, called information for the number of the shul, then sat by the phone and pushed buttons but didn't lift the receiver. It was nearly nine o'clock. He took the phone number and walked back to the kitchen, finding Diane at the table, sorting through plastic utensils, separating the knives, forks, and spoons.

Trying to sound relaxed, Adam said, "If you feel well enough to be left alone, I'm going to take a ride to the old shul in Gramercy. I'll be back by noon."

Diane bit the inside of her cheek and pointed a plastic spoon at him. "You don't want to just call first?"

"No. I'll just go there." Adam was sure he would walk into the basement and find The Devil right where he had left him twenty-five years ago, primed to catch Adam and his friends drinking wine in the cantor's study. If he called, it would give that sinister man a heads-up. "You're all right to be alone?"

271

Sunday morning and the Long Island Expressway was empty. Driving like a wrongly accused man—one step ahead of the FBI—Adam flew through the Midtown Tunnel and worked his way downtown to Twentieth Street in less than half an hour. Parking alongside the temple he saw the old brown-brick building now had a blue and white canopy over the entrance, and a huge signboard with white-lettered announcements and schedules. Next Sunday night: Anna Quindlen Speaks, Benefactors' seats sold-out/ General Admission tickets still available.

Adam drifted into the tumult of mothers and fathers as they threaded through a side door with toddlers who were skipping and laughing or tugging and crying, depending, Adam guessed, on their attitude toward Torah for Tots. Every adult looked very young. So many years had passed; Mike Devlin could not be inside. Adam experienced a pronounced certainty that the man was dead.

The hallway was dark. Adam found his way to the old office, occupying the same old space. The heavy oak door was closed, so he knocked. When no one answered, Adam turned the knob and the door swung open, revealing a fully lit room with three desks in a row and new file cabinets, their manufacturers care-tags still attacked. The first nearest desk was clean, supporting a computer with a Western Wall screensaver, a telephone, and a pile of outgoing mail in a box. The second desk was messier with a child's box-drink dripping from the straw, and the third desk looked like a storage shelf. File drawers along the wall were pulled open and full, appearing no more organized than the desks. Adam scanned the drawer fronts with his eyes looking for a label hinting of employee records. In the corner was a metal vertical file; the drawers said: *W-2's, Insurance Claims, Contracts.* This had to be for personnel.

"May I help you?"

Adam jumped. A woman the size of an eight-year-old stood at the front desk, with white hair pulled into a bun, her square vintage gray suit hanging from her shoulders. Adam said, "Hi there. I'm Adam Oppenheim. I used to be a member. My uncle was Cantor Kaplan?" He felt his charm oozing from him.

Her face stayed cool; it did not express any love lost. "Hmm. I heard he died recently. In China." She rolled her eyes.

"Yes. He was very sick."

"I know. I'm the office administrator. I did his health insurance and Medicare forms for years. You need more forms?" Her tiny shoulders dropped, imposed upon.

"No. I need the phone number of his friend, Michael Devlin, if he's still alive. He worked here for years." Adam smiled with clamped lips, forbidding himself from using the expression Shabbas Goy. All charm drained, he could feel the iridescent-cherry color of a thief shining from his face.

"Uh huh." The woman looked Adam up and down as though she were the Gestapo. "I don't know where he is," she said, shrugging as if Devlin was insignificant. "If you want you're welcome to dig around for his old file in there." She pointed to the W-2 drawer. "I got a card from his wife a year ago telling me his pension fund got straightened out, so I know he was kickin' until then." She turned to leave the room. "You've got until noon. I lock-up right after the last Sunday schooler is out the door, at twelve-o-five and not a second later." The door slammed behind her.

Adam sifted through the voluminous records of employees, insurance claims, contracts, and finally found a scant amount of paperwork on Michael Q. Devlin. An old union contract listed a Staten Island phone number and address. Adam went into the lot behind the shul, where he could get cell phone reception, to dial the number. Kicking some cigarette butts around in the dirt, and unearthing a used condom, he waited for someone to pick up the other end of the phone.

The youthful voice that said "Speak" could not have been Devlin's wife. Adam said, "Hello. I'm looking for a Michael Q. Devlin. Is he in?" He walked to a cleaner spot.

"What are you selling?" she asked.

"I'm not selling anything. Is this still his home?"

"No. He moved. What do you want with him?"

Knowing he was asking to get disconnected, Adam went ahead and asked, "Who are you?"

"Who are *you*? You called here! I'm hangin' up."

"Wait! I'm a lawyer. I represent a friend of Mr. Devlin, Cantor David Kaplan. I'm also Mr. Kaplan's nephew and a former congregant from the shul. You see, he died and Michael's in the will. I need to find him." He didn't know where that came from but he liked it. Sneakiness had found a clean room in his character.

The woman instantly warmed and told Adam she was Mike's daughter. Softer, she asked, "You weren't one of those boys who called my father 'Devil' are you?"

"Oh, goodness, no. I never heard that one."

Too savvy to accede to Adam's request for Devlin's home address or phone number, she said, "You can have his email. But that's it."

"He has an email address?"

Adam heard her drag on a cigarette. "He's got a computer like other Americans." She giggled. "Did he leave my father money or just the key to his liquor cabinet?"

"I'm not at liberty to say." He asked for the email address and hung up without giving his name, insuring that a return call was impossible; he was un-star-sixty-nine-able.

274

Adam flew into his house, grabbed Diane from under the bathroom sink where she was emptying the cabinet, directed her to the computer, and dictated his email as she typed.

To:MQDEV@southjerzy.com
From:TheOpps@nervisenergi.com
Subject: David Kaplan
Dear Mr. Devlin,

My name is Adam Oppenheim. I trust this message finds you well. Unfortunately, my uncle, David Kaplan has just recently died. I thought you would like to know as I am told he was your friend. I apologize for lying to your daughter and telling her I am an attorney for his estate, but it is imperative that we speak. Please respond as soon as possible with an address or phone number. Thank you.

Devlin's reply at one in the morning consisted of only an address in New Jersey. Adam took the liberty to assume that meant he was invited to visit. He immediately notified Liora, risking waking her and releasing the wild animal within, and she demanded Adam and Diane boycott the funeral Seth had arranged and later go to the cemetery with her and Eli. Otherwise, she would leave immediately. Adam promised Liora he would wait until they could all go together; his dedication to resolving his conflict with Eli was his only true motivation. Once Liora was satisfied with the deal, she told him when and where to pick her up in the morning.

Monday morning at nine o'clock, while Adam was putting on his socks from the edge of his bed, Elana called him from the cemetery. Her words flowed in an even toned assault. "How *dare* you not come after Rabbi Giacalone has gone to this extreme?" By eight-thirty that morning, David's

275

body had apparently arrived at his gravesite to be greeted by Seth, Elana, and a minyan of strangers. "How dare you ignore the mitzvah my husband accomplished?"

Adam just let her keep talking.

"Poor Eli is sick and you insult David's memory further...letting his first son be unrepresented by you, at the grave! I'm exhausted by your shenanigans. We try to bring the family together and you spit in our faces."

"Elana, I'm sorry you're hurt, but Eli is in shock! This isn't about spitting in your faces."

"I understand that, Adam" — she lowered her voice — "I understand about resentment and anger, of course. But this is about memorializing David before God."

Did he owe anything to David? A ferocious sense of betrayal racked his cardiac system before he said, "I have someplace urgent I have to go today. Please call me later. Please. We'll talk it out."

After a long pause she said, "That might be helpful, an opportunity for the rabbi to express himself." Elana sneezed and cleared her throat. "I have a heart, you know. I feel badly that you resent my husband. But you have to rise to the occasion." She sneezed again. "I will get the rabbi's okay, but you should invite him over and apologize personally."

Adam looked around his room as if to check for incriminating evidence they might find if they came to his house. "Please come! Absolutely! Call me back only if you *can't* come." Under even the worst circumstance, he was excited at the thought of seeing her. "I want you and Seth to come. Diane and I want you to come." He felt short of breath. "Give me a time to expect you." At the very least, he owed them an invitation to break bread in his home.

"Six o'clock."

He started calculating the timing of his round trip. "That's perfect."

She took his address and hung up.

Diane had been listening in the doorway and scrunched her face, dramatizing her confusion. Adam left his hand on the phone a few seconds and then said, "That was Elana Giacalone. They may be coming for dinner at six."

"Oh Jesus, they're pissed at us, aren't they, for not showing up for his funeral party."

"They sure are," Adam said seriously. "She thinks this is all about Seth and David's honor."

"So, you invited them here to explain to a rabbi and his wife about humanity?"

"No! She said I should apologize to Seth personally for not showing up. Look, I've got to get dressed and get to Liora. You'll have time to get to the deli? Kosher with a capital K?" He didn't wait to hear her answer. The thought of Liora waiting for him was more frightening than the prospect of disappointing Elana with inedible food.

Liora was staying at the Marina Motel in Sheepshead Bay, Brooklyn. Adam was on the road to retrieve her by nine-thirty. His collection of rubber-banded notes sat on the back floor of his car. Maybe Devlin's memories, the ones Liora was sure he'd have, would acquit Liora. Whether paroled or not, he wanted her to feel welcome to come home.

She was standing under the motel's short canopy as Adam pulled up, her head topped by the purple beret, her neck wrapped with the colorful scarf. With the lavender coat hanging long below her knees and her black boots high, she looked religious and she looked striking.

She shuddered with cold before slamming the car door closed and turning to face Adam. "I want to get home in time to visit Eli."

Adam tried to be reassuring. He told Liora that the exact address Devlin emailed to him had been entered into his navigation system and should lead them right to the man's condo in Tom's River, New Jersey. The trip should take about two hours. Adam knew they would have to talk about something and wondered which distasteful subject would come up first.

Seconds after starting on their way, "Havah Nagilah" started to play from her handbag between her feet, and Liora scrambled, her hand emerging with her cell phone. Happy chattering in Hebrew ensued, and Adam was left relatively anxiety-free while she talked for ten minutes. Slapping the phone's lid closed, Liora looked at Adam. "My youngest daughter, Ariella. She sends her regards."

"She called you from Israel?"

"Cell phones and phone cards. We talk everyday. Every-single-day." She held the small phone between her large folded hands in her lap.

"Really nice." Did she know that Ariella and Jamie spoke regularly? "Everything is well?"

"Wonderful. She is seven months pregnant with her first child."

Jamie had mentioned that.

"So, your son, Jamie, he's married by now?"

He thought she redirected the conversation rather quickly. His heart dove into darkness and he questioned her prior knowledge of Jamie. "Jamie is only twenty-four. And he's gay." He waited.

Matter-of-factly, she said, "My son, Edo, with the one leg, he's gay too." She drew a deep breath, glared, and nodded deeply at Adam, as if her son's orientation was somehow, genetically, Adam's doing. "Is that why you sent him to live in Colorado?"

"I didn't *send* him. He left on his own." He was injured but not surprised by her reservations of him as a father. Did she think he was unloving like David?

"But you didn't stop him. You didn't keep him near you." Liora hummphed. "Real shame you aren't closer. And just one son."

There was only one way to end this discussion, and that was to bring up an even more distasteful topic. "I have a sincere apology to make to you," Adam said, steeling himself for her sarcastic retort. But she said nothing and stared through the windshield. He said, "The letter you mentioned at the hospital, the one you sent to me when I was twelve and you left New York, well, I just read it for the first time a few nights ago. I'd never opened it. So, I didn't know you wanted my help." They were getting onto the Goethals Bridge that would bring them into New Jersey.

For a moment, Liora wept quietly, then she blew her nose. Adam apologized, repeatedly, and felt the urge to reach over and dry her face with his sleeve, but she was so still, so stiff inside her winter costume, that he left her alone and they drove, listening to an oldies station, until Adam felt he had to speak. "We have another hour to go. Tell me what it's been like for you in Israel." He hoped that wasn't pathetically insufficient.

She clapped her gloved hands, which made a dead thump of a sound, and grinned at him. "Oh. So we have an entire hour! Well, let's see. Which week of the last thirty-five years should I describe?"

Adam was ensnared by her sarcasm but he said quickly, "How about the first week."

"Do you hope to give me a gift of self-repair, or do you want me real strong so I can drag your sorry ass out of the mud?"

Adam saw Liora's eyes widen, smart alecky, and she seemed struck silent. He felt his conscience tearing. After a few painful moments he said, "Let's agree I've been a schmuck. A genuine prick." He gripped her arm gently. "Tell me from the beginning."

First she pulled her gloves off, washed her fingers across her face, and then began to speak as if she had walked off the plane yesterday, a teenage girl in Tel Aviv, alone and exiled. "The sun was so strong I could barely see the tarmac. The reflection blinded me." She covered her eyes with her hand. "Across the fence, my aunt Reba waved to me with a little blue and white flag. I was thinking, Is she supposed to be my mother? She kissed me and hugged me and I cringed under her touch." She turned to Adam and soured her mouth. "She smelled like stewed prunes. I cried and wanted to go home. I yelled in her face, I want to go home!"

The tollbooths onto the Garden State south were clear and Adam barely came to a stop to toss his thirty-five cents into the coin basket.

"Her house was a big white stucco box. I had to share a small room with her two little girls. Right away my cousins came to look at me, pull at my hair, to feed me and give me other clothes appropriate for the weather. I never felt such heat. I smothered in it."

Liora talked rapidly for the rest of the drive. Adam learned about her school and her first spark of interest in nursing, and how she met her husband who was an injured soldier in the hospital where she trained. He died last year of a heart attack. She sounded love-struck and heartbroken and Adam thought of Diane.

Liora was resting when the car's navigation system yelled at Adam and told him to turn around the first chance he could. He had missed the jug-handle to make a U-turn across the highway. He was humiliated, not humiliated in front of his cousin, but in front of the *navigation woman*. While he made his U-turn he said, "It's only a voice, you know. Why do I feel as though she's disappointed in me? Like the woman knows who I am."

"What on earth are you talking about? What woman knows who you are?"

Adam explained to her about the satellites and about this wireless system. "They know I can't follow directions."

"You must have a guilty conscience." She whispered to herself, "He is a shmuck." Mildly stung, except when Adam turned to respond he saw the dimple of her smile. They drove a few more miles, Adam following the computer woman's directions more carefully, until they came upon Devlin's townhouse, a single story white-shingled cottage connected on one side to an identical house. The neat grass was brown from the winter. Adam got out of the car, came around to Liora's side. She sat until he opened her door. He asked, "You coming with me?"

"Would I trust you to do this alone? Go ring the bell!"

Adam suggested she keep her volume reasonably soft. "They have security patrolling these places. You'll get us thrown out again." His sarcasm felt good, but he didn't want trouble. He wanted to find answers, some kind of exoneration for both of them, get this over with and get home to Seth and Elana. He had thrown David's notes into the car, thinking he and Liora would talk about them during their drive. "Wait one minute," he told Liora, then opened the back car door, and scooped David's lunacy from the floor.

FAIRYTALES DO COME TRUE

There he stood, the Shabbas Goy, staring blankly at Adam. Adam did not recognize the man; his face very wrinkled and red-veined, he was bald, and had either lost height or was not as tall as Adam remembered. Adam introduced himself and Liora. Mike Devlin smiled at the two visitors. He held himself straight and waved them in. Like the lawn, the living room had a benign and neat appearance, nothing too fussy or especially horrible. As Adam passed him walking into the house, he smelled the alcohol on his breath.

Mike told them his wife had recently passed away and it was good to have visitors. Condolences were extended.

Liora, frighteningly quiet, asked for something to drink. There was nothing bottled but club soda or scotch. Mike filled a tall glassful of scotch for himself while his guests sat on the sofa sipping tap water. Adam took it upon himself to remind Mike of Liora's birthright, to explain how David died and in whose company. The man responded by wiping his mouth and saying, "My sympathies. Death is always a sobering surprise." He lifted his glass, and took a sip.

Adam suspected someone else must have used that expression to Mike regarding his wife's death. Adam nodded his head, made his *it's so tragic* face, and spurred by the thought they might get into a conversation about losing a spouse, rushed into his motive for the visit. "David's son Eli is well and living on his own in Brooklyn, but we have some questions regarding

282

David's will. Would you happen to know anything about his relationship with another woman...someone who could have had another child of his?"

Mike gave them a long look, then began to laugh so hard he started to choke. Once he caught his breath, he pointed at Liora. "You want me to nail the girl who had your baby brother? What d'ya know about any of this?"

Adam leaned forward. "So you know then, for certain, that David had another child."

"But I ain't givin' the man's secrets away." He looked at Liora. "You seem kind of quiet and sweet. You must have had it tough, leaving your daddy"—he wagged his thumb toward Adam—"but how bad do you want this man to know what your father was doing?"

"I want everyone to know who he was and that I am his victim," Liora said.

Mike took a crumpled handkerchief from his pants pocket and wiped his nose. "Honey, lovely as you've grown up to be, you did try to hurt that little Eli. Your daddy was not very good at keeping secrets when we *socialized*." He shook his glass and took a sip of his drink. "Why do you need me to drag up all the old shit? Excuse my language."

Liora said, "To hell with your fucking language, sir. I need you to tell my cousin here what you know, that my *daddy* was a drunk and a womanizer. You think I was comatose all those years? I wasn't. Do you think Eli believes me about our father? He doesn't!"

He smiled broadly. "Mind your respect. He did plenty hard work for that synagogue. But your daddy did like the girlies, and this"—he held up the bottle of scotch—"and schnapps didn't help his situation much." Then he sat, closed his eyes, and nodded his head.

Adam finally cried out, "Mike!"

Mike smiled. "Just thinking about stuff."

"Yeah, that's really nice. Pleased with something you and David did?"

"Nothing in particular. We were close friends. I was his *confidant.*"

Adam felt the paper bundle heavy in his inside jacket pocket. "But listen to me. David left me and a few other people obscurely detailed notes about his life. Things he obviously wanted someone to know about. If we read some of David's notes to you, you think it would kind of stimulate your memory? You might share a few confidences?" Adam rubbed his fingers together to signify money.

Liora gasped. "What are you talking about? Notes? As in messages in a bottle?" Her warm breath fell on Adam's face, stoking up his anxiety.

"Excuse me, Mike," Adam said. "I have to take Liora out of the room." He stood and she allowed Adam to elbow her into the kitchen, where he told her calmly about his thievery in Shanghai of the scraps of paper David had left behind with Seth. "Eli has some too." He decided not to verbalize Seth's suggestion that her father's notes were probably written to her. "I'm begging you to follow my lead and let me fill you in later."

"Follow *your* lead?" Liora's voice was shaky. "You tell me this shit now?"

"I didn't know if I would have to use them here with Mike. I had brought them to discuss with you in the car. I'm sorry I held out on you." He saw her eyes water. He had cheated her again.

"You think you have one up on me? Well I have news for you, buddy, I already know whatever that drunk could possibly

tell you, so show him the damn shit-worthy scraps and" —
grabbing his sleeve, she pulled Adam close to her face — "get that
bastard to speak!"

Adam couldn't look in her eyes. "The notes spell out some
pretty unattractive sides to your father. I understand you know a
lot, but, all due respect for what facts you know, you didn't
know about Seth."

"And we have yet to see if that claim is fact or fairytale." She
turned and walked into the living room. Adam followed her.
They reoccupied their places on the sofa and Adam held out the
notes to Mike. "You think you can tell us if there's more to the
story than what's in these? At least fill in? They're in Hebrew.
It's somewhat open to misinterpretation."

Mike gave a one-shouldered shrug. "I don't know if that
would be right. Me and the cantor spent many, many hours
together talking about his life." He looked at the ceiling and
smiled. "He had an awfully powerful voice and he did write
some interesting poetry. I didn't always know what it was
about, but it sounded nice." He folded his hands across his
chest.

Adam knew what he was waiting for and pulled two
emergency hundred-dollar bills from his wallet, then set it next
to Mike's glass.

Mike slipped the bills into his shirt pocket and said, "Let's
hear what he says." He lifted the sweaty glass and waved his
free hand at Adam and his papers.

Adam held the packet of notes, carefully stretching and
removing the elastic band, opened to the page he'd marked with
the toothpick the night he quit reading, and handed the rest of
the bunch to Liora. "Do you want to read it? I stopped in the
middle because I don't think I'm translating accurately." He
hoped he was wrong about everything.

She turned her face close to Adam's and clenched her teeth, whispering directly at him. "What's in here? What am I going to hear about?"

Adam focused on Liora's eyes and tried to exert a force he did not feel he had. His entire face grew hard. "Another woman, the woman who might be Seth's mother, and maybe why he sent you away. You've got to listen to this. For everyone concerned, but especially for yourself."

"Give me a glass of scotch," she said.

After finding a glass in the kitchen, Devlin handed it to her and wiped his hands good and dry on his pants. As Devlin keenly watched, Adam unfolded three tightly squared-off sheets of yellow legal paper, two large white index cards, and finally a cream-colored sheet with a jagged edge that seemed to be the torn-out page of a bound book. "You'll stop me if it's too hard to hear," he said to Liora. Adam gulped his water and then began reading the text slowly in English.

The first yellow paper:

More than a year after Miriam's death, at three o'clock in the morning, it was difficult to convince myself, while standing on a street corner I have never before seen, that I am a righteous man, a thoughtful man. I believe it was then that I lost my faith in God. For how had I never learned contentment?

I had been walking since I left minyan. By now the bars on the Bowery knew my drink, they knew the kind of woman I wanted. She had to be anything that Miriam was not.

Liora choked back tears and poured more scotch. Adam's voice remained steady.

I first went with women after nine months of mourning. I met them at bars. I was in need of touch. I do not know to this

286

day the ages of the young women, but I allowed myself to follow them into the back rooms. I continued to meet women this way for several months. It pleased me to look into a woman's eyes, and I found it especially gratifying to be looking into their eyes on Shabbas. I had no fear of He who had abandoned me. And I had surely been abandoned.

The sheet was finished and Liora took the paper and stared at it. She trembled and shook her head at Adam. He held her hand, squeezed tight and she begged again, "Please, just read."

Mike waved his glass at her, "Don't stop now! We're gettin' to the nitty-gritty."

Adam was so intrigued he couldn't help but to read on.

One crisp and brilliant spring night I walked across the Brooklyn Bridge. At the other side the sun set over the Promenade, and the air chilled, but I felt peaceful and calm. Walking toward Fulton Street, inattentive to my surroundings, I was maliciously accosted by three hoodlums. They took my money, my gold watch, and my wedding band. They kicked my stomach and punched my face, ripped my shirt, and tore my tsetse. They left me on the sidewalk bleeding from my nose. I moved forward as if I knew where heaven laid its bed for me.

Liora lifted the page from Adam's hand, pulled it closer to her face and began to read aloud, her voice weak.

Feeling more deranged than the boys who had just attacked me, I scrambled down the nearest subway steps onto the IRT line and rode the train until I got to Nostrand Avenue in Flatbush. I knew the area as a boy and I felt a sense of safety. It was near nine o'clock, and the first face I can recall under the floodlights of the exit was June's.

BETH SCHORR JAFFE

Liora looked at Adam, as if to ask, you know about this?
Adam took her hand. He knew only that Seth's mother's name
was Jericho, but little else. He said, No, and squeezed her hand
to continue.

> June was of small stature with brilliant green eyes and a
> ruddy complexion; I would never have known she was a Jew.
> She was some years younger than me, but old enough,
> sweet-faced, not shy. She immediately appealed to me.
> She later told me that as soon as she saw my torn tsetse,
> she knew I was not a threat and that she could approach me.
> I explained what happened to me. She reached into her wallet
> and handed me a twenty-dollar bill and insisted I call a cab to
> take me home. I would pay her back, I told her. I would call her
> and pay her back. And this is how it began.
> It was several weeks before I had the courage to call her.
> She told me to mail her the check but I would not for fear that
> my payment could be traced and I would be caught in my
> night lies to my son about where I had gone. I would not send
> cash in the mail. I wanted to see her. She agreed to meet me
> at the same train station for the money.
> June took the twenty dollars from me but her fingers
> lingered in the palm of my hand. She led with her smile as we
> walked across Nostrand Avenue, through the quadrangle of
> Brooklyn College, past the students and their laughter. Her
> apartment was in the basement of a large red brick house on
> Twenty-fourth Street and I followed her into her lavender-
> scented and lilac-colored rooms.

"Adam," Liora asked in an almost childlike tone, "how much
filthier does this get?"

"Honestly, I didn't get this far. I was afraid of misreading it."
Adam turned so that Devlin couldn't see his lips. "It's meant to
be read by you, or by his children. He must have used some
discretion."

288

A cough came from Mike. He waved his hand in a gesture that suggested she should go on, as if he knew.

> June opened the oven door, switched on its interior light and it shone onto her bed that lay unmade in an alcove next to the kitchen.

Liora slapped her hand to the sofa and shoved the paper at Adam. "Do the best you can. I can't do this anymore."

Adam felt lousy for Liora, but he knew if he read it with his scrappy Hebrew, they would at best get scraps of truth. "You can skip it," he told her. "But I can't read this accurately." He rubbed her hand. "I'll be here for you now. I promise. But we have to know about Seth. For you, for Eli."

Liora pulled the paper back from Adam.

> Her white body was netted in freckles, as if her skin was trapped in woven points of velvet. Often times thereafter I would stare at her face and match the perfect sphere of bones shaping her cheeks and chin to the shape of her breasts, compact and warm as her breath. June guided my hands down the slight curve of her waist and put my fingers to rest on the knot of her navel. She had a small rounded mound there, as if once pregnant, long ago. I was in awe of her tenderness.

"Poetic. I told you," Mike said. Liora raised the third yellow sheet to her face briefly, then read while the paper sat loose on her lap.

> June was generous and joyful, quiet and easy, and God would not be gone those nights. I found Him within her. It was more than enough holiness for my life. She accepted no gifts, nor did she want to know anything about my family. She spoke little of her wishes. We were together exactly

eight times a month for the course of three months. Each
time we met, my desire to live strengthened, my
demoralization evaporated.

In admitting this affair, I trust that the inheritors of this
personal—albeit sentimental—journal of my conduct will try to
understand how captivating she was, and will travel willingly
with me into the glory that was her skin on my skin and the
excruciating pain of nothingness upon breach.

Adam was stunned but kept his mouth safely shut.

"So, is this supposed to be her, the mother?" Liora asked
Mike.

"I need to hear more. So far, it's still a blur."

Adam waved his finger in a friendly threat. "I'm not giving
you any more money. I don't have any more money."

"Quiet, you," Mike said to Adam. "Read on sweetheart."

Before she began, Liora pressed her lips together as if blotting
lipstick.

The affair ended the instant I confessed my love for her.
She said she was in love with a man she had long known. I
don't know why she bothered with me if she loved this other
man. They soon married, June and the Italian man named
Joseph.

Adam heard "Italian man named Joseph" and thought
Giacalone. He looked at Liora. They both looked to Mike. Mike
said, "I don't know no Joseph," as if responding to a criminal
interrogation.

"You think?" Liora whispered in Adam's ear.

"Keep going." Adam saw the terror on her face.

Often during the first year of her marriage I would walk
around her neighborhood and look for her. When I finally

crossed her path, six months later, I saw she had the belly of a woman in middle pregnancy. When she saw me she turned and ran away. It wrenched my gut to think she and Joseph had made so potent a physical union that she had conceived quickly. The birth of her child would throw her into the drowning pool of motherhood, a world that would leave no room for estranged bedfellows. I wished even then that this could have been a new brother or sister for you, Liora, and I wondered if it were.

Liora's voice had diminished to inaudibility as she heard the dead man say her name. Adam took the remaining index cards, which seemed to be scribbled with dates and times, and the cream-colored sheet from her lap, folded them into their little squares, and put them back in his pocket. "You don't have to go on, Liora. Enough is enough."

She caught her breath, grabbed the unread sheet from Adam's hand, and whispered its words back.

Though June's departure left me lonelier than ever before, her absence set so profound a course in me, she enlivened my again faithless life with the occupation of regret and contrition.

Liora sat breathing hard, until she belted out, "This is absurd! Why in God's name would my father try to describe these obscene behaviors to us? Why would he want us to know this about him? It can't be true." She looked at Adam.

Why would David detail such a story for his daughter? Poetic license is one thing, Adam thought, but this David didn't sound even remotely familiar. "It doesn't seem to make sense," Adam said. "He was too proud to leave this as a last impression." He wondered though, if this were at all true, why the hell didn't David proclaim the boy his and name him as Seth and June as Jericho? Seth had read this in Shanghai and presumably hadn't disputed it. Adam looked at Mike. "What do you know about June?"

Mike rubbed his face hard, rolled his neck around, and looked at Liora for several seconds without blinking. "Your father had a special talent for writing. It was like listening to a fairytale. Beautiful words, beautiful story, really."

"Yes," Adam said, "he was a talented, poetic man. So, do you know who June is?"

Mike covered his mouth to squelch a burp. "Forgive me—I said it was *like* listening to a fairytale. But it actually was a fairytale. There was no one named June in David's life. I would know."

A buzz of panic vibrated between Adam's ears. He prayed the man would be just drunk enough to talk more than he wanted to and give up names, correct David's fiction. "Are you sure?"

Mike laughed softly, winked at Liora, stood, and stomped his feet. "No doubt to me, this is the story he wants you to believe, because the real story is more"—he grimaced, appearing to be searching his mind as his head wobbled a little—"more nightmare than fairytale. This girl, your father's *girl*friend, the one who had a kid"—he tilted his head closer to Liora—"Jericho? Remember her, Liora? Cute little twig of a thing. Her father had linen stores all over. Sold sheets and tablecloths."

Liora sat mute. Adam asked Mike to excuse them one more time to talk privately for a moment in the kitchen. Liora rose and followed Adam. Devlin rumbled to the air about truth being the only way to live, did an impressive impersonation of Jack Nicholson saying, "You can't handle the truth!" laughed, and turned on the television.

"I knew that whole meshugganah Stein family," Liora told Adam. Adam watched her face light up as if she were awaking from amnesia. She did in fact remember more of the drama from the spring of her sixteenth year. Immediately after David caught her assaulting Eli, her father punished her by merely slapping her face. A few days later she was finishing up her clerical chores in the shul's office, and went looking for her father to take her home. He was with Devlin, both of them drunk, as usual, in the basement of the shul, but this time Liora found them conspiring in whispers. She stood at the doorway a long moment—trying and failing to figure out what they were saying. "I didn't overhear much, but I kind of remember hearing *she* this and *she* that. I thought they were talking about me." When her father saw her he jumped up, mad as hell that she was listening. Three days after her eavesdropping she was on a plane to Israel. She knew the whispering between Mike and her father happened after her father caught her slapping Eli's face, because she had to apply her aunt's cover-up foundation to her enflamed slapped cheek before leaving for the airport. Apparently, David thought she overheard something. Apparently it was something not very nice.

Adam asked, "You think that Mike and David were talking about Jericho, and that had to do with you leaving? They had to think you heard something terrible to bounce you out like that. You think that's what Devlin means?"

"I have no idea. My father was a drunk and a sleaze, but I thought he loved me." She put her face up to the sun through the small kitchen window, as if waiting for the answer from heaven. She suddenly perked up. She whispered assuredly, "I don't think Mike's a liar. Obviously, there is a discrepancy in the name of my father's whore. If Seth is the result of the affair, we should know who his mother is."

"Would that make a difference to you?"

"If he's going around as a rabbi, I'd like to be sure the woman was at least Jewish."

"Oh," Adam said, bothered by her ulterior motive: look to make Seth relinquish his Judaism, his identity.

She hooked Adam's arm and walked back into the living room. They found Mike watching *The Price Is Right* and shouting "Yes!"

Adam sang out, "We're back!"

For Liora's sake, Adam said delicately, "Can we hear your version of David's romance? We have to get home soon." He would have waited as long as it took, but he thought he'd light a fire under the guy before he changed his mind about talking.

Liora told him she remembered a drunken basement conversation. "I have no recollection of what was said, if I ever actually heard anything to begin with."

"*I* was *not* drunk and never am," Devlin scolded her. "David? He was cockeyed. He was scared. Scared for you and Eli."

"*My* father was scared? What on earth could scare him?"

"If he wanted you to know that, sweetheart, he would have told you." Mike lit a cigarette and offered the opened Camel's soft-pack to his guests. Adam shook his head but Liora took one. He turned to Adam. "I do have a poker game at one. You think you'll be on your way soon?"

Adam planted himself on a chair closer to the television. He folded his hands in his lap, looked up into Mike's face and said, "Mike, my man. You have been a tremendous help today. But this woman here"—he lifted his hand toward Liora—"she has lived a rough life. Israel is no playground you know. Lots of wars."

"It is a beautiful country," Liora said.

Adam threw her a look of impatience. "Please, Mike. Your friend is dead. His widowed daughter has six children, one of whom is pregnant, and several grandchildren waiting for her to come home to them. Eli's heart is broken over the prospect of an illegitimate brother. We're not leaving without the rest of the story." He looked at his watch. "You say your game is at one? I hope you don't have to travel very far." What he really hoped was that Mike remembered the two hundred dollars.

Mike simmered for a few seconds, but then broke his face open with what looked like more revelry than reluctance. "Jericho Stein," he said, "known to her friends as Jeri, was a sixteen-year-old daughter of a congregant." Mike scratched his neck and stretched his jaw. "Jeri sang with the temple's women's choir. She was a sweet girl, but confused and loved this Giacalone kid. Giacalone? Yeah, Giacalone. An Italian boy in Brooklyn."

Adam went electric at the name. Liora hugged her gut.

"Her father found out about it and he threatened Jeri that unless she stopped seeing the Italian kid, he was going to send her to live with some religious aunt in Toronto."

Adam glanced at Liora to gauge whether or not her expression mirrored his horror: Jeri was a teenager. David. Oh Jesus. Liora's face was white and damp and Adam knew exactly what she was thinking.

"Jeri was fond of the cantor. He, you know, directed the choir and she decided to trust him with her troubles. Ask for his advice. After all, her father was an arrogant pig. She came to the cantor and told him she would rather die than move to Canada and live with her aunt."

David and Jeri met in his office after school, Devlin went on, two or three times a week for several weeks, and soon met in places other than the synagogue office. "It's not that your father kissed and told, but after the mess, he told me stuff."

"What stuff?" Adam asked spontaneously.

Devlin told them. Stuff like, they met in his car and parked on dark streets. They drove to motels in other boroughs, and they met in the attic of her father's house. Devlin nearly smiled at the memories. "Hate to tell you so bluntly, Liora," Mike said, "but how do you say it? Your father was schtuppin' her for months."

Liora's face changed from white to red and held perfectly still. Adam knew if she gave in and moved a muscle she would lose her grip on her dignity and fall apart. Adam rolled his free hand in a forward motion and said to Mike, "Fast-forward to the baby."

"I'm thinking it through," Mike said. "She got pregnant and she swore to her parents that the Giacalone kid wasn't the father, and she told them who the father was. She kind of offered the cantor to her father like it was better than having an Italian grandkid." Mike rubbed his eyes. "I don't know if that made things worse, because next thing, Jeri's father, Mr. Stein, came to the shul, found me and David in the basement, and threatened him." Mike stood up to dramatize. "Stein walked in, in his black coat and hat, his mouth already opened, like he was howling! He told your father he was not going to report him to the temple," Mike shook his finger in the air, and whispered, "No, cause then everyone would know his kid was a slut. He was not going to make David leave his job, his house. He wasn't going to humiliate his own wife. Instead, Stein was *only* going to make the cantor lose his mind."

Adam grabbed Liora's hand and squeezed it tightly, as if it was David's throat. Mike looked hard at Liora. "He told your father that he should watch his daughter's back every day of the week, every minute of the day, because he was going to have her raped by a pack of goons and leave her pregnant, carrying a pig fetus, if it was the last thing he did on earth."

Liora shot up from her seat. "You can't be telling the truth!"

Adam stood and put his arm around her shoulders, but held his tongue; words would have come out as gibberish.

Mike sipped from his glass and held his finger in the air, his eyebrows peaked, remembering an important fact. "And Stein said, 'That pathetic, bent son of yours is good as dead. Lock them up because their lives are worthless.'"

Adam cringed at the words but he urged Liora to lower her trembling body to the sofa, where she sat like a broken branch.

Mike shook his head. "Your father was losing his mind, all-righty. He was terrified of that man. Then that little girl, Jeri, ran away from home and lived with the Italian boy in Brooklyn."

Mike sat back exhausted. "And you?" He pointed to Liora, "I never knew what he told you, but you were on the next plane to Tel Aviv. And Eli, well." He shook his head and it fell forward. "I never got to see that sweet boy again. Your father just kept telling me how sick he was and how he couldn't go outside."

Couldn't go outside. "But David let him out later on, with Sharon," Adam said.

"Don't know about him then. After a while, your brother just faded away. Mr. Stein died about five years ago. I retired seven years ago and never think about it." Swig. "Still, it's a relief to hear the boy made it out of the house safe."

Adam found it strange no one seemed to regard Eli as a grown man. "And, how sure can we be that this is the real story?"

"Never taped any conversations or took pictures, like someone would nowadays. Not something anyone would want to remember. But until Jeri passed from breast cancer, poor young thing, she kept in touch with my wife. Maybe she was thirty-six, thirty-seven when she passed."

So, the part about her dying of cancer was true. Jeri was older than Adam was and he couldn't picture her as a girl, but he did remember her short, fat father, with his home cut hair hanging out of his yarmulke, and his patchy beard. Ruby had more than once dragged Adam as a young boy on the bus to Ocean Avenue in Brooklyn to get tablecloths and sheets from Stein's schemata store. He knew Liora accompanied him and Ruby on at least one occasion; he remembered she bought monogrammed hankies. A big blue L was stitched onto the corners. Adam called them her Laverne and Shirley snot rags.

Devlin tapped his finger on the sofa arm. "Thinking about it some now, I guess except for the way he met her and who she was, the rest of his fairy-tale was true. He was never the same after Jeri. Not only was he obsessed with protecting you and Eli, but he wanted to have that other child of his. She wouldn't let him near the boy." Mike shrugged. "He was full of the Lord with her." He rolled his eyes. "I doubt the man believed in anything holy by the time Eli reached five years old. His line to God was disconnected." Mike smiled slyly and said nothing more.

Once inside the car, taking a moment to catch his breath before beginning his drive, Adam looked tenderly at Liora, seeing the pink shawl of frailty fall over her eyes. "You'll be okay," he said.

"I'm doubtful." She turned her hands up toward the sky, with her weak smile seemingly to mock herself. "I wait and wait for a clear sign, life is O-K. But the struggle. Recuperation from loss upon loss. There is just no hope." She broke down, crying into her scarf.

He knew that, in exposing her hardship, she was giving him a gift. "Your children? I know they bring you hope and fulfillment."

She nodded in slow motion. "Six times," she said, and then gazed wearily at her cousin. "I filled my emptiness six times and with each child thought I felt real hope. But *real* hope lasts more than a moment. As you see, I bore no hope by bearing children." She straightened her beret and pulled her chin up. "Loving them has been a challenge. *Not* loving is a challenge. The only thing I truly bred is *doubt*. I am doubt-full." She opened her arms to reveal herself.

They drove for half an hour before they spoke again. "I guess I should let you know that Seth and Elana are coming to my house tonight," Adam finally said. He didn't look at Liora. "She called me from the cemetery." He squinted, as if protecting his eye from a punch she hadn't yet thrown.

She sat silently for a few seconds and then she exploded. "Maybe I'm an idiot, but I am unable to understand how you could host them! You made me a promise!"

"It will give me the opportunity to feel them out. Protect you and Eli by befriending them."

"You're going to protect me?" She bleated an exaggerated laugh. "You can't even keep a promise. Seth is a man who wants my blood. Nobody gets my blood." She raised her voice, "If he's coming to your house then so am I! I'll be there after I visit Eli."

"I didn't break any promises. I said I wouldn't bow down to him and I'm not." Deception and thievery were the accusations made against his father, and easily as dishonesty had seemed to work its way into Adam's talk, he realized that from his first deception in Shanghai he d been in a constant state of anxiety. He reached for Liora's arm. "You have a right to be there tonight. If I'm too busy to pick you up, how will you get there?"

"There's a bus, I presume? Subways?"

"Take a taxi. My treat."

"Thank you, but I don't need your money. I don't need anybody's money."

Adam knew whose money she wanted it made clear she didn't need.

Liora's armor faded before his eyes.

He fiddled with the knobs on the dash, making damn sure that navigating, manipulative bitch of a satellite would not be yelling at him again. Not today.

LITTLE BLUE LINES

A s Adam took her cape, Elana whispered, "I'd love some hot tea. I'm freezing." The temperature in Queens had risen to a mild and partly clear forty-five degrees—Adam figured Seth must have arranged it with God—which made Elana's shivering suspect. Her full-length cape removed, Elana was left dressed in a straight flannel skirt, a gray flannel turtle neck sweater that was far too fitted for a rabbi's wife, and a gray flannel hat with a black ribbon around the brim. She could have been a fashion model for a depressed Russian designer. She was gorgeous.

Adam peered out the window to the bus stop across the street. Knowing Liora, she would take the bus just to prove it was not too difficult for her. Adam looked back to Elana. He thought about the allegations she had hissed at him that morning when she called from the cemetery. He tried to read contrition in her eyes; there appeared to be some. "I hope you'll feel warmer soon. I'll put up water for tea and raise the heat," he said.

Elana turned to Diane and spoke as if she were a familiar member of the family. "I just feel so chilled." She coughed gently into a tissue. "I think I'm coming down with the flu."

"Do you want me to get you some aspirin?" Diane asked and walked her and Seth into the living room, holding her arm.

Seth, wearing a black suit, overcoat, and the satin yarmulke that was no doubt a freebie from the cemetery, blinked his eyes with heavy lids and smiled politely at the women. "Let's not

301

make this meeting a medical consultation. She'll be fine. We're staying at my aunt's house for the remainder of the week and I'm sure Elana will receive all the tender care she needs."

A sheet of icy possessive anger fell through Adam. "Diane was just trying to be helpful."

Seth's body tightened yet further when Elana took his hand, tugging on him, bringing him out of the living room to look at the framed photographs placed along the walls of the foyer. Family photos, including David in his long tallis, standing tall behind Adam in his bar mitzvah portraits, were sheer humiliation. Adam didn't remember David being so much taller than his father. He squinted at the photo to see if David were standing on a platform — he didn't appear to be — and then he urged Elana and Seth into the dining room. He helped Diane set the table with plastic disposable plates — Diane was afraid the holiday china was not kosher enough — and served the deli platter from the caterer's tray. Elana folded the cloth napkins and set them around the table. Once seated, Adam watched as Seth blessed and then ate the Russian rye with a side of coleslaw, while Elana took two slices of corned beef and ate them plain off her plate. After eating in near silence for a while, Elana — graciously encouraging Seth to join her in the conversation — talked passionately about their work in China, teaching Hebrew to children in the Lubavitch nursery school, helping the few remaining Chinese Jewish Diaspora understand their Judaic customs, though Elana admitted they were hopeful to one day return to New York to live. "I miss my family," she said. "By the time I have a baby, I'll want to be with them." She blushed.

Adam thought of Yin but buried his questions for now.

"Family is vitally important to us," Seth said. "Elana has three sisters and now I have Liora and Eli. What I'll do about that will require more thoughtful considerations, now that he is ill and Sharon seems determined to undermine me."

"Undermine you? How? Why?" Diane asked. She looked appalled.

"We spoke yesterday. I called her at Eli's house," Seth said, "because I want to see Eli before we leave."

"And was she difficult?" Adam asked, thinking, Thank god she was difficult. The woman is a saint. Seth did not have to see Eli.

Elana sat forward across the table and said softly, "She doesn't want anyone to speak to Eli outside the presence of his lawyer. Apparently, she thinks the rabbi is a thief."

"Oh, I doubt she thinks that, Elana," Diane said. "She's just incredibly devoted to Eli."

Since they bonded at the hospital, Adam noticed Diane was protective of Sharon's honor.

"She says she'll order a DNA test from Seth before anything is discussed with him," Elana said.

Adam was grateful someone else mentioned that before he or Liora had. "There is a last will, legally drawn. What does she think you could steal just by *talking* to him?" Adam was not as worried about the theft of goods as he was determined to emphasize to Seth the needlessness of addressing Eli in person. Like a surface he intuitively knew was too germ-suspect to touch, Adam had decided, and the decision was stuck in his head, he could not allow Seth and Eli in the same room, in the same country, ever.

Everyone sat still, watching Seth as he rose and composed himself. "The last will and testament is specific when it comes to Eli's care, but that was before the onset of his current condition." Seth rubbed the side of his mouth with his thumb, as if grinding a crumb into his skin. "I spoke with Eli's primary doctor at the hospital."

Adam's heart jumped, realizing he had witnessed how the family's hierarchy had just altered. No wonder Seth is so tolerant of thievery, Adam thought. He stole the throne right from under Eli's gurney.

Acting unaware of Adam's tension, Seth went on. "Eli is neither intellectually nor emotionally incompetent and Sharon knows this." He looked around the table. "Her powers over him allow her way too much freedom with his inheritance. She needs to be monitored, or we need to reclaim the job of his care until he is willing to care for himself." A thin band of moisture collected on his lower lid. "My father seems to have raised a boy and turned him into a golem." He sparked with, "Pinocchio in reverse. He created a healthy child, protected the life out of him—and then magically, enter Sharon to re-animate him."

"And you told her this?" Diane asked.

"In so many words. She knew David well. But unlike my father, she is not Eli's creator or his protector." Seth straightened his shoulders. "I just don't think she should have the right to handle his so-called *health* expenditures."

"And you think you should?" Adam asked. He thought if they were on the same page about anything, they should be uniting to get Sharon to relinquish all control over Eli, never mind transferring the control to Seth! He only wished Eli would speak to him again so he could do what his cousin wanted. "You don't even know him," Adam said. "I'm his closest relative. Just ask for what's yours and leave well enough alone. For Christ's sake." Adam looked at Elana and said softly, "Forgive me."

A few tears seeped out and puddled in the corners of Seth eyes. "Whether I know him as well as you do is not in question. The fact is, I want to see to it that Sharon does not take advantage of him. That's all I want."

Adam didn't know what to make of those tears, but relented and said to him, "I agree, to some extent, with you about Sharon. She could, I suppose, find a way to misuse funds. But you don't even live in the country. Until it's legally challenged we have no choice but to leave Sharon alone and just keep an eye on things." Adam averted his eyes from Seth's.

"I'm in the process of legally challenging her," Seth said.

Adam fumed. "To what end?" he demanded. He thought, go ahead, challenge her, while we test your blood, you fucking asshole.

"To a safe end for Eli," Seth said.

Safe end? It sounded ominous to Adam and he was all the more determined to keep that man away from his cousin.

Elana sneezed into her napkin three times in a row.

"God bless you," Seth said. He turned to Diane and said evenly, "I'm sorry I was so rude when we arrived. Of course you were right to offer her some aspirin."

"I'm okay, Seth," Elana said. "Don't make a fuss."

"I confess," Seth said. "I was angry, I *am* angry about being the only one of David Kaplan's family to attend his burial. I knew Eli would be unable to be there, but why, Adam, after making such an effort to bring your uncle home, did you stay away from the service?"

"Which was lovely and respectful," Elana added. Her long disheveled hair, her face that glowed from a probable fever, and her mixture of submissiveness and bravado combusted in Adam's head.

Obligatory kindness forced a statement. "I didn't come to the cemetery today because it would have devastated Eli that you were there and he wasn't." It bewildered Adam that Seth was going to such lengths to honor a father who—out of his own desires, grief, and guilt—screwed over all his children.

What did Seth really want? Did he even know the truth about his mother and father? Uncomfortable about keeping his visit to Devlin a secret from Seth, Adam found it all the more difficult to also keep secret the fact that Eli was not speaking to him.

He looked at Seth. "With all due respect, Eli's feelings are paramount to me. Diane and I decided to wait until he's healthy enough to go with us to the cemetery." After all he'd learned from Mike Devlin today, Adam didn't know if he could actually ever face David again, even buried and covered with dirt.

Adam peered out the front window into dinnertime's flat amber dusk. Citrine streetlights shone like rude interruptions; light faded unevenly through the gray limbs and purged the sidewalks of a warmer winter day, and any promise of calm. Diane remained quiet and exchanged shy smiles with Elana. Seth sat, his lips glued closed. Adam wondered where Liora was. She should be here to evaluate Seth's MO. If he were her brother, maybe she would sense some kindred spirit. He looked up and caught Seth's eye. "Does it bother you what your father wrote about your mother?" He was pierced by his own lack of restraint; his cruelty.

Seth's lips turned upward, as if smiling, but his bulging eyes showed he was stunned. "You mean the lies?"

Elana was not as gentle. "Of course it bothers us. But what is it you want to know, exactly, about David and Seth's mother? May they rest in peace."

"David apparently used a fictitious name for your mother." Embarrassed for Seth, Adam coughed.

"You used the plural, *lies*. There were parts besides your mom's name that weren't true?" Diane asked Seth. "I just want to know who your family, my family, is."

Seth showed her his smile. "And this inquiry is not prompted by some natural desire to entertain yourselves with the sordid details? You are discussing my mother."

Adam felt his stab, and wondered what part of Seth's contempt grew from feelings about his father. "Well, for starters," Adam said, "what's the story you think is the truth?" Come on, he groaned in his head, you're here already, dump the shit!

Diane looked back and forth at the two men. "I'm sorry if we sound rude. It's been a rough few days. Adam and I only want to help Eli and see this family come to terms with its future."

"Eli's future," Adam said.

"Eli's future," Seth said, "has nothing to do with my mother. The story David wrote about falling in love with this freckled-face June is all make-believe." Seth lowered his chin, looked to his wife, put his finger on his lips, seeming to instruct her to stay silent, and then rested his eyes on Adam's face. "My mother told me everything about their love affair." With a less vile delivery than Devlin had, Seth relayed the account of his mother's relationship with his father, David, that Adam and Liora had heard that afternoon. "She told me in the emergency room while we waited for my father, Joseph, to come out of surgery. He never did." Seth was fifteen, he told them, when his father Joseph died after a car accident on a family vacation in Maine.

"I'm sorry," Adam and Diane said simultaneously. Adam did feel terribly sorry for the man. Car accidents, breast cancer, being orphaned, then dumped on by David—and then only when he was too sick to be a real father to him.

Though Adam already knew the story, it was more painful hearing Seth tell it. Diane grabbed Adam's arm murmuring, "Do we have to keep talking about this?"

A fleeting pout on Seth's mouth morphed into a smile. "She didn't seem to harbor resentment, my mother. She willingly raised me under a protective tent of lies, a story David concocted, and she agreed to tell me, about my real Jewish father dying when my mother got pregnant and Joseph rescuing her, only delivering the truth to me while the man who loved and raised me, the father I loved with all my heart, was dying. It was a generous thing she did all those years, for everyone."

Adam was puzzled that the terms of Jericho's life seemed to have created in Seth the kind and unusual effect of empathy for his mother. Amazed by his candor and calm, Adam had to assume Seth did not yet realize how his mother's affair, and his birth, had such catastrophic effects on Liora and Eli.

Diane prodded. "What else was in the notes David left with you in Shanghai?"

Seth seemed only to want to further excuse his father's tender lies about his mother. "I was not about to further David's shame by revealing to him that I knew the truth about the shady circumstances of their romance." He felt David believed that their bond as father and son depended on the notion that his parents' affair remained as clean as possible. "I let on only that I realized he had substituted Jericho's name with June for her protection."

David had given the notes to Seth because he still wanted control over the incidental details of his conduct. He wanted to make sure Seth still believed in the fairytale. While they cared for David during those last months, they allowed him to perpetuate the written lies about Jericho. Seth said, "Naively, I admit, I'd hoped, for Eli's sake, for Liora's sake, David's little story would remain intact." Seth grimaced. "I pitied David."

Stunned by his hostility, Adam saw it was solely Seth's mother who harbored no resentment. Adam had only wanted to see Seth in order to insure he agree to leave Eli alone, yet now he was being bombarded with Seth's world of sorrow that the others share. Adam thought Eli would be pleased to know Seth suffers part of the huge pain he and Liora suffer.

"You didn't seem at all surprised by the telling of my mother's statutory rape." Seth said. The tone of his voice sounded as if the rape was a pesky rash his mother had had: bothersome, but not terribly serious.

Adam took a breath, and then lied. "There were whispers over the years. Bits of stories here and there."

Diane moved to the arm of Adam's chair. He hadn't had time this afternoon to retell Devlin's history lesson, and hoped she understood his motive and wouldn't ask him right here and now about these so-called stories.

Elana asked Diane, "Do you think the fact that Seth's mother was a teenager, that the circumstance was," she looked at Seth compassionately, "unconventional, would help in any way to soften Eli's heart about his brother?" Elana gazed, one at a time, into Diane and then Adam's eyes. "I think Seth should at least meet Eli."

"No! No, no, no." Adam exclaimed. "You cannot meet Eli yet. Eli is in a compromised and extremely vulnerable position. He could not possibly have the strength or wherewithal to express and conduct himself competently. Please, Seth. You have to slow the pace. He can't know the truth about his father and your mother yet." Here Seth sat exuding compassion for his half-brother, yet it was a familial malice that Adam feared from him. Did Seth even know about his grandfather's threats to David?

Seth said, "My wife is over-anxious and spoke thinking only of me." He smiled at Elana with apologetic warmth in his eyes and lifted their entwined hands to kiss hers. "The truth is best," Seth said, "but even factoring in David's intention, the truth is, his decisions concerning Eli will never change. Outcomes from misguided choices always remain intact." Seth tapped the tabletop. "Should Eli be left now to pity his father as I do? I'd rather I was left angry with him. Over time, anger diminishes."

Adam's anger at Seth was turning into pity as well, though he was ever more suspicious. Seth seemed a little too contained. "Well, Seth. Maybe before you leave New York there'll be an opportunity to see Eli." Over my dead body. Adam wished he could get the image of David fucking a teenager out of his head.

A queer, flat silence hung over the table for at least a minute before they heard the sound of footsteps approaching. Adam's eyes instinctively focused on the precise height at which he knew her eyes would be. Liora's hair was pulled back and piled atop her head, and her eyes shone like two wet, oval sea stones. Adam's heart came as close as he'd ever felt to lethal tachycardia. He sprang up from his seat and choked out, "This is my cousin, Ms. Liora Roth."

Diane popped off the arm of his chair. "How did you get in? How long have you been here?"

"Your bell doesn't seem to work, so I let myself in." Liora, scowling, bitter lines around her eyes, marched to within one inch of Seth. "Does this look like the face of diminished anger?"

Adam knew she had been there too long and had heard too much. He was sure she snuck in on purpose.

Seth and Elana stood and drew together as if someone had tugged on a rope laced through their bodies.

Almost Seth's height, Liora yelled as she pointed at his eyes. "Do you know how long I've waited…you have the balls to want to talk to Eli! He wouldn't even see me today!"

Adam scooted around the tight table to stand beside her. "Come into the kitchen with me. I'll get you a drink."

"Fuck you too! You don't even defend your uncle from this bastard's slander? He called my father a rapist!"

"We're just listening, Liora," Diane said. "No one's accusing anyone of anything." She scooted around the table and whispered to Adam, "I'm going to lock the front door."

Liora pushed Adam away and peered at Seth. "You want some kind of control over this family! Well you don't get any." She spun and pointed to Adam. "And you don't get any!" She broke into a kitten-like cry and pounded her fist on the table.

Adam used all the strength he could muster to grip Liora in a hug. He felt the rawness of her anger scratch his eyes. "Come and wash your face." He pushed her into the bathroom. He watched as she dried her face with her hankie. Adam asked, "What do you expect to happen here? Seth has legal leverage, your father made him executor. You're going to make him angrier. I need him to agree to stay away from Eli."

"Why? So *you* can control him? Control my father's estate? You're all pirates!"

Adam was stung. "You can't believe that."

"Seth's mother was a whore." She used her sleeve to swipe the mucus sliding from her nose. "Her father was a thug. Why should Seth be any better?"

"Liora. Stop saying his mother was a whore. She was a girl. Just a girl. The same age as you, for God's sake." She hadn't heard the horrible way Joseph died, and how much Seth loved the man who raised him. "And I don't think Seth even knew his grandfather. This Mr. Stein disowned them, didn't he?" Bullshit sidetrack. Adam really wanted her to hear about Seth's sad past.

She threw his hand off her shoulder. "Ask him if he knows his grandfather was a goon and threatened our lives." She covered her face with her handkerchief, cried "bastard" into it, then wiped her eyes and caught her breath.

"Okay. Just calm down," Adam said, patting her back. "We'll go back in, but you let me talk. You hear me?"

"Oh, shut up."

"Liora!"

She muttered, "I just want to kill him."

They found Elana in tears, Seth pacing around the living room, and Diane draining the remains of the wine bottle into her glass. She looked at Liora, poured half the contents of her glass into Adam's and handed it to her.

"Let's go sit in the living room," Adam said. "Everyone is going to remain calm." He kissed Diane's cheek and he whispered, "Sit next to Liora. Keep her down."

Adam watched from the archway until everyone found a seat. He smirked for the group. "There's a lot at stake here. It's time for all of us to share."

"Share what?" Seth asked instantly. "I hope you mean productive discourse and you're not going to try to alter David's last will. It's already in probate."

Odd. That had not been even the seed of a thought, yet this was the first thing that came from Seth's mouth when confronted by David's formidable first child. Since meeting Seth in Shanghai, Adam had thought he was obsessed with order and the dictum of his responsibility as a rabbi; until earlier today he had not even realized how emotionally effected Seth was from losing David. But was Seth's doggedness a manipulative charade to get the Kaplan goods? As for Elana, he was sure she was simply a manipulator by nature; her behavior was an innocent degradation from perfection, as Jamie might have put it.

Liora was whispering to Diane argumentatively, her face tight. Adam walked to the middle of the living room. "Here's the deal. Liora doesn't care about her father's money."

"She deserves his money," Diane said.

Adam reprimanded her with a look. "Regardless, she doesn't give a crap."

Seth laughed. "Hooray for me! Are you expecting me to put on my coat and leave because you think that's all I do give a crap about?"

"No. Of course not." Adam was embarrassed "What Liora wants," he said, "is for everyone to know the truth. So far we have lots of truths, scattered information and hearsay, and no one seems to know the whole truth. I'm the most ignorant, but I know more than I did yesterday." He nodded at Liora. "Do you want to ask Seth anything?"

"You ask," Liora said, looking at the floor.

"Do you know why Liora went to Israel and Eli was kept inside?" he asked Seth.

Seth shrugged, an of-course-I-know shrug. "I make no judgments about how Liora treated Eli. I'm sure she was suffering."

Liora hummphed. "And Eli? Was he too debilitated? Is that what *Dad* told you?"

"Well, yes that is what he told me. I admit I'm confused about that. There seems to be issues surrounding his evaluation."

"Yes. Issues," Liora said. Adam watched as she leaned forward and Diane grabbed her arm and tugged her back.

Adam looked at Diane. "Can I light a cigar?"

"Sure. Kill yourself."

He lit his cigar from Rhoda's dinner. "Liora and I already knew what happened between your mother and father," Adam began. He told the Giacalones about his trip with Liora to see Mike Devlin; he related a cleaner account of what Mike said about Jericho and her father. "I had to listen to this horrible story, Liora had to hear it, and will deal with it for the rest of her life." Adam was immediately sorry he said the story of his mother's love affair was horrible. He asked, "Did you know your grandfather?"

"No. We never met. My mother said he was evil and I was never to contact him. I never did. I know he's dead."

Adam rolled the cigar between his fingers, then stomped it out in the potted dirt of Diane's dead plant. He looked at Seth and Elana, saw the fear in their eyes and felt as though he was delegated to tell twin kindergartners that their parents had been run over by a train. "Jericho's father—I don't even know his first name."

"Irwin," Seth said.

With a mixture of compassion for Seth, contempt for David, and great regard for Liora's heart, Adam described how Irwin threatened to have Liora and Eli hurt, very badly hurt. If Liora being "raped by a pack of goons" or threats to murder Eli hadn't made it clear enough to them, he explained how terrified David was, how quickly his daughter was deported and how completely his son was hidden.

Seth somehow managed to remain deadpan, let go of Elana's hand and pulled a cigarette from his shirt pocket. Adam watched as Seth struck a match, lit the cigarette, inhaled what seemed like a suffocating amount of smoke into his lungs, and then rose and walked toward the entry foyer. His right knee buckled and it seemed he was going to tumble to the floor, his leg bent beneath him, but Seth straightened quickly, opened the door, and drifted out.

Elana said, "He'll be back. I don't know what this is going to do to him." She closed her eyes. "He still thought his mother left David only because she loved Joseph. Seth believed David always wanted to raise him."

"She did love Joseph and David probably did want to raise Seth," Adam said. "David has done to him what he did to all of us. Seth has no idea how much suffering David caused."

Elana spoke succinctly, but to no one in particular, "Is that Seth's fault?" She turned and looked at Liora. "Liora? Should he pay because you were all mistreated?"

Liora said loudly, "He can't come here and expect to take over a family that's overcome so much, survived so much. With*out* his help! What? Does he think he can perpetuate my father's lies? Keep Eli captive and me excommunicated? Become David's clone?"

"Oh course not," Elana said. "Can't you see? He wants to be a part of his family. It hasn't been easy for him either. Joseph and his mother are dead. Knowing David forfeited him to Joseph, and now this with his grandfather..." She began to cry.

"And the inheritance? He doesn't want the money?" Liora asked.

"It isn't about that. But Seth deserves something from his father, since he never had *him*."

"And we had him? Eli and I? We lost him too," Liora said, her voice almost softening. "We lost everything."

Adam looked at Liora and felt included in her losses. He put on his down jacket and walked out to find Seth. As soon as the screen-door snapped closed, he peered down over the porch railing and saw him standing against the neighbor's garage door, huddled under a shallow eave. With his arms twisted around himself he seemed smaller, homeless. Adam went back in the house, grabbed Seth's coat, brought it outside and heaved it over the railing. Seth caught it and put it over his shoulders. He looked up to Adam and shouted, "My father. He ruined your lives."

"Not your fault." More than sharing mere sorrow and loss with his siblings, Seth was bearing the guilt of being David's bastard child, and was also now aware of being the grandson of a mad goon. Adam walked toward him, feeling his weight stepping soundly up the snowy driveway toward his cousin, his feet finding the pavement and touching down with a solid footing. Adam spoke softly. "Did you know my father committed suicide?"

Thirty minutes after Seth walked out of the house he seemed to finally know what his birth did to fracture this family. Adam wondered if the revelation would soften him, if a man like Seth could be softened, knowing that he, like the others, is an innocent party to the sins of the previous generations. But when Adam saw how quickly the rabbi was ready to get back into the house with his wife, he wondered if Seth had really empathized at all with him, or had Adam, in the telling of his father's suicide, only weakened his stature in Seth's eyes. He felt ashamed.

Adam and Seth reentered the house to find Elana and Diane sitting silently next to each other on the sofa, each clutching small throw pillows.

"Shalom," Seth announced himself to his wife as he came through the door. "I'm fine." Elana shot up from her seat, threw the pillow onto a nearby chair and ran to hug him.

Adam asked Diane, "Where's Liora?"

"She's taking a nap in our bed," Diane said. "We'll drive her back to Brooklyn later."

Elana had to use the bathroom. Seth asked Diane to be so kind as to brew some good old-fashioned American coffee and then he gently pulled Adam by the elbow onto the sofa to sit beside him. "You will go ahead and do your best to comfort Eli. Tell him what he needs to know about his father. Elana and I will go home and take care of the will from Shanghai."

"By take care, you mean—"

"I mean, Liora will get her third of David's life insurance. There are numerous other concerns though. Sharon has not gone away."

Elana came back from the bathroom to witness the men shaking hands, though Adam was tentative about what he was agreeing to. Adam stood for Elana. "Everything okay?"

"Fine," Elana said, smiling. "Seth? Are you all right?"

"Nothing a little time won't heal. Come, Elana, sweetheart. We need to a call a cab." He waved her closer to him.

Diane walked in with a carafe and some Styrofoam cups.

"They're gonna go now," Adam said, turning his face out of Seth and Elana's line of vision, and twisting his mouth for his wife.

Diane put the coffee and cups down on the lamp table, then scurried to open the hall closet to get Elana's cape while Adam pulled Seth further down the hall out of Diane's earshot. "Could you, every once in a while…"

Seth finished Adam's question, "Check on Yin?"

"Would you? I'd like to know she's being taken care of."

"No change will take place in the child's life due to your constant worry and ill-founded guilt." Seth laughed and patted Adam's shoulder. "I'll email all and any news."

Adam patted him in return. He whispered, "You just have to know, Eli is not up for grabs. Unless he comes to you, you have to leave him alone."

"My intention was never to grab him."

With worries about Seth still unresolved, wishing he would have stayed longer to clarify his intention, Adam was nevertheless relieved to see Elana go. She elicited compromising desires, and he was happier when he and Diane were alone again with each other. Once the door locked behind them he told Diane that he missed his father. "I told Seth what happened to my dad. It may have been a mistake, but I just felt like he needed to be included in my family secret."

"Either include him or else one-up him on hell-as-I-knew it."

"I think he wins the hell game." Adam sprawled across the sofa, his head propped up on the armrest, and dozed, beginning to understand why Seth's knee-jerk reaction was to keep his father in Shanghai with him, steal him, punish him, and punish the family who thought David was all theirs. Seth is one sick puppy, Adam thought. Fits right in.

Diane slept with her head on his belly and her body lying between his legs.

They awoke an hour later to find Liora standing at the kitchen sink on the cell phone talking to Ariella. When Adam's eyes met hers, she ended her call. "Do you want to stay the night, or would you rather go to your motel?" he asked.

"I really have to go pack. I'll be leaving tomorrow."

"So Eli wouldn't agree to see you this afternoon?" Diane asked.

"No. They'd moved him to another room in the hospital and the visitor's desk was under orders. No passes. So, I tried." She shrugged. After drinking tap water in her cupped hands, she said, "My children need me. I just want to go home."

Joey had called at midnight to say the PTA of the local Junior High School was ready to start a bonfire in the gym rather than capitulate to the frozen pipes and keep the kids home one more day. At dawn, Adam rolled out of bed, ready to spend the day working. Diane was nowhere in sight. Adam yawned her name loudly as he shuffled his way into the bathroom. The light over the sink had been left on and he saw the blue box sitting on the counter. He looked in the wastebasket at the cup and the blue dip-strip. Adam picked up the entire basket and walked with it into the kitchen. Diane was sitting with her head in her arms at the table. He heard her whimpering. "What's this?" He held up the basket.

"A garbage pail."

"Why are you crying? Is all this a pregnancy test? What are you doing?"

"The box has two tests. I took the first one yesterday. That was the second one." She cried harder.

"And?"

"And I was pregnant yesterday, but not today."

"The vomiting," he said.

Yes, when no one else got sick Sunday morning and Adam had run to the city, she ran and bought a test pack. Her period came this morning, three weeks late. "How could I be so stupid?"

"You aren't stupid." He realized he had never stopped hoping either. Adam held his wife and felt the bereavement rattle through her. "You were not wrong to hope." He smelled baby powder on her skin. She had already bought supplies.

THE HARM IN TELLING

Eli was more angry with Adam than with anyone else. He was the closest thing to a real sibling Eli had ever had, and his convenient repression of Liora's attack on him was all the more hurtful. Eli cared less about whether or not Seth was related, and more about the fact that both his father and Adam, men he had loved and trusted, were masters of deception. Eli felt pumped to slap their moral disabilities in the face.

A few days after his father's funeral, Eli came home from the hospital. Once he was comfortably set up in his bed, Sharon told him that Liora tried to see him before she left for the airport. "She said she'd gladly leave her blood sample with that lab in Coney Island. If she calls from Israel, would you speak to her?"

His stitches suddenly sizzled through his abdominal wall. "My sister is dead. Don't even suggest I speak to her." The only business he had with her was to receive the results of her blood sample, along with his own and Seth's. Eli refused to speak to him as well. He was uncomfortable answering his own phone until he was assured Seth had returned to China.

The weeks spent waiting until the lab reported the results of the DNA tests were, ironically, some of the most luminous days Eli ever lived: he was home from the hospital, finished with his shiva responsibilities, and free from his family's bothersome phone calls; especially the long-awaited call that would announce his father had died. The hospital stint had depleted his physical energy, but his spirit and determination were soaring.

320

"If Seth is a liar and has no legal claim to this family's estate," Eli told Sharon, "than all this talk will have been a waste of our time together. To hell with him and anyone who tries to take time from us." He prayed that Seth was lying, but even so, he let himself entertain fantasies about the playful childhood the two of them might have had. "We need to make our plans," he told Sharon. "A real home. Careers. Travel."

It took exactly twenty-seven days to hear from the lab. Eli got the news while gluing the final part, a metallic yellow square with the black prancing horse emblem, to the hood of his 1/18 scale model of a 2001 yellow Ferrari F50. He'd heard only two rings of the phone and figured someone else had answered. When he saw, peripherally, Sharon standing in the doorway to his room he felt a hot tremor discharge from his fingertips. He continued to place the part, concentrating on the steadiness of his hands. "Was that for me?"

"The lab. You're ready to hear?"

"Ready and able." He felt about as ready and able as the day Sharon first forced him to go outdoors. But he had done that and he could do this. He gripped a sharp piece of scrap plastic in his hand.

"Well hon, the results are very positive." She didn't enter the room. "Everyone's blood has the same father."

Eli felt the plastic dig into his palm and dropped it quickly, then played calm and brushed some dried glue from his pants. He stood and faced her. "Well. My proud, proud father." How many more bastards were out there? He took a few steps toward Sharon and kissed her mouth softly. "You'll call the lot of them, then. The lawyer first." He thought about what she might say to Seth. "Tell Seth his claim has been proved legitimate and he will collect his share of my father's money."

Sharon asked, "And Adam and Liora? You'll call them yourself later on?"

"Absolutely not! Just tell them the test result, and send him the painting and rug my father left to Diane, and that's it. Ask Liora how she wants us to send the jewelry." So much for cousin and sister. "Let me know when you've reached them all. I'll be here, in my room." Envisioning any one of them receiving the gift of an inheritance from his father turned his stomach. He was both too humiliated and angry to listen to Sharon's portion of the phone conversations and started to close the door in her face, when shame blushed over him. "I'm sorry that I'm ordering you around. I can't listen to these calls. Frankly, I feel like screaming."

Eli didn't scream. He sat on his bed and held on.

Sharon blew a kiss and told him she loved him. She would leave him alone.

Sharon wrote down everything everyone said so that Eli could review the conversations verbatim. He held Sharon's memos in his hands during her report, but he never looked at them. Sharon said, "After leaving the information with your attorney's paralegal person, I phoned Adam. He pleaded with me to make you call him. He said he had to talk to you about Seth's mother."

Eli was sitting on his desk chair. At the mention of Seth's mother his body squirmed. He fought to erase any thoughts of Seth's mother as a real person, as though Seth were borne from only his father's blood. "She's irrelevant," he said, and stood to gaze out the window. "In fact, anything Adam has to say is irrelevant. Next?"

Sharon stood next to him, tall and pale by the window. "And then I called Liora, who listened to me, mumbled something in Hebrew, I don't know what, then told me to donate the jewelry to the United Jewish Appeal, and hung up."

"Do exactly as she says. Next?"

She took a deep breath and snarled sarcastically at Eli. "And I made the call to Seth. He asked how you were feeling, thanked me for my *polite*, though *delayed* report, but reminded me that he already knew what the results would be" —her voice became shaky—"and that he is now in a stronger position to revoke my power of attorney regarding your care."

"What!"

She broke into tears, sniffling through the rest. "He's also going to ask David's attorneys to divide the insurance money to include Liora."

Eli was first stunned, and then flew into a rage of the sort he had not shown Sharon since he was a teenager. He ripped pillows and blankets from his bed, he threw his garbage can with its model scraps across the room, and he hit his fist hard enough against the wall that a poster fell from its nail and slid down to the floor, cracking the glass.

"You're scaring me, Eli." Sharon put her hands to her ears. She shouted, "Handle it like an adult."

He turned to see Ludie standing behind her. "Go away," he told her. "Go down to the others and keep them there."

Sharon could instantly shame Eli. He shook his hands in frustration. "I'll clean it up!"

"It's not quite the point."

"The point is—I'm a lunatic." Eli sat on the edge of his bed and clenched his fists in an effort to level his temper. Taking a deep breath, Eli hung his shoulders and gave in to his exhaustion. When he felt his hands relax, he said, "I am perfectly calm. I will call Seth."

Standing with her arms folded across her chest, Sharon said, "What have you learned about pressuring yourself? You are never going to be *perfectly* calm."

They glared at each other. "Hand me the phone book," he said. "I'm about as close to calm as I'll ever be again."

"What are you going to say to him?"

"To leave us the hell alone and leave the insurance alone. What is it his business what Liora gets?"

"You're not calm enough. Wait a while."

It was the end of March. Eli waited.

By May Eli was physically strong enough to start his summer courses at Kingsborough Community College. His attorney informed him that Seth had not yet filed legal papers but had engaged their respective attorneys in a dialogue about why Eli had fallen so far behind for so long under Sharon's care. Seth, his attorney told him, was also committed to getting Liora her share of the insurance money.

Eli would not cooperate. The estate remained in probate. He talked to Sharon endlessly about how Adam had deserted him, had left him in the care of his sister's vicious hands, and the atrocity that had resulted from Adam's weak character. Adam kept calling to tell Sharon he was willing to do anything to mend his relationship with Eli; Eli was willing to do nothing.

"Your cousin is only human," Sharon said gently to Eli. "If you're going to condemn everyone who did something ill-considered, then you will have to condemn me as well."

There was no fault Eli could find with Sharon.

"For all those years that I was a student with you, I knew better," Sharon said. "I should have been more aggressive with your father sooner."

"Ridiculous. You were all I lived for." He remembered what she had forced him to do at the time and he shuddered at the thought of having been pushed to do more.

In July, Eli successfully completed his first college course, "Intro to Abnormal Psych"—an evening session, to which Sharon insisted on escorting him. While still in the parking lot of the college on that last night of school, Eli asked her to marry him. She said yes, with two conditions: he finally return Seth's call, and insist he leave their arrangement as is, and that she and Eli make love.

"In that order?" he asked.

"Any order you wish. Preferably, not in that order."

Relieved that she was the one who asked, confident, and desperate to marry her, Eli took her hand and led her from the open parking lot to her car. In the backseat, he touched her face with light fingers, unbuttoned the two tiny buttons near her neck, and lifted her blouse and stretched her bra over her head in one forceful swoop. He moved his hands along the curve of her body, keeping his own nearly motionless. He kissed her throat and playfully pushed on her breasts, pulled gently on her nipples so that her small breasts stretched to a point, then lowered his face to taste them while he moved his fingers across her pelvis and pressed his palm hard against her groin. She unzipped his pants and his entire body stiffened with the fear of ejaculating too soon. Once she touched him close enough, and had slid her hand down past his navel, he could not hold himself back and was deeply humiliated by the mess he made on her stomach. He caught his breath, revolted at the sight of his semen on her. "I'm sorry."

"Eli. It's fine. It's not like you peed on me." She smiled, and then reached to her handbag for tissues. She wiped herself and then kissed his mouth. Eli could feel himself smiling.

An hour later they made love in his bed. He tried to go slowly. When she was breathing so hard that she grabbed him and directed him to penetrate her, he entered her and with a few pumps brought her to orgasm. Then Eli released himself.

Eli stood facing the mirror in the second floor bathroom, the telephone cord stretched and flattened through the closed door. The slightly odd jingle of Seth's phone ringing was enough to rattle him. Would he sound familiar? Would he have an accent? He prayed he had a lisp.

Seth answered the phone with a soft but deep hello that sounded to Eli like the first note of an aria. Eli was momentarily silenced, but when Seth said Eli's name, somehow knowing who was calling, Eli responded. "This is Elias Kaplan. Is this Seth, what is it, Giacalone?" His annoyance at the absurdity of this man's vocation was instantly revived.

"Eli. How are you feeling? From your surgery, I mean."

"Fine," he said firmly, then tightened his grip on the phone. "I just want to let you know that you have certain rights, being an heir to my father, but those rights do not extend to tampering with his final will or my life. Is that understood?" Eli's heart was pounding. He held his mouth shut when he heard his heart ask, What do you look like? What do you feel about me? Can you love me?

Seth cleared his throat. "Yes. I understand. But do you understand that I have a responsibility to our father. Do you understand that he came here to get his thoughts about his life straightened out? I think most importantly, he sought to make sure all his children knew how much he loved them."

The tears were forming in Eli's eyes. "I lived with him my whole life. I know he loved me." The tears fell.

No one spoke for a second. "That's good if you know that. Because he loved you and Liora very much."

And you? Eli wondered, Did he love you? "Liora is beyond the scope of your concerns. And even my father knew not to leave her an equal inheritance." He turned his face away from the phone so Seth wouldn't hear him sniffle.

"That wasn't right. David was confused. He used historical fabrications. It was easier for him to publicly shun her and avoid explanations. In that, he was selfish and wrong."

Eli didn't want to hear about his father's fiction or Seth's hypothesis. Eli raised his voice. "My reason for calling is to tell you to leave me alone, to leave the will alone, and to leave Sharon alone. She will be my wife by the end of August, and I have no need for you or any other man to impose another thought, another opinion, about my well-being!" He slammed the phone into its cradle.

Striding into his room, he slapped at his model cars and stomped on the pieces. Feeling the crunch of plastic under his feet did nothing to alleviate his anguish. He felt unloved, and worse, unloving. This man was his brother. After half an hour of pacing, raging among the four corners of his small room, Eli threw open his door, stepped carefully toward the phone in the hallway and redialed Seth's number. He heard the same beautifully toned hello. "It's Eli. I just want to say" — he stared outside and watched a leaf hanging by a thread-like twig, refusing to let go — "I don't need your help, but if you come to New York, for something, call me. We'll meet." Eli hung up, and panicked, as if he had just said something obscene to a rabbi, realizing that although the thought felt right, the invitation became terrifying once actually spoken.

Mid-July heat baked their bungalow. Eli and Sharon strolled on the boardwalk of Brighton Beach and talked of one day moving to an air-conditioned apartment in the city. Ocean breezes were all Eli needed to cool his head and think rationally. Seth had called back that morning, a week after Eli called him, to say he and Elana decided to stop questioning Sharon's motives. Obviously, Eli's marriage to her negated any challenge Seth offered, though Seth said he would keep the inheritance in probate as long as it took to get Liora what she deserved.

Eli and Sharon wanted to get married in August. They wanted out of Brooklyn. There was only one way to do that. They agreed to split the money from the insurance three ways.

August 9, 2001, on the night before their intimate summer wedding, Eli called Adam, telling him he did not want to ruin his new life with the stale taste of his cousin's deceit. The truth being, he'd had a taste of parity with Adam, a delicious though tiny sample of family warmth, and he wanted more. For a few moments in the hospital, he was the dear brother and close cousin that had to be nurtured through a rough time. Eli invited Diane and Adam to witness his and Sharon's marriage. Adam and Diane accepted his invitation.

September 9, 2001, before Adam's guilt was stored away long enough to get cobwebs, he received a message. Seth had kept his word. As requested, hospital officials notified him that there was a major change in Lucy's condition. Seth emailed Adam: Lucy never regained consciousness before expiring from a cerebral hemorrhage. Yin was an orphan.

September 11, 2001, a month after the wedding, children were back at school, Adam and Diane were urgently thinking of how to rescue Yin, and Lower Manhattan was set on fire.

On a clear and warm October night, overwhelmed by the enormity of loss, constancy of fear and vulnerability, and his recent news from Shanghai, Adam took Eli for a drive along the Belt Parkway and parked in a rest area near the Bay Eighth Street exit, beside the shadows of the Army's Fort Hamilton and the Verrazano Bridge. The vast span was lit from Brooklyn to Staten Island. Over the seawall, cargo tankers drifted in the moonlight. Adam hoped the motionlessness and mist would soften Eli.

His cousin leaned forward and put his chin on the dash. "Beautiful scene, Adam. What are we doing here?"

"I thought you'd like the view. We could relax and talk about things." Adam was bursting to tell him that he'd spoken to Seth about Yin, but there was Eli's business to take care of first.

"We had to come here to talk?" Eli asked. "You're not going to try to kiss me, are you?"

Adam laughed. "I'm counting on the fact you're joking." He wondered if that was a jab at Jamie, turned his head toward his side window and then to Eli. "Can you handle some difficult but important details about your father?" Adam didn't know how angry or frightened the truth might make Eli, but he hoped passionately it would free him. "I can't stand that you still feel so heavy-hearted about the past. You know how sorry I am. You have every right to be furious with all of us, but if you somehow, someway, came to believe that your father was desperate and sorry, could you let go of your anger?"

"Now you're going to start explaining my father to me?" Eli said. "I'm doing okay. What magic explanation do you think can erase someone's *entire* memory?" Eli pointed to the now regularly patrolling Coast Guard. "Considering everything, and now this, don't you think I'm doing well?"

"Extremely well!" Adam wanted him to do better. "I know you don't want to hear about what David did to you and Liora.

You've told me. I know. But if you are serious about meeting Seth one day, you really should know about his mother and your father, and why he got so far away from the man he once was."

"No more post-mortem, Adam."

"You're a grown man and you can stand to hear about other people's torments." Adam watched Eli's face to see if that was too harsh. "You're my captive audience, Eli."

Eli looked nonplussed. "And if you tell me about his mother, will that be enough for you? This need all you people have to stone me with everything you know. Like knowing something rinses the deed clean, and life becomes fresh as a baby."

"But your father's unveiling will come. And if you do meet Seth, how will you understand him if you don't know his history?"

"Did I say I needed to understand him?"

"Why else did you tell him to call you if he's in New York? Think for a minute about what you need."

Eli sat and appeared to be thinking. "I need to understand my father, not Seth. So if you think knowing about his mother will help toward that end, lead me O great guardian to your brilliant understanding." He bowed his head.

The towers falling was more unbelievable than most people could integrate into their normal patterns of thought, but personally, seeing Eli here with him in a car, talking as if it were nothing for them to be together shooting the breeze, was equally surreal. And he thought, Anything is possible. Adam believed telling Eli about Jericho was the right thing to do. Holding still and poker-faced, he described the day of his visit to Mike, delicately and discreetly revealing the story Mike told about Jericho — Adam referred to Jeri as David's "woman-friend" — and about the choices David made to protect his children.

After a few torturously mute moments, Eli pounded his right fist against the car door, then turned to look at Adam, but still said nothing.

"Anything?" Adam asked. "Does the truth change anything?"

"It brings me tremendous suffering" — Eli choked on tears — "merely thinking about my father...that he took such blatant advantage of that girl. You are talking about my *father*. My father, my sole guardian, was a vile man who continued to write self-serving notes about love. My father, who chose to leave me, to die with the child that his disgusting and sinful behavior conceived." He took a few seconds to contain his anger. "Am I supposed to feel better now?"

Adam knew that David's shame, a life in which all integrity had been bartered away, would haunt Eli for many years before it freed him. They rode silently back to Brighton Beach. Adam parked in front of Eli's house and hoped he would say he had an epiphany and was now relieved to know the truth. He waited to hear his cousin breathe for the first time in open air. Eli opened his door, leaned over to kiss Adam's cheek and said, "Drive home safely. My love to Diane."

It fixed Adam's heart into a slow rhythm of capitulation, thinking how David — a religious and intelligent man — and Eli — a motherless, challenged child — should have been so well paired to feed and fill each other's lives. Adam thought, How tormented worlds become when a simple unit as father and son don't fit.

Adam watched Eli move from the broken curb and climb his concrete stairs. To what degree were the workings of desire and sorrow responsible for the conciliation of two brothers and a cousin? And Liora? Was she the sacrificial child?

Among the Stars

LIGHT READING

The last Saturday evening of February 2002 brought Diane and Adam back to the curb outside arrivals at Kennedy Airport. Jamie and his new boyfriend, Sean, walked through the exit door—each lugging a garment bag and a backpack. It was the first time they had seen Jamie since he left a year ago. Diane murmured to Adam that their son looked beautiful; his face was fuller, and so was his girth. She said, "Maybe he's pregnant."

"You're an insane woman with a one track mind."

Jamie had made the trip to New York for the unveiling of David's headstone that Sunday morning. The important thing for Adam and Diane was that the plane arrived safely; after that, they wouldn't have to concern themselves with terrorists again until the day the men left. Adam watched his son's interaction with Sean from his new perspective as the father of an affirmed homosexual. Aside from Jamie and Sean's exchanges of tenderness as they all inched toward each other, a rub on the shoulder, a shared squint after an inside joke, there was also restraint evident between them, in an embarrassingly obvious effort to keep Adam and Diane comfortable.

Diane peeked in the car window to check on her little girl, napping in the back seat.

Taking advantage of his contacts with local government officials in China, religious affiliations and diplomats at the American Embassy, Seth had been able to assist Adam and Diane in their adoption of Yin. Even with expedited paperwork and approvals, they were not allowed to go to China to get Yin until January. They knew Jamie would love her from the moment he saw her.

Handsome, an inch taller than Jamie at about six one, with wavy, sandy hair and a skier's tan, Sean could have stepped out of an L.L.Bean catalog. He was also a thirty-five-year-old pediatrician who in his twenties had been married for five years, and after the birth of his daughter had an emotional collapse. With a year of therapy and a divorce to his credit, he was able to accept and live a gay life. Jamie was not his first romance, but there had not been many priors, and Jamie had confided in his mother, who later shared the information with Adam, that their son was reasonably confident about Sean's faithfulness, and he felt safe. "Sean," Jamie said, "has a deep commitment to healthy living." Four months ago, he moved in with Sean, and Jamie told his father that Sean made him feel exquisitely positive about himself.

When they reached the car, Jamie introduced Sean, whom Diane and Adam had spoken with several times by phone. Adam shook his hand and Diane let him kiss her cheeks. Sean said, "Let's take a look at your new daughter."

Jamie put his arm around his mother's shoulders as they stared at the sleeping Yin. "She's big for a newborn," Jamie said. "I didn't think China made you wait that long to adopt."

Diane ignored his wit. "Isn't she lovely? I just love her so much. Your father was right about her. She is so precious. And she adores him." She beamed.

"I'm happy for you, Mom."

Adam was happy too and smiled to himself, warmed by Sean's respectfulness. He directed Sean to take the front passenger seat next to him, and watched the rest of his immediate family squeeze into the back.

That night at the house, Adam thought Jamie appeared relaxed around Sean. Sean touched various tchachkas, fingering glazes gently and drawing his hand back into his pocket, realizing perhaps he shouldn't touch everything. Adam could see Diane's pride when Sean, *Doctor* Sean, offered to look down Yin's red throat. She'd had a runny nose ever since they brought her home from China. Adam was reassured by Sean's dismissal of anything more serious than a cold. Sean wrote out a list of vitamins he recommended.

Sunday morning at ten o'clock, Adam, Diane, Yin, Jamie and Sean piled into the Volvo once again and drove to the cemetery. Everyone in the car sat subdued until Jamie coughed. Diane turned around to look at him behind her in the backseat, and Adam caught his son's eyes in the rearview mirror. He asked, "Everything okay?"

"I just wanted to let you know before the weekend gets away from us that with Sean's encouragement I've enrolled in Denver State," Jamie said. "I have Colorado residency status, so the tuition is reasonable." He looked at Sean and Adam saw Sean nod. Jamie continued. "Sean is gonna help with the tuition. I'm a psychology major."

Adam was pleased that Sean had offered even a portion of Jamie's tuition; it had to mean some form of hard commitment to his son. "Terrific, Jamie. What do you plan to do with it?"

"I'm thinking about forensic psychology." He laughed. "You know, I could get a part on your beloved *Law and Order*."

"I don't watch much television. Is that the show with Brad Pitt?" Sean asked.

"No, no, Benjamin *Bratt*. You know, he went with Julia Roberts," Diane answered.

"Well, she made a movie with Brad Pitt. The Mexican," Jamie said.

"Stop this!" Adam said laughing. He really wanted to hear more about Jamie and school. "We are not playing six degrees of Kevin Bacon."

"What does this have to do with Kevin Bacon?" Diane asked.

"Never mind! I want to hear about Jamie and school!"

He heard Sean say under his breath, "I love Kevin Bacon."

Adam would wait until classes actually began in the fall to tell Jamie that both he and Eli had enrolled at The City College of New York. If Adam could manage to keep up, Eli would graduate only one year ahead of him.

Liora had been notified of the unveiling, via Sharon, but could not attend due to more urgent obligations; her country was at war and her children were the warriors. Seth and Elana could not come due to Elana's difficult first trimester, but, "God willing," they would come back to the states for good soon after the birth.

Eli and Sharon, the rabbi that married them, and members of their congregation were gathered at David's gravesite, making small talk in front of the covered headstone. Adam focused on Eli, who was making sure the rabbi didn't look when he sneaked a second peek under the cover to check the stone. A middle-aged man, a stranger to Adam, put his arm around Eli's shoulders and gave him a supportive squeeze. While Diane led Yin out of the car, straightening her hat and describing where they were and what the surroundings looked like—as she did with her as a rule, at every scene they entered—Adam tried to give Jamie attention, kidding his son about his added weight. Sean had to reassure Jamie he wasn't fat.

Adam felt a melancholy fly a threatening circle around him. What sorrow, no matter how deep, could take a man away from his family, lead him to a dark basement to cleave his body and let all his blood? David did at least stay with his sons until illness killed him. At least Eli would have that, Adam thought.

Sean took Yin's other hand and along with Diane walked to the gravesite. Jamie was trailing behind, looking at something in the distance. Adam grabbed his elbow, then pulled him back toward the line of cars along the gravel driveway. The damp air smelled of upturned dirt. The scent was strangely calming. Adam said, "We miss you, you know. Your mother and I wish you'd visit more often."

"I will. It's been a hectic, crazy year."

Adam saw Jamie smile and he melted. "Until the day I die, of natural causes, I'll be here for you. You left town. You pulled away. It's okay, but nothing in this world could take me away from you. I could lose everything else in my life and be ruined, but if you were here, I would stay to be with you." He started to cry.

"You're being morose." Jamie put his arm around his shoulder and gave a manly tug. "It's because we're at a cemetery. Lighten up. I love you too. I'm here for you too."

"You don't have to be here for me. I'm the father. I, I"—he couldn't think fast enough; he could hear people chatting, approaching them. He turned and saw Diane, Yin and Sean returning. He held his palm up, motioning for them to stop. Adam put his hands on Jamie's broad shoulders and hugged him tightly.

"Any closer you'll be behind me," Jamie said as if he were Groucho.

Adam chuckled, and looked over Jamie's shoulder to the crisp wintry cemetery, a level vista of browned grass, gray granite monuments with Stars of David, and Diane, Yin, and Sean gaining ground.

"Eli did the entire arrangement for the unveiling himself," Adam said to Diane as they drove. He had to speak loudly because she was in the backseat with Sean and Yin. Adam said, "I know he was disappointed." He thought about it. "Because Seth and Liora weren't there." They weren't there to see the evidence of his manhood. To see Eli standing tall beside his father as the schemata is lifted from his tombstone. "So you're sure their reasons for not coming were legit?"

"Seth wouldn't lie about his wife's pregnancy. And Liora? Does she need a more legit reason than war?" Diane asked.

"It's the only thing that could have ruined this morning for Eli. Could have, but I don't think he let it."

"They'll come around some day. Seth, I think, will come to Eli," Diane said.

Eli's anger toward his father seemed to lessen over the course of the year, and as Seth had predicted, *pity* for their father became the toy he and his brother shared, as they began to play the lifelong games of siblings.

Adam heard Diane smacking kisses on Yin's cheek. Then she kissed the back of Jamie's shoulder. "I love you."

"Me too, Mom."

Now that David had been left to rest in peace, the family was to congregate at Eli and Sharon's New York City apartment for lunch. Eli and Sharon had moved out of Brooklyn with the things they had taken from the old house in Gramercy Park. Sharon's private practice was just beginning to build, and Eli had several years of school left before he would earn a living. Adam was gleaming with pride while he listened to Eli explain his plans the week before the move, spending evenings together painting and cleaning the apartment. The oriental slip-covered sofa was reupholstered, the hardwood floors were polished, and Sharon, a closet water-colorist, filled the walls with her seascapes.

By the time the truck had carried the last old chair through the doorway, the contemporary and bright apartment on the eighteenth floor, with "Benjamin Moore, Navaho White," paint on the walls, already bore the clean scent of Sharon's hand and body lotion. Adam smelled cucumber and melon wherever he walked.

As Adam drove from the cemetery on Long Island through the Midtown Tunnel, he listened to Sean reading nursery rhymes to Yin. His head became lighter, and he felt a smile breach his face. He and Diane hadn't yet told Jamie their other exciting news. Yearning to once again have a family home—of sorts—that would somehow knit closer what was left of the Oppenheim/Kaplan clan, Adam bought a two bedroom co-op in Eli's building, and he, Diane, and Yin would soon move into their new home, two stories below Eli and Sharon. Yin would be able to easily ride the elevator to visit her aunt and uncle.

The three couples and Yin assembled around deli platters set up on the dining table. Eli wanted to make clean up easy on Sharon by using paper plates, but after seeing their flimsiness in his guests' hands, he became apologetic about his decision. "I'm not used to having so much company. These disposable things are not as strong as advertised." Everyone told him not to be ridiculous and piled sandwiches high on their plates.

Jamie and Sean ate hurriedly. Jamie had surprised Sean with matinee tickets to "The Producers" that afternoon and Sean wanted to go downtown to see Ground Zero afterward. They would take the train back to Queens that night. At the door, Eli went to shake Jamie's hand but Jamie pushed it aside and grabbed Eli wholly. Sean followed Jamie's lead, then came back in from the hallway to kiss each of Eli's cheeks. Eli stood as stiff as a framed poster. The door closed with a solid thud and Adam saw Eli jump. "That sound jars me," Eli said.

Without excusing themselves from the women, Eli pulled Adam to come with him into the spare bedroom. A row of framed Ferrari posters was propped against the walls, like wainscoting that had yet to be nailed down. Books were still boxed in the middle of the floor, and two computers sat side by side on a makeshift desk. Eli opened the closet and pulled a brown hat-sized leather box off the shelf. "It's filled with my father's papers," Eli said. "From you, plus Seth sent his." He shook his head and rested against the wood plank desk. "The personal treasures my father depended on to propagate his integrity," he said out of the side of his mouth. Eli unlocked the box. "His attempt to make peace." He lifted the note David had written on the backside of a student's practice haftarah, neatly folded in a separate envelope. "I kept this from everyone until I believed him." He ushered Adam out the bedroom door.

In the living room, Diane and Sharon had moved to the sofa to sit with cups of coffee and Yin sat next to Diane listening to her cassette with earphones. Her head bobbed with some beat she heard as her fingers were going through the motions of counting.

"I beg your indulgence on my father's behalf one last time," Eli told the group. He looked at Sharon. Adam thought she looked poised and beautiful, her feet propped up on the small ottoman.

Eli caught a quick sharp breath, and stood as straight as he could manage. "I don't know at what point during my father's last year this was written, but in my mind they sound like the true voice of the father I knew and loved. I read this as his eulogy." With both hands gripping the white sheet of paper, in a crisp and deep voice, Eli read:

My life is not without love. I tell my story, not arbitrarily but economically, for the details are abundant and my time is not. I owe nothing to the world as my life story is my privilege to keep, my privacy is my right, but the desire to expose my passages of relief, my yearnings for the woman I loved, have grown desperate, driven daily by my need to be understood by my children, who will no doubt be the beneficiaries of this treatise, and to explain how I interfered with their peaceful existence, how my own defenses led me to seek gratifications, through drink and lust and how this beautiful numb existence brought with her the ganef who made me take your freedom.

Miriam died in a flash of a moment while fulfilling my dearest hope: to bear my son. A shattered man, I brought Eli home. I was heavy with hollowness, as abandoned as a man in a birth-sack that had been delivered but not birthed.

Unborn, I tried to bear witness to her spirit returning, looking always, listening always, for signs that Miriam was trying to reach me. A sign. A loose nail that caused her favorite painting to fall to the floor had me believe she came to visit. Within months I found myself driven mad with my perverse attention to movement and sound. The rabbi could bring me no solace and God was unable to enter my heart. My faith drained away. I had little trouble accepting His departure. I was, in truth, relieved to let Him go. His presence had become a frightening cap around my heart.

When Miriam did not visit, I had to leave the house to divert my near-insane attentions. I walked to streets she had never walked, prowled the neighborhoods she had never smelled, touched the hands of women she had never known. I strove to distance my mind and body from the nothingness her death had brought to me. Now as in the past, I find myself a fractured soul, a ghost, alternating between self-righteousness and self-contempt. I credit my instinct for affording me the sense that my most loving responsibility was to Eli, yet curse that same instinct for creating my too vigilant guardianship over an imprisoned son. And could find no recourse for dealing with Liora but to send her away, as both criminal and victim. She was forsaken, my daughter, whose absence hurt me so I could not think of her without feeling all fibers of life incinerate. Was there no other solution? I am positive that no alternate solution ever occurred to me. I am also positive now, as I lay my undoing before you, burned to nothing by sorrow, an alternative should have been so brightly seen it would have illuminated me with the fires of parental decency.

ACKNOWLEDGMENTS

I could not have succeeded in completing this work without the generosity, patience, words, and wisdom of my editor, poet David Groff. I regard him as a gift in this world. Several fortuitous degrees of separation brought me to my wonderful editor. They each know how it worked. For the connection and all that grew from it, I thank Alvin M. Schmidt, M.D. for his kindness and sensitivity, and Roger B. Granet, M.D. for the constancy of his support and respect.

Many thanks to all my courageous early readers who dared to break my heart with their critiques: Henriette and Aubrey Tadman, Carole Gaunt, Joan Rosenthal, Rona Goldfarb, Lynn Mancinelli, Mari Jaffe, and Beth M. Jaffe.

My deepest gratitude to the women who not only read my work but read my mind as well and keep me laughing through my wildest thoughts: Shari Korenstein, Ruth Davis, Myra Evangelista, Valerie Sterlacci, and my personal writer in residence Sande Boritz Berger.

Many people helped with the research for this book. I would like to especially thank Sharon Kepniss for sharing her knowledge and insights on cerebral palsy, and Rabbi Shalom and Dina Greenberg from the Shanghai Jewish Center for responding to my numerous emails asking about contemporary Jewish life in Shanghai. Kudos to the kind professionals at Llumina, for successfully walking me through this publishing forest.

For me, all truth is forever held within the hearts of the three incredibly loving men in my life: My husband Len, and my sons Rosh and Steven. Thank you for always answering my phone calls.

www.ingramcontent.com/pod-product-compliance
Lightning Source LLC
Chambersburg PA
CBHW030154200626
46812CB00017B/1917